SWEETHEART, SWEETHEART

by Bernard Taylor

In this novel of bloodchilling seduction and unearthly love, David Warwick returns to England when he senses his twin brother Colin is in danger. There he discovers that Colin and his young bride have both died grisly deaths, the victims of a ghastly evil. Soon the evil overpowers David and forces him to embark on a journey into the macabre that he might not survive.

"The best ghost story. . .I have ever read, and am ever likely to read!"
—Charles Grant, bestselling author of *Stunts*

"*Sweetheart, Sweetheart* is a dandy story in which the normal dissolves into the bizarre without a skipped beat."
—*Houston Chronicle*

"Ingenious and well-crafted — a most satisfying chiller!"
—*Grand Rapids Press*

"Taylor is a master!"

—*Publishers Weekly*

Other Leisure Books by Bernard Taylor

THE GODSEND

BERNARD TAYLOR
SWEETHEART, SWEETHEART

LEISURE BOOKS　　NEW YORK CITY

This is for my mother and Tom.

A LEISURE BOOK®

January 1992

Published by special arrangement with Souvenir Press Ltd.

Dorchester Publishing Co., Inc.
276 Fifth Avenue
New York, NY 10001

For further information, contact: Souvenir Press Ltd., 43 Great Russell Street, London, England, WC1B 3PA

The name "Leisure Books" and the stylized "L" with design are trademarks of Dorchester Publishing Co., Inc.

Printed in the United States of America.

SWEETHEART, SWEETHEART

1

I can't see the sun right now; there's an angel in the way.

As I lie here in the short-cropped grass with my eyes just half open a butterfly alights on the carved angel's head. It stays only a few seconds—its wings opening and closing—then takes off, fluttering away, dancing up and down over the grey stone wall.

Everything around me makes a picture of the greatest calm and serenity. And so it *should*. This spot, I tell myself, should be peaceful by definition. Yet often I wonder about that . . .

I remember how I told Shelagh I'd find peace by coming back to England. And the irony of my words returns to me every moment. As if this gravestone isn't enough there's the old man further off who stoops, lovingly tending his roses. The roses are not white, though. They're red, blood red. But still, they're roses.

Yes, it's all calm. To any onlooker it must whisper only of peace. But to me it shrieks of things that are best not thought about—if I want to survive. But it's impossible, that—*not* to think about them.

The horror didn't begin when I returned. It had started long before. Even in New York, so far away, I'd had signs—though I hadn't recognised them as such. All I was certain of was that I had to come back again, to England. And the only thing I'm certain of now is that I should have stayed where I was, with Shelagh. If I had, this story would be different; at least it would have a different ending. But I couldn't stay. Not when there was that *need* in me—to see Colin again.

There in Manhattan I never really found contentment. Never anything *lasting*. But was that what I was looking for when I went off those eight years ago? I

3

don't know. Something. I certainly didn't go with any great hope. I went leaving behind me vague feelings of unhappiness, of not belonging; yet having no reason to imagine I'd find elsewhere the answers I sought. I chose America because I liked American people, because there'd be no language problem, and because I felt the British were closer to that people, spiritually, than to any other. But there was nothing really *positive* about the exercise—unless escape is such. And that's really what it was, I suppose; I can't be sure now; I wasn't so much going to what was new and strange and exciting, as getting away from the scene of so many failures.

I look back now in some surprise, wondering that I should have stayed for so long—while being aware of my lack of contentment—certainly until Shelagh came along, anyway. But I'd had six years there, alone, until she came to share my life with me. So why had I stayed? Was it the need to assert myself?—to prove that I could get along without any help or encouragement from my father? Not that he was about to offer any. Perhaps it was just that—some impotent up-yours gesture to him. If so, it was pretty futile.

Shelagh, though, during those last two years, *did* give me a positive reason for being there; if only so that we could be together. And if my brother had never met Helen then we might be there still . . .

But he did meet her; and then began that *draw*, that *need*, that reaching out to me, and I couldn't rest once that had started.

And there was no explaining my feelings to anyone. Not even to Shelagh. I think she saw it all just as some kind of vague homesickness, and that was something she couldn't understand.

"Why are you so anxious to go back?" she asked me. "You can't be *that* desperate to see your father. Or your home."

"What home?"

"Exactly. And it can't be Colin. I mean, you never saw him that often."

It *was* Colin—but I didn't say so, then. "I shall find peace," I said after a moment. The words sounded so foolish, but she didn't smile.

We had met when she came to teach at the private school where I was a teacher of history and English. I can remember my first sight of her as she walked into the staff room that morning wearing a light-blue pinafore dress over a white blouse. It was her colouring that struck me first: rich, copper-coloured hair, very straight, heavy, brushing her collar; and the bluest, bluest eyes I'd ever seen—evidence of her Irish ancestry. I was drawn to her warmth right from the start, and day by day in her company I grew happier, feeling the warmth and friendship between us grow and blossom. And over the weeks our mutual attraction and our friendship grew into something more: richer, stronger; and inevitably we made our decision, looked around for a bigger apartment, and moved in together. I'd never felt about any girl as I did about Shelagh, and I was aware of that from the beginning.

"Couldn't we," I asked her now, "at least go to England for the vacation. We could leave as soon as the semester ends."

"We're going to teach summer-school. You know that. We've already agreed."

"We can get out of it. Christ, I've had enough of teaching, anyway."

"We can't get out of it now," she said. "It's too late. Wait till summer-school's over. It's only for a month. You can't be *that* restless . . ."

I could sense the petulance of my expression, feel the sullenness in the set of my mouth. "Marry me, Shelagh," I said. Same old tune. "Marry me and let's get away to England together . . ."

". . . We've been through all this before . . ."

I said, making a laugh:

"It's because I can't dance, isn't it?"

She looked at me very steadily for a moment without any trace of humour, and went away, into the kitchen. I watched her go, the phoney smile on my face congealed, then followed her, more than a little aware of my limp as I crossed the carpet. Leaning in the doorway I looked at her as she busied herself with the coffee-percolator.

"I'm sorry," I said. "I didn't mean that, and I've never thought it—even for a moment."

"You're different lately," she said softly. "You're a different person. Over this past year you've been getting steadily more and more—introspective." She shook her head. "I don't know . . . I've watched you daily getting more uptight and jumpy. And even at night you're no better. You can't sleep without taking those damn pills. And when you *don't* take them you just lie awake, tossing and turning. A year ago you'd have laughed at the idea of taking sleeping-pills . . ." She turned away. "My God, Dave, you're starting to make *me* nervous. I just don't know what's come over you."

I shrugged. "It's probably the school . . . and this place . . ." I waved a hand, taking in the apartment. "Everything . . ." I forced a smile. "It's a phase. I'll get over it."

She came over to me, reaching up, arms about my neck. "Sure you will." She kissed me. "But I worry about you . . ."

"Marry me . . ."

"Look . . . I've known you for two years, and half that time it's like you've been in another world. Before—that first year—you were not like this, and I know—" here she smiled, "—at least I *think* I know—that this isn't the real you." She paused. "Anyway, I'll marry you when you're *more like you.* I'm not about to be the solution to somebody's problem." She eyed me steadily, then added:

"I know when this whole thing started."

". . . Go on . . ."

"Well . . . with Colin . . ."

She touched that nerve again with the mention of my brother's name.

"I'm sure that was it," she said. "He writes that he's getting married and you go straight into a decline."

Yes, that was true . . . At almost exactly that time, I saw, my uneasiness had begun to grow. I hadn't been aware of it before—the precise time of its beginning, but now I was, now that Shelagh pointed it out. And looking back over the past year I could see how increasingly nervous I had become; unable to settle to any-

thing—in the classroom or at home; all the time growing more short-tempered and irritable. Yes, that's when
it had begun—a year ago when Colin had married Hel-
en and moved in with her.

But why should it be? What connection could there
be? Nevertheless, that's when my headaches had
started, my growing feelings of anxiety . . .

In the bedroom I got out some of the letters Colin
had sent. The last one was dated March 2nd. Weeks
ago. It was quite brief—just telling me that he and Hel-
en were well, and asking when Shelagh and I planned
to visit them. His earlier letters had been more frequent,
and much longer.

There were photographs too. Snapshots of himself
and Helen; pictures taken after the marriage ceremony;
pictures of them standing in front of the cottage. There
at the gate they stood, arms entwined, smiling at some
anonymous camera-holder. So many pictures had arrived during the first few weeks of their marriage; all
those views of the cottage; the shots of the Berkshire
village, Hillingham; images of Colin: Colin reading,
Colin lounging in the garden, Colin sitting at the wheel
of his gleaming red MG, and, in every one of them,
Colin looking happy.

More numerous, though, were the photographs of
Helen. I looked at them again, wondering what she was
like beyond her physical appearance. She looked tall
and slim, her hair a rich dark brown, falling past her
shoulders. Her eyes looked almost black against the
fairness of her skin, and in their expression there was
something not to be fathomed by the searching camera's
lens. Her mouth was wide, the lips full and hinting at a
gentle humour . . . Was it humour? The clothes she
wore looked rather modish. Her dresses were long—
when she wasn't wearing blue jeans—and her neck and
wrists were hung with beads and heavy-looking bangles.
She looked very much what Colin said she was—an artist . . . And that, I realised, was about all I knew of
her. By all accounts she had appeared in his life quite
suddenly, and they had married less than two months
after their meeting . . .

Shelagh had followed me into the bedroom and now

stood looking at one of the snapshots of the old cottage.

"It really is a lovely house," she said, then, smiling, added: "But if *you* want a cottage in the country you're going to have to save your pennies and buy it yourself. *Then* you can have that bit of—peace you're looking for. I can see you, teaching at some village school and spending your time hovering over tomato plants and building rustic walls . . ." She hesitated a moment, and then went on:

"You are . . . *glad* for him, aren't you?"

"For Colin?" I nodded. "Of course I am." I was. "He's happy. He's got what he wanted. Of course I'm glad for him." He had married Helen, and if Helen was also the owner of a beautiful country cottage then more power to him.

I picked up the snapshot of that beautiful country cottage and straightaway I could feel that sensation again—that near-physical force pulling at me, pulling me towards him—Colin.

Colin . . .

I have never understood why. Or how. How could there be such a bond between us? I'll never understand it. I only know that it was always so.

It's even more strange, I suppose, when considered in the light of our upbringing, and in the fact—as Shelagh had said—that really I'd hardly known him. But it was always there. Always like that between us. Colin and me. There has always been, no matter how far apart we might be, a bond between us—some invisible string that draws us together. *Well, twins,* people say—as if that accounted for it. And they relate stories to illustrate those strange ties. But they don't explain anything, anything at all . . .

Shelagh, knowing me better than she thought, said, "Dave, you mustn't worry because he hasn't written lately. His whole life has changed. He's got new things to think about. You wait—he'll start writing again soon."

But he didn't write, and my inner disturbance increased with every day. I tried telephoning, but that didn't get me anywhere, and after being told for the sixth successive time over several days that the telephone was out of order I gave up trying. There was nothing I could do but wait. And in the meantime I'd make a concentrated effort not to dwell on it. Perhaps then that nagging nervousness I felt would fade . . .

Well into May I looked forward impatiently to my birthday. The 15th. Colin and I would be thirty-two years old—he the elder by some hours. Monday, the 15th. Surely then I must hear from him.

Monday's mail brought a bill and four birthday cards. One card was from Shelagh, one from the school principal, Jefferies (well, wasn't the faculty One Big Happy Family?), one from the students in my eighth grade English class, and one from my father. This last was like those other cards that had arrived from him over the years, each one appearing as regular as clockwork, and bearing the single word, "Father". No message.

There was no word at all from Colin.

"Maybe you'll hear tomorrow," Shelagh said. "How can you guarantee a letter's arrival time after a three thousand mile journey . . . ?"

That evening, by way of celebrating my birthday (I never felt less like it), we went out to eat at a small, favourite restaurant on the Lower East Side. And I was miserable. I sat across the table from Shelagh, toying with the fish on my plate, forcing down the occasional mouthful and trying to wrestle with a strange pounding that had started up in my head. At the same time, in front of me, all around me, was a descending cloud, thick as a curtain.

"Aren't you going to eat more than that?" Shelagh's smile was touched with frost, and her voice had a slightly brittle edge to it.

"I'm sorry . . ." I raised a hand to my temple. "I'm just not very good company."

"That's the truest thing you've said all day."

We sat in silence. I could think of nothing to say and I had no wish to make conversation. I could feel her eyes on me when the waiter came and took away my

half-eaten, picked-over food. Avoiding her glance, I sat
concentrating on my cup while the coffee was poured.
A strange sensation was coming over me; a feeling of
warmth, while the ends of my fingers had begun to tin-
gle. The pounding in my head was growing stronger and
I could sense an enormous pressure building up behind
my eyes. I seemed to be cocooned in haze, a fog that
was enveloping me, seeping into my pores. I watched,
as if in a slow-motion film, the movement of my hand
as I slowly ground out my cigarette. I could see my fingers trembling . . .

And then the density was lifting again and I became
aware of Shelagh's voice coming to me through the
fringe of the haze. I looked at her blankly.

". . . I'm sorry . . .?"

She was reaching for her bag, her mouth tight.

"I was saying I'm going home." She had already paid
the bill (it was her treat) and now she counted out the
tip, snapping coins onto the plate. "I asked you a question three times, and you can't even be bothered to listen to me."

"I'm sorry. What did you want to know?"

"It's not important any more." She clicked her purse
shut and stood up. Her voice lowered to a whisper.
"I've had it with you tonight. And now I'm going home.
I can get better reactions from the Late Show."

"How are you feeling now?" She murmured the
words to me, her mouth close to my ear on the pillow.

"Okay. How about you?"

"Okay."

After a moment she added:

"I'm sorry. I was a bitch."

"I'm sorry, too. Really. If only I could explain what I
was feeling . . ."

"You don't have to try."

I turned to face her, and held her. After a time my
hands moved up and touched her breasts, and she
pressed herself against me. My fingers moved lower,
brushed aside the silk and touched her bare skin, gentle,
caressing . . .

I hadn't had much in the way of sexual experience

before I met Shelagh. I seem to have missed out somewhere. I'd had less than my share of furtive fumblings in back rows, and very little success when I *was* presented with any golden opportunity. My leg—and Aunt Marianne's influence, probably. I had never been at ease, really at ease, in any sexual situation, that's for sure. I remember once watching a blue movie; it left me feeling, in a way—as well as strangely, almost mind-blowingly excited—almost totally confused. Surely all that thrusting and sliding was done only to give value for money. Those people up there on the screen couldn't have any connection with *ordinary* people—with me.

With Shelagh, though, I felt no such confusion. I suppose that what I knew I had learned from her, and I made love to her in a pattern that we, ourselves, had established. And within the limits of that pattern I felt safe, secure. Her demands matched my own, mostly, and she never made me feel threatened by any sense of inadequacy.

The more cliché-ridden love stories speak of unbridled passion. I wasn't sure that I had ever experienced such a thing; not where Shelagh and I were concerned, anyway—and I had never known anything better than that which I experienced with her. But still, if our passion was bridled, even so it was good. Very good. And while we weren't about to set the place on fire, it was enough. It was enough for her, and it was enough for me, and we were happy . . .

We lay there side by side. Long since spent. Shelagh was sound asleep, while I felt that pounding in my head starting up again and getting louder and louder. I had already taken two sleeping-pills, but obviously they weren't going to do anything for me. I felt hot and feverish. Feverish, yes; it was as if some strange malady I was suffering from was swiftly coming to a head . . .

In the end I got up, went to the bathroom and shoved my head under the cold tap. It didn't help. I still couldn't rest. When the dawn came up I was still awake, and I watched it lighten the window, saw Shelagh's soft features taking shape in the receding gloom.

After coffee I just sat there while she got her things together ready for school. Seeing me hunched over the table, not moving, she said: "Are you taking the day off?"

"No." I shook my head. "I'll be in later. Make some excuse for me, will you?"

She came to me, put her hand on my hair.

"Dave, what's up . . .?"

"Nothing. I just want to wait for the mail . . ."

I did wait for the mail. When it came it was just one single item. But that one item was a card from Colin.

"I told you so," Shelagh said when, later on, in school, I showed her the card. The picture on it was a reproduction of Rembrandt's *The Night Watch*, and there inside, beneath the little printed message of greeting Colin had scrawled his name, and added: *Will write soon.*

"Well," Shelagh said, watching my face, "are you happy now?"

"Yes, I am."

But it was a lie. Colin's card had brought me a sense of relief. But it was an intellectual thing; it didn't do anything for the way I really *felt.* And as the morning wore on, endlessly, I felt inside me a tightness that grew and grew, as if my whole body were being constricted by some invisible bands—and the greatest tightness was in my head. I had an insane urge to just leave my desk and walk out of the building. But that wouldn't have helped; the panic was a part of me, in me; I couldn't leave it behind.

The afternoon was even worse. I saw myself irritable and snappy with my students, so that they approached me warily, conscious of my tenseness and not eager to push their luck. And all the time that black cloud was descending, growing closer and more stifling, till I thought I would do anything to escape its numbing, saturating presence.

But at long last the final session of the day came and

went; all I had to do then was get through the weekly faculty meeting.

Once begun, I thought the meeting would never come to an end. Jefferies started it off in his usual flowery, adjective-ridden manner, leaning back in his chair at the head of the refectory table, fingers steepled, holding forth on the most trivial matters as if he really had something to say. I wasn't touched by any of it. Sitting beside Shelagh I looked at the bright smiles, the bright eyes and the agreeing, sycophantic nods of the other faculty members and couldn't even summon up my usual feelings of contempt.

And the minutes ticked by. Slowly, so slowly. Eventually, glancing at the clock, I saw that it had turned half-past five. Varley, the gym instructor, all brawn and no brains, was adding his two cents' worth to the problem of Sinclair—one of the students where there was "a little behavioural problem that needed attention". I tried to listen as questions were put to him, but my mind wouldn't settle. I just sat there, staring down at my briefcase before me on the table and feeling as if the top of my skull was about to open. Somewhere, as if from far off, I heard my name mentioned, and dimly realised I was being asked a question. I tried to collect myself, took a breath and opened my dry mouth to speak. And that was it.

Suddenly, after all the months of increasing tension I felt, inside my head, a tingling, searing sensation. The fuse had finally ignited. As if I could physically run from it I staggered to my feet. Behind me my chair was sent clattering to the floor. And it was then that the blow hit me.

When the explosion came it was like a kick, aimed deep inside my brain, so powerful that I felt my head jerk on my neck. For a split second everything was a shower of scarlet sparks and splashes against the blackness. I heard a roaring in my ears, like a rushing of wind. And then there was a pressure against my body, so strong, so agonising that I felt as if my ribs must give way beneath it. And the pain continued, changing, as if some hand was at my chest, reaching inside me, grasping my heart and squeezing . . . squeezing . . .

It was the terrible pain in my chest that pushed the sound out of me, forcing it up through my throat so that it echoed in the room and rang in my ears.

"*Don't . . . ! No-o-o-o-o!*"

I saw, dimly, through flickering eyelids, Varley's face before me; saw his porcine features take on an expression of wonder and consternation.

Then everything stopped.

2

❧ ❧ ❧

I came to with Shelagh's face bending over mine. There was a pillow under my cheek. I put up a hand and gingerly touched the side of my skull where I could already feel a bruise coming out.

"Somebody's gone to get some ice," a voice said, and then Shelagh, as she pressed my hand:

"You'll be all right, darling. Don't worry."

I looked up into her eyes. She was crying.

"I've got to get away," I said. "To England."

"Hush," she whispered. "Hush. Don't talk now . . ."

The next day all I had to show for those months of tension was the bruise on my head. Apart from that I felt as well as I ever had. I couldn't understand it. I went back into school the day after and got down to my work with renewed energy and an unusual feeling of mental and emotional freedom. That *tightness* had gone—and along with it all the feelings of irritableness, the poundings in my head. Shelagh saw the change in me and relaxed. For her it was all over.

I took her completely by surprise when I told her, the following week:

"I meant what I said."

She was sewing a button on the sleeve of her coat. She looked at me, frowning, puzzled, needle poised.

". . . About what?"

"When term's over at the end of this week, that's it—I'm going."

"I thought all that was finished with." She paused. "So what do you want me to say . . . ?"

"Tell me you'll come with me. Jefferies can run his summer-school without us if he has to."

"It's too late to change it all now."

"I've done it. I told him yesterday. I told him I've got to get away, to rest. He understood."

"We can't *both* go. We can't *both* just—leave them in the lurch."

"So you won't come with me . . ."

"That, I gather, means you intend to go anyway."

"I nodded. "Yes.""

She looked at me for a moment, then: "This past week you've been perfectly okay. Like your old self. And now you're harping back on *this* again." She shook her head. "I don't get you at all."

Late Friday evening I lingered in the hall with my suitcases, packed, beside me. I could hear Shelagh in the kitchen as she went about her work. Then, as I waited there with my hand on the door-catch she came out, wiping her hands with a cloth.

". . . I'm off then," I said awkwardly.

"So I see."

". . . I'll call you when I get there."

"Okay."

I opened the front door, picked up my cases and started off towards the lift. As I pressed the button I heard the sound of her feet as she came after me. I opened my arms and she threw herself into them. I held her tight against me, kissed her.

"Oh, Dave . . . why are you doing this?"

"I shrugged, mouth set. "I don't know. I only know I have to. I feel okay, but nothing's changed. I still have to go.""

She nodded, leaned her head against my shoulder. "I don't understand it. But if you have to, then I guess you must." She smiled as she looked up at me, smiled as if I were a hopeless case. "I'll miss you."

We stood looking at each other. "Here's the lift," I said, and she grinned, clicked her tongue.

"Eight years in the New World and you still haven't learned to say elevator. And your accent's just as English as ever."

Behind me the doors slid back. She stretched up, kissed me lightly, quickly, one last time.

"Go on now, or you'll be late."

I found it impossible to sleep on the overnight plane. I couldn't even relax. All I could do was repeat to myself that I was going back. Back to England. Back to see Colin again. I woundered how he had reacted on getting my wire. Was he as excited as I was . . . ?

I remembered how I went to see Colin, to say goodbye to him all those years ago before I left for New York. Having met so infrequently during our lives up to that time I'd had no real hope that any last moments spent together could do anything to make up for the lost years. I stood with him in the street outside the restaurant where we had met for lunch, facing him, while the office workers swarmed about us; seeing a mirror-image of myself and, at the same time, almost a stranger. And through it all I could feel that tie between us. But we just stood there and, as we had done throughout the meal, talked of unimportant things—unimportant at that moment. He spoke of his work as an architect, I of my work as a teacher, and we answered one another in platitudes, neither of us having the courage to go near the heart.

I felt bound, constricted by emotion. At the loss, at the terrible waste. I wanted to embrace him, just put my arms around him; to be, just for a second, close to him as I had wanted to be all my life. But I didn't. Of course. I simply stood there. And he stood there. And we smiled, grinned at each other and said we'd keep in touch. And in the middle of it all I felt this great resentment of my father stir up in me. Colin and I could have—*should* have—grown up *together*. We should have shared our boyhood, our games, our friends, adventures and secrets. There should have been an *accepted* bond between us, so natural as never to be questioned. But that special closeness of brothers or friends had been denied us, undeveloped, left to atrophy. Before I was a year old I had been shipped off to Bristol, to be brought up by Aunt Marianne—childless, severe, abandoned Aunt Marianne—and as a result there I was, years and years later, saying goodbye to my twin brother who was almost unknown to me. Though, I thought on reflection, it surely hadn't been necessary for us to have *remained* apart—not from the time we were adults, anyway. But that was probably *my* fault, I reckoned. If I had been more courageous, more sure of myself—and less in awe of my brother's seeming perfection, then I could have done *something* about it. As it was I had used reasonable excuses: it was a long, long way from Bristol to London and (until I met Shelagh, anyway) I wouldn't go near the driver's seat of a car. My leg, of course. So, with one thing and another, set on the course we were, Colin and I had hardly ever got together. Even so, in spite of that, I loved him. I loved him even though I hardly knew him.

Perhaps my visit to him, meeting him in that awful restaurant, was my way of saying that. I know *he* was affected by it. I could see by the way he brushed his fingers over his jaw; it was one of my own mannerisms. I know that as we formally shook hands he was near to tears. He let go my hand after a long, long moment and aimed a gentle fist at my left shoulder—and that was his embrace. Then, in a voice that was an echo of my own, he said goodbye.

My farewell to my father only underlined my feelings of resentment.

I went to see him straight after seeing Colin. He answered the door to me, looked at my raincoat, my packed suitcase and Co-op carrier-bag, said, "So, you're off then," and retreated to his chair before the television screen. His welcome was no surprise.

I hung in the doorway for a few seconds, wondering whether I should just turn and go, but I wondered too long for the gesture to be effective and in the end moved into the room and sat on the arm of a chair.

"I've been to see Colin," I said. "To say cheer-io . . ."

There was a second or two before he registered my words, as if the images on the screen were more interesting and he had to be torn from them.

"He's a good boy," he said, his head not moving in my direction, and I thought, You're classic, you really are.

On the sideboard were pictures of my mother. My mother a young girl; my mother sitting on a five-barred gate; my mother standing with him, arms around his waist, laughing; a studio portrait—all taken before I was born. And it all amounted to about as much as I knew of her. I had long ago learned not to ask *him* for information.

"No gardening for you today," I said fatuously, and he gave a brief look at the teeming rain and said, "Doesn't look like it, does it."

I got up. ". . . I'd better be off."

"What time is your train?"

"An hour . . ." I headed for the door, scooping up my belongings. "I'll let you know how I get on. I'll write as soon as I get settled . . ."

"Yes, I'll be interested to hear." His voice was so casual. I might have been going to the shop at the corner.

And I did write to him. Twice. He didn't answer either letter.

Colin kept in touch, though, regularly—at least up to the time of his marriage. It was only after that that his letters began to grow short and infrequent—eventually coming to a dead stop. But until that time we went on corresponding and exchanging our bits of news. I told him about Shelagh, my meeting her, my feelings for her, and later on he wrote telling me that he had met Helen. His following letter with the news that they were getting married came, surprisingly, only weeks later.

And if the news was a surprise to me I could only guess at the shock it must have been for my father. I'm sure he'd reckoned on Colin staying around forever—as *I* had, I realised, when I came to think about it. I suppose I'd come to the unconscious conclusion that Colin probably wouldn't marry. God knows my father made him comfortable enough at home. Oh, sure, Colin had had his share of short-lived liaisons—the odd names in his letters showed this—but they never amounted to anything, and I thought it was likely to go on that way. But then Helen came on the scene.

I wondered about Helen. She had to be someone pretty special if Colin's marrying her wasn't just a gesture for freedom from our father. I didn't think it was. She probably *was* different from the other girls he'd known. So I was naturally curious, and eager to meet her. I wanted to meet the girl who, in the space of a few weeks, could prove herself strong enough to break Colin's ties with my father. And seeing from his early letters how happy he was, I wanted to meet her more than ever. I'd never received such letters from him as those he sent around the time of his marriage. They were brimming over with happiness and hope for the future. It was just after Christmas when they'd begun to tail off, and in the early spring when they stopped completely. Except for his card—but then, the letter he had promised to follow it up had never arrived . . . Still, here I was on the plane, going to see him. There'd be no need for letters now . . .

The trip mercifully over at last, I alighted, bleary-eyed, in need of a shave, and followed the other travellers through Passport Control, then Customs, and then out of the restricted area to where people waited in anxious, eager knots, milling about, craning their necks to catch first glimpses of loved ones. I moved among them hesitantly, trembling with anticipation, looking everywhere at once. I could see no sign of Colin's tall frame—but there, when I'd cabled I hadn't asked him to meet me, and also I'd arrived at very short notice. My disappointment temporarily smothered, I got in line and changed some dollars for sterling, then caught a bus to the air terminal. Once there I went straight to a telephone and dialled the number of the cottage. Still out of order. After I'd replaced the receiver I just stood there. I felt let-down and a little annoyed. All around me people were moving about with purpose and determination, while I could only hover, nervously smoking and feeling my excitement evaporate. I wasn't even sure that Colin and Helen were *at* the cottage. They could be away somewhere and not even have received my wire . . .

I pondered for a while on whether to take the chance and just make my way to Hillingham in the hope of finding them in. But what if they weren't? Then I'd be stuck in a small, strange place, knowing no one . . . No, I wouldn't risk a wild-goose-chase . . . I'd go first to see my father.

For some reason I didn't want to examine I was glad of the excuse to go and see him. All the way here on the plane I'd had it in the back of my mind that I wouldn't see him. I wouldn't. I didn't feel up to facing again that indifference in his eyes; hearing it in his voice. I didn't even *want* to see him, I'd told myself; I knew I'd be unhappier for any confrontation. Nothing would have changed, I was sure. There wasn't any reason why he even had to know I was in the country. He wouldn't care, anyway . . .

All these things I had thought about—and there I was, stubbing out my cigarette, climbing into a cab and giving my father's address in Hampstead. No phone call first, either. That would have stopped me; he would have said something, or not said something, that would have been sufficient to keep me away . . . I sat gazing out at the strange streets of London. I was a fool, I knew it. I didn't, couldn't, give up. Thirty-two years of it and I still didn't know when to call it a day.

I avoided looking at his windows as I went up the front steps—just in case he might happen to be looking out. I rang the bell and waited. I looked at my watch. It was just after two-thirty. I rang again. And at last I heard his foot-steps, and there he was, inching open the door.

He looked at me, saying nothing, then, with a sudden movement, held the door wider. I stepped past him into the darkened hall and then followed him into the living-room. I stood looking at his back as he gazed from the rear window onto the garden—same flowers, same greenery.

"How are you?" I asked.

It was as if I hadn't spoken, and I thought, I was right, nothing has changed—even after eight years. But I hadn't really expected it to, had I? No, but I had hoped . . .

"You didn't waste any time, did you," he said without looking at me.

I didn't understand him. "I've come over for a holiday," I said. "I thought I'd just—call in and see you. Before I go on to see Colin . . ."

"Yes," he said, "you go and see him."

And here I am. Now. With Colin. And we're probably closer than we ever were before, since the time we shared the space of our mother's womb. We really are together again now. He won't go away, and neither shall I.

I turn to lie as he is lying. I can hear birds singing, smell the scent of the flowers. I close my eyes against the sun, feeling its warmth on my face. It's what I came back for—to be with him.

The only difference is, I'm on top of the earth and he is under it.

3

❧ ❧ ❧

When my father said Colin was dead I thought for a moment I'd heard wrong. I stared at him, but his face remained impassive and I knew there was no mistake. I felt my lips beginning to twitch in the beginnings of a hysterical smile, and I stood clenching my hands, my eyelids, my teeth, in an effort just to be still.

Opening my eyes again I could see the enormous change in my father. Not just the change wrought by the passing of years; it was much, much more. He stood silent, almost leaning against the back of his armchair, thin hands gouging the fabric like gnarled tree roots. His face was deeply lined and his eyes, red-rimmed, looked past me towards the rear window, seeing nothing. After a little while he turned his head and peered into my face, then let his gaze move down my body to my unmatching feet. He looked away again.

I sat down on the sofa, tears welling up in my eyes, spilling and running down. When I could speak I said:

". . . When . . . ?"

"The funeral was a week ago."

"How did it happen . . . ? Was he—ill?"

"I don't want to talk about it. It's over."

"I've got to know."

"It can't make any difference to you, one way or the other, what I tell you . . ." And then he was leaning over, opening a drawer in the sideboard. His hand had moved and a little bunch of keys fell on the carpet. I picked them up.

"What are these for . . . ?"

"His place in Hillingham. It's yours."

"Mine . . . ? The cottage?"

"In his will. There's probably a letter on the way to you now—from his bank in the village—they're his executors and trustees." He nodded towards the keys. "He left that spare set with me."

"And that's the way I would have heard," I said, "from his *bank*?"

He said nothing. I looked down at the keys in my hand. "Anyway," I said, "it was Helen's house. How come *I'm* getting it? What about her?"

"Don't talk to me about her."

It was clear then from the sound of his voice, his expression, how much he disliked her. Perhaps hated her. And he probably thought he had reason to. There Colin had been, safe, resisting all outside influences for over thirty years. Till Helen had come along. And Colin had gone away with her and now he was dead. Yes, my father could hate her for that. I wondered what Colin had really felt for this ageing man who now sat hunched in his chair, his mouth pressed into a thin, bitter line. Had he loved him? Perhaps. Even so, his love for Helen had been stronger.

I fingered the keys. There was a small tag attached with words on it: *Gerrard's Hill Cottage*.

"You'll also get whatever else he had," my father was saying, "in time. Anyway, the house is yours. I wish you joy of it."

"But what about his wife?"

"*Wife*." He almost spat the word out. "*She* doesn't need it." He looked at me with his lip curled. "I'd be glad if you wouldn't mention her to me—that neurotic—*bitch*—with her artsy-craftsy ways."

I just stared at him. Could she have done so much to rate such vitriol? Were my mother and my brother the only two people my father had found it possible to love?

"Was he ill?" I asked.

There was a long pause, then he said, "He had an accident. In his car . . ."

So it was as simple as that. Colin had ended up just one in the year's statistics.

"If he'd stayed here he'd have been all right," my father said, "but he had to go and meet *her*; marry her. And he knew next to nothing about her." He shook his head in disgust. "He moved in with her—before they were married, I mean—and she already had one man— her fancy man—living with her."

"Did he tell you that?"

"He didn't need to. I *saw*. I went down there; I met the man. Some layabout or other. A painter, too." He made it sound like a dirty word.

"Colin never mentioned him," I said.

"Well, it isn't exactly something you'd want to shout about, is it. Anyway, he didn't stay long after Colin got there. That was something, I suppose."

"I still can't believe that—that Colin's dead," I said. "I can't seem to—take it in."

"No," he said slowly. "It's not easy."

I felt sorry for him. Though he didn't need my sympathy and would never have asked for it. But he was suddenly pathetic.

"When did you get here?" he said. He sounded tired, as if it required effort to speak.

"Not long ago. I came straight from the airport . . ." Who would have thought he was my father? I didn't even know how to address him. "Father" sounded too formal and a joke, while "Dad" would have been a ludicrous lie . . .

"You should have stayed in America," he said. His voice had taken on a slightly softer tone; he might have been trying to be pleasant; I couldn't tell—I just didn't know him. "You'll never know what a shock it was," he said. "You—you're young. You're resilient . . ." He shook his head, bewildered. I had thought I would never understand him, but perhaps I was just beginning to—or maybe I didn't even *need* to. Just accept. I felt suddenly less resentful—he had only been blind; all sensibility and no sense.

"I can't really expect you to understand," he said. And then: "How could you? He was everything to me."

The feelings of sympathy and forgiveness in me died.

"Where will you be staying?" he called after me as I strode into the hall.

Ironically I had hoped that I might stay *there* with *him* that night. Colin's death might have brought us together. No chance at all. I just wanted to get out.

"I'll be in touch," I said. I was at the front door, wrestling with my suitcases. He came up behind me.

"Where are you going now?"

The front door was open. I was moving through into the sun. I shrugged. "Hillingham, I guess."

"Hillingham." He nodded. "You don't let the grass grow under your feet, do you."

At Paddington I caught a train to Reading, from where, I'd been told, I could get a bus to Hillingham. Waiting from the bus I killed time in a pub, drank a scotch with one meagre piece of ice floating in it, and asked myself what I was doing, what I hoped to achieve. Colin wasn't at the cottage. Colin was dead. There was nothing to go there for. But still I sat there on the grained-plastic seat, sipping at my drink and watching the clock. Of course I would go there. I had to do *something*.

It was after six when I got to Gerrard's Hill. The friendly taxi-driver who had driven me from the village was heading back the way we had come, leaving me standing on the grass verge, my cases at my feet. I looked over the hedge, looked at the cottage.

It was beautiful. Far more beautiful than it had appeared in any of the photographs Colin had sent, and for a while I stayed quite still, relishing my first sight of it. It was all so *complete*, I thought—so *right*. There was the tall, steep, peg-tiled roof, with the moss growing in the crevices; there were the dormer windows, the stout stone walls, the roses that climbed the walls and grew in profusion over the gate's arch; there all the colours of the garden that lay around the house and stretched out, away, beyond; and the very lines of the house itself—not one of them precision-straight—all of them showing the personal touch of the hand—the laying on of stone on stone, tile on tile. I thought of the ugly blocks of flats I had passed while coming here in the train—great tall buildings of regimented slots; great grey slabs of concrete—buildings that would never mellow; to which a thousand years could not add, through age and weathering, a single touch of grace . . . Not so this place. This place, Colin said, had brought him happiness, peace. And standing there, I understood. Birds sang, leaves rustled. The only sound of man's making came from the taxi as it disappeared into the distance. Before me stood the cottage. Helen and Colin's cottage. Now mine.

Pushing open the front gate I went in underneath the roses and, ignoring the front door, followed the flagstoned path that led to the rear. At the back of the house a green lawn, framed by flower borders, swept up towards what looked to be an orchard. The air was full of the scent of growing things.

The second key I tried fitted the lock of the back door, and I went in,—very quietly—almost consciously so—as if afraid of disturbing occupants.

I found myself in the kitchen. Everything very neat. Someone had done a very thorough job of tidying up.

The next room, about the same size, was green-carpeted—the dining-room; and from there I went into the hall, from which a staircase rose to the upper landing. I went up the stairs and looked around the three

bedrooms and the bathroom—the house was decep-
tively large.

In the bedroom that was obviously *theirs* I saw photographs ranged on a bedside shelf—all of Colin,—but
no, the last one, I realised, was of me. There I was,
grinning, looking around at the camera, cigarette in
hand; a picture that Shelagh had taken just over a year
ago. I'd had longer hair then.

Around the walls were oil-paintings, and in the lower
right-hand corner of each one I read *R. Helen Cartwright*. The pictures were good—so they seemed to
me; not the result of some Sunday-painter's flair, but
the result of talent, real talent. There were two near the
bed that particularly impressed me. One was a study of
the back garden; I recognised the shape of the lawn,
and by the orchard the white-washed wall with the rose-
trees against it, all the flowers in tight bud. I recognised,
too, the shrubs, and the silver birch that cast its purple
shadow on the side of the house.

In the next picture there were two figures,—young,
laughing people standing in a garden; but an unidenti-
fied garden, this one, shown only by splashes of green,
and the blues and pinks of unspecified flowers. The figures might be Helen and Colin I thought—idealised
versions, perhaps, but there was something very much
of Colin in the man's thick black hair and slim pose.
Helen's style of brushwork was loose, her images
formed by quick touches of colour, so that the detail
was only gathered from a little distance and from the
overall effect. I could clearly see, though, the bluebird
(was Helen such a romantic?) that hovered in the air
above their heads.

The other paintings were nearly all figurative, and
the background in each of them was urban—relics from
her art-school days, I imagined. I saw a child standing
in the snow; a woman lying in a park; silhouettes of
people standing out sharp and clear against the grey of
city bricks and mortar. I stood before the pictures for a
long time, admiring her composition and vibrant colours. If these works reflected Helen's personality, I
thought, then I knew I would like her.

On the top of a bureau were several pieces of pottery,

decorated with studies of flowers, exquisitely drawn. A patchwork counterpane covered the bed; hundreds of tiny pieces—striped, chequered, polka-dotted, flowered hexagonals, all sewn together with infinite care and patience. Helen's mark was everywhere.

Just before I went out I turned in the doorway and looked back. My glance took in the books, the paintings, the photographs. Just for a second a little needle of disturbance nagged somewhere at the back of my mind—and then was gone. I went back downstairs.

In the hall I turned right and found myself in the living-room. A large room, the width of the house, and softly carpeted in a deep, warm grey. A small piano stood against one wall, while the opposite was lined, on each side of the chimney breast, with books. I let my eyes range over the titles—art books, novels, histories, biology, famous trials and famous criminals.

At the side of the sofa, beneath a heavy antique sword fixed to the wall, a small table stood, bearing a vase of roses. There were more flowers in a vase at the front window. All fresh.

I went over by the window, leaned down and put my face to the roses. Soft, creamy white with the most delicate perfume. I closed my eyes while the scent lingered under my nostrils. Somehow the situation seemed so unreal. I felt I shouldn't be there. It was *their* house—Colin and Helen's. And it should be hers now as it had been hers before. But, my father had told me, she didn't need it, and I recalled the expression in his eyes as he had spoken.

I couldn't get over the feeling that I was an intruder. And yet, at the same time, strangely, I felt in no way alien. There was a gentleness about the house's atmosphere that was positive in its warmth, its acceptance of me. I felt welcome.

The scent of the roses seemed to fill the air around me. Gently I touched the soft milky petals. They were not completely white, I could see when looking more closely. Around the edge of each petal was the palest blush of pink, only just barely discernible. Had Helen put the flowers here? She must have. And very recently. Then where was she now? If she was no longer staying in the house, where was she staying? Somewhere nearby in the village? I had a sudden picture of her letting herself into the cottage, carrying armfuls of flowers from the garden, arranging them in the vases . . .

"They're beautiful, aren't they?"

The words came so suddenly into the stillness that I started. I turned quickly.

"I'm sorry," the woman said. "I didn't mean to make you jump." Her voice was soft, shy, coloured by the West Country, words delivered slowly. She stood in the doorway, face in shadow, her body a dark slim silhouette against the light that came through the window beyond. I could see the darkness of her hair, long, past her shoulders. I smiled.

"I was wondering where you were," I said.

4

❧ ❧ ❧

"Hello, Mr. Warwick."

She came forward into the light as she spoke and I saw at once that she was not Helen.

"I'm Jean Timpson," she said. She put her head slightly on one side, gave me a shy smile. "Don't worry about me being here. I come in every day to make sure everything's all right."

". . . I see." I nodded, smiling back at her. I didn't see at all.

"I give you a bit of a shock, didn't I?" Her eyes flicked over my face without settling, nervous. "It wasn't a shock for me, though—seeing you. For some people I suppose it would be—you being so like him. But he said you'd be coming here one day." She seemed to find it impossible to look into my eyes. Her glance, on meeting mine, fell quickly away to focus somewhere in the region of my left shoulder.

She had a warm, earthy look about her. Her teeth were very white against her suntanned skin; her nose was dotted with freckles, as were her bare arms. Her hair, much too long for a woman of her age—she had to be somewhere in her late thirties, I reckoned—was slightly frizzy and kept back from her face by a pale-blue ribbon that matched the colour of her blouse. The ribbon, tied on top of her head, seemed somehow at variance with the rest of her appearance, giving her almost the look of an overgrown child. I smiled again. "I'm very happy to meet you, Miss Timpson," I said.

"Jean. They always call me Jean."

Silence fell between us and I was aware suddenly that the clocks had been kept wound.

"Are you going to be staying here from now on?" she asked.

"Perhaps—for a few days. I've only just arrived."

She nodded. "From America. I know. Your—your brother often talked about you." She paused. "I used to come in every day. I did some cooking, cleaning, tidying up . . ." More silence, then she said: "Would you like a cup of tea? I expect you would."

"Thank you. I'd love some."

Pleased, she turned away, and I followed her into the kitchen and sat at the table. When the tea was made she handed me a cup and took one for herself. She drank standing near the window, her profile very dark against the flowers and the grass outside. She said to me suddenly: "You know, you're exactly like him; just the same voice, the same brown eyes and black hair." Then she lowered her eyes. "I shouldn't talk like that. Reminding you . . ."

"It's all right," I said. I finished my tea, got up and took my empty cup over to the sink. She began: "There's more if you——" and then stopped. I saw that she was looking at my feet, my limp. Her eyes came up, caught mine and looked hastily, guiltily away.

"You see," I said, "I'm not *exactly* like him."

I felt sorry for her, for her inability to cope. I looked away from her embarrassment, gazing out onto the garden. She said, after a moment, "I . . . I expect you're hungry too . . ."

I hadn't eaten in what seemed ages, but the thought of food hadn't occurred to me.

"Yes, I am, rather."

"I'll go on home and get you something." She picked up her basket.

"No, please," I protested, "I can find something in the village."

"It's no trouble at all for me. We only live at the bottom of the hill. Won't take but a few minutes." She was already moving towards the door. Quickly I took a step towards her.

"My brother . . . Can you tell me where he's—buried . . . ?" The last word stuck in my throat.

". . . The cemetery's on the other side of the village." She spoke slowly, as if choosing her words. "You go down the hill, turn right and follow the main road. Over the bridge, through the village square and straight on." She had opened the door, was standing on the step. "Are you going there now?"

"I thought I might."

"It's not marked—the grave. Not really. I mean—no name, or anything." She moved back past me, tore a piece of paper from a small notepad and wrote on it with a pencil attached to a string. "Here . . ." she passed me the note. "The grave is just on the other side of the wall. You can't miss it. It's the newest one there. A few yards from the path, on the left of the gates."

I looked at the paper, at the figures written in her childlike hand. I wasn't used to death. "Is that all you get?" I said. "Just a number?"

She looked briefly at me then moved back to the door. "I won't be long. But you take your time. Your dinner'll be ready when you want it."

"Tell me something," I said.

". . . Yes?"

"Is Helen—Mrs. Warwick, in Hillingham?"

"Well, yes . . . of course . . ."

"My father said that she . . ." I stopped, started again. "This place is *mine*. My brother left it to me . . ."

She only nodded. Obviously I wasn't making sense.

"Well, I don't understand it," I said. "It was *hers*. And you said she's still here—in Hillingham . . ."

"Yes . . ." Her voice trailed off.

"Isn't she?"

"Yes, but I meant . . . in the cemetery."

I was still in the kitchen when she came back about fifteen minutes later.

"I thought you'd be gone," she said.

"I feel a bit tired," I mumbled. "I'll go in the morning." It wasn't my tiredness, although it was very real. I just didn't want to go, not when it came to it.

She began to unload the contents of her shopping basket, stacking things in the refrigerator. I could hear from the dining-room the delicate sound of the clock as it struck seven. I checked the time with my watch. In New York it would only be two o'clock in the afternoon. I hadn't called Shelagh.

"The phone's still not working, is it?" I asked.

She shook her head. "It's forever going out of order. It's a nuisance." She nodded in the direction of the village. "There's a phone box down by the bridge and a couple more by the post-office . . ."

"I'll wait till tomorrow."

Quietly, expertly, she was preparing vegetables. The brilliance of the day was dying, slowly dying. I felt lost, suspended; I'd have let a blind man lead me.

"How did the cottage get its name?" I asked, making conversation. "From the hill, I suppose."

"No, the hill was named after the man who built the cottage—Gerrard." She pointed to the wall and I saw there, left uncovered by the surrounding plaster, a brick with markings on it. I went closer and saw what was written: *A.G.*, then a heart with an arrow through it, then *A.G.* again, and beneath it, the year *1796*.

"Pretty old . . ."

"The main part. The extensions were added by his son, a few years later."

"I said, looking at the first *A*: "Arthur? Alan?"

"Adam. The other initials are his wife's—Ann. He was a blacksmith. And according to your brother, a tall man."

"How would he know that?"

"He said because the ceilings and doors are very high for a place this old. And Gerrard built it to fit hisself."

She shrugged. "Anyway, that's what your brother said. I don't know much about it."

"Do you come from these parts?"

"Yes. I haven't lived here all the time, though." She concentrated on the contents of a saucepan. "I moved away when I was younger. To Marshton Ridge. Then I come back a few years ago . . . to stay with Dad again."

I nodded. "Did you know my brother's wife well? I never met her."

"She came to Hillingham while I was away. When I came back she asked me if I'd come up and—you know—lend a hand around the place."

"And you've been lending a hand ever since . . ."

"Well . . . at the beginning I didn't do it for long because . . ." Her voice faltered, then she went on: "But I came back later—when your brother came here. *He* was *nice*. They both were. It was only after she got married that I really got to know her." She sighed. "She was—a lovely person."

What a change, I thought, from my father's comments on Helen. Remembering his words, I thought of the man—Helen's "fancy man" as my father had called him—who had been living here with her. Now, after a moment's hesitation, I asked:

"Did you know the man who lived here—*stayed* here—before? Before my brother came?"

I thought for a moment she wasn't going to answer, then she said, avoiding my glance:

"Alan De Freyne. Oh, yes, I knew him." She added shortly, "But he didn't last long once your brother was here."

"Who was he—De Freyne?"

"A friend—or relative of hers, I think . . ." She wanted off the subject, I could tell. I made an effort to move the conversation in another direction.

"I never heard of Marshton Ridge," I said.

"No, well, you wouldn't. It's a quiet little place. Pretty much like this. Everybody knows everybody else. And what goes on. And what they don't know they make up."

Her last words had taken on a slightly bitter tone. I

wondered at it. I looked at her but her face was averted.

"Why did you come back?" I asked. "Did you get tired of the place?"

"Something like that." She paused, then said suddenly, with a quick smile, "Why don't you go and rest a bit? I'll call you when it's ready."

I got up from my chair. "I'm asking too many questions."

"Oh, no, no," she said, but I knew it was so, and I didn't want to add to her discomfort. I moved to the door.

"If you want a drink," she said, "there's various bottles of this and that . . ."

"That's a good idea." I poured myself a scotch-and-water, added plenty of ice, and carried it into the living-room. There I sat back in a comfortable armchair and put my feet up on the footstool. I needed the rest *and* the drink.

The steak, potatoes and salad were delicious. After I had eaten—and after Jean Timpson had gone, with a promise to return the next day—I turned off the lights and went upstairs. There in the bedroom I found my suitcases open and partly unpacked, and my pyjamas neatly laid out on the turned-down bed.

I took a soothing bath, put on my towelling robe and walked, tip-toe-on-my-left-foot, back to the soft-carpeted bedroom. In spite of the coffee I'd drunk I felt so sleepy that I debated for a moment whether or not I'd need a sleeping-pill. But I took one; I'd been caught out before. I walked over to the open window and stood there in the darkness, the bedside lamp switched off behind me. I looked down towards the village where the windows winked their yellow lights in the summer night. I yawned, closed the curtains, went to my bed and climbed in. I whispered, "Oh, Colin . . ." into the dark, and fell asleep.

I awoke with the sunlight streaming in through the crack between the curtains. I hadn't set the alarm-clock at my bedside and I'd also forgotten to wind my watch. I dressed in a pair of faded blue denims and went downstairs. The clock in the dining-room told me it was just after eight. I made myself a cup of instant coffee and carried it out into the garden. The morning sun was so bright, the air so warm and clear—no hint of the New York humidity I had never grown accustomed to. I wandered over to a wooden seat on the rolling lawn and sat there sipping from my cup. Later on, I told myself, I would go to the village, to the cemetery. And I must phone Shelagh, too. But there was plenty of time for that—in New York it was still the middle of the night. For the moment I could take in the morning, feel the soft grass under my bare feet and enjoy my new sense of freedom.

Over in a little round flower bed I saw some small rose-trees bearing the creamy-white flowers I had seen in the house. I went over, leaned down, taking in the almost-familiar fragrance. As I straightened up I heard Jean Timpson's voice behind me.

"Good morning . . ."

I turned, smiled at her. She half lifted the basket she held in her hands.

"I brought you some nice fresh eggs for your breakfast."

"You'll spoil me," I said.

And I said the same thing to her half-an-hour later as I sat at the dining-table with scrambled eggs and toast before me. And it was a real possibility—the food was so good. When I had finished I got ready to leave for the cemetery. As I opened the front gate I heard her calling after me. I stopped, waited while she came round the side of the house carrying scissors and paper.

"I wondered . . . well . . . per'aps . . . per'aps you'd like to take some flowers with you . . ."

"I should have thought of it myself," I said. "Thank you." I watched her then as she leaned over and snipped away at the roses, pink, yellow, white. Carefully she wrapped them in the brown paper.

"From their own garden," she murmured as she handed them to me. "I think it has more . . . meaning."

I could feel her eyes on my back as I started down the hill. Just before I turned the bend in the road I glanced back and saw that she was still watching me; I could see the movement of her blue blouse as she moved back behind the cover of the hedge. I wondered about Jean Timpson . . . Was it her intention to look after me while I was here? I wasn't so sure that I wanted her around the place all the time. Still, it wouldn't be a problem; I wouldn't be staying any length of time.

Following her directions I took the winding road that led into the heart of the village, coming into the square almost before I was aware of it. Last night when I arrived there by bus I hadn't been in any frame of mind to take note of my surroundings. Now I did. It all looked as if it hadn't changed very much over the years. There were a couple of hotels, the usual pubs and, in between, rows of shops in which only the goods displayed seemed to give any real evidence of the progress of time—this apart from the other signs of the century: the cars, and the inevitable television aerials sprouting from the weathered rooftops.

The few people I had passed on my way from the cottage prepared me now for the curious, surprised looks I got as I walked across the square. Being so like Colin, I knew I had to come as something of a surprise to the passers-by. But word would soon get around . . .

Above the houses I saw, reaching up into the sky, the spire of the little church. Then, rounding the bend, there it was before me, surrounded by the cemetery with its green, green grass, and stones like uneven teeth. I turned in at the gate.

Jean Timpson was right—the grave was easy to find. I saw it at once, the little marker bearing the number, the newness of the freshly turned earth, the vase holding roses, and delphiniums of the most exquisite blue. Jean Timpson's work, you could be sure.

I stood for some moments looking down, picturing Colin lying there with Helen beside him. I knelt and put the flowers along with those that were already there. The combined scent of the blossoms was strong, heady stuff.

Colin . . .

I couldn't get my breath. Beyond my tears the flowers were a blur.

After a while I got up and brushed the bits of dead cut-grass from my trousers. An elderly man came wandering along the little paths that ran between the graves. He walked slowly, going nowhere in particular, looking calmly around him with proprietorial gaze. As I looked at him he nodded a silent good morning, then came leisurely towards me. When he was close he stopped and looked down at the grave over which I stood, lost, and then up into my face. His eyes were cool, unruffled. Death, burial, were nothing new to him. I didn't say anything. The tears were still wet on my cheeks and I knew that with my first words I would go completely. I turned away, waiting, gaining time. He waited too. He'd seen it all before. When at last I faced him again I saw his faded eyes were full of sympathy and understanding.

He was the sexton, Harrier, he told me. Could he help me in any way . . . ?

"Thank you . . . No . . ." It was beyond help.

"I didn't know them," he said. His accent was very broad.

"My brother and his wife . . ."

He nodded. After a few moments he turned to go, his mouth framing a farewell. I said, stopping him:

"I only found out about it yesterday—the car crash. I still don't know when it happened."

He looked at me in surprise for a second, then took a small notebook from his pocket and flipped through the pages.

"The sixteenth of May."

I stared at him. He looked back at me with concern.

"Are you all right, sir?"

"Yes. Yes, thank you . . ." The sixteenth of May. The day following my birthday. *Our* birthday.

"Do you know what time?" I asked, knowing what the answer would be.

"About eleven at night, I believe." He was a mine of information.

About eleven at night. In New York it would have been about six. The day of the faculty meeting. It was then that Colin had been killed. While I had been at the refectory table, with Shelagh beside me and Varley's voice droning on. It was then. Colin, in his red MG had crashed, had died. And in the moments of his death I'd felt that explosion in my brain; I could remember it so clearly; and that terrible pressure on my chest, that wrenching at my heart, that vicious, piercing, rending inside me, so that I had gone down like a felled tree . . .

Colin and I—we had been closer than I could ever have dreamed.

I gestured to the newly dug plot at my feet. "The funeral was a week ago, I understand . . ."

He nodded. "*His* was, yes . . ."

"*His* funeral?" What did he mean? "You mean they had *separate* funerals?"

His notebook was open again. He flicked the pages. "That's it—Friday, the twelfth. She was buried ten days before." He nodded confirmation, while I just stared at him. I didn't get it.

"I thought . . . I assumed . . ." I began, then ground to a halt. I took a deep breath. "What happened to *her*? How did *she* die . . .?"

He hesitated before he answered. "I—I just looks after all this, sir. You best go and talk to somebody else." He turned away. Dimly I heard his murmured good morning, and he was off, moving along the narrow, angular, short-cropped paths.

5

❧ ❧ ❧

There was no sign of Jean Timpson on my return to the cottage. I went back outside, across the lawn to the seat and sat thinking on what the sexton had told me. It was too much to deal with . . .

As I sat there my eye was caught by a small lithe shape that crept amongst the flowers. A small cat, little more than a kitten. Against its glossy black fur the poppies showed up an even more brilliant red. I leaned forward, my hand reaching out, fingers moving on thumb.

"Here, kitty . . . here, kitty . . .

The cat stopped, one white paw raised, and looked round at me. I saw the snow white bib, the alert, observing eyes, and then she was moving on again, on up towards the orchard.

I leaned back and, squinting against the sun's glare, looked at my cottage—my cottage. It was what I'd always wanted. Everybody's dream house. But that I should have come by it in such a way . . .

There was a blackbird perched on the chimney, very dark against the sky. He sang. His tune was made up of straight notes and trills, cascading, every few seconds the same song repeated, over and over. The sound, so pure, so effortless, seemed so much a part of everything around me—part of the newness of my being there, the trees, the flowers, the house, the garden. He had surely sung for Colin, too . . . Below the singing bird the steep roof pitched down in an uneven sweep—so much lower on this side of the house—to the walls, in places being met by the hollyhocks that reached up, and the honeysuckle that climbed around the door, the windows. The ground close along one section of the wall had long ago been scooped out to form the basis of a small sunken garden where blue, white and pink blossoms grew thickly among the stones. Everything looked so perfect. I sighed, stretched, then took off my jacket and let the warm sun get to my bare arms.

Over to my left, at the end of the very long gravelled drive, stood what once must have been stables. I walked over and looked closer. Part of the old building had been converted into a garage, a smaller section into a kind of tool-shed, and the remaining large section into a studio—Helen's studio. I could see her easel there, the canvases leaning against the walls. After a moment I went in.

There were shelves all around bearing jars, bottles, books, papers, etc. There was a table with tins and tubes of paint. Paint-brushes and painting-knives stood in a large coffee can. Her easel stood near the window getting the best of the north light. Drawings and working-sketches were still pinned to the wooden frame for reference, and an unfinished painting of a face was still fixed there, abandoned, cancelled out by rough brush-strokes that zigzagged its surface.

When I went into the kitchen a few minutes later I saw that Jean Timpson had returned and was making preparations for my lunch. "Won't be too long," she said, and I nodded at her briefly-, half-turned profile, sensing her discomfort as I stood watching her work.

"Would you like a drink?" she asked.

I thanked her and said I'd like a gin-and-tonic. She nodded. "You go and sit down. I'll bring it in to you."

". . . Okay." I went.

There were paintings in the living-room, too. Paintings of Helen's, all in her own very special style; I no longer needed to look for her signature to know they were hers. And there were other pictures, by other hands. I saw a large abstract in blues and reds, garish and hard-edged and, a few feet away, flanked on the other side by a photograph of an elderly women surrounded by cats, a rather primitive oil portrait of a man and a woman. They were both quite young. She looked somewhat self-conscious, but behind her shyness I thought I could read a gentleness, a humour there in her eyes. She was shown sitting, while the man, tall, dark-haired and rather stern of aspect, stood slightly behind and to one side, his left arm hidden behind her shoulder. The woman held a bouquet of roses in her lap. In the background was the cottage. The picture was probably the work of a local artist, I thought. It possessed a certain childlike charm; there was an endearing naïveté in the meticulous attention to detail—the ring on her finger, her brooch, the buttons on his jacket.

"I brought your drink . . ."

Jean Timpson stood there holding my gin-and-tonic.

"Thank you." I took the ice-cold glass from her. "You even remembered to put in lemon."

She gave me her shy little smile in acknowledgement. Then she said, nodding towards the painting. "That's a nice picture, isn't it?"

". . . Yes. He looks a bit—forbidding. Though she looks pleasant enough. Who were they?"

"Named Temple. Robert his name was. His wife was called Bronwen. She was a Gerrard before she married him. He was no good to her at all. Went off and left her. And she died."

"You mean of a broken heart? I thought that only happened in the old English folk ballads."

She glanced at me blankly, not understanding. "They found her dead . . ." She turned her attention to the photograph of the woman who sat knee-deep in cats. "That was Miss Merridew." She added after a beat: "She liked cats."

"So I see." I couldn't help smiling. "This—" I indicated the abstract, "—who did this?"

"Oh . . . Alan De Freyne."

There was something in her voice that made me turn and look at her, but her face showed nothing—except her awareness of my glance. She avoided this by pointing to a framed sampler that hung on the wall. "Look at that . . . how beautifully it's done . . ."

I read the embroidered words of a poem:

> *Fall, leaves, fall; die, flowers, away;*
> *Lengthen night and shorten day;*
> *Every leaf speaks bliss to me*
> *Fluttering from the autumn tree.*
> *I shall smile when the wreaths of snow*
> *Blossom where the rose should grow;*
> *I shall sing when night's decay*
> *Ushers in a drearier day.*

And there in the same neat stitches with their harmonious colours, *By Margaret Lane, April, 1904.*

"Strange," I said, "and all these years I thought that was by Emily Brontë."

My feeble humour was lost on Jean Timpson. She said, "Oh, it just means it was *sewn* by Margaret Lane." She paused, added: "Your brother didn't go much on it, I don't think. He took it down. Put it in his study. I put it back just a day or two ago. The wall looked—wrong without it." She looked suddenly doubtful. ". . . You don't mind . . . ?"

"Of course not."

"There's lots of things down in the cellar," she went on. "From the different people who've lived here over the years. Your brother spent ages down there poking about—and when the antique man came. I'm afraid the place is a bit of a muddle down there right now, so you must excuse the state of it. Your brother said not to bother trying to tidy it up." Still looking at the sampler, she added, "*She* didn't have a very happy life either. She had a sad end, too . . ."

Silence. I said suddenly: "I went to the cemetery. What sort of end did Helen have?"

Jean Timpson's discomfiture was so apparent it made me wince. And then she was turning, looking from the window, saying too loudly, too quickly: "You left your jacket out there, look. And it's going to rain, I'm sure." And she hurried away, through the doorway.

I caught her up outside as she got near the seat.

"You didn't tell me," I said, "that Helen died at a different time. The sexton told me. He said she was buried ten days before Colin. I thought they'd been killed together in the car. Why didn't you say?"

She shrugged, nervously picked up my jacket, handed it to me. I went on:

"That's all he told me . . ." Then I asked: "What happened to Helen?"

". . . She had an accident. A fall . . ." She looked up and I followed the direction of her eyes.

". . . From the *roof*?"

"It was an accident."

I looked down into the sunken garden, the rocky well with the flowers growing amongst the stones.

". . . And she fell down there . . . Oh, Jesus . . ."

Jean Timpson took a step away, eager to be gone. Not yet, though. "Please," I said softly, "tell me what happened." More silence. I saw the ripple of her throat muscles as she swallowed. "What was she doing up there?" I asked.

"She had this kitten. Girlie. A little black and white thing . . ."

"I've seen her around . . ."

"Well . . . it got up on the roof, and got stuck up there. Mrs. Warwick tried to get her down. She fetched the ladder and put it up against the wall and climbed up." She gestured. "—From the other side. It's not nearly so high there. She got right up to the top and then—then she—slipped . . ."

". . . Did you see it happen?"

"No . . ." Then she said with a rush, "It wasn't my fault. It was late. I thought she was sleeping."

"So you were here in the house at the time."

"Yes . . ." Her voice grew stronger, a little shrill. "—But I didn't know *that* was happening. I didn't know what she was doing. I just heard all the noise—the shouting, the screaming. When I came out it was—all over."

"You say it happened quite late . . ."

"About ten or half-past . . ."

"Where was my brother at the time?"

"Up by the thicket, I think he said. He heard her shouting, like I did."

"What was she shouting . . . ?"

"—For someone to help her, I think . . ." She paused. "I was supposed to be keeping an eye on her. And I *had* tried. I'd stayed for three nights—but I'd hardly got any sleep, myself. All night long she'd be getting up, doing this, doing that . . ." She rubbed at her eyes with the heel of her hand. "I tried," she protested, "but there wasn't no telling what she'd do any more." Her glance flicked to my face, then away again. "I'm not speaking ill of the dead. I liked Mrs. Warwick, I really did. But it's true, she was . . . *different* . . . towards the end. You just didn't know what to do with her . . ." She sniffed, dabbed at her nose with a handkerchief. "When I looked in on her I thought she was asleep. I went to have a bath. It was the first time I'd had to myself all day. I felt sure she'd be all right. I never dreamed. I wouldn't have let her climb up there. Never. But I didn't know . . ."

"What was my brother doing outside?"

"They were talking, I s'pose. I don't know."

"They . . . ?"

"Him and Mrs. Barton. She'd only got here that evening. When I ran outside they were both there. He was holding Mrs. Warwick . . ." She clenched her eyelids tight shut. "Mrs. Warwick was still alive then, when I got there. It was terrible. There was so much blood. I saw her die." She stared before her as if seeing the scene being re-enacted in the well of the sunken garden. "I watched her eyes go—glazed. I knew then she was dead."

The tears were streaming down her cheeks. And all the time the blackbird went on singing.

6

❧ ❧ ❧

I stood silent. Somewhere in the trees a wood pigeon rose up, clattering, squeaking on rusty-sounding wings. It settled again, and then I was only aware of the rippling trill of the blackbird's song against the broken sound of the woman's weeping.

"It was an accident," she said. "They said so at the inquest."

"You mustn't blame yourself . . ." I felt useless.

She put her hand to her mouth in an effort to still the sobbing. "I heard her, but I just couldn't get out fast enough."

"It's over now . . ." I reached out, let my hand fall back to my side. ". . . Don't cry . . ."

"But I'm sure he thought it was my fault. He must have done. I should have been watching her . . ."

"How was he—afterwards?—Colin . . . ?"

"He sent me away." She stood there like a child whose doll has been taken from her.

"—How do you mean?"

"He told my father, too. Dad had been coming up, helping with the garden. Your brother—he told us not to come back. He said he didn't need anybody any more. But he *did*. He should have had somebody looking after him. He wasn't looking after hisself, that's for sure. And I don't think he was doing his work or anything . . . He went away at the end, but then he come back again. And that's when he—died." Her tears ran stronger—for herself?—for Colin?—I wondered.

"Who is Mrs. Barton?" I asked.

"A friend of theirn. A widow. She used to live in the village till she moved up to London. She come back to see them sometimes. She come back after Mrs. Warwick died. But he should have had somebody with him *all* the time." She sighed, shrugged—gestures of helplessness. "I only saw him three times after Mrs. Warwick was killed," she went on. "The first time was when I come round that next day to ask if I could do anything. That's when he said he could manage on his own. So . . . I didn't come round no more—not till after *he* was dead . . I felt then that I *ought* to . . . The only other times I saw him was at the inquest and at Mrs. Warwick's funeral." She raised her head, gazing past me, unseeing. "He looked terrible. Like he was in a dream, almost. Mrs. Barton was with him then. And the doctor."

"That's a local doctor?"

"Yes. Doctor Reese. He'd been looking after Mrs. Warwick. They sent for him straightaway when—when she fell . . ."

After a moment she turned and began to move away from me. Her voice, more under control now, came to me across the grass as she stood in the doorway.

"I'm—I'm so glad . . . I'm so glad you're here, Mr. David . . ."

"I'll come by in the morning," Jean Timpson said after dinner while I sat over my coffee. "—Just to see you've got everything you want."

"It isn't really necessary," I protested gently. "I can look after myself."

"I always used to," she said. "for them. And I—I like to do it . . ." She waited a moment, eyes directed at my left shoulder, but I put up no further resistance.

"Okay." I smiled. "We'll have to work out some arrangement as regards payment and so on."

"Oh, that don't matter . . ." She paused. "I'll get Dad to come up and see you, if you like. Maybe there's something you'll want done with the garden."

"I don't know anything about gardens."

"That's what your brother said, at first. He soon wanted to learn, though."

"I can't *stay* here," I said. "I have to go back—to New York."

"Ah, but per'aps you'll like it so much you won't want to go back."

"I thought of Shelagh. "No," I smiled. "I have to go soon. Quite soon." Then I added, "But I shall come back again, one day."

After she had gone I realised I *still* hadn't phoned Shelagh. I had just let the day slip by. Ah, well, it would have to wait till tomorrow . . .

Opening off the dining-room was Colin's study. Quite small. I hadn't investigated it before. I went in there now though, softly opening the door, switching on the light that banished the hushed, grey-blue dusk. I stood in his little hideaway; looking at his desk, the pictures around the walls, the shelves laden with books, rolls of stiff paper,—obviously various architectural plans and things—his typewriter on the desk's polished surface. Everything very neat. Somehow it all appeared just as I had imagined it would.

On the desk next to the telephone I saw a little pile of unopened mail. My sense of guilt as I sorted through it was unrealistic, I told myself; it was something that had to be done. There were various bills,—for gas, electricity, etc., an invitation to a party in London (the date of the party had come and gone), a postcard from someone called Hal who was having a wonderful time in Rome, a couple of circulars, a letter from me (how strange to see it there, still sealed, after its long journey, ending up in my own hands!), and three or four other letters that told me nothing—from people I'd never heard of, and who didn't—going by what was written—appear to figure very strongly in the lives of either Colin or Helen. The wire I had sent was there too. And

a number of birthday cards. Among the cards I saw the
familiar one from Shelagh and me; one, very warm,
from my father; one from someone simply signing herself *With love—E,* and one from Jean Timpson. *Happy
birthday from Jean,* she had written, adding two kisses.
Baby rabbits on the front. There was nothing that
seemed in any way remarkable. Certainly if their mail
was any indication, Colin and Helen had led very quiet
lives. I stacked the pieces together again and put them
back on the desk . . . Who was *E*?

Unrolling a sheet of paper that lay there I saw on it
some sketches and a finished plan for a little gazebo or
summer-house. Obviously something to do with his job,
I assumed.

As I turned to go I saw beneath the window two suitcases with Colin's name on them. I lifted the nearest
one and found it full. The other also. I snapped open
the catches. Whoever had packed the cases had done so
in pretty much of a hurry. The contents seemed to have
been thrown in without any kind of order—all very
haphazard. My hands moved amongst various items of
clothing. I found papers and drawings relating to his
work—what looked like unfinished projects; I saw his
passport also, his birth certificate, several other documents. It looked as if he'd been packing to go away . . .
and in a hurry.

At the top of the cellar stair I flicked the light-switch
several times, but no light came on. I went back to the
kitchen, searched around there and eventually came up
with a pocket torch. Returning, I flicked on the beam
and went carefully down the steep cellar steps. At the
bottom I stood still, shining the light around me.

I could understand what Jean Timpson had meant
when she'd spoken about "the state of it" . . . The
whole room seemed to be jam-packed with the cast-offs
of the house's inhabitants over the years. I saw boxes,
crates, chests, old pictures, picture-frames, discarded
lamps and assorted pieces of furniture. There was so
much junk there that it would take a week to get
through—if one had a mind to try.

I wandered over, squeezed between an enormous old

Welsh dresser, an old clothes-horse and a chair and lifted, at random, the lid of a chest. The smell of moth-balls rose up from the clothing neatly packed away there forever—protected from the moths for what purpose?—the clothes would never be worn again. Another box held just piles of books. I directed the light onto some of the titles, recognising none; I saw the names of unknown authors printed on pages speckled with time and yellowed around the edges. The book I took up felt dry and unpleasant to my touch. I dropped it back with the others and a small drift of dust rose up, the scent of brittle, decaying paper lingering under my nostrils.

As I turned, moved away, the arcing beam of the torch reflected in two round eyes that stared into my own, and I jumped so violently that I hit my elbow a sharp blow on the corner of the dresser. I swore. Then I saw where the eyes belonged. What on earth was the cat doing down here? I wondered . . . My heart still pounding, I called softly:

"Here, kitty . . . here . . ."

She didn't move. I remembered the name Jean Timp-son had mentioned and I called again, my voice cooing:

"Girlie . . . come here . . . Come on, Girlie . . ."

Still the cat didn't move; just crouched low there, mouth open in a silent snarl, baleful eyes unwinking in the beam of light.

And then I saw that it wasn't Girlie at all. I went nearer and looked more closely. I saw the stuffed robin between its dry claws; saw the dead, dry look of the cat's dead hair, the coldness of those round, glass eyes. Under its crystal dome it stared out, past me, impassive, rigid, a decaying, moulting monument to Miss Merri-dew's love for her pets.

There were other treasures there too from Miss Mer-ridew's occupation of the house: sepia photographs in cracked and dusty frames. I found also another sampler from the needle of Margaret Lane—so much painstak-ing work, and all so meaningless now. From Keats this time; I recognised some of the last lines from *The Eve of St. Agnes:*

And they are gone: ay, ages long ago
These lovers fled away into the storm.

So exquisitely wrought, but torn and discoloured behind its cracked and broken glass.

My torch beam swung around, slowly; it picked out another old chest, delicately carved on the lid with flowers and the letters *BDG*; I saw a stack of canvases with their faces to the wall, an enormous old brass pot, more books—and then my torch went out.

Futilely I flicked the thumb-switch back and forth, but nothing happened. In the end, giving up, I carefully groped my way back to the stairs and up again into the fresh air and the light.

As the evening deepened into night I sat in the living-room, poured myself a scotch and set myself to relax in the stillness.

I should, by rights, have been sitting there with Colin and Helen. We should have been talking happily over our drinks, time flying so fast we'd have been unaware of the swiftly darkening night. Perhaps Helen would have played the piano; we might have sung old songs, our voices joining in together, and we growing closer—Colin and I—dispelling the awkwardness bred by the years of separation, making up for lost time, and making it up irrevocably so that there would never be that distance between us again . . . But I would never see him now. He was dead. I said aloud, "Dead," and wondered at the fragility of our bodies—and why death should be so final . . . Wounds, blood spilt, holes in flesh, organs torn—adding up to the ceasing of our being—so that we became just *things,* soulless, rotting flesh, clay . . . *dead.* And Helen was dead too. Both dead. It was more than I could conceive of, even now; I could only pay lip-service to such knowledge.

I could understand now why Colin hadn't written, hadn't even opened my last letter to him. The wonder was that he had, somehow, through his grief, remembered to send my birthday card . . . That part, I could see him shutting himself off, avoiding the pain of any outside contact that might only add to his sorrow and bewilderment. It would be my own reaction, I was sure. We'd follow the same pattern.

Had, I asked myself, Helen's death contributed in any way to his own? If she had not died might he still be alive tonight, talking to me, smiling at me across the room . . . ? If Colin *had* died because of Helen I could begin to understand, in a way, my father's resentment, even hatred, of her. Poor dead Helen, to have heaped upon her even now, in the grave, such a passion of enmity, when probably all she had sought had been love and understanding . . .

As I sat, the light in the room had grown steadily dimmer. Outside in the garden the leaves and flowers became silvered by the moon, the same light that filtered into the quietness around me, palely shining on the frame of Margaret Lane's sampler and the roses. The rest was nearly all a shadow. I turned on the small lamp at my elbow and the garden fell to a blanket nothingness while I sat surrounded by the relics of the house's history, relics that covered so many, many years—from the old portrait of Temple and his wife to the new cigarette-butts in the ash-tray at my hand.

From a shelf I took at random a book and flicked through its contents. Names I saw there, some well-known, some more obscure; the coiners, the thieves, the killers. Accounts of those different few who had gained their own kind of immortality by their acts of passion or greed. There was Christie, Haigh, Madeleine Smith; the great criminals and the not so great. Colin's name was scrawled on the fly-leaf. I laid it down beside a little white statuette—a knight on a charger. On the base of the statuette were Helen's initials. Helen and Colin . . . they were everywhere.

When I had finished my cigarette I turned off the light, went upstairs and got ready for bed. Jean Timpson had been there before me and turned back the coverlet. On my pillow lay a perfect rose—white, with just the softest touch of pink on the edge of each petal. I picked it up, smelled it. Silently, through my surprise, I thanked her.

When I lay down at last the scent of the rose was still there on the linen. I relaxed, comfortable between the smoothness of the sheets. I remembered I hadn't taken a sleeping-pill. To hell with it; perhaps tonight I could get by without one.

I would. It was my last clear thought before I slept.

Leaving Jean Timpson busy with the washing-up after breakfast the next morning I made my way towards the village. There had been a moment, earlier on, when I had almost thanked her for her thoughtfulness with the rose, but I had let the moment slip by and it was too late.

In the square I stopped at a phone box and reported the cottage telephone still out of order. As I replaced the receiver I asked myself why I had bothered; by the time they got around to fixing it I would probably be away again. Still, if they did it promptly, then at least for a short time Shelagh and I would have easier means of making contact with one another.

There was only one bank in the village, so it didn't take much working out that it was the one that must have looked after Colin's affairs. Mr. Jennersen, the manager—after he'd offered me his condolences—confirmed at once that they were, indeed, the executors and trustees of Colin's will. "We've written to you about it," he told me, consulting his file, and I said that his letter must have arrived in New York after my departure. He nodded, passed some papers across the desk to me. "Your brother's will. As you see, you are the sole beneficiary."

"Yes . . ." I didn't read the paper. Didn't try to. I couldn't. Not then.

"It's quite straight-forward," he said. "The house will be yours and, after the various expenses—the funerals, the administering of the estate, Estate Duty—there'll be some money, too; quite a considerable sum." He added: "Eventually."

"Money?" I said. "I didn't think my brother had very much."

"No, but his wife did. She was what you might call 'comfortable'. And now whatever's left will pass to you."

"I had no idea that she was—was wealthy," I said.

"Though I knew she didn't work for a living—apart from her painting, I mean."

"I believe she was quite successful," he said. "But that only formed a part of her income. She'd also inherited some very profitable shares."

It was a bit too much to take in all at once. "So I've got money *and* a house," I said.

"First the will will be discharged. That might take two or three months."

"I'm living at the house now."

He smiled. "I don't think that need worry us. I hope you enjoy it. It's a beautiful place—the cottage." I nodded agreement, and he asked, "Do you intend to stay there?—to live there?"

"I've got to get back to New York, soon . . ."

"Well, if you should decide to sell the cottage we can arrange the sale for you . . ."

"Thank you. I'll give it some thought."

On leaving him I followed his directions, crossed the square and found the door with Doctor Reese's nameplate beside it. I rang the bell and waited. His wife answered, tall and well-groomed. I could see she knew at once who I was—though she did a fair job of concealing her surprise. I told her I wanted to see the doctor, and she said he'd be starting his consulting hours in a few minutes if I'd care to sit in the waiting-room.

"I'm not sick," I said. "I don't want to see him professionally—not in that way . . ."

She hesitated for just a second, then said, adding a smile, "I'll see if he can spare you a couple of minutes first, then," and led the way into a small sunny room facing the square. She left me there and after a short time the doctor appeared, cheerful-looking, tall and round-faced; and obviously fresh from the bathroom—he dabbed with a tissue at a small bloody nick on his chin. He smiled at me, we shook hands and he urged me to sit down, his eyes straying to my foot as I did so. That didn't take him long.

"I haven't got very much time, I'm afraid," he said apologetically, sitting on the arm of the sofa. "Tell me—how can I help you?"

"It's about my brother—and his wife . . ."

He nodded sadly. "Of course. Let me say how very sorry I am." I thanked him for his sympathy. He went on:

"I didn't know your brother that well. As you know, he'd only been here about a year. I knew Mrs. Warwick better. I saw her several times towards the end . . . treating her for one or two household injuries. Nothing serious: burns, cuts . . . She always seemed to be doing odd bits of damage to herself out in her studio. An occupational hazard, I suppose. But mainly, of course, I saw her because of the baby."

"The baby . . . ?"

"She was three and a half months pregnant when she died."

"She was pregnant," I said, "yet in that state she goes climbing up on the roof—in the middle of the night."

The shrug he gave said there was no accounting for some people's actions. I said, after a moment:

"You were at the funeral with my brother . . ."

"Yes. He was in a very bad state, naturally. I wanted him to go away—leave the house for a while—get away from all its sad associations—if not for always then at least for a holiday. It wasn't the place for him, not then, not at that time. That house—there's been so much unhappiness there."

"What are you saying?—that the place was getting on his nerves? That he was in some way—responsible for his own . . . end . . . ?"

He said simply, "Aren't we all—to some degree or other?"

"Was anyone else involved in his—accident?"

"No. As far as anyone knows, anyway. There was no one else in his car, and no other car involved." He looked at his watch. I pressed on. "How did it happen? Do you know? Was he—drunk . . . ?"

"Definitely not. Most certainly not."

"Look," I said, "I'm asking because I don't know *anything*. I'd just like to *know*."

He shrugged. "It seems to have been one of those—freak accidents. It appears he just drove down the driveway of the cottage at a tremendous speed—and in that car of his you could get up to a high speed over a very short distance. It appears he just went straight down the drive and right across the road. There's a beech-tree facing the entrance—you must have seen it. He—drove right into it—head on. I got there a couple of hours after it happened. He was quite dead."

In my mind I had a sudden picture of Colin lying smashed and bleeding in the wreckage of his car, and I thought again of how in school I had felt the impact of his collision—strong enough to knock me over.

"The sexton told me he probably died around eleven . . ."

"Yes . . . A local taxi-driver found him. I arrived about the same time as the ambulance."

"If someone had found him earlier he might have been saved . . ."

"No," he said softly. "He was quite beyond any help. He died outright. You can be sure of that."

I sighed. "It all seems so—*unfair*. They were so happy together. And now you tell me they were even having a baby . . . Everything was going so well for them . . ."

He nodded. After a moment he looked at his watch. There were still so many questions I wanted to ask but I forestalled his forthcoming polite dismissal, thanked him for his time and got to my feet. As I followed him to the door I said, "I'm told that my sister-in-law . . . that she behaved rather—oddly before she died . . ."

He looked at me steadily. "Who told you that?"

"The woman who was looking after them. Jean Timpson."

He gave a resigned nod. "Listen, if you stay here for any length of time you're going to find that there's—talk. In a place like this there always is. Rumours breed like bacteria. Sometimes they can even destroy . . ." As if slightly embarrassed, he added quickly: "I'm just trying to—prepare you . . ."

"To ignore any kind of talk, you mean."

He gave a reluctant nod.

"What kind of talk?" I said. "What about?"

"Look," he said, "your brother and his wife were a lovely young couple who died tragically. It's terrible, but it's true. And it's over, the inquests are over, and it's *all* over now. Finished."

". . . The inquests . . . I suppose the verdicts were 'accident'—'misadventure'—that kind of thing . . ."

"Yes." The briefest pause. "Of course."

As I stepped past him into the hall he said: "I suppose you'll be going back to America soon."

"Well, there's nothing to keep me here. Except the house. But I didn't come for that . . ." I felt his eyes on my feet as I moved to the door.

"What happened to your foot?" he asked. "Accident?"

"I was born like it."

"Oh . . ." What else could he say. Then he smiled. "Is Jean Timpson looking after you, too?"

"Very much so." I smiled back. "She's capable. Very good at her job."

"I'm sure she is." He nodded, preparing the moment for parting. I thanked him again, we shook hands again and I stepped out onto the worn, hollowed step.

For some moments after the door had closed behind me I still stood there. I had hoped that my visit to the doctor would have settled some of the disorder in my mind. But it hadn't. I'd had a few answers, but they'd only set more questions buzzing in my brain. I was more confused than ever.

7

∾ ∾ ∾

The note which I found lying on the kitchen table, written in Jean Timpson's round hand said: *Gone to the shops to get a few things. Will be back soon to get your lunch.*

I changed into a pair of shorts, took one of Colin's books and went out onto the lawn. There I spread a rug on the warm grass and lay down, spreading myself out in the sun. I read for a while the story of Doctor Crippen and his pathetic, stage-struck, ill-fated wife, but the tale seemed somehow so unremarkable now. Overexposure would do it every time. There were no surprises left in the story; no mysteries there. In the end I closed the book, slipped it under the edge of the rug away from the sun's glare, got up and wandered over the lawn and into the orchard.

Not covering that large an area, it was of an irregular shape, finishing in a tag-end that stuck out like the boot of Italy. Beyond it on the other side of the hedge that marked its boundary I could see more trees—not fruit-trees, though, but elms, birches, ashes. There was a sizeable gap in the hedge and, stepping through, I found myself in a small wood. In complete contrast to the garden, everything here was wild. The smells were different too. Such a mixture of scents. No scent of roses or poppies, but subtle, indistinct smells, shaded, moist. Was this where Colin and Mrs. Barton had been talking on the night Helen died . . . ?

I wandered where the trees were more widely spaced, my path a downhill one. Then, fifty or sixty yards further the ground dipped sharply, and at the foot of the steep slope I found myself on a flat grassy area facing a large pond. Beyond the screen of willows on the far bank the wheat-fields stretched out, rolling across the hills.

I followed the rim of the pond for a while in a wide half-circle, then turned to my left and moved away from it, back up the wooded slope—the trees grew thicker here—and onto the flat where it flanked the orchard on its southern side.

Then, all at once, coming out of the shadows, I came upon a clearing where the sun got through with ease and shone down on a large, freshly-dug-looking area next to a rectangle of broken paving stones on which stood a little stone bench. All around grew rhododendrons and spindly rambling roses, all looking forgotten amid the ferns and the encroaching wild shrubbery. Someone, some time in the past, had found a retreat here . . .

I crossed the clearing and stepped once more into the dappled shadows of the leaves. Over to my left now I could see that the orchard had become the garden. Then only a few yards further and my feet found a narrow path which led me through the thicket, and out, under a rose-covered arch, to the familiar territory of the lawn and the flower beds. I moved across the grass to pick up the rug, and as I did so Jean Timpson came around the side of the house pushing a pale-blue baby's pram loaded with shopping.

"Hang on, I'll help you," I called out, and went towards her. I lifted one of the bags of groceries and nodded down at the pram. "Very practical."

"Oh," she said shrugging, "I've used it for years . . ." She paused. "It was new once . . ."

As we carried the provisions through into the kitchen I said, "You've got enough stuff here to last a month. I'll only be here a couple of days."

She looked slightly crestfallen for a moment, then, "Ah, well," she said, "it won't go to waste. Anyway, it's better than not to have enough."

I remembered I hadn't cashed any traveller's cheques when I'd gone to the bank. I'd have to go back after lunch. "I must settle up with you for everything," I said. "And you must work out how much I owe you for all your work."

"Oh, no . . . only for the things I've bought. I . . . I like to have something to do."

"But not for *nothing*. Anyway, it isn't right that you spend all your time round here looking after me. You must have plenty of other things to do."

". . . Don't you want me here?"

"That's not it at all," I protested. "But—what about your father . . . ?"

"Oh, I looks after Dad, all right. I'm there when he needs me."

"Fine . . ." It was all I could say. "Fine . . ." I hesitated a moment longer, then turned and went back out onto the lawn.

After lunch I went upstairs to get my traveller's cheques. Sorting through my wallet I came across a snapshot of Colin. It showed him sitting at his desk. Although the picture was a little dark I could see clearly his happy expression as he sat there looking up from his papers and books. About to return the picture to my wallet, I suddenly stopped. I looked at it again, closer. Then I went back downstairs and into his study.

His desk was as I had seen it first—no disorder there as was shown in the snapshot; his pens and pencils lay neatly in their trays and the typewriter hidden beneath its cover. It wasn't the neatness that disturbed me, though.

I opened the top drawer of the desk and looked quickly through its contents: more pencils, more draughtsman's paraphernalia, files, notes on various projects. Nothing there that I was looking for.

The second drawer was locked, but a key that lay next to the telephone fitted the lock. Beneath a jumble of papers I found a bundle of letters tied together with string. Without undoing the knot I slipped one out, took it from its envelope and read: *My sweet, darling Colin* . . .

A love letter from Helen. I felt my heart churn, thump, like someone discovered in a guilty act. I thrust the letter back into its envelope, put it together with the rest of them, put them all back in the drawer and slammed it shut.

Up in their bedroom again I looked at the same paintings, the same photographs. The drawers and cupboards I opened still didn't show me what I was looking to find . . .

I stood very still in the middle of the room where they had slept, made love together. And I looked again at the photographs.

In the snaps Colin had sent me of the interior of the cottage there had been photographs of Helen all over the place. They had stood on his desk, hung on the walls, stood on the bureau here in this room.

Now there wasn't one. I hadn't seen a single one anywhere in the house.

Poor Colin . . . had the memory of her face caused him such anguish . . . ? I pictured him in my mind's eye, saw him moving, stricken, through the rooms, taking down Helen's photographs, hiding them away out of sight. I hadn't realised just how much he had loved her.

After I'd cashed some traveller's cheques I went into a phone box, dialled the operator and made a collect call to Shelagh. When she came on the line she didn't bother with any greetings but just said at once, "David, what *happened* to you?! I thought you were going to call me as soon as you got there." She didn't sound as if she were in the next room, or even in the next town; she sounded fully three thousand miles away and as if her voice were only a foot above the Atlantic. I was sorry, I told her, but the phone in the house was still bust, and also I'd had a few things on my mind.

"That's nice," she said, "a few things on your mind. Wasn't I one of them?"

"You sound like everybody's idea of a Jewish mom."

"Where are you calling from now?"

"A phone box in the village."

"Well, anyway, I'm glad to hear you. At *last*. How are you? How was your great reunion with Colin?"

I tried to speak but no words came out. I heard myself gasp and felt the tears streaming down from my clenched eyelids. Far off I could hear her voice, warm, full of concern, calling my name. "David! David—oh, my darling, what's *wrong*?" And I told her, and stood in the narrow confines of the phone box and wept.

Coherent again at last, I said: "I'm okay now . . ."

"David . . . ?"

"Yes . . . ?"

"Come on back. Come on home."

"Yes." I nodded, puppet-like. I felt drained. "Yes, yes . . ."

"There's nothing to keep you there now, is there?"

". . . Not now . . ."

"Then come on home."

"Yes. Tomorrow. I'll come home tomorrow."

"And will you call me when you've got everything fixed?"

"Yes, I will."

After I'd hung up I lit a cigarette and stood for a couple of minutes waiting for the time to pass. In the small discoloured mirror next to the dialling instructions I could see my eyes still red. I went out, flicked away my cigarette and crossed the square to the small travel agency I'd seen there. I booked a flight for the next day then returned to the phone box and called Shelagh to give her the details. My decision—a positive action—made me feel better, and her voice, and the happiness in it, made me feel better still.

I pictured her as I walked back across the square, remembering the way her hair went, her blue eyes looking up, smiling her own special smile of welcome. She was reality. Maybe not mine as completely as I wished but, nevertheless, reality. This, here, in contrast, was as substantial as smoke. What did I have to do here? Nothing. What did I have for company?—memories, the people of my imaginings.

And even when I did go tomorrow it wouldn't necessarily mean goodbye to this place. Not forever. I'd be back one day, and then Shelagh would be with me. And together we would discover the cottage, the village, the countryside around. We'd do it together, the way it should be. And it would be *ours*, the cottage—as it had been Helen and Colin's—not mine alone. And when that time came—maybe next summer—the memories that shuffled through the place would have had a chance to settle.

A dark blue Ford slowed up beside me as I walked. I saw that the driver was Reese, the doctor. He pulled to a halt, leaned across and wound down the window.

"You want a lift?" He was being, I thought, over-considerate—about my foot. But maybe not. Maybe I was just being over-sensitive. I thanked him, opened the door and got in beside him.

"I'm going back to New York tomorrow," I said, watching as the trees and hedges rolled by.

"I'm sure that's the best thing. Come back when you're not so—affected by—everything. You can enjoy the place then."

I nodded agreement. We sat in silence for a while and then we were drawing level with the cottage, slowing down in front of the flowered arch. He stopped the car, we shook hands and he wished me luck. I thanked him, said goodbye, then got out and watched as his car wound on up the hill and disappeared from view. I opened the gate and went round the side of the house. As I stood looking out over the lawn Jean Timpson appeared from the kitchen, carrying trash to dump in the bin.

I said to her: "You told me your father used to give my brother a hand on the garden . . ."

"Yes."

"Do you suppose he could get up to see me some time this afternoon? Just for a few minutes."

"I'm sure . . ."

"You see, I'm leaving tomorrow."

". . . Going back to New York?"

"Yes."

"Oh . . ." she said, then nodded, standing silent, her lips pressed together.

"I have to get back," I said.

"I—I thought you'd be staying on a bit longer . . ." A pause. "What time are you leaving?"

"In the afternoon." I added— a salve to her obvious disappointment, "I'd be glad of some lunch before I go."

"Of course." She began to turn away, stopped. "Oh, I forgot to mention—the phone's working again now. They rang up and tested it while you were out."

"Great," I said, "now that I don't need it."

I remembered suddenly the money I owed her. I took out my wallet, counted out notes and pressed them into her hand. She accepted them reluctantly, put them into her pocket and picked up the trash-can. Her eyes looked past my shoulder.

"I'm sorry you're going," she said, "but anyway, thank you."

"What for?"

She shrugged. "Well . . . for letting me come here."

When she had gone back inside I followed the path that led to the side gate, opened it and stepped down the single step onto the long gravelled drive.

The garage, empty, stood behind me as I turned and looked out towards the road. This had been the route of

Colin's last journey. On the far side of the road stood the huge beech-tree that his car had hit. I walked down the drive, crossed the road and ran my hand over the scarred surface of the tree's bark. It had withstood the impact so easily it seemed, escaping with little more than a scratch—while Colin's life had been wiped out of existence. A freak accident, Reese had said. And it must have been that—a *real* freak accident. Every day people died on the roads and the motorways, their deaths making up the factors of our everyday lives—but Colin had died almost in his own driveway—just yards from his own front door.

I crossed back behind the house, went under the rose-covered arch at the side and wandered aimlessly to the clearing in the thicket. There I sat on the stone bench and lit a cigarette. My mind was full of questions. But I must have no more of them. What had happened was finished and done with. Over. For Colin and Helen it was over. For me it was over, too. Tomorrow I'd be back with Shelagh. Think about that.

A man's voice was calling my name. Beneath my sandal I flattened the remains of my third cigarette and stood up. When I got back into the garden a small, wiry old man came towards me with hand outstretched. He gave me a slow smile as he approached. He had thick white hair, cropped close, and against the deep tan of his skin his eyes were very bright and alert. He had to be Jean Timpson's father. We greeted each other, shook hands. I said I was hoping that he and Jean could keep an eye on the place for me while I was gone. "I'd hate to return and find it all gone to ruin," I said.

He nodded. "Don't you worry about it. We'll look after it." He paused, then said, "Your brother and his wife . . . I really liked them. Sad business. Very sad." He sighed, looked out over the garden. "Him and me were really getting to know each other. And he was really getting to know about all this . . ." He indicated the garden. "Mrs. Warwick hadn't bothered with it—kind of let it all go—but your brother—well, he really took to it. It was nice—seeing somebody take to it like that. Finding out about things, making all kinds of discoveries about plants and stuff . . ." He pointed to an overgrown, neglected patch over to the left of the path. "When we started on it most of the garden looked like that. It takes time to get it all up together again once it's been forgot for a time."

"Yes, and I don't want that to happen. It looks so beautiful now."

He moved away from me and crossed the lawn to where some young rose-trees stood. I followed, watching as he looked down, nodding his approval.

"You wait," he said, "give 'em another year and they'll be a picture. Very acid, this soil. Good for roses."

They were the white roses—the kind I'd found on my pillow. "They're very pretty," I said.

"Oh, ah . . . The ones out front are a bit past it now—a bit old, but these—well, you wait and see . . ." He took a leaf between his broad calloused thumb and forefinger. "Good, strong young trees."

"You must be quite an expert."

He smiled. "Well, you can't live in the country all you life and not learn nothing."

Side by side we made our way slowly into the orchard. He gestured up to where the fruit hung. "They need pruning bad. It had all been left too long. Old Miss Merridew really let it go towards the end, and then it was empty for a year or so afore your sister-in-law bought it. And as I said, she never done much with it."

"What about De Freyne?" I said. "Was he interested in the garden?"

He answered me quite shortly. "I don't think so." Then he smiled suddenly, but it was a forced, slightly awkward smile. "Well, both of them being artists, like—well, they're not the most practical type of people, are they?" He pointed to some roses that trailed down among the branches of an apple-tree. "See, wherever you look—flowers everywhere. And all got so out of hand." He sighed, and then smiled—this time with real pleasure. "Now there was a gardener for you—Gerrard."

"Which one was that? There were several, weren't there?"

"I'm talkin' about Bill. The last one—that's if you

don't count his daughter. He was a master where this garden was concerned. A wonder with flowers." He waved a hand, taking it all in. "Mind you, there was a lot more to it once." He pointed off beyond the fruit-trees, beyond the thicket into the distance where the fields lay. "That all belonged to the cottage once. Them fields. Shrunk through the years. Bits sold, hacked off, piece by piece, till this is all that's left."

"The little wood . . ." I indicated where I had been walking, where the rambling roses and rhododendrons grew, ". . . That still belongs to the cottage, doesn't it?"

"Oh, yeh, that's yourn, all right. Though I doubt there's much you can do with it. Clear it, maybe—extend the garden a bit—if you wanted to." His tone told me he didn't think it would be a good idea.

"No, I like it as it is." I thought of the clearing where I'd sat on the stone bench. "There's a little part of it that's already been cleared."

"Oh, yes." He nodded. "That's where the old summer-house was."

"It's a good spot for a summer-house. Very secluded."

"Yeh. Bill Gerrard built it for his daughter. Your brother was going to build one right next to it, he said."

"Ah, yes . . ." I remembered the drawings I'd seen on his desk.

"He marked it all out, and made a start, but he didn't get very far. I s'pose he had other things on his mind." I looked quickly at him at these words, but there was nothing to read in his face.

"I guess," I said, "the house has seen quite a few occupants in its time."

"Ah, a few . . ." He pressed his left thumb with his right forefinger, counting off names. "There was Adam Gerrard at first, o' course—who built the main part of the place. Then you got his son, Tom, who lived on here afterwards, and then you got *his* son, William—Bill. Bill was a bit different from the others. He wasn't content to marry any local girl. He ups and marries a Welsh party. They didn't have no sons—just the one daughter."

"Bronwen," I said. "The one in the painting, with the dark-haired man."

"Right—Temple." He nodded. "He was her father's handyman." He gave a little chuckle. "Handyman," he repeated, and chuckled again. "He was known locally as Handyman Temple—partly on account of he only had one hand—or part of one. A little incident with an axe. I think Gerrard felt somehow responsible, so he kept him on. Even let him marry his daughter."

"But he—Handyman—went off and left her, right?"

"Ah, buggered off to America. Just three-four years after they was married. Went off with a dairymaid from one of the local farms . . ." He gave a little shake of his head. "Oh, you don't want to hear about all the sad things of the past . . ."

I inferred from that that he felt I had enough sad happenings of the present to think about. But it couldn't hurt me, anything that had gone so long before; my sadness over Colin was the only real thing, and whatever Timpson told me of other people, of other times, was like so much fiction. "I want to know everything about the place," I said, and he nodded, "Well, natural, I s'pose. Your brother was just the same."

Turning, I looked back through the trees and saw, through the green, green leaves, the walls of my house. Reese had said, of my brother: "*I wanted him to go away—leave the house for a while—get away from all its sad associations . . .*" *Had* Reese meant that those associations had got Colin down . . . ? All *I* had found in the house was an atmosphere of warmth and welcome . . .

"Tell me about them," I said, "—those sad happenings in the past . . ."

"You mean the Temples and the Lanes . . ."

"Ah, yes—Margaret Lane. What happened to her?"

He gestured towards the thicket. "The summer-house got burnt down. She was trapped inside."

"My God, that's terrible. But how could a thing like that *happen*?" I thought of her sampler on the living-room wall . . . "Was it an accident . . . ?" Her death wish was stitched in all the colours of the rainbow.

"Nobody really knows. For sure. There was talk at

the time; you know how it is. But there's always talk."
He sighed. "Anyway, it was a very sad business. A
young couple they were. Just moved in. Hadn't been
married very long. After that happened he—John
Lane—turned a bit—funny, you understand? Like he
didn't go out hardly at all. Kept hisself to hisself all the
time."

"How come you know so much about it all? I guess
the stories get passed on."

"Yes. Partic'ly the scandals." He chuckled. "My family's been here for ages, and they didn't have no wireless
or telly then."

We had turned at the lower end of the orchard and
now began to walk slowly back. Timpson said:

"If you really want to know about the house or the
village you should go and have a chat with old Jim Pitkin. His folks have been here since the year dot. Farm-
ers. Though not him. He've got a shop in the village.
Sells antiques. Oh, ah, what old Jim can't tell you about
Hillingham ain't worth knowing, I don't reckon."

"I'll look him up." I said.

As we neared the orchard gate I saw, close to the
hedge, what looked to be part of a small stone pillar. I
went over to it and pulled aside the branches of the
rambling rose that nearly obscured it. It looked very
old.

"It was a sundial," Timpson said. "Got broke when a
tree come down. Worst storm hereabouts for ages. In
the summer of 1902. My mother remembered it, talked
about it. Also that was the mornin' that Handyman ske-
daddled." He paused, added, "Just as well he did too, I
reckon."

I let go the thorny stems and turned back to him.
"Why do you say that?"

"Well . . . if he wanted to save his neck . . ."

"Oh—because of his wife—Bronwen?"

"Yes . . . A few days after he went somebody went
into the house and found her lying on the floor. Dead.
She was in a terrible state, too—I mean the look of her.
Her clothes all stiff with dried water and mud, and bits
of dirt and leaves sticking to her."

"Somehow I gathered—from Jean—that her ending

was a—a more—romantic one," I said. "More like—pining, dying of—well, a broken heart . . ." I smiled as I said it. The old man shook his head at the notion.

"Her heart? No, it was her skull that was broke."

"And they reckon her husband did it . . ."

"Ah." He nodded. "Course, they couldn't catch him. It was too late by then. He was gone. Safe on his way to America."

"How do they know he went there?"

He gave me a little sideways look. "Ah, well, if you wants to know any more you ought to go and have a talk with Jim Pitkin."

I smiled at his closeness. We were just passing through the orchard gate onto the lawn. My house, before me, stood drenched in sunlight. Looking as it did it was difficult to associate it with the tragedies that had occurred there. Margaret Lane had died horribly in the burning summer-house; Bronwen had been struck down and left dying from a broken skull—dying deserted and alone. And then Helen . . . and then Colin . . . Was it possible, I wondered, for a house's past history to influence the lives of its inhabitants? I thought of Helen's restlessness and strange behaviour. And not only hers. John Lane's, too, for that matter. And Colin's . . .

"Tell me about Miss Merridew," I said, "What was *she* like? What's *her* story?"

"She came after the Lanes. Here over sixty years. A funny old biddy, but nice enough. Bit eccentric, I suppose. All she thought about was her cats."

On the grass I halted, looking up at the steep roof and then down into the sunken garden. I thought of that night. Helen falling. Colin cradling her in his arms. The other woman there . . .

"Did you know their friend, Mrs. Barton?" I asked.

"She used to live in the village once." Then after a moment he said,

"Jean's right disappointed that you're going so soon. She took it very bad when Mr. Warwick died . . ." He paused, then said in a tone that would deny any contrary opinion:

"She's a good girl, Jean. She's been—lonely. She's had her share."

Share of what? I wondered. Loneliness? Unhappiness? Troubles? Sympathetically I nodded. He went on:

"She've got no real friends. Not in the village. She don't mix with them—hardly at all. Well, neither do I. There's things they don't understand. Things they don't know the ins and outs of. And what they don't know they'd as soon make up." He sighed. "Ah, well, we manages all right, one way or t'other." He was silent, thoughtful for a moment, then he added:

"Course, they talked to her then, all right. Never had more'n a couple of words for her before, but when *that* happened—to Mrs. Warwick, well, they was all ready with their questions then." He shook his head. "She didn't say nothing, though. She kept quiet. Let 'em think what they likes."

I wanted to ask what those questions were. And what had she kept quiet about . . . ? Instead I said:

"Does Jean have any kind of regular job?"

"Not any more. She used to work at the stables for a time. A long time. But that came to an end. More's the pity."

We moved on in silence. From behind us came the sound of a thrush. It heightened the stillness that hung there. I stopped to listen. Timpson stopped at my side. "That sound," I said, "it's so pretty . . ." I could see the shape of the thrush against the leaves of an apple-tree. The old man nodded. "Ah. Not much to look at, but most of the good singers never are."

We turned and I led the way round to the front of the house. There we discussed terms, settled on an hourly payment, and he promised to let me know how much time he put in on the work.

"I won't be able to make a start for a week or so," he said, facing me across the gate, "but rest assured everything'll be done."

We shook hands, sealing the bargain, and I watched him as, back straight as a board, he walked away down the hill.

In the kitchen I put on the kettle for coffee, sat down, kicked off my sandals and let the cool tiles get to my bare feet. My right leg ached slightly. From the stairs I could hear Jean Timpson at work with the vac-

uum cleaner. It was just as I'd begun to pour boiling
water into the cup that the telephone began to ring.

The sound, next to my ear, was so sudden, so unexpected that I jumped. Scalding coffee slopped over onto
my thumb, and I cursed, almost dropping the cup, and
spilling even more. As I turned, much too quickly, the
cat was suddenly there, weaving between my feet, and I
lurched, reaching out for balance, my other hand con-
necting with the milk-pitcher and sending it spinning to
smash on the floor. I followed it down, falling heavily,
awkwardly, cup and kettle clattering and sending up
splashes of coffee and boiling water. Next moment I lay
sprawled on the tiles, feet tangled in the rungs of the
kitchen stool, and a deep cut, made by the broken milk-
pitcher, in my left arm. The cat, startled by the catas-
trophe, had fled. The telephone went on ringing.

With the blood welling from the cut in my arm I got
to my feet and lifted the receiver.

"Hello?"

A man's voice came on the other end of the line. It
said with deep loathing:

"You bastard, Warwick."

8

❧ ❧ ❧

I was so stunned that I momentarily forgot the searing
pain in my arm.

"Who are you?" I managed to say at last. "What do
you want?"

"Don't play the innocent with me," he said, "you
bastard."

I said again: "Who are you? What do you want?"
and the sneer in his voice came over quite clearly as he
answered, "You sound like a fucking gramophone record." After a short pause, he added:

"Well, are you happy now? Now that you've got what you want?"

"Look," I said, "I don't know who you are, and I don't know what you're talking about."

"You're sitting pretty now, aren't you? Now that you've got everything. And you've also got your freedom."

". . . Who are you?" My hand holding the receiver was wet with sweat. I could feel my heart thumping.

"I heard about her death," he said. "An *accident*. Very convenient, that. Leaves you all set up, doesn't it? Or so you think."

"Listen," I said—I was starting to get control of myself now—and not before time—"I don't have to stand here and listen to all this crap. None of it makes any sense to me. What are you—some kind of madman?" While I spoke now I was aware of the blood that was running down my arm and dripping onto the floor. "If you've got anything to say," I said, "I suggest you come round here and say it in person."

He gave a short, humourless laugh. "Yes, you'd like that, wouldn't you? Well, maybe I will, one day. But in the meantime there's one thing you can be sure of: you haven't heard the last of it." There was a deathly little silence for a second, and then he finished:

"I'll get you for this, Warwick."

He hung up, and I stood there with the dial tone in my ear and my blood making patterns on the floor.

Jean Timpson poured hot water into a bowl, added disinfectant and, with cotton-wool, gently bathed the cut. After she had blotted the wetness away she held a pad of gauze and lint to the wound and secured it with a bandage. Then I dialled Reese's number and told him about the accident. He said he'd see me right away, and then asked me if I could get there under my own steam.

"It's my *arm*," I said shortly. Much too touchy.

When I went upstairs to change out of my ruined, bloodstained shirt I noticed again how neatly Jean Timpson had laid out my clothes in the wardrobe and drawers. Shame—I'd have to start packing it all up again as soon as I got back from the doctor's.

On the landing I paused, looking in at Colin and Helen's room. I saw his face smiling at me from the frame on the bedside table.

Downstairs I found Jean Timpson hard at work clearing up the mess I'd made on the kitchen floor. I stood watching her for some moments, then I said:

"I haven't seen any photographs around the place of Mrs. Warwick . . ."

"No . . ." She was crouching, carefully picking up bits of china and glass.

"But they used to be around—on his desk, in their bedroom. I know because of the snapshots he sent me. Was he . . . in that much of a state?"

"Pardon?"

"My brother . . . All her photographs being taken down like that . . ."

"Oh," she said, "Yes . . ."

"I mean . . . was he in that much of a state after she died . . ."

"I wasn't here afterwards. Don't you remember? I told you."

I nodded. "Yes, of course . . ."

"He sent me away." Her back was towards me; I could see nothing of her face. I moved to the door. Her voice came, stopping me as I reached for the latch.

"The photographs was be*fore* . . ."

". . . Before . . . ?"

"He . . . he took 'em down be*fore* Mrs. Warwick was . . . be*fore* that night."

". . . *Are you sure* . . . ?"

She nodded, got to her feet, stood looking down at the dustpan in her hand. I could hear the gentle hum of the refrigerator.

"She was crying, Mrs. Warwick was, I remember. I heard her say something like, 'All my pictures— what have you done to them . . . ?' Something like that . . ."

". . . And . . . ?"

"Nothing." She shrugged. "He didn't say nothing. She asked him again, but he didn't answer."

"He must have said something."

"No. No, he just—just turned and—walked away."

"Let's have a look at it . . ." Reese was unwinding the bandage. "Did you put this on?" he asked.

"Jean Timpson."

He nodded approval. "She did a good job." Now he studied the cut. Nodded again. "You don't do things by halves, do you? I'm afraid you'll need a couple of stiches."

"How many is a couple?"

He grinned sympathetically. "In your case, seven or eight."

"Damn."

There was a knock at the door and his wife entered bearing a tray. She smiled at me, set the tray down and quietly went away again. She had set out two cups, I noticed. "So, I interrupted your tea-break," I said to him.

"It happens." He gestured towards the tea. "Help yourself to sugar."

"Is this under the National Health Service as well?"

He chuckled, drank from his cup and finished setting out antiseptic, a hypodermic needle and other items over which I didn't allow my eyes to linger. I didn't look, either, when he started work on my arm; I kept my head turned as far away as possible. His hands were large with broad-ended fingers, yet his touch was surprisingly gentle and sure. As he worked with the needle he hummed softly under his breath.

"What do you use for stitches?" I asked. Any question to pass the moments.

"Silk."

"Not catgut."

"Isn't that what they use for tennis rackets? Or is it violins?" He went on humming. I said:

"Do you know whether my sister-in-law was very happy with my brother?"

I felt his fingers falter, very slightly. His tune came to a halt. I prompted him.

"Do you know?"

"Why do you ask such a thing?" He resumed his work. "Don't *you* know? He was your brother."

"I thought I knew, but now I'm beginning to think I don't know anything at all."

My arm was finished. He lightly covered it, secured the dressing with tape and began to put his instruments to one side. "How does it feel?" he asked.

"Fine . . ." I paused. "Perhaps there's something you *can* tell me . . ."

"What's that?"

"Why is it that the people I've talked to are so—evasive? The sexton, Jean Timpson, *you* . . . As soon as I start to ask questions I get the devil's own job getting an answer. Why is that? Is there something I shouldn't know?"

He had begun to wash his hands. "Look," he said, "you're going back to New York tomorrow. In a few days, weeks this will all be behind you, and you'll be able to view it all more—rationally . . ."

"See, there you go again. I can't get a simple answer to a simple question."

"Questions." He gave a slight shake of his head "Why don't you leave it alone. Your brother and his wife are at peace now. I know that sounds very sentimental, but it's true. Whatever troubles they had are over. Can't you leave it like that? Your questions won't help them now. And they certainly won't help you."

"There are things I want to know," I said. "Helen was in a pretty bad way before she died—and I want to know why. According to Jean Timpson, Helen wasn't in a fit state to be left on her own. And another thing—my brother removed every single photograph of her."

"That doesn't really surprise me. I know he was knocked sideways by her death."

"He removed them be*fore* she died."

He said nothing to this, just looked at me for a moment then turned away, reaching for a towel. I watched him as he dried his hands. Very methodical.

"Why?" I said. "That's what I'd like to know. What had she done to make him behave in such a way? You were treating her. You must know something."

He hung up the towel. I asked, as the silence continued:

"Did you know Mrs. Barton?"

". . . She's just a woman who used to live here in the village."

"Is that all you can tell me? *I* know more than that. I know that she was there at the cottage on the night Helen died."

"It's no secret," he said. "What else do you want to know about her? She's a widow. First name Elizabeth . . ."

Elizabeth. I thought of the *E* on Colin's birthday card.

"She lives in London now, so I'm told," I said.

"Yes, but I don't know where."

"That's all right. I'm sure her address will be at the cottage . . ." I had already decided I must write to her. I had to contact—even if it was only by letter—someone who had been close to Colin and Helen. "I'll get in touch with her," I said.

He gave the slightest nod—which told me nothing at all.

"Helen was already living with a man when she met my brother," I said, "Did you know him?"

"Well, Alan De Freyne was certainly living *at* the cottage. I don't know about living *with* her."

"Did you know him?"

"Yes. He was a patient of mine. I knew him fairly well. Good-looking, fair-haired man. About forty . . . He was a painter also, I believe." He looked at me obliquely. "Why are you asking about *him*? He wasn't even here at the time any of this—the—business—happened . . ."

I shrugged. "Even so, I want to get in touch with him."

"I don't see how it would help you. I told you—he'd gone." When I said nothing he added, "Ages ago. As a matter of fact I can tell you the exact day. I can remember because it was my wife's birthday, the 28th of April." He reached up to a shelf and took down a large desk diary with last year's date on it. "I was taking her out for the evening, and Alan De Freyne hadn't turned up for his appointment . . ." He was riffling through the pages. "I didn't want to waste any more time so I phoned your house to see what had happened. Your brother answered. When I asked where De Freyne was your brother said he had left—gone from the village that morning." He prodded the page before him. "There it is, yes. His appointment was for six-fifteen— my last one of the evening.

"28th of April," I said, "that was only about four or five days before Colin and Helen were married. Why would De Freyne leave so suddenly—just then?"

Reese shrugged. "Your guess is as good as mine. I was damned annoyed because he hadn't bothered to let me know, but had just left me sitting here. Still," he put the diary back on the shelf, "I shouldn't think your brother was much put out."

"Why do you say that?"

He hesitated. "I don't believe they got on very well together."

"Go on . . ."

"I *know* they didn't. Only the week before that they had a bit of a bust up."

"How do you know that?"

"De Freyne told me." He paused, shrugged. "I don't see why I shouldn't tell you. I was treating De Freyne— just for some minor disorder—and when he came round to see me he had a split lip and a bruised eye. I asked him how it had happened, and he said he'd had a fight with your brother."

". . . Did he say what about?"

"I didn't ask him." He frowned. "Look, I wouldn't go reading too much into it all."

"How can I not read anything into it? Up till recently I thought Colin and Helen had been totally happy together."

"The fight was with De Freyne," he said dryly, "not Helen."

"But De Freyne had been living there with them, so of course Helen was involved. Bound to be."

"Not necessarily."

"Anyway, I shall find out. As soon as I know where he is I shall write to him."

"Why? What good will it do to start chasing after him and Elizabeth Barton? What can you hope to gain?"

"A bit of peace of mind."

"I don't understand."

"Then I'll tell you."

And I did. God knows why, but I did. I told him about the phone call. "Whoever it was," I said, "he thought I was Colin. And he believes that Colin was responsible for Helen's death. That he killed her . . . for her money."

Reese was very quiet as I talked. When I'd finished he waited for a moment, then said:

"But *you* know that's not true."

"Of course I know it's not true." I put my head in my hands. "God—I just don't know what to do."

"Nothing. Do nothing. It was just some crank, that's all. The world's full of them. Forget it."

"How can I. I can't."

He sighed and shook his head. "That's the trouble," he said, "you begin by knowing just a bit of the story, just a few of the facts, and you start writing the ending yourself. A few questions about Alan De Freyne and Elizabeth Barton, then one crank's phone call and you've already built a saga out of nothing."

"Hardly nothing. If it's enough to make people talk. And you said yourself there's been talk—rumours."

"Well . . . yes . . ."

"About Colin."

He nodded reluctantly.

"What are they saying about him?" I asked, "The same as in that phone call?"

"No, no, no . . ."

I didn't believe him. "What then?" I said. "Something to do with him and Elizabeth Barton?"

His silence told me I was right.

"So that's it. They're saying that he and this woman were having a bit of a fling together."

He said, with the slightest touch of defensiveness: "She's a young, attractive woman. You don't think that escapes people's notice, do you?"

"And are they still saying all this?"

"No, not now." He shook his head. "You'd be surprised—people can be amazingly generous and well-thinking of the dead."

"But they *did* think that. That's the point."

"People say and think and do all kinds of things. But that doesn't mean any of it has to be right."

In my mind I was back on the phone call again. The man had clearly implied that Colin had killed Helen for her money and now, here, I had come up with an additional motive. Elizabeth Barton. I sat there, staring down at the table. "What do *you* think about it?" I said at last.

"I *don't* think about it. Look, I'm a doctor, and I just do—or try to do—a doctor's job. And at the risk of sounding sickeningly pious in the extreme, that job is to help and not hinder."

"But they're all so wrong," I said. "He loved Helen. I know it. His letters . . . he couldn't fool me like that. He *loved* her. They loved each other."

"Good. Then just hang on to that. If you believe that then you have no need to go on torturing yourself with all these speculations."

Although I didn't look at him I felt his eyes on me in the silence that followed. Then he said:

"There was an inquest. You know that. And a verdict of misadventure."

"I'm not talking about the inquest," I said. "I'm talking about what the villagers have been talking about. What they think. And they think Colin killed her. That's it, isn't it?"

Without giving him time to say anything else I picked up my jacket and walked from the room.

9

Outside in the square I stood still, at a loss. Why had I over-reacted so? After a while I turned and walked away, in the direction of the churchyard.

Amongst the graves I wandered about, looking at the

carved headstones, reading the inscriptions there. All those names, all those dates, all those monuments to grief, love, memories, self-pity, guilt . . .

I looked at the tended graves with their fresh flowers and weed-free earth. I looked at the forgotten ones where the headstones had tilted over the years, and where the encroaching grass and weeds said there'd be no more roses, no more daffodils, and where the creeping moss and lichen all but obliterated the carved lettering.

It told such sad tales of life, that place. And the illustrations were everywhere. From the tiny, throat-catching graves of the children: *Simon. Aged six. Into Thy Hands O Lord* (with daisies, fading)—to the dusty plastic tulips, to the empty, overturned rusting pot, to the carved child-angel with her texture like soap who bent her head, gently smiling in her vigil of everlasting prayer . . .

There I saw some of the Gerrard graves, adults and children. They were among the forgotten, the writing on their stones eroded by the years, but still readable. I found the grave, too, of the last of them: *Bronwen Denise Temple. Born 1867. Departed this life August 1902.* Only a few yards away I found the grave of Margaret Lane, the sampler-maker. Another forgotten one—laid to rest at the age of twenty-five. She lay beside her husband, John. He had survived her by only four years. I thought again of sad Margaret burning up in the summer-house—and then again of the melancholy words of the poem she had so delicately sewn,

> *I shall sing when night's decay
> Ushers in a drearier day.*

—and wondered at a young girl being so concerned with thoughts of death. But why should I wonder?—it was nothing new. And certainly Emily Brontë herself hadn't exactly been what you'd call a laugh a minute.

At the side of the path I found a seat and sat there smoking one cigarette after another while the evening grew mellower. I thought of Jean Timpson's tears as we'd stood on the lawn while the blackbird had sung on unconcerned. I thought about all that Reese had said to me—and what he hadn't said. And through it all one thing was becoming abundantly clear: my brother's marriage was appearing less and less idyllic all the time. I had insisted to Reese that Colin and Helen had truly loved each other. And now I could only wonder whether they had ever loved each other at all . . . Not only was there all that business with Alan De Freyne, ending with the fight and De Freyne's sudden departure; I had also the knowledge that Colin's relationship with Elizabeth Barton had caused gossip in the village. And, it was certain, the talk had not stopped at *that* . . .

After a long, long time I got up, left the path and picked my way slowly between the graves to that other one.

I stayed there for ages, it seemed, leaning on the nearby cemetery wall, aware of the silence, the stillness all around me. In the strengthening moonlight the gravestones merged into a general pale luminosity, relieved only here and there where the moon's light was directly reflected. Colin and Helen's grave, without a stone, was only a dark shadowy mound from where I stood.

"You should have a stone," I whispered to my brother. "You must. You shall."

He does have a stone now. It's simple, but it's enough. And next year the flowers won't have to be placed in pots; the ones I've planted will be growing, from the earth—from *him*, from *them*, in a way.

And I shall plant *more* flowers. I haven't decided which, though. It's something I'll have to think about. I could plant some roses, I guess, but I'm not sure whether that'd be right; whether *she'd* like them. Ah, well, it'll come to me. There's time and, after all, Rome wasn't built in a day. It's just that now the earth still looks rather bare with only the cornflowers in the glass vase. It looks so new still, the grave. The flowers are new, the earth looks newly turned (as it is), and the stone is new. The stone is very new, and the lettering on the stone looks the newest thing of all. All that precise chiselling; so sharp, so clean.

On the other stone I can see a spider, quite small, climbing up the edge. He doesn't really climb; he just walks. He accepts being there; doesn't find the newness off-putting . . . I turn over to lie on my back and move my head to watch his progress. After leaving the edge of the stone he begins to walk over the face of it, across *Beloved Wife of* onto her name, moving first to the *H* and then the *E*, and stopping, resting in the groove of the *L*. There is a little shade there in that little groove. And it's a hot day.

At the foot of Gerrard's Hill I saw in the dimness the figure of Jean Timpson coming towards me. As she drew near she put her head on one side and gave me her shy, eye-avoiding smile. I smiled back.

"Good evening," I said.

"Good evening." She shifted her basket from one hand to the other. "I just thought I'd look in . . ." She nodded back in the direction of the cottage. ". . . Just to see how you were—if you needed anything . . ."

"I'm okay, thank you."

". . . What happened about your arm?"

"Eight stitches."

"Oh, dear."

"It feels all right."

She nodded, began to turn away. "Well, I'll . . . get back home. Dad'll be wondering where I am."

I said, stopping her, "You told me Mrs. Barton was with my brother at Helen's funeral."

". . . Yes."

"And my brother's funeral . . . did she come to that?"

"No."

"But they were good friends . . ."

"She wasn't there. I was there and I didn't see her. The last thing I saw of her was on that—that last night."

"Which last night . . . ?"

She fiddled with the handle of her basket, shifted her feet.

"Which last night?" I repeated.

"The night he died."

"She was here *then*?"

A nod in answer, lips set.

"But you said you hadn't been up to the cottage. So how do you know?"

She turned, pointing up the hill. "Behind those trees opposite the cottage there's a little clearing—hidden from the road. I can see it from my bedroom window."

". . . Yes?"

"She was there that night. I saw her car parked there."

"Are you sure about that?"

"Positive."

"What time was that?"

"Close on ten o'clock."

I went to speak but she answered my question before I could ask it.

"And it was still there at eleven, too."

I waited. After a moment she went on:

"See, that was the time I heard the bang. Of course it was only later that I realised what it was—the car crashing. I didn't know at the time. I'd gone to bed early—and the noise woke me up. I got up and looked out. I thought perhaps I'd imagined the noise. I could see her car still there; it was very bright moonlight."

"The ambulance wasn't called until nearly two hours later," I said. "By a taxi-driver. If Mrs. Barton was there—as you say—then why didn't *she* do something?"

Jean Timpson shrugged. "Well . . . she was there all right." Her face was in shadow as she dug her thumb-nail into the weave of the basket-handle. She didn't look up.

"Does anyone else know she was there?"

Another shrug.

"Did you tell anyone?"

"No."

"Didn't you even tell them at the inquest?"

"I wasn't at the inquest. I wasn't asked to go."

"But—but didn't you feel you should have told—somebody?"

"Wasn't none of my business. Not really, was it?"

"Wasn't it?"

"We keeps ourselves to ourselves, Dad and me . . ."

I nodded. "So I guess you wouldn't have heard anything in the village . . ."

"Heard what?"

"The talk. About my brother. About him and—Mrs. Barton . . ."

She looked at the ground. Her voice came low with melancholy and old bitterness.

"That would be like them. Talk, talk, talk. They don't leave nobody alone." She raised her head. "He didn't do *nothing*. Nothing at all. *I know*."

The vehemence in her words moved me. I was grateful to her for her belief. I said, after a moment:

"Perhaps there's something you do know . . ."

"What's that?"

"Where I can write to Alan De Freyne . . ."

Even as I finished speaking I saw a hardness come into her face. "I don't know." she said, "—and I don't want to."

I'd never seen her quite like that before. She was all controlled anger and hurt. I said hesitantly:

"You sound as if you knew him—*well* . . ."

"Yes, I knew him." She paused. "More's the pity."

I watched her as she turned the corner and walked down the lane. Heavy-footed, I made my way on up to the cottage.

In the kitchen I saw, so neatly set out on the table, ham, cheese, butter, bread and pickles. Being mothered like this was a new experience for me. I just picked at the food. I wasn't hungry.

I went upstairs afterwards. The first things I noticed were my cases—half packed, and then the rose lying on my pillow. I was grateful for the work on my luggage; I wasn't so sure about the rose.

Strange, even with so many thoughts, so many new questions that threatened to scramble my brain, I still managed to get off to sleep without taking a pill.

From the study the next morning, early, I telephoned Doctor Reese. I could tell by his voice that he hadn't been up very long; he sounded slightly put out. When he heard my voice his own took on a wary note.

"Hello . . . what can I do for you?"

"I'd just like to—to check on something you told me . . ."

". . . Yes . . . ?"

"The night my brother died—you said a local taxi-driver was the first one to find him . . ."

"Yes, that's right. He called me, and the ambulance. Why, what's wrong?"

"Did you know—Colin had someone with him on that night?"

Silence at this.

"I've just found out that Elizabeth Barton was there when it happened," I said, "So why didn't *she* call you?—or the ambulance? You said he'd been dead about two hours when you got there . . ."

"Yes."

"Elizabeth Barton was close by when he smashed up his car. But she did nothing. He just—just lay out there for two hours. He might have been *saved*." My voice was rising in anger. "He *might* have."

"I told you," Reese said, "he was gone beyond any help. He died outright, I know that." There was a brief pause, then he said, "Are you sure Mrs. Barton was there?"

"Yes."

"That's . . . odd . . ."

"Yes, it *is—odd*." I wished I could see his face. Was he as bewildered as he sounded? I prepared to hang up: "Well . . ."

"How's the arm today?" he asked.

"Oh—okay, thanks. Fine." I remembered the way I had stalked out of his house. "I'm afraid I was a bit steamed up when I left you . . ."

"Forget it. You were naturally upset. Believe me, I do understand."

"I didn't even thank you—not to mention I didn't pay you."

"There's no charge."

"Of course I must pay you. I'm not one of your regular patients. I don't believe in free treatments. Tell me how much I owe and I'll send it to you."

"It's on the house. Forget it." He was sounding quite relaxed now. "Just have a good journey. You can send me a postcard."

"Oh, I didn't tell you," I said. "I changed my mind. I'm not leaving now."

10

❧ ❧ ❧

At eleven-thirty I phoned Shelagh. Her voice came slightly slurred as if I'd wakened her from sleep. Which I had. She mumbled, yawning:

"David, do you realise what *time* it is here?"

"I'm sorry," I said, "but I had to be sure to catch you while you were in."

"It's half-past six in the morning. Where would I be going at *this* hour?" There was a short pause, then she added: "Something's wrong. What is it?"

"Nothing, except—I won't be coming back today after all."

"What's happened?" she sounded wide awake now.

". . . There are one or two things I have to sort out."

"What kind of things?"

"Oh . . . Look, I'll write to you . . ."

"I don't want you to write to me. I want you to come home."

Home . . . "I'm sorry, I can't. Not just yet."

"What's going on? I don't think you're in a fit state to be there alone."

"I'm okay. I'm all right now, believe me."

"How can I? And when I think of how you were yesterday . . . I mean, you've had a bad shock. How *can* I believe you're all right?"

"I am . . . Look, I'll try to call you later. The cottage phone's working okay now . . ." I tried to make my voice sound casual, reassuring. "Go back to sleep now . . ."

"You don't fool me with that tone," she said. "Dave, I think you should get away from that place. I don't think it's good for you."

"I'm okay. Really." We were going round in circles now.

"Well, when do you think you *will* be coming home?"

". . . Soon . . ."

"How soon?"

I fumbled for words, gave up. In the end I said, "Go back to sleep, Shelagh. I love you. I'll talk to you soon." I put down the receiver before she had a chance to say anything else.

Earlier on I had telephoned the firm of architects where Colin had worked. I knew that at the time of his marriage he had given up full-time employment there in favour of a part-time arrangement that would enable him to strike out on his own in a freelance capacity. All I learned now, speaking to one of his former workmates, Ingham, was that Colin's appearances at the office had grown fewer and fewer, and that towards the end of his life they had hardly seen him at all. Colin had last shown up, Ingham told me, just a few days before Helen's death . . . And that was all they were able to tell me . . .

It was after that that I had called the travel agency and cancelled my plane reservation. And that made it final, my decision to stay on.

Now, after speaking to Shelagh, the reality, the awareness of that decision brought with it a sense of peace. I could feel it stealing over me. I wondered at it. My reasons for staying were tied up in a whole string of questions, each one as disturbing as the next; and yet there was this peace. And somehow it had nothing to do with the rest of it. It was a separate thing—quite apart.

And I realised then that I took that warmth, that contentment from the cottage and its immediate surroundings. But no—*not quite*. I didn't *take* it—it gave of itself . . . It's hard to describe my feelings. I sat there, very still, my bandaged arm on the smooth polished wood of Colin's desk, and let the love and the welcome that was there surround me, enclose me. I looked at the room, smelled the smell of it, the faint scent of furniture polish; I smelled too the scents that drifted in from the garden—the grass, the shrubs, the flowers; and everything—by touch, sight and smell— and even by sound, with the gentle creak of my chair— brought me a sense of well-being. I would go back to New York at some time, of course. I must. I would have to. But not yet. Not yet. Later.

In a drawer of the desk I found Colin's address book. Alan De Freyne wasn't listed there, but in the B section I saw Elizabeth Barton's name and below it an address in Hillingham, which was scored through. Underneath that there was a London address and telephone number. When I dialled it the ringing tone just went on and on. I'd try again later . . .

Looking from the window I saw, over to the side, the patch of ground that still lay wild and choked with weeds; a bit of Colin's unfinished work.

Clearing the patch didn't prove to be as easy as I'd anticipated. By the time I sat down to eat with snagged fingers and aching back-muscles only half the area had been cleared. Still, I was pleased with it. Pleased with myself.

Jean Timpson was pleased too. Pleased that I was staying on. I could tell. As she set down my lunch she looked at my bandaged arm and said, "You mustn't overdo it . . ."

In the living-room afterwards she brought coffee in to me.

"Don't go," I said as she moved back across the room.

She stopped, waited; and in spite of all my good intentions I blundered in. "Would you say," I said, "that my sister-in-law was—was—generally unhappy . . . with my brother . . . ?"

She didn't answer. Well, she must be sick of my questions. Since I'd got here I'd done nothing but give her the third degree; continually raking over the ashes of the painful memories she wanted to consign to the past. All I was doing, over and over, was reminding her of a bad time, and bringing back to her the guilt she had taken upon herself. Was it any wonder, I asked myself, that her fingers clenched as she stood there?—that one hand lifted and twitched uselessly at the ribbon in her hair?

"I have to ask you," I said. "You're one of the few people who was in any kind of regular contact with them. There doesn't seem to have been anyone else— apart from Mrs. Barton and Doctor Reese. But it was you most of all . . ."

She nodded. I said:

"Doctor Reese had apparently been treating Helen for some time."

"Well, she couldn't sleep."

". . . And he knew that, I suppose."

"Well, it's a natural thing, I should think, to want some kind of medicine when you can't sleep."

"How bad was it?"

"Towards the end she wasn't sleeping at all. And it was really getting her down, you could see. I remember I heard her on the phone, asking the doctor for sleeping-tablets. I don't think he gave her any, though, not going by what she said."

"What was that?"

"She just got very—angry, sort of. She put the phone down on him."

"Did you know she was going to have a baby?" I asked.

She nodded.

"Perhaps," I said, "that's why he wouldn't give her any sleeping-pills."

"I expect so." She was so eager to be gone, I could see. She was almost wilting under my eyes. I moved my gaze, focused, beyond her head, on the portrait of the Temples. "I wonder how *he* made out in the United States?" I murmured. I was thinking of my own time there, my own departure, my father's scornful goodbye. We had something in common, Temple and I, I reckoned; we had both chosen America to escape to. But had his reasons for going been any more positive than my own? Had he gone in search of a new life in the New World—or had he gone only to escape the hangman's noose? Had he been running *to* or running *from*?

I shifted my glance and re-read the words of Emily Brontë's poem; I wasn't at all surprised that Colin had taken the sampler down. I wasn't at all sure that *I* could live with such depressing sentiments—beautifully though Margaret Lane had wrought them. I passed on, away from her sadness, and latched on to the photograph of Miss Merridew as she smiled her sepia smile and cuddled her cats. And that brought me on to Girlie, Helen's kitten—and so back to Helen. There was no end to it.

"Helen's cat," I said. "You told me she was trying to get it down from the roof . . ." I paused. "Did you see it?"

Jean Timpson shook her head. "Well, no, I can't remember that I did. But does that matter? I mean, it was there."

"How can you be so sure?"

"Your brother—he told me."

After a good deal more work I left a finely raked patch of soil—redeemed from part of that minor wilderness—and rang Elizabeth Barton's number again. This time I got the engaged signal. After that I got, from the operator, the numbers of the only two De Freynes in the London directory. Neither turned out to be the one I was looking for, but there, experience had taught me that things just didn't happen as easily as that. Still, at least I knew where Elizabeth Barton was . . .

After I'd cleaned myself up I called the local garage/car hire/taxi service and asked for a cab to take me into Reading. Once there, at the station, I didn't have long to wait before I was sitting in a train bound for London.

From Paddington I got a tube to Turnham Green and, with the aid of my street guide, eventually stood before a neat little house with tubbed trees standing on either side of the front door. I rang the bell, and just moments later the door opened and a rather pretty woman stood there wearing a light sweater and blue jeans.

I saw recognition leap into her eyes, and even as I opened my mouth to speak I saw another woman appear in the background of the hall. For a second our glances met. I watched her eyes widen, a hand lifting to her mouth. I saw her mouth open, her head go back as she gave a frightened cry of alarm.

The next moment she had run forward, snatched the door from the grasp of the other woman, and slammed it in my face.

On my way back a light spattering of rain fell. It only lasted a few minutes but I could see in the skies there was more up there, waiting to come down.

I looked forward to my return to the cottage with a feeling of slight impatience mixed with a vague, unexplainable sense of excitement. Behind me lay my abortive attempt to see Elizabeth Barton. And there had been nothing I could do about that. I had rung the bell twice, and waited, knowing all the while that my waiting was pointless; they weren't going to open up to me again. I had obviously been a most unwelcome visitor . . . It only made me more determined that at some time Elizabeth Barton and I would meet. She had the answers to several questions that *must* be answered . . .

For now, though, I could do nothing further about it. So for now—forget it. Before me lay my cottage, my own sanctuary—safe, secure; *there* I would feel welcome and at home.

No Jean Timpson anywhere around when I arrived. I was glad. Glad to have the place all to myself. It still wasn't five o'clock. In the kitchen I made a cheese sandwich and a cup of tea then went out into the garden. Over to the west I could see the dark clouds still moving up, but at the moment the air was sweet and dry. A cool breeze blew. When I'd finished eating I left my plate and cup on the seat, picked up my rake and walked to the patch of ground I'd been working on. As I approached I saw that the shower of rain had given the soil a deeper, richer colour. Perhaps tomorrow I could finish my work on it—and maybe then it would be ready for planting—with something or other; I'd have to talk to Timpson about that.

Then, as I drew closer, much closer, I saw the large round letters that had been scratched into the earth:

WELCOME HOME

11

❧ ❧ ❧

Jean Timpson, I silently asked, what are you playing at . . . ?

The sight of the words there brought a slight panicky feeling. I could feel my heart beating faster. It wasn't fear—I don't think so—unless it was the fear of simply not knowing how to cope with the situation . . . I felt strangely disturbed.

While I looked down at the earth I saw its colour darken still further as the heavy clouds obscured the sun. At the same moment I heard, faintly, the ringing of the telephone.

It was Shelagh.

"What's up?" I asked her.

"I'm hoping you can tell *me* that. I just want to know whether you've decided when you're coming back."

Through my other ear I heard the rumble of thunder, coming nearer, and the first splashes of rain on the window-panes.

"I don't know," I said.

"You must have some idea . . ."

". . . No, I don't know . . ."

"It all sounds so—vague. I wish you'd come on home. You don't belong there."

She was wrong. This was exactly where I belonged; where I stood now, in my beautiful cottage, with the rain lashing the windows, and the birch- and elm-trees complaining in the wind. "I'm perfectly fine," I said.

"I think it's rather—morbid," she said. "Before when you called you couldn't wait to get away, and now you don't seem to know *what* you're doing."

"Please," I said, "try to understand."

"I'm trying to. But—what are your plans? Am I included in your plans?"

"Of course."

"How?"

"Oh, Shelagh——" I said—and dried up.

"Are you still there," she said.

"Yes."

"Oh, to hell with it."

The dialling tone sounded in my ear as she hung up on me.

I poured myself a large scotch and sat there in my comfortable armchair watching as the wind whipped through the boughs of the trees and hurled against the glass in sudden gusts. I thought about the people who had sat in this room in the past looking out at the rain: the first Gerrard and his young wife; his son, his grandson with his Welsh bride and their daughter, Bronwen—who had married the handyman who had loved the dairymaid. Then the Lanes—Margaret and her husband, John—whose newly-wedded bliss was so soon blighted; then Miss Merridew, the cat-lover. Then Helen. Then Helen and De Freyne. And then Helen and Colin. And now me . . .

By the time I'd finished my second drink the rain had stopped. I opened the kitchen door and the smells of the garden came to my nostrils, lingering gentle in the rain-washed air, sweet, fragrant. I moved wonderingly along the path that skirted the lawn while the raindrops fell from the overhanging leaves onto my hair. I breathed it all in, that scent, so special, so completely indescribable, that comes from a garden on which rain has newly fallen.

When I got to where my rake lay beside the patch of earth I could see no sign of the words any more. The rain must have washed them away. Perhaps, I thought for a moment, I had only imagined it . . . My head felt light after the heavy scotches I'd drunk; I'm not sure that I was even thinking very clearly. But anyway, somehow it no longer seemed important whether the words had been in the soil or in my imagination . . .

I found myself smiling. So what if Jean Timpson had overstepped the mark; it had been the nicest, most original welcome card I'd ever had.

That night, after Jean Timpson had cleared away my dinner things and gone home I settled down in front of the television. I might never have been away, I thought; there was a party political broadcast where the opposition party said they had the answer to the country's ills; following that a documentary about the rising crime rate—not nearly so amusing—and after that a play in which all the characters seemed to answer each other with questions. Switching to another channel I was just in time to catch the climax of some British horror movie where there was a battle going on for some poor girl's immortal soul. Lots of blood, flashings of crucifixes and cries of anguish. I left her to it, flicked the off-switch, went up to my room and found another rose on the pillow.

I got up late—after lying in bed reading for an hour—and made my breakfast of toast and coffee. Jean Timpson had told me she couldn't get in until late afternoon—and that was fine by me. I liked being there alone.

Looking from the window I saw that the rain had begun to fall again, benevolently, gentle, roscid—and revelled in it. I knew that to have stayed in our New York apartment with the rain falling would have depressed me immeasurably. Here, though, it was different. And I held the difference to me, savoring it—the solitude, the peace that stretched before me; I hugged it to me like a wanted, but unexpected gift . . .

When Jean Timpson arrived about five-thirty she found me stretched out with the pieces of a jigsaw puzzle spread on and about a large tray that lay on the carpet before me. My left arm ached slightly beneath the bandage and I concluded that, with my attempts to play the gardener, I had possibly overdone things.

Earlier I had begun a letter to Shelagh—and then

tore it up half finished, not really knowing what I wanted to say. Or maybe it was just that I didn't know *how* to say what I wanted to say. I had then taken a crack at another of the real-life criminal cases from Colin's bookshelf: yet another theory, though well-argued, on the everlasting mystery of how Charles Bravo had met his gruesome end in Balham. But somehow it was all too much at a distance . . . It was after closing the book, replacing it with the others, that I had come across the jigsaw puzzle.

I found it (bought for rainy evenings by the fireside, I supposed) in Colin and Helen's room. Bringing it downstairs I opened the box and shook out the pieces. Ah, those memories of my childhood—those memories of my past jigsaw puzzle days,—those days when the other boys had been out hiking or climbing and I wouldn't have been able to keep up . . . But I had no anger, no bitterness now. It was simply a fact of life— my life.

The picture on the box-lid showed a reproduction of a painting by Fragonard, *The Swing*. A woman in a pink dress, her petticoats billowing, was being swung back and forth by a shadowy man in the background who seemed to be having a great time pulling on the swing with reins. In the foreground, lounging in the middle of a rose-bush, a fellow in a grey suit was getting his kicks by looking up the woman's skirts. He was smiling. And she was smiling too, and she knew he was there. One of her legs looked quite malformed—she had an unbelievably long left thigh (How had Fragonard passed it?); her other leg was kicking off into the air the dinkiest pink slipper. It was all incredibly romantic, made for chocolate boxes, and quite ridiculous—but the colours were pretty, and the garden in which the frantically happy trio frolicked with their insane revelling grins gave me a feeling of added peace.

Jean Timpson knocked at the living-room door and I looked up and smiled at her from my low vantage point. "I'm having a lazy day," I said.

She gave me her shy smile, the same one as always, eyes slipping away from my face. She looked at the puzzle.

"Mrs. Warwick bought that. She thought she might do it while she was resting . . . I don't think she ever got round to it, though . . ."

The implication was saddening. So many plans made every day—for which there'd be no fulfillment. All those train-, boat-, theatre- and plane-tickets bought, the tennis courts reserved, the holidays planned—and nothing coming of any of it. Death had no consideration for arrangements.

"I'll do a bit of tidying up and then get your dinner." She was giving me her smile again and retreating to the kitchen. I concentrated on finishing the Fragonard-woman's malformed leg. We had something in common, she and I—though if she was aware of her deformity she certainly wasn't put off by it—and neither was either of the two smiling men. As I worked I was vaguely aware of Jean Timpson moving back and forth carrying cleaning implements, putting fresh flowers in the vases by the windows. I didn't pay much attention, though.

I got up after a while and went upstairs for more cigarettes. I saw that Jean Timpson had been there and made my bed.

I saw, too, another rose.

It took me completely by surprise—because here it was, still daylight; outside the sun still shone on the raindrops that clung to the leaves.

It was a perfect rose. Just opening, exquisitely formed, tiny jewelled beads of moisture lying on the soft petals.

Going back downstairs I hovered in the kitchen doorway and lifted the rose to my nostrils. There was no chance that Jean Timpson, working over the stove, could miss seeing it . . .

"The rain," I said, "brings out the scent of the flowers . . ."

She turned, her eyes lingering on the rose for a second, then looked away again. She began to gather dishes and cutlery together. "Roses were Gerrard's speciality," she said. "Bill Gerrard . . ." She gave a little sidelong glance at the flower—unreadable. "Beautiful, aren't they?"

In the living-room I put the rose into a vase along

with the others. There were those of the same creamy
white and some of a pale yellow, a larger strain. Then I
turned my attention back to the flowers in the jigsaw. I
wasn't making much progress with it, but after a good
gin-and-tonic I didn't mind very much.

When the phone range just after midnight I'd had
several more drinks, was feeling a bit the worse for
wear and was on the point of going to bed.

"David . . . ?"

Shelagh. I answered her heartily casual, aware of
how sickening my tone must sound. "Oh, hi! How's it
going?"

"Fine, just fine." Her words were measured. "And
how's it going with you?"

"Fine. Did you have a good day?"

"It's a bit early to make an assessment." Pause.
"Have *you* had a good day?"

"Oh, yeh. Okay, I guess."

Another pause, then she said, "I don't believe this
conversation."

"What?"

"You heard me. David, what are you doing? Do you
know when you're coming back?"

I started to tell her that I didn't, and hiccupped. I
took a deep breath. "No . . . I don't know when."

"You're drunk."

"Oh, Shelagh, come on . . ."

"I don't know what the hell's happening with you.
Really, I'm starting to imagine all kinds of things."

I said abruptly. "Well, there's something *I'm not* imagining . . ."

"What? What's that?"

". . . Skip it."

A little silence, then: "David, darling, this phone call
is too costly to spend it playing games. What are you
talking about?"

"Colin . . . and Helen . . . There are people
who—who believe that—that Helen's death wasn't
an—accident. They believe that Colin—killed her."

". . . *What?*"

"It's true. I'm not making it up . . ."

"Oh, my darling . . ." Her voice was suddenly all warmth and compassion. "Come on home. You've been through enough. Come home. For my sake. I miss you so much."

"I miss you too. But I can't. Not yet."

"What do you hope to achieve by staying there?"

"Well . . . I can find out the truth. Show them."

"Aren't you—taking this whole thing a bit too far? I mean—you're under a strain . . ."

"I probably am—but that has nothing to do with it."

"How can you be so sure? Why don't you—well, have a talk to somebody. Somebody who's—understanding . . ."

"I'm talking to *you*."

"No, I mean . . . a doctor, maybe . . ."

"Oh, I get it. You mean a shrink. Keep up that kind of talk, it'll get us a long way."

"I'm trying to *help*." Was she near to tears?

"Shelagh, listen," I said gently. "I've got to do this. Please . . . bear with me . . ."

"Okay, David." She sounded weary of it all. "Whatever you say."

I had a hangover the next morning, waking late with a dry mouth, a monumental thirst and heavy head. Jean Timpson was already there when I got downstairs, ready for me with coffee and orange juice.

Feeling slightly more human I went out into the sunshine where the smells of the garden rose to meet me. I wandered idly to the patch of earth I had cleared. And saw that the message was still there after all . . . the rain *hadn't* washed it out.

No, I was wrong. There was a message there. But it was a different message. Just one word.

STAY

I didn't leave the writing there as I had before. No. I got the rake and scratched away at the letters, obliterating every mark. I wanted it over with, done, gone. The first time I had turned it into a joke, but now it had gone far beyond that. And I had enough to think about without dealing with the strange behaviour of some frustrated country woman.

I had difficulty facing her as she served lunch. When it was over I went into the living-room and sat down before the jigsaw puzzle—only about an eighth finished—that still lay on the tray and surrounding carpet. I fiddled with odd bits, adding a touch of the sky, part of the woman's skirts; but my mind wasn't on it.

As I sat there Jean Timpson came in and moved to the vase of flowers by the front window. I didn't look up.

"Shame . . ." I heard her murmur.

I did look at her then. She was gazing at the flowers.

"The roses," she said, "they're dying. They don't last like the others."

"Yes . . . shame." I returned to the puzzle, feeling her glance on the back of my head; she had to be conscious of the flatness of my tone. And then she was moving out of the room, the dead yellow roses in her hands.

So little I did that day. I walked out into the countryside and back through the village. And I talked to no one. I realised that I was just letting the time slip by; in spite of my intentions I was doing nothing really constructive. I was staying on, I had told Shelagh, to prove Colin's innocence and still the gossip—yet apart from that one attempt to see Elizabeth Barton my efforts amounted to very little. Her strange, unexpected reaction to my visit should, I was aware, make me more determined that ever—but there I had been for the past two days—just wandering about the house, about the garden. It was almost as if that, alone, were the purpose of my being there. Well, tomorrow I'd start, I told myself. Yes, tomorrow I'd really begin . . . But for now I was glad that the rest of the day was mine—to spend as I wished . . . I quickened my steps, heading back to my safe haven on Gerrard's Hill.

Jean Timpson had gone for the day when I got there. I fixed myself an early dinner and settled down for another evening alone. I loved this solitude. I felt utterly secure. When at last I turned off the lights ready to go to bed I moved up the stairs with my feet knowing, surely, every inch of the way. I had been there less than a week, yet I might have been there always.

In my bedroom I switched on the soft light of the bedside lamp, took the rose from my pillow and got into bed. The clock said eleven-thirty. I saw my untouched sleeping-pills there; I wouldn't be needing one tonight, either . . .

I tried to read for a while, but my eyes refused to focus properly after a time so in the end I put the book down and flicked off the light.

I remember nothing more until I was awakened by the ringing of the bell. I started to reach out to depress the button on the alarm clock and then realised that the ringing was coming from the front door. The time was just coming up to one o'clock. Who the hell could be calling at this time of night?

The ringing grew more insistent. I climbed out of bed and got into my robe.

The ringing persisted as I went downstairs. Like an alarm bell. But I didn't take the warning . . .

As I opened the front door the hall lamp rayed bright onto the figure standing on the step. I moved back in surprise.

"Well," Shelagh said, "aren't you going to ask me in?"

PART TWO

The lunatic, the lover, and the poet
Are of imagination all compact:
One sees more devils than vast hell can hold.
"A Midsummer Night's Dream"—
William Shakespeare

12

❧ ❧ ❧

Across the kitchen table Shelagh smiled at me over the rim of her cup. I looked at her, so pretty and neat in her yellow blouse and slacks, and could hardly believe it was true—that she was really there.

"I'm terrified of meeting your daily," she said. "She'll know we didn't sleep in separate beds."

"So what? She'll get used to the idea."

She nodded, and then said: "You wouldn't believe the panic I was in. I thought you were really sick. I was so worried."

"So you pressed the panic-button and gave up summer school—for what—to come and save me?"

"Something like that. I mean, you've had a couple of pretty hard knocks, and then after your phone call when you were so upset, and then all that stuff you were saying . . . Well, I didn't know what I'd find when I got here. A basket case, maybe."

"And what do you think now?"

She studied me for a moment. "You seem very—pulled-together. I was sure you'd be a nervous wreck at the very least. And look at you—you have a tan that's really fantastic and—well, you look better than you have for ages."

The sun was streaming in, touching her bare arm. I reached across, pressed her fingers. "You're not going to rush away now that you know I'm okay, are you?"

". . . That means you really intend staying on here—still."

"Yes . . . I told you."

"Well," she said after a moment, "having told Jefferies that I won't be available I guess I've got nothing to hurry back to. And this is a lovely place . . ."

I leaned back in my chair and stretched my arms. I felt the contentment in my fingertips. I felt suddenly, all at once, the first real touch of happiness since I had arrived back in England.

The night before, after Shelagh's arrival, we had sat for hours, talking, talking, till almost three; and we had grown closer again with every minute.

Leaving out all mention of Jean Timpson's odd behaviour, I told Shelagh what had happened since my arrival—of the discoveries, the shocks, one upon the other. And I had cried, and she had held me, arms around me, close. And the worst was over then. I had needed someone there—Shelagh, it had to be Shelagh; someone who cared, who would understand. And when my tears were dry I knew that everything would be all right.

Now, sitting in the warmth of the morning sun, I was more certain than ever.

We left our empty coffee-cups and I led her out into the garden. Holding her hand I proudly showed her over my newly-acquired property, taking her along the path by the lawn, skirting the flower beds, pointing out the flycatcher's nest and—airing my growing knowledge of their names—the various flowers. From there we went into the orchard, ducking beneath the clustered apples (the size of cherries) where the birds sang, and then beyond it into the thicket and so down to the banks of the pond.

And all the time I revelled in her joys of discovery; her ohs and ahs of delight made *me* see everything as if for the first time again. And the same inside the house as she moved wonderingly from room to room. I said nothing, prepared her for nothing, but just watched. In Colin and Helen's room she looked at the paintings on the walls and nodded her appreciation. Gently she touched the intricate design of Helen's patchwork quilt.

"There was a lot of love in this house," she said, and I grinned at her sentimentality. "I mean it," she said. "I know I sound sickening, but it's true. You get a feeling about the place. You can tell. It's everywhere. The house is full of it."

That was Shelagh—right on the nose.

"I don't think she likes me," she whispered.

"Nonsense. Why wouldn't she?"

Jean Timpson had arrived at the cottage to get my lunch to be greeted with the sight of Shelagh changing the bandage on my arm. The look on the older woman's face was a study. After I had made the introductions I added, so that there could be no possible doubt: "Shelagh will be staying here with me. Probably until I—till we go back to the States."

Jean Timpson's smile had remained a little wooden. From what?—embarrassment?—because Shelagh and I would be staying here together? Possibly. Or maybe it was just shyness at meeting a stranger—there was certainly some of that—evident in the way she twitched at her lilac hair-ribbon. But whatever it was, I wasn't about to allow it to matter.

"She'll be all right," I said now to Shelagh, standing behind her as she sat at the piano. "Just give her a chance." Jean Timpson had just gone by with her cleaning things, muttering a soft, awkward "Excuse me . . ." as she sidled through.

"I reckon she could be a little jealous," Shelagh murmured. "She's had you all to herself for days and all of a sudden there comes some pushy American female on the scene, making your breakfast and lighting your cigarettes. Etcetera." She smiled with the last word and then, more seriously, added: "And when you think about it, maybe she feels she's had you here much longer."

"I don't get you."

She looked into my eyes. "You look *exactly like* Colin, so . . ."

". . . And for her, perhaps, it's as if Colin has never left . . . ?"

She shrugged. "It's a thought." Her voice was almost a whisper. "Though I'm probably being too clever. But I think she could be a bit jealous. I don't miss much—especially when I get the fish eye like I did this morning when she came in."

"You're imagining it."

"Well, we'll see." She turned from me and bent her

head over the stack of sheet-music on her knee, flipping through the romantic covers with their hearts and flowers and sunsets. "Anyway," she added, "I'm not complaining. She's certainly been looking after you." She grinned. "And there was I rather looking forward to being your ministering angel. Some kind of cross between Florence Nightingale and Pollyanna. Now I'll have to think of some other role." I laughed, touched her hair. She lifted her face and I leaned down and kissed her a long kiss. She said softly, "I never thought I would miss you so much. But dammit, I did." Her eyes were very steady on mine. "I didn't realise," she said, "just how much I love you."

She turned from me again then, smiling, pulling her blouse closer at the neck—"It's chilly in this room"—and began to play Cole Porter's *Night and Day*.

She didn't see my smile—which I couldn't stop, but her efforts at a piano had always amused me, Probably because she would insist on playing whilst knowing all the time how mediocre was her ability. Listening to her as she crucified Cole Porter's evergreen, I reflected that the word mediocre was possibly too generous a description. Her style, if it could be called that, was erratic to say the least as she rippled through the easy parts and slowed up for the more difficult ones. I sharply drew in my breath when she solidly hit a wrong note and she looked at me with a fierce expression, daring me to complain. "Don't start," she warned.

"I didn't say a word."

"Just as well." She turned back, eyes torn between the printed page and her fingers on the keys. "*You* can't play at *all*. I *can* play a *little*."

"You're right, Miss Eyre," I said in my best Orson Welles voice, "you *do* play a *little*."

Undeterred she played on, more flamboyantly. "Oh, Mr. Rochester, you smooth, sweet-talking bastard, you." I grinned. She added: "You know, your Miss Jean Timpson makes me think of a rather rustic Mrs. Danvers."

"Wrong book," I said. "Mrs. Danvers is the creepy housekeeper in *Rebecca*. *You* mean Mrs. Fairfax—or was it Grace Poole?"

"That's the one." She stifled a laugh. "Grace Poole. That's who she reminds me of. There's something a little—strange about her. Well . . . maybe not strange exactly . . . *Different.*"

Before dinner I sat out on the lawn while Shelagh, in the cottage, fixed cocktails for us. When she appeared she handed me a vodka martini then watched while I sipped it and nodded my appreciation. She said, "I've been having a little chat with Jean."

"Oh?"

She sat beside me on the seat. "Just—an effort to be friendly. I mean, I'd like us to be friends." She sighed. "She doesn't make it that easy."

"I thought you were getting on okay."

"Oh . . . I'm not so sure." She took a sip from her glass. "And you know something?—I was right."

"What about?"

"She said having you here made it almost seem as if your brother had never—gone . . ." She watched my face, looking for a reaction.

"What else did she say?"

"Nothing much. Maybe I was trying too hard but—I can't seem to reach her. She's *so* shy . . ."

"Give it time," I said.

We sipped our martinis while the birds sang and the shadows lengthened across the grass.

"This place is heaven," Shelagh said. "It's easy to see why Colin loved it so."

Her words ruffled the calm I was feeling and I thrust them away, concentrating on the warmth, the gentleness and the peace around us. And then Shelagh was giving a small cry of pleasure and leaning down to the little cat that had appeared, as if from nowhere, to rub its nose against her ankle, tail waving high.

"Now where did you come from?" Shelagh cooed, and took the cat onto her lap, her fingers stroking the soft fur. Purring, it nestled against her hand.

"Her name's Girlie," I said. "She comes with the cottage."

At that moment the kitchen door opened and Jean Timpson came towards us across the lawn with the information that dinner was ready. I picked up our glasses while Shelagh continued fondling the cat. She held the animal closer, her cheek against the softness.

"She was Mrs. Warwick's," Jean Timpson told her. "After they were—gone she wandered off. I thought she'd gone for good." She smiled, watching the movements of Shelagh's smoothing hands. "She likes company."

"I hope she stays now," Shelagh said, and I thought of the kitten up there on the steep roof, clinging on, afraid to get down, and then Helen fetching the ladder, climbing up . . .

"I roasted some lamb," Jean Timpson was saying to Shelagh. Although she was avoiding eye contact (when did she not?) I thought I saw an attempt at friendliness—and I was glad of it. There was, she then told us, fruit pie and cream to follow, ". . . if," she added, "that's all right . . ."

"Sounds great," Shelagh said, accepting the gesture. "David will tell you, I have a very sweet tooth."

"And how," I said. "Ice-cream, chocolate—you name it . . ." I laughed, but I was still seeing Helen up there by the chimney, losing her hold—slipping, falling . . .

"Come on, dreamer . . ." Shelagh touched my shoulder. She had put the cat down and now it ran off across the grass. "Let's go eat."

After dinner we wandered down to the village and called at a pleasant pub overlooking the river. We bought pints of beer and took them out to the small back garden where we sat at old rough-wood tables. A slight breeze came off the water; not scented by exhaust fumes or garbage, but the smells of the countryside.

Shelagh, reaching in her bag for cigarettes, brought out three envelopes and handed them to me. "I keep forgetting, these arrived for you after you left. There were other things, recognisable as bills and such. I reckoned you could live without those."

"You reckoned right."

One of the letters was from an old friend, the second from the landlord of our apartment. Both were unimportant. The third, air mail with an English postmark, was from the bank in the village, signed by the manager, Mr. Jennersen. He was offering condolences and advising me of the contents of Colin's will. No longer news.

Shelagh was studying my face. I put the letter in my pocket. "It's from the local bank," I told her, "about Colin." I smiled at her serious expression. "It's all right, it can't shock me now."

"No?"

"No, not now. Except . . ." I came to a halt.

"Except what . . . ?"

"That—that phone call I told you about. I can't forget it."

"Dave . . ." She touched my sleeve. "Helen's death was an accident. What does it matter what a few ill-informed, malicious individuals think?"

"It matters."

"It should only be important what *you* think. What you *know*."

I nodded. She went on after a moment:

"And you know they were happy together . . . don't you?"

"Do I?"

"Well, all his letters. He sounded so content . . ."

"You're forgetting, I heard hardly at all during the last half of their year together, and nothing at all towards the end."

"So you think they *weren't* so happy, maybe. That perhaps Helen was so unhappy that she—that she killed herself . . . ?"

I didn't answer, just studied my beer.

"You're afraid, aren't you?" she said.

". . . Leave it, Shelagh."

"You're the one who should leave it." Her eyes were very steady on mine. "You *are* afraid. God knows what's going on in your head; what your wild imagination's putting you through."

"You're forgetting that phone call," I said. "He's *sure*—that Colin—killed her . . ."

"And you're beginning to think he could be right. Right?"

13

"Don't even suggest it," I said through gritted teeth.

"Why not?" she said calmly. "It's what's in your mind." Her fingers pressed on mine. "And you must know how ridiculous it is." She paused. "It is, isn't it?"

I must hold on to the cool sound of her reason. It was what I needed.

"Yes," I said.

"Dave, it *is*. It *is* ridiculous. You'll go on searching, tormenting yourself, looking for answers. And when you find them—*if* you find them; you might not—you'll see that you've been eating your heart out for nothing at all. There'll be a reasonable explanation—and it won't involve coming face to face with some—some awful truth about . . . Colin."

"You really believe that?" *I* wanted to believe it, so much.

"I do. Honestly I do."

"But that phone call . . ."

"Somebody getting his kicks. Somebody who didn't like your brother, that much is obvious. And you should take notice of somebody like *that*?"

I nodded. She was right. She went on:

"And don't forget there *was* an *inquest*. And there they were presented with all the facts. That's what inquests are *for*."

"Yes."

"It makes sense, doesn't it?"

"Yes."

And it did. It did make sense. I smiled at her. "I needed somebody to talk to." I said. "Or rather, somebody to talk to *me*. I know I haven't been able to see straight."

"I'm not surprised, under the circumstances. I'd have been climbing the walls." A little silence went by, and then, "So what are you going to do?" she asked.

"About what?"

"About Colin. Helen. All your questions, your worries."

I held her fingers tighter. Held tighter to the persuasive sound of her common-sense words.

"I shall forget it," I said.

"Good." Her smile was so warm.

I tipped my glass, finished my beer.

"You want another?" she asked.

"No. Let's go home."

We took cups of coffee out into the garden—all moonlit, soft, warm air, sweet-scented. Ducking under the arch at the side we wandered through the shadows of the thicket, following the narrow path to the clearing where Bill Gerrard had built a summer-house for his beloved daughter and where, years later, sad Margaret Lane had burned to death inside it.

I felt no lingering melancholy there now. Why should I? I didn't know its secret . . . then . . .

No, I felt, then, only an increasing happiness. A relaxing that grew and grew.

"You'd like to come back here, wouldn't you?" Shelagh said. "To stay?"

"If you were with me."

In the dim light I could see her eyes on mine. Her hand on the bench moved and rested on my hand. I thought again of my declared reasons for staying on in Hillingham. And they no longer seemed important any more. It was just Shelagh.

And she had been right in all that she had said. All those worries about Colin, and Helen—they *were* ridiculous.

Putting my arm about her shoulders I drew her closer to me. She rested her head on my shoulder. I took a last drag on my cigarette and dropped the glowing end onto the stone at my feet. I watched the red spark become smaller and smaller till it was quite gone. And with it I would let go all those wonderings, those doubts about my brother and his wife. Reese, too, had been right. He had said it was all over. And it *was* over. I couldn't help Colin or Helen with my emotional probings. Colin and Helen were far beyond anything I could do for either of them. I thought about De Freyne and Elizabeth Barton . . . I wouldn't bother them . . . now . . . Wherever De Freyne was I wouldn't try to find him. What was the point? And Elizabeth Barton, who had appeared so afraid at my sudden appearance on her doorstep . . . Whatever were those reasons for your fear, I silently said, you can keep them to yourself. I won't probe any more . . .

"I *am* going to leave it," I said, "about Colin. What I told you about—about finding out the truth. I *know* the truth. Let people say what they like. I'm going to try to forget it. I *shall*." I smiled, demonstrating my new-found sense of freedom. "I just want to enjoy being here with you. Let's live for the living. Colin is—*dead*."

I felt a great, overwhelming sense of relief, as if at last I was released from some age-old tie; as if the knots were loosening, falling away, the blood surging freely once more through long-restricted veins. I was finally acknowledging that Colin, my brother, was gone, really gone, would never reach me again. Perhaps I had lived far too long in his towering, distant shadow. Now, finally, it had faded. I would make my own way.

I became aware of the beauty of the night. Up above us the Milky Way was brilliant in the clear sky, while all around us the leaves were rustled by the breeze and the movements of night creatures.

"It's a lovely secluded little spot, this," Shelagh murmured. "I'd like a summer-house here myself someday."

"That means you want to come back."

"How could I not?"

I kissed her. "Then you shall have your summer-house."

Before Shelagh got ready to go upstairs I went ahead and looked in the bedroom. The scent of flowers drifted in through the open window, but there was no rose on the pillow. Somehow I had known there wouldn't be.

Jean Timpson had evidently got the message. Not before time.

When I got downstairs I found Shelagh sitting on the carpet leaning over the jigsaw puzzle.

"You haven't got very far," she observed. I agreed with her, then she said, looking at the picture on the box-lid: "The filthy beast—he's looking right up her pants."

"Some people are like that."

"Maybe she's not even *wearing* pants. That could account for his smile."

"Disgusting people." I reached out, lifted her up. She came close against me, arms moving around my neck. "Let's go to bed," I said.

I carried a lighted kitchen candle into the bedroom and turned off the bedside lamp. "Just this and the moonlight," I said. "That's enough."

As I lay down beside her she pressed herself to me. Our arms wrapped each other, holding closer, closer still, so that we were flesh against flesh the length of our bodies. I kissed her, touching, caressing, and she moaned softly against me, little animal sounds, pulling me nearer.

"I love you," she breathed against my cheek. "I love you. Oh, my dear, dear Dave . . ."

A gust of air, brief, sudden, flicked across my shoulders, hit the candle flame and snuffed it out. I paused for a moment, an orchestra conductor momentarily losing his place, my rhythm faltering. Shelagh was a pale shadow now, lit only by the moon.

"Don't stop," she said. "Oh, don't stop . . ."

14

❧ ❧ ❧

On our way back from the cemetery we stopped at a shop that sold antiques, the goods on sale ranging from rubbish to some really beautiful pieces. There was a lovely Victorian shaving-mug patterned in blue and green that I coveted; also a porcelain statuette—a rather erotic study of Leda in an embrace with her swan.

"It's gorgeous," I said to Shelagh.

"It's rude."

"I don't care. I love it."

"Then buy it."

I examined the price label on the base. "I'll think about it." Always the cautious one.

"We'd only have to hide it," Shelagh said, "every time some maiden aunt called around."

"We don't have any maiden aunts."

"Just as well."

She went back to picking around amongst the bits and pieces—like a hen scratching for corn. "You've got so much stuff here," she said to the old man who sat behind a big old desk, and he looked up, moving his eyes from their focus on my leg. I saw him nod his grey head and smile, his cheeks crinkling. He looked sharp. He wore a brown suit of old-fashioned cut, a brilliant white collar, and a precisely knotted tie with green stripes. In his gentle, lined face his eyes were alert and, as they turned back to me, soft with kindness. His old voice, when he spoke, was strong with the sound of the West Country. "I knew who you were," he told me, "the minute you walked in."

I smiled back at him. "I know about you, too. A little. You're Mr.—Pitkin?" He nodded, pleased. I added: "Our neighbour, Mr. Timpson, has spoken of you."

"Oh, ah, I should reckon they all know me," he said. "I've been here longer than most . . . ." He paused. "I met your brother a few times. Got to know him pretty well."

Shelagh came over carrying a little china cream pitcher with daisies on it. "How much is this, please?"

He looked at it for a moment, told her a price and she converted it into dollars and cents and said. "I'll take it." He began to search around for a piece of wrapping-paper, and it was as he got up that I noticed that he limped slightly on his left leg. Not quite as pronounced a limp as mine, but still, a limp. That, I realised, probably accounted for his interest in my own uneven gait.

"That looks like one of Sad Margaret's, doesn't it?" Shelagh took my thoughts away, pointing to a framed sampler on the wall.

"How can you tell? I should think one looks pretty much like another."

The old man turned to us at this. "No, she's right." He smiled at Shelagh. "If you mean Margaret Lane, you're right. It is one of hers." Shelagh looked at me with a superior I-told-you-so lift of an eyebrow. He went on: "Miss Merridew sold it to me. It's been here for ages. I bought another one from your sister-in-law—that was before she was married. Sold that one, though. She sorted out quite a few bits and pieces she didn't want. Things that had been kept at the cottage—hoarded over the years—from the previous owners. I didn't take that much—just a few odd things."

"Did you know her very well?" I asked, and sensed Shelagh shooting a glance at me; I knew what she was thinking: that I was harping on Helen's death again—and after my professed intentions.

"I've known everyone who's lived at that cottage—since I was born," he said, "nearly eighty-six years ago. I doubt there's much that's happened here in the village that I don't know about. I've seen it all here." He sighed. "Oh, yes, a lot of changes—and not all for the better. But I suppose it's what they call progress. Nowadays people come and go, and you don't know who they are or where they're from. From different places; different countries, like as not. When I was a lad you took it for granted that everybody knew everybody else. Different now. Harder to keep track. One time, it seemed, half the people in the village were related to each other. Nobody went further than the next town—hardly ever. Well, you couldn't, could you?" I began to shake my head in agreement, no, but he answered his own question. "Course you couldn't. Not when the only means of getting anywhere was by foot—unless you were lucky enough to have a horse. But people today, they fly off here, there and everywhere and think nothing of it . . ." He seemed to have forgotten Shelagh's purchase. The cream pitcher lay before him, unwrapped on its sheet of wrapping-paper. I stole a glance at her. Her expression was all the encouragement he needed to go on. He smiled at her, said she was from America, wasn't she?—he could tell by her accent. "Course, we're used to foreigners coming here now. In fact they're buying up half the village, sometimes it seems." He added quickly, shaking his head, "Oh, don't misunderstand me, I am not including you." I said I realised that. He went on:

"Oh, we're used to different accents now, but years ago, well—it was something to talk about. Like when Bill Gerrard went off and come back with a Welsh girl for a wife. That was quite an event."

"He was the gardening one," I said.

He grinned. "You've been studying your history."

"Mr. Timpson—he gave me a quick lesson."

"Oh?" The old man looked at me quizzically. "And what did he have to say?"

"Not a great deal. He said you were the expert."

He just looked at me for a moment, as if trying to see behind my words. Then he said: "She, Bill Gerrard's wife, brought with her a beautiful Welsh dresser—a real craftsman's bit of work."

"I think it's still there." I recalled my brief exploration of the cellar.

"Ah, it is." He nodded. "I know it is. Yes, she

brought it all the way from Wales along with her trunks and stuff."

Shelagh said: "That would be Bronwen?"

"No, no, she—Bronwen was their daughter."

"Who married Handyman Temple," I said.

"Right, old Handyman." He shrugged. "I don't know why I say old. He wasn't old."

"He was the one who skipped off to the States, right?" Shelagh asked.

"Yes."

"With a dairymaid."

"Yes." For all his former loquaciousness he didn't appear very eager to take up the subject, this subject.

"All told," I said, "he didn't make out too badly for a guy with only one hand, did he?"

"Oh, no, he did all right. He was clever enough." He shifted the cream pitcher on the paper, began to wrap it. "Imagine—bringing her Welsh dresser all the way from Wales." He grinned. "There's no doubt about it—your cottage has seen a rare collection of females in its time."

Did he, I wondered, include Helen in that collection? "How well," I asked—too quickly—"did you know my sister-in-law?"—and saw Shelagh give me a pained look that clearly asked could I never let the matter drop.

"I knew her," he said thoughtfully, "about as well as most people did, I suppose. But it seemed to me that nobody really knew her *that* well . . . She called into the shop a few times; she was very pleasant; we chatted. And a couple of times I saw her there at the cottage. Mind you, I knew your brother better, although he wasn't here nearly as long. I asked them if they'd sell me that Welsh dresser. He said they would. He'd had it moved down to the cellar, out of the way, but then, before we actually settled the deal she—she had her accident." He gave a sad little shake of his head. "Terrible shame . . . terrible shame . . . I didn't see your brother after that happened. But before then he came into the shop many, many times. And we'd always get talking about the cottage—the folks who'd lived there, this and that—you know how it is. I suppose it was natural he'd be interested . . . as anyone would be . . ."

There was an unspoken "but" at the end of his sentence. I said, after a moment:

". . . But . . . ?"

"Well . . ." he shrugged, "he seemed just—fascinated by it. I got to thinking that he came here just for that—to talk."

Was he saying that Colin had become obsessed by the house? I recalled again Reese telling me how he had urged Colin to get away from it—*away from all its sad associations* . . . Had Reese made the same implication?

"He'd ask me," Pitkin said, "the same questions over and over. I think probably the place was getting on his nerves. It could do, too, if you're of an imaginative turn of mind . . . at all highly-strung."

Highly-strung? Did that describe Colin? I watched as the old man resumed the wrapping of the cream pitcher. Shelagh had moved over to the sampler. I turned and read over her shoulder the words that were embroidered there.

> *My true love hath my heart and I have his,*
> *By just exchange one for another given;*
> *I hold his dear, and mine he cannot miss,*
> *There never was a better bargain driven.*

"That's by Sir Philip Sidney," Shelagh said airily, turning back to me. "Did you know that?"

"No, I didn't know that. But one thing I'll say for it—it's more cheerful than her other one."

"She was obviously happy when she made this one. She wasn't always sad."

I looked at the date on it, stitched in blue: "December, 1903 . . . It wasn't that long before, either."

"Oh, we must have it, Dave," she said. "It belongs at the cottage, doesn't it?"

I nodded. "If you say so."

Pitkin quoted a price to her—a very low one—and she did her conversion job again and told him happily that it was a deal. While she picked over coins and notes in her bag the old man carefully wrapped the framed sampler in paper. When it was done I thanked him, said goodbye and led the way to the door. He followed us. As we said goodbye again I heard the sound of horse's hooves and, looking out, saw a woman go by on the street leading a large chestnut mare. Shelagh said rapturously, "Oh—!" and hurried out past me, in pursuit. From the doorway I watched as she caught up with the woman about twenty-five yards along. They fell into conversation together. As I watched, the old man, at my side, said:

"I hope I didn't say anything—to upset you just now."

"Not at all." The sampler was coming unwrapped in my hands and I pulled it into shape again. "I don't know why she wants this," I said for something to say. "The place is chock-full of mementos already."

"And Margaret Lane is hardly the happiest person to want reminders of."

"Yes . . ."

We were silent then. Both of us. We were back to death again and, athough their names were not mentioned, back to Colin and Helen. I said, forcing a grin, putting an end to the conversation—and, hopefully, its associations: "She'll moon over that horse all day if allowed to . . ." and stepped away. Quickly he said:

"Oh . . . that Welsh dresser . . ."

"Yes?"

"I would still like to buy it. If you'd consider selling it . . ."

"I don't know. I haven't even looked at it properly." I shrugged. "I'd have to think about it."

"I'd be glad if you would . . . think about it. Then perhaps I could drop in and—well, have a chat about it . . ."

"Any time."

"Tomorrow afternoon?"

He didn't let the grass grow under his feet. "Fine," I said. We shook hands and I stepped away from him for the second time.

"Oh," he said, "just one other thing . . ."

I could tell what was coming by the expression on his face. "What's that?"

"If you don't mind me askin' . . . Your leg . . ."

How'd you get like that? . . . *Do* you mind me askin'?"

Usually I did mind. Not with him though.

"I was born like it," I said.

"Ah . . ." Briefly his eyes closed as he gave a little nod of understanding. I wanted to ask How about you?—but for some reason I didn't have the courage. For a second I thought how rather strange the situation was—both standing there considering one another's limp. Quite ludicrous, really. Then he said, patting his thigh:

"Me—I had an accident. It never set properly. Ah, well . . ." His expression said it was no longer important. "It doesn't bother me. If it happens when you're young you have a good long time to get used to it, don't you? It doesn't matter so much, does it?"

I agreed, no, no, it didn't matter that much. Though inwardly I didn't agree at all. It did matter. It did.

Up ahead I saw the woman and the horse continuing on their way and Shelagh walking back towards me. "Well, we'll see you tomorrow," I said to the old man and, with a final nod of goodbye, went to meet her.

As we headed across the square she linked her arm in mine. "God, what a lovely animal," she said, still thinking about the horse. "Mrs. Stoner—that woman—she's got several horses. She says I can take one out any time I like. Isn't that marvellous? I'm going to take her up on her offer." She was silent for a few seconds then she said:

"Why did you ask that old guy those questions?— like how well did he know Helen? You're still pursuing it, aren't you?"

"No, I'm not. But I'm just—naturally curious—to meet anyone who knew them—anyone who can fill in the gaps." I smiled at her. "I don't intend—going any further than that."

I led the way towards the garage tucked in one corner of the square. A sign there told us that there were taxis and cars for hire (the same firm that had supplied the taxi to take me into Reading. Maybe the same firm whose driver had found Colin's body . . . ? But don't think about that.). One thing was certain—if we were going to stay on for a while, then a car was an absolute necessity.

The man who came out to us as we reached the pumps was the dark, swarthy one who had driven me from the bus on that first day. I told him what we wanted and he said doubtfully, clicking his tongue, that all he had available was an old Vauxhall. Though it was, he added, very reliable. I told him it would do and, while Shelagh took off for the ladies' room, followed him round to the back yard where every inch of space seemed to be filled with various bits of cars of every make and description.

His name, the man told me, was Bill Carmichael. He obviously knew mine. We chatted, walking side by side across the yard, and suddenly I came to a dead halt. The next moment I had moved away from him. Some yards over to one side I stopped and stood staring down at what was left of my brother's MG.

It bore no relation to the smart shining machine in the photographs Colin had sent me. It lay there now a twisted, snarled up wreck, the bonnet concertinaed, one side almost completely ripped away, just hanging by the merest slender strip of jagged metal. I saw at once that anyone who had been in that driver's seat could not possibly have survived.

I remembered how proud Colin had been of his MG. I remembered the picture of him sitting at its wheel, the happy smile on his face, the warm sun reflecting in the brilliant red paintwork. I had to look away. I felt almost sick. I could imagine for the first time just how violently, how sickeningly he must have died. I felt sudden tears well up in my eyes—those tears I had thought were a thing of the past. I couldn't help it. They were not for his passing, though—they were for the manner of his passing. I stood still while the tears coursed down my cheeks, trying to get my breath without making a complete idiot of myself, my face turned away so the man, Carmichael, shouldn't see. When at last I'd got control, after a fashion, I went over to him. He was studiously examining the oil level of the old Vauxhall. He looked round at the sound of my approach but—out of deference to my emotions, I know—avoided my eyes.

"Were you . . . the one who . . . who found him?"
I managed to say, at last.

"That's right, sir . . ."

I looked back in the direction of the wreckage. The
tears stung my eyes all over again.

"I never dreamed," I said, "it would be like that."

There was a note lying on the kitchen table when we
got back. I read it then said to Shelagh: "From Jean.
She says she'll be back later. She's done the shopping,
she says, and there's ice-cream for you in the fridge."

Shelagh smiled. "Isn't that nice of her. She remembered my sweet tooth."

After finding a good place to hang Sad Margaret's
sampler we changed our clothes (shorts for me; shorts
and bikini-top for Shelagh) and set about preparing
lunch. We made sandwiches and iced tea and, while
Shelagh fed Girlie I carried the loaded tray out onto the
lawn and set it down next to the rug I'd spread out
there. As we ate, Girlie came to us across the grass and,
smelling of cat-food, nuzzled around us for a while before being distracted by the flight of a passing butterfly.
She dashed off in mad, scampering pursuit, leaping up,
missing the red admiral by a hair's breadth, while we
laughed at her insane antics. Then, suddenly exhausted,
she came back to us and lay down, sides heaving, in the
shade of Shelagh's body.

Later, when the sandwiches were finished Shelagh
got some of Jean Timpson's ice-cream from the fridge. I
lounged back as she ate. "I don't know how you can
touch all that sickly stuff."

"You don't know what you're missing." She grinned
at me and took another spoonful. "That really was so
thoughtful of her . . ."

I drained my glass of the last drop of tea and lay
down, prone, my head on my forearms. I closed my
eyes.

It was Shelagh's short cry of pain that snatched me
back from the edge of sleep. Quickly I sat up. She was
holding her hand to her mouth, spitting out melted ice-
cream that ran, tinged with red, between her fingers. I
knelt before her. Tears shone in her eyes. Pain and

fright. When she took her hand away from her mouth I could see that her lips were smudged with blood.

And in the hand she held out to me was a long sliver of glass.

15

❧ ❧ ❧

When Jean Timpson arrived I asked her where she'd bought the ice-cream.

"The big shop in the square . . ." She smiled. "Was it all right? I thought Miss Shelagh would like it."

I held out to her the sliver of glass. "This was in it." She stared at it, face set. ". . . Was she . . . ?"

"She cut her gum and the inside of her lip. Not too badly, but painful for all that."

"You give that to me . . ." she held out her hand, "and I'll take it and show them."

"No, I'll do it. First thing Monday." I studied the glass. It was about three-quarters of an inch long, very thin at one end with a point as sharp as a needle. If Shelagh had swallowed it . . . well, I dreaded to think what might have been the result.

"Is she in there now?" Jean Timpson asked. Yes, she was, I said, and she went past me towards the living-room. I followed.

Shelagh was sitting on the floor sorting through records. Girlie was in her lap. Jean Timpson stopped just inside the doorway.

"Oh, Miss Shelagh . . . I'm so sorry." She paused. "I just don't know what to say . . ."

All concern, Shelagh got up and moved towards her. "It's not *your* fault. And I'm perfectly okay."

"They ought to be more careful. I'm sorry, I really am." Jean Timpson's hands were working, writhing nervously.

"Please . . ." I said as I dropped the piece of glass into a small dish on the mantelpiece, "you mustn't get yourself into a state about it. As Shelagh said, it was no fault of yours."

When she had gone, back to the kitchen, Shelagh said, "Poor thing—she feels worse about it than I do."

With the house to ourselves again after dinner we talked, listened to Neil Diamond and Simon and Garfunkel and then, on television, watched Judy Garland make it from rags to riches in *A Star is Born*. Before bedtime came I went upstairs and checked our room. No rose there.

The room was very warm. I opened the windows and felt the welcome cooling night air drift in through the lace curtains. Later, when I followed Shelagh there from the bathroom I found her in bed with the sheet pulled up around her chin and one of the windows closed again.

"I thought I'd freeze to death," she said.

"You," I told her, "are a spoilt American brat. All that air-conditioning and central-heating—and faced with the *real* elements they're too much for you."

"Balls."

"You think you've got an answer for everything with your university education."

I put out the light, got in beside her and held her. But when I began to caress her she stayed my hand. "I'm sorry, darling," she murmured, "but I don't feel all that good, really."

"Your mouth—where you were cut?"

"No, not that. Just . . . generally. I'll be okay tomorrow."

"Sure you will." I smoothed her hand in mine. "Poor baby . . ."

I slept soon after. The next thing I was aware of was surfacing, only half with it, to the sound of her voice as she cried out beside me. She was trying, with difficulty, to sit up. One of her thrashing arms, catching me a blow on the shoulder, brought me fully awake. I sat up beside her and put my arms around her, but she shook my touch away, moving, twisting wildly, fighting me off.

"It's all right . . . it's all right . . ." I held her again. "You've had a bad dream. You're safe now . . ."

She turned slow, puzzled eyes to me. Reality was getting through to her; you could see it dawning, settling. She lifted a hand, touched my cheek, so gently, as if reassuring herself of my presence: safety. I never loved her more than I did in that moment.

". . . Just a dream," I said softly. "It's all right now . . ."

She nodded, wordless, then lay down again and closed her eyes.

This time I stayed fully awake until she was asleep.

She was still sleeping when I crept out of bed the next morning and went downstairs. At the kitchen table I drank coffee and orange juice and smoked a first cigarette while the sound of church bells drifted up from the village and birds and butterflies flew about their work in the garden. Another very warm day. I made fresh coffee, poured more juice and took it upstairs. Shelagh was awake now. "How do you feel?" I asked her. "Better?"

She smiled at me. She felt perfectly all right now, she said.

After lunch: omelets (Jean Timpson wasn't coming in till later), Mr. Pitkin arrived. I'd forgotten all about his arranged visit and when he rang the bell just on three-thirty I wasn't prepared. I hadn't given the dresser a single thought since meeting him, let alone having come to a decision as to whether or not I wanted to hang on to it. But there he was, all spruce and smiling on the doorstep, hat in one hand, walking stick in the other.

"I have to tell you the truth," I told him once he was inside. "I haven't made up my mind about it yet . . ."

"Oh, that's all right." He smiled. "There's no rush. And anyway, I enjoyed the stroll." Politely declining Shelagh's offer of coffee he waited a moment then asked if, while he was here, might he take a look at the dresser . . . ?

"Certainly," I said, and then, remembering the duff cellar light and the faulty torch, added: "But it'll have to be by candlelight, I'm afraid."

I lit candles and led the way to the cellar door. "Be careful—the steps are steep," I warned him, and he smiled and said, "Oh, I know," and followed me down, with Shelagh bringing up the rear. She hadn't been down there before and when we reached the floor and stood in the circle of light she stood looking around at the accumulation of past possessions and ahead with delighted surprise. And she wasn't in the least fazed by Miss Merridew's stuffed pet.

Pitkin had moved to the dresser. I followed him with the candles and looked at it then, really looked at it, for the first time.

Standing at least eight feet high with a length of almost six feet it was an impressive piece if only by its size. I said to Pitkin, "It must weigh a ton! They must have gone to so much trouble to get it here. How on earth did they manage it?"

"They'd have brought it on a cart. Along with all her other bits and pieces." He ran his fingers along the carved edge of one of the lower shelves. "But you can see *why* they went to so much trouble, can't you." It wasn't a question. "I'd reckon her father made it for her, or else it had been in the family. Be given to her for her bottom drawer, I should reckon." Shelagh looked at me questioningly at this and I said, translating for her: "Bottom drawer. Hope chest to you," and she said, "Hope chest to you too," and aimed a pathetic fist at me. "The genuine article, this is," Pitkin said, "and a specially nice one as well. And solid. Not like those flimsy little copies they churn out today."

There was certainly nothing flimsy about this one. I put my shoulder to it and tried to shift it, but I couldn't budge it an inch. "No," the old man said, watching me, smiling, "you'd never move that on your own." He seemed in his element. He began pulling out and pushing in the smoothly gliding drawers. "Look at that," he murmured. "The fit. Perfect . . ." He touched it lovingly, caressing it almost; he didn't care about the dust. "Something like this," he said, "would stay in the family for years, being passed down from one generation to the next." He turned to me. "I remember seeing this when I was a boy. First when the Temples lived here and then later after the Lanes moved in. Course, it was upstairs in the kitchen then. And all the china was set out of it, all the plates in neat rows, the cups hanging from the hooks. It really looked a picture. All polished. Beautiful . . ." He paused, as if seeing it as it had been. "Mind you, Bronwen Temple was the one for having things looking nice. She took such a pride in everything. Very fastidious. Everything had to be just so. Her clothes—everything—it all had to be so right, so perfect, not a mark anywhere. Your cottage here—well, it was like a palace."

"Maybe that's one of the reasons," I said, "why her husband went off and left her."

He nodded slowly. "Very possible. After all, a home's for living in, not looking at," and Shelagh said, "You're right," as if he'd dropped some pearl of wisdom at her feet. Remembering my previous conversation with him—and with Timpson—I said: "But he was having a little bit on the side, wasn't he? He went off with one of the local girls, a dairymaid, didn't you say?"

"Effie," Pitkin said. "She was *our* dairymaid."

"Ah, yes," I said, "Mr. Timpson said you were the one who would know all about it."

". . . I don't know that there's anything to tell. He went off and left his wife. Went to America."

I asked the same question I had asked Timpson: "How does everybody know he went there? Did he tell people he was going?"

". . . No. Not as far as I know . . ."

I shook my head. "Wasn't it enough just to leave her? Did he *have* to kill her first?"

"You can't be . . . sure that he did. When she was found the doctor said she'd only been dead a few hours. And Handyman had been gone three days by then."

"Even worse," I said, "if he—hit her and just—just left her to die . . ."

"No one ever proved that's what happened. It was never proved."

"What do you think happened, then?"

For some reason the old man avoided my eyes. When he answered me his voice sounded slightly strained, his tone reluctant. He shrugged. "I was only a boy at the time . . ."

He didn't want to go on with the subject. I couldn't imagine why, but for some reason I clearly felt that he didn't want to talk about it. It only made me more curious. I approached him at a tangent.

"Did you know them well—the Temples?"

"Oh, yes, I knew them. I used to run errands for them. For both of them."

He turned a little away at this and gave his attention to the dresser again. I said, changing the subject:

"Tell us about the Lanes . . ." And it wasn't just an empty question. I wanted to know. "What were they like?" I asked.

He was more forthcoming when it came to the Temples' successors. After a moment's pondering he said:

"I remember . . . I met them first when I went round there with my father. There was a tree had come down . . ."

"Ah, yes," I said, "Mr. Timpson mentioned that." It was the tree that had broken the sundial, I recalled, the one that had fallen the same day as Temple's hasty, guilty departure . . .

"It'd come down in a storm," Pitkin said. "And it *was* a storm, too. Trees coming down all over the place. Really bad. Anyway, since the Temples were gone this tree just stayed there. So after the Lanes moved in we all went along to help cut it up, move it." He grinned. "They wouldn't have been short of firewood that coming winter, that's for sure."

"Why," Shelagh asked, "did you and your father go round to help them?"

"Oh, wasn't just us. A lot of the local people went. Living out in the country, folks are always ready to lend a hand if they can. Not like in the cities. In the country you never know when you might be called on. And in the same way you never knew when *you* might be needing help. And of course, them being newcomers—well, it was the neighbourly thing to do."

I remembered what Timpson had told me about John

Lane—that he had become something of a recluse after the death of his wife. "How was he?—Lane—then?" I asked.

"That's a long time ago. Oh, he seemed all right. Tall fellow. Dark. Not unlike you, I s'pose. By all accounts he caused quite a flutter with the young women in the village when he first arrived here. But he was only interested in his wife, so I believe. She was a very quiet young woman. Shy, gentle, placid soul. It was quite a shock when *that* happened to her."

"How did it happen exactly . . . ?" This was Shelagh.

"Who can say . . . ? Nobody knew about it till it was over. John Lane come down into the village one morning in July and said his wife was dead. He said it had happened just a few hours earlier. Apparently he'd woke up, missed her and gone outside looking for her. And saw smoke coming from the summer-house. Well, it was blazing all right. He broke the door down and managed to drag her out but it was too late. She was dead. According to him she'd got into the habit of going out to the summer-house at all times of the day or night. He reckoned she must have knocked over the oil lamp she'd taken in there."

"And they believed him?" I asked.

He hesitated, then: "Some did. He was burnt pretty badly himself—in trying to get her out. And there wasn't really any reason you could think of as to *why* he'd—do away with her. Besides that, she'd begun to act a bit strange, so to some people it didn't come as such a great surprise."

"And the *other* people?"

"Well, of course they had their own ideas. And they let it be known, quite clearly, what those ideas were."

"What was the official verdict?" Shelagh asked.

"Accident." He nodded. "Which it probably was, I reckon. Anyway, one thing there was no doubt about—it finished Lane. Oh, yes. He never got over that. In spite of what some people said, I think he was devoted to his wife. I saw him just a day or two after it happened. He was like a changed man. He *was* a changed man. He was like . . . well . . . broken. And from there he just went steadily downhill. Stopped going out, stopped seeing people. When he was ill my mother came down and nursed him, but she said she didn't think he wanted to go on very much. Well, whether he wanted to or not, he didn't. He died while she was there."

"What was wrong with him?"

"Smallpox. That was about three or four years after his wife's death."

"Four," I said. "I saw their gravestone in the cemetery."

"It's such a sad story," Shelagh said.

"Yes . . ." Pitkin nodded. "After that Miss Merridew moved in." He tapped the dresser. "I asked her to sell this to me—oh, not long before she died. She wouldn't sell it." He turned, looked at me expectantly, hopefully. I shrugged. "I just don't know . . . not right now."

"But if you do decide to sell it . . ."

"I'll give you first chance, you can be sure."

"Thank you." He gave an apologetic little smile. "I think it's such a shame to have a lovely piece like this and just—leave it down here gathering the dust."

I watched his old hand resting lightly on the dusty wood. I looked at the dresser again, the whole enormous size of it; one thing was certain, we didn't have room for it. "And you could find a good home for it, could you?" I said.

"Oh, yes. No fear of that."

I nodded. "Well . . . I'll let you know in a day or two."

"Good," he said. "Fine . . . fine . . ."

In the open doorway I stood for some moments after he had gone from sight. "What's up?" Shelagh asked me.

I shook my head. "Nothing . . ." But there was something the old man had said down in the cellar that hadn't quite added up. At the time it had been too fleeting for me to grasp, and now I couldn't put my finger on it at all . . . Ah, well, it probably wasn't important . . .

In the living-room Shelagh read for a while and I sat on the carpet and tried to make some progress with the jigsaw. I wasn't getting anywhere with it, though, and in the end I gave up and went outside to mooch around the garden. It was while poking about in the toolshed that I came across an old croquet set. Back in the house, over tea, I studied the little time-discoloured book of rules. It was a game calculated to bring out the worst in people, I reckoned—though it didn't appear to demand much in the way of energy.

Shelagh said, raising one eyebrow, "You're dying to have a crack at that, aren't you?" Then she nodded. "Well, why not. I've always fancied my chance at croquet."

"It's pronounced 'crokey'—not 'crokay' . . ."

"Arkansass to you."

On the lawn we hammered in the metal hoops and the sharp-pointed, colour-banded stake that was the finishing-post, and then began.

Shelagh caught on quickly. Too quickly. After an hour-and-a-half, during which time I hadn't managed to get beyond the third hoop, and in which time she managed to slam my ball countless whacks across the lawn in the wrong direction, I decided it was time to stop for a drink and a cigarette. Then our one drink became two, and by that time Jean Timpson had arrived and almost finished preparing dinner. Our croquet game was forgotten. After we had eaten, as we were drinking coffee in the living-room I looked out and saw that dark clouds had begun to gather. And in no time at all they were well and truly overhead and threatening. Not for long, though, the threat; the rain began to fall, gently at first and then, after a short respite, very heavily in a sudden downpour. I remembered the mallets out on the lawn and got up to fetch them in, but Jean, thoughtful Jean, had beaten me to it. "It's all all right," she said as I headed through the kitchen, "I saw them out there . . ." and she nodded to where the mallets and the hoops stood neatly stacked by the door.

She went home soon afterwards and Shelagh and I settled down for another quiet evening. Beyond the window-pane the rain continued to fall, whipped by the wind that had sprung up, so that it spattered in sudden gusts against the glass. And the wildness outside only served to make me feel, there in the cottage, more secure.

And Shelagh, too. While the rain lashed at the windows and the thunder growled in the distance she looked across at me and smiled, hugging herself. "I love it, I love it."

I find it difficult to describe how I felt my contentment growing, but it was, it really was. The cottage, I felt, was hourly becoming more and more *ours*—as if our presence there was forcing those ghosts of the past to relinquish their hold upon it. Those relics all around us, of the former inhabitants, were becoming only relics—objects, and nothing more; more interesting in their own right, increasingly divorced from the associations that had caused them to be kept and treasured. I found I could look on Sad Margaret's samplers and be aware only of her exquisite needlework, and I could forget—though, granted, not all the time—my awareness of her unhappy days and her grotesque ending. If we stayed there long enough, Shelagh and I, the house, I knew, would one day be ours completely. They would *all* be gone, those past dwellers of Gerrard's Hill Cottage—*all* of them. And that meant Colin and Helen too. And that I wished for most of all.

It would only be a matter of time, I thought, and I'd be able to think again of Colin as he had lived; to take pleasure in the few memories I had of him, memories that would always be touched by the sadness of his death, but nevertheless, pleasurable. As it was, right then, he was still too close, still too much an occupant there; the loss of him still much too real and too near to the present; the book I took from the shelf was, I was so aware, *his* book, and when, a little later, Shelagh and I began a game of chess, it was with his chess set . . .

Our game of chess went the way of our game of croquet. We packed it up just before ten and, yawning, Shelagh went on up to bed. I stayed down and watched some of the news on television, but it was just one story of gloom, doom and despair after another—proof that man hadn't learned a damn thing for all his ages of evolution and progress—and, deciding that enough was enough, I switched off and started up the stairs.

I was just setting my good foot onto the landing when I heard her cry out.

I rushed in, put on the light and held her, trying to still her madly thrashing arms. I soothed her, rocking her in my arms like a baby. After a minute she stopped fighting me and relaxed again.

"I had another bad dream," she said. There were tears in her eyes. She reached out, grasped, held tight to my sleeve. "Don't go. Come to bed now . . ."

After breakfast, while Shelagh washed the dishes, I went into the living-room to get the piece of glass and hand it back to the shop along with a piece of my mind. The glass was gone.

"Probably Jean moved it," Shelagh said, "when she came in with her feather duster, doing her Mrs. Danvers bit while we were at dinner last night."

"Yes, I expect so." I watched her as she dried her hands; watched the slim line of her body as she reached for the jar of hand cream on the shelf near the sink. She smoothed the cream into her hands, fine, slender fingers working.

"Are you going somewhere?" I asked.

She grinned. "I thought I'd go down and have a look at Mrs. Stoner's horses. You want to come with me?"

"No, thanks."

When she was ready I walked with her round to the front of the house. We stood on either side of the gate, framed by the arch of climbing roses over our heads. She reached up, lightly ran the tips of her fingers along my jaw. "I'll see you later."

We waved to each other when she got to the bend in the hill road. When she was out of sight I took the croquet mallets, hoops and balls and put them back in the toolshed. Then I exchanged my sandals for a pair of Colin's wellies, took a fork, a rake and a hoe, and made my way towards the patch of unturned earth. I wanted to have it cleared and all finished for the rose-trees I would order which, according to Colin's catalogue, would be planted in the autumn. Timpson would take care of that part of it for me. I thought about how it would be—my own roses blooming when Shelagh and I returned next year . . . The house would be more than ever mine . . .

I found myself whistling as I walked along past the rear of the house, past the sunken garden. I whistled until I was close to the patch of garden I'd already cleared. Then, my feet and my tune came to an abrupt halt.

Clearly in the fresh, still rain-damp earth new words had been written. Large round letters, childish and uncertain in the forming of their character, but by no means uncertain in the message they spelt out:

SEND HER AWAY

16

In Doctor Reese's waiting-room I sat down facing a fat woman who was trying to amuse a peevish child who refused to be amused. We all had problems. In my own mind I could still hear the words I had muttered as I'd stood by the garden patch: "*Jean Timpson, this is it. You're through.*" And while the anger had still boiled inside me I had hacked at the earth until all trace of the message had gone . . .

My thoughts now were interrupted as Reese put his head round the door and called to me. I laid down the outdated *Sunday Times* colour supplement back on the coffee table and went in to him.

"Oh, yes, that's fine," he murmured with satisfaction as he examined my arm. Then, while I averted my eyes he began to remove the stitches. I could feel him snipping at them, deftly pulling them out. "I understand you've got a visitor," he said, and I glanced at him and saw that his eyes were smiling. I shook my head. "My God, word here travels faster than Western Union."

"A friend of yours from America, so I understand."

"Shelagh, her name is. Shelagh O'Connell. Twenty-five years old, a hundred and twelve pounds, five foot five, eyes of blue."

"You forgot to say what kind of toothpaste she uses."

"Mine."

He grinned. He was swabbing my arm, studying the scar. I said:

"I saw what was left of my brother's car. It was such a mess. I never realised before just how hard he must have hit that tree. How could he have had such a crazy accident?"

He shrugged. "What can I say? That's what it was. What else could it have been?"

I didn't want to face Jean Timpson until I'd fully decided how to tackle the situation. For the moment I had no idea how to go about it.

Standing in the hall on my return I could hear her at her work in the kitchen. I turned away from the sound, went into the living-room where Shelagh put Girlie down and came towards me.

"How is it . . .?" She examined the fierce red scar for a moment, then said, "It'll fade." As I sat down in my armchair she added in a near-whisper:

"Jean's been so sweet to me while you've been out. Her basic trouble *is* her shyness. That's all. We had quite a long chat. Poor thing—she feels so bad about that ice-cream."

The ice-cream . . . And suddenly the words I had found scratched in the earth took on a whole new, quite sinister connotation. Yet surely she wouldn't go *that* far . . . But the thought preyed on my mind. I hardly listened as Shelagh went on talking.

"Did you know that *she's* something of a horsewoman herself?—Jean? So we have something in common. *She* didn't tell me about it, though. Mrs. Stoner did . . ."

. . . I was seeing again that thin, razor-sharp sliver of glass in Shelagh's palm, her palm stained with her blood . . .

"Apparently," Shelagh went on, "Jean worked at the stables when she was younger. She left, though; her dad went up there one day and created a fuss about one of the guys who worked there . . ." She went on talking, but I was absorbed in my own thoughts. How anxious, I wondered, was Jean Timpson to have Shelagh gone? The ice-cream had come in a plastic tub with a lid that just pulled off. It would have been the easiest thing in the world for someone to have pushed in the glass, smoothed the ice-cream over again and replaced the lid . . . Did she resent Shelagh's presence enough to do such a crazy thing? Was she capable of doing it . . .?"

"David," Shelagh said, "you're not listening to a word I'm saying."

"I'm listening. I'm listening already . . ." And I was still wondering how anybody could put glass into someone else's food . . . The thought made me shudder . . . "You were talking about Jean working at the stables," I said.

"I'd finished with that ages ago." She came to me, placing her hands on my shoulders. "You're in a strange mood. What are you thinking about?"

"Nothing important." I shook my head.

"Something's up. I can read you like a book." She moved to the piano. "You need soothing . . ." She lifted the lid and struck a loud chord. "A little music to soothe the savage beast."

"To soothe the savage *breast*." I laughed. "It's *breast*."

"I'd never use such a word," she said primly, and began to play *Home on the Range*.

I barely spoke to Jean Timpson as she served us at dinner. I just found it too difficult. I don't know whether she noticed my reticence, but Shelagh certainly did. And I think she tried to make up for it.

"Leave the washing-up," she said to her. "We'll do it."

"Oh, no . . . that's all right."

"I insist," Shelagh said. "David and I will do it. You go on home."

Jean Timpson turned her gaze to me, wavering, uncertain what to do. I nodded, only half looking at her.

"Yes, you go on home. We can do it." I suddenly wanted her gone; I wanted never to see her again.

"Oh, well, if you're sure . . ."

"Quite."

Her eyes flicked directly to mine from a moment, then moved aside again. "Well . . . thank you . . . I'll see you tomorrow afternoon . . ."

Minutes later, after she had gone, Shelagh said:

"What was all that for?"

"All what?"

"With her—Jean. You sounded so sharp. Almost angry. Didn't you see the way she looked at you? Is there something wrong?"

". . . No. It's just been a long day . . ." I got up from the table. "Come on. Let's get the dishes done."

As she washed the china I methodically dried and stacked it. All the time I was making a positive effort to be cheerful, not to give away any hint that there was anything on my mind. But I couldn't stop the thoughts from creeping in. Tomorrow, I had determined, I'd see Jean Timpson and make some excuse so as not to have her back again.

"That's about it . . ." Shelagh shook water from her hands. "I'll just get the ash-trays." She went out of the room, I dried the last plate then recapped the washing-up liquid and replaced it on the shelf over the sink. As I drew back my hand my fingers brushed the jar of hand-cream and it fell with a dull crash onto the tiles.

I was crouching over the mess of thick white cream and shattered glass when Shelagh came back into the room. "What happened?" she asked.

"I owe you for a new jar of hand-cream." I could hear the stiffness in my voice.

"Oh, well, never mind."

Taking an old newspaper I got the mess onto it, then wadded up the paper and threw it into the trash can. As I wiped the floor clean I could feel my heart racing. I looked up at her and she turned in that same moment and saw my face.

"David . . . what's the matter?"

"Is something the matter?" I forced a smile. "Nothing's the matter."

Nothing's the matter, I had told her. And I saw her again as she had been that morning, taking the lid off the jar, shoving her fingers into the cream. Had I not broken it she'd be doing the same thing just seconds from now.

Nothing's the matter, I had said. I wouldn't tell her that along with all that mess of cream and broken glass I had found two double-edged razor-blades.

17

❧ ❧ ❧

"Are you sure you feel well enough to go riding today?" I asked Shelagh over breakfast. She had awakened again in the night, crying out, clutching at me, and it had been some time before she could be persuaded to go back to sleep.

"Really, darling," she said to me now, "I feel perfectly fine. And I'll feel better still having a good long ride over the hills. Be marvellous." She paused. "Why don't you come with me?"

"Riding?"

"Yes. It wouldn't make any difference." She meant my leg. "They could find you some quiet old nag who's on the point of going to the knacker's yard; one who couldn't manage more than a slow trot."

"No . . . really . . ."

She put a teaspoon of honey into her mouth, then offered some to me. I shook my head.

"It'll set you up," she said.

"No . . . it's too sweet . . ." And I immediately thought of the ice-cream. I had told Jean Timpson that I never ate ice-cream. There was never a chance that that sliver of glass could have got into *my* mouth . . .

"Now what's wrong?" Shelagh asked.

I stared at her for a second, then said:

"Marry me, Shelagh." I loved her. I wanted to keep her safe. Safe. "Please marry me."

"I was wondering," she said, returning my gaze, "when you were going to bring that up again. I've been giving it some thought."

"Oh . . . ?"

"I've realised that most of the trouble before was a failure on *my* part. I just didn't understand what was going on. All your—moods and—depressions. See, I understand it now. All that stuff with you and Colin— why you were like you were all that time. You know . . ." she gave a little, slow nod, "you're much stronger than I thought. Oh, I know you're upset still, and confused—but you have a certain—strength about you. Yes . . . I see you differently now."

"So what are you saying . . . ?"

"I'm saying, yes, let's get married, dummy." She grinned. "If you still want to."

"*Yes, ma'am.*"

She laughed. We leaned across the table to one another, kissed, and I could taste the lingering tang of honey on her mouth. A breeze from the open window brushed her hair against her face. The window flapped against the frame and I got up to secure it. She came over to me.

"When?" she said.

"Well, let's find out." My smile sounded in my voice. "I'll phone the nearest register office."

Half-an-hour later we were heading for Millingford, a little town about five or six miles away. For the second time I patted my pocket, checking that my birth certificate and passport were safe; I probably wouldn't need both but the registrar had said that I must furnish the necessary documents so I was playing safe.

"You've got your passport, all right?" I asked Shelagh.

"Yes, I've got it. And just to be sure, I've also brought my driver's licence, my Blue Cross Insurance card, my Social Security card and my Mickey Mouse Club badge."

She was playing safe too.

"Good girl," I said. "So we're all set."

"All set."

When our arrangements were made we were all set for Saturday morning at eleven. My smile kept coming back.

Returning to the cottage, Shelagh changed into her blue jeans and a light-coloured shirt. "I thought you had to wear jodhpurs and all that stuff," I said.

"Mrs. Stoner's got some gear she said she'll lend me." She slung her canvas bag over her shoulder.

"I'll walk with you down the hill," I said. "I want to call in and see Jean Timpson."

"Are you going to tell her?"

"Oh—about us, you mean . . ."

"Of course. What else is there?"

The thought of Saturday, our wedding-day, filled me with happiness, but the thought of an imminent encounter with Jean Timpson filled me with dread. I knew what I wanted to say, but wasn't sure how I'd get it said. Still, it had to be done.

We left the house and walked down the hill together. When we got to where the road bent round towards the village she kissed me on the cheek, said, "See you soon," and went on her way. I watched her for a while then turned into the lane that led to Timpson's house.

There were several houses along the lane and at first I had no idea which one was theirs. But then I saw Jean's old blue pram parked in a garden and I let myself in at the front gate and walked up the narrow path with the neat flower beds on either side. At the front door I steeled myself then let fall the heavy door-knocker. The door was opened by the old man.

"I saw you coming up the path," he said, ushering me in. "I'm afraid you've missed Jean. She won't be back for a while."

I felt a great feeling of relief at his words—a temporary reprieve. Foolish, though—I was only having the unpleasantness delayed.

He gestured to the table where I saw the remains of ham, cheese and bread laid out. "I'm just finishing off me dinner afore I get back up to the farm . . ." He paused. "I've just made some tea if you'd like a cup."

Thank you, I told him, but I couldn't stay long—and remained standing there, in silence, while the tension I had built up lessened, to lie simmering just below the surface.

"You want to leave any message?" he asked.

I grasped the chance, coward to the last. "Yes, thank you. I'll leave her a note if you don't mind."

He nodded towards an old desk in the corner. "You'll find paper and stuff there." He sat down before his interrupted meal. "If you'll excuse me I'll get on . . ." I nodded, "Of course," and moved eagerly to the desk.

I was so glad of the cop-out he had given me. And I hated myself for being glad. But even as I took up the pen I was able to tell myself that I was only doing the logical, sensible thing. The *only* thing.

On a small, cheap-papered writing-pad I wrote, after a few moments' thought:

Dear Jean,
 Now that my arm is quite better again and I am quite able to look after myself—and also since She-lagh will be staying with me until we return to New York I have to tell you that there is really no further need for you to spend your time helping us as you have so kindly been doing. I am enclosing a little money which will reimburse you for anything you have spent on our behalf and also pay you for your generous help.
              Many thanks.

I read it over. It was so badly done, so crudely done. But it got the message across. I signed my name to it, hovered another second over its curtness and then put it in an envelope together with more than enough money to cover anything I might owe her. Then on the front of the envelope I wrote her name.

"All right?" the old man asked with his ingenuous smile. I nodded, yes, and he held out his hand and I put the envelope into it. "Depend on it," he said, "she'll get it as soon as she comes in." He put the envelope beside him on the table.

I thanked him, took a step away, preparing my departure. I couldn't cope with the warmth in his face. "Give me a few more days," he said, "and I'll be through at the farm and be able to come up and give you a hand."

I thanked him again. I felt such a hypocrite. In half-an-hour he'd find out I'd just fired his daughter. I could only hope that he'd take the letter at its face value.

"You're the one who ought to be thanked," he said. I looked at him in surprise and he nodded his short-cropped head. "It's meant a lot to our Jean, being able to come up and see you; to have somebody else to look after apart from me. It's good for her too, to be with younger people, and to feel . . ." he paused, ". . . needed."

I couldn't think of anything to say. I stood there with one hand reaching up to the doorhandle.

"She's been telling me about your young lady. Shelagh, is it?"

"Yes."

"She sounds—well—a very nice young lady."

For no reason at all, I said, "She's gone off riding."

He nodded again, smiled, and turned, gazing from the window. "I'm glad Jean goes up to see you. She needs friends, people she can trust. The folks in the village—they're no good to her." He twitched at the sleeve of his shirt. "Some people won't let up on the past, that's their trouble. Won't let a body forget. Even some of the folks she's known all her life. Funny how people can change. And it hurts. Of course it do. It's because they don't understand. She don't say nothing, but you can see it hurts . . .

"I expect," he added, turning to me, "you've heard about it. You'd be bound to in this place."

I wanted to say, I'm a stranger here; people haven't told me very much about anything . . . but I just shrugged, noncommittal.

"Oh, ah, no doubt." He shook his head. "They *think* they know the truth, and that's as far as they want to go." He sighed, looked away again. "That's why she left here in the first place. I knew what talk would do to her. That's why she stayed in Marshton Ridge long after she—after she lost her babby. That took a good bit of gettin' over, that did, I don't mind tellin' you. Some women take it specially hard, something like that. But she began to pick up, in time. And then when she got the job there—with those well-off people—well, she started to do just fine." He paused, looked at me earnestly. "I'm only telling you all this because—well, to get it straight, sort of. Like I said, you've been kind to her. She likes you. She trusts you. So it's as well you know the truth about how it was with the boy—rather than believe what you might hear elsewhere."

Not understanding, I said, "Yes . . ."

"I don't know why that should have to happen," he went on. "Four years she looked after him without a speck of trouble. And then it was all over in seconds. Well, there was talk then. You couldn't get away from it." His mouth looked resigned; it matched the sadness in his voice. Surprisingly there was no trace of bitterness there. "She suffered," he said. "There was no living with her, my sister said, and that's a fact. You could see what was going to happen. A couple of years later on, when she came back to me, she was all right, but—but different . . ." He looked into my eyes, as if trying to make me understand. "Quieter. She was—deeper inside herself. More . . . private." He gave an ironic smile. "They do say as time heals all wounds, but meself, I ain't so sure."

Silence went by, marked off in seconds by the solemn tick of the grandfather clock. Into the quiet he said, his smile growing, warmer:

"You wouldn't believe the difference it made when your brother came here and married Miss Helen. And once he was here, well, the other one, he didn't hang around very long—and Jean was glad about that. She suddenly got an interest in life again. And she was that excited about the baby coming. You can imagine how she felt when it all—ended, but . . . well, anyway, now *you're* here, with your young lady—even if it is only for the summer. And I can see the change in her. She's getting more like her old self every day."

I couldn't see straight for my convoluted thoughts and emotions. Was I wrong about her? I thought of her melancholy, shy face topped with the bow of coloured ribbon. I pictured her coming home, finding the note I had left for her. *She needs friends,* he had said, *people she can trust.* And she trusted me. I remembered how she had told me of the time when Colin had sent her away. Here was I, doing exactly the same thing, but less courageously.

But I couldn't be wrong. How could I? The glass in the ice-cream, the razor-blades, the words scrawled in the earth . . . She trusts you, Timpson had said. *She trusts you* . . . I was so confused. Suddenly I didn't feel sure of anything any more. And suppose I was wrong . . .

I looked at the letter lying on the table. I took a step forward.

". . . My note . . ." I began. And he followed the direction of my eyes, then picked the letter up.

"Don't you fret yourself," he said. "I'll make sure she gets it." He tucked it securely down in the pocket of his shirt. "As soon as she gets back."

It was out of my hands.

18

   ન   ન   ન

At the end of the lane I lit up my last cigarette (bought duty-free on the trip over) then walked down to the village where I bought another carton.

Coming out of the tobacconist's I saw Jean Timpson emerge from the supermarket carrying a small bag of groceries. I panicked; I knew I could never—considering the note I'd just left her—face any kind of conversation with her right then. And she was heading in my direction—though as yet she hadn't seen me.

Without hesitation, or giving more than a passing thought to my cowardice, I dodged around the pub on the corner into one of the streets behind the square. I stopped outside Pitkin's shop and saw, reflected in his window, that Jean Timpson had turned the same corner. Whether or not she saw me this time I had no idea, though I couldn't see how she could miss me. Still, even so, she didn't know that *I* had seen *her*. And I kept it that way. The door to the shop was open and without looking back I went in.

Pitkin had obviously seen me arrive outside and now he said good morning and asked me how I was. Fine, I told him, just fine. For long seconds I continued to stand there like a bump on a log and he nodded towards the street, saying, "Oh, there goes young Jean . . ." Anyone under fifty, I supposed, would be young to him . . . I didn't turn but watched, in a mirror, her progress as she hovered at the window, looking in at me. I saw her go away . . .

What—Pitkin asked me then, with an anticipatory smile—could he do for me . . . ? Seeing his smile I realised all at once what he took (hoped?) to be the reason for my visit. I decided I couldn't disappoint him.

"I just . . . just dropped in to say you can have the dresser," I said, and as soon as I'd spoken I was glad I had. He was so pleased.

Well, he said, after thanking me three or four times, we would have to work out a price, wouldn't we? Oh, I'd leave that to him, I said; having no knowledge of such things I'd leave it to him to give me what he thought was right. I asked him when he wanted to collect it. It would, he said, have to be at the weekend; he'd try to arrange it, then phone and let me know.

There was nothing really to say after that. But I didn't want to go just yet; not while there was a chance I might run into Jean Timpson on my way back to the cottage. He saved me, the old man; asked me if I had time to have a drink with him at the corner pub. "Yes, I'd love to," I said, meaning it, and he got his stick and followed me out into the street.

After he'd locked the door after us we went into the corner pub where he ordered each of us a pint of bitter.

We carried our drinks over to a table in the corner. He lit his pipe, I a cigarette. I relaxed in his company. He was a nice old man and I liked him very much. He was so easy to be with. I had still felt fairly tense after the business with the letter and my talk with Jean Timpson's father, but now, sitting chatting to Pitkin, the tenseness was quickly going. When we'd finished our beers I bought scotches. I felt he was unwinding too. He became more talkative, more open. I reckoned he was probably rather lonely, and glad of the company I briefly offered. His wife, he told me, had died some nine years earlier. His only son had been killed in the war. I asked him how he'd gone from farming to antiques. He smiled. "I s'pose it does seem a bit of an odd step, doesn't it? The shop was in my wife's family. We just got too old to work the farm, so we sold it and opened up the shop again. I can't say I regret it."

I got up and got two more drinks. When I put his down before him he protested for a moment, saying he wouldn't be fit to work, but he was enjoying himself, I could see. As I sat down opposite him again he lifted his glass, smiled at me over the rim and said, "Your good health."

"Cheers."

"Do your parents live in England?" he asked me.

"My mother's dead. My father lives in London."

"He must have been glad to see you get back from America. Particularly at a time—well, like this."

"No . . ." It would have been much the easiest thing to have said yes. But I said no, and he looked at me in surprise.

"We've never got on," I said with a shrug.

He gave a sympathetic nod. "Nor me, with my father." He looked off into space. "A very strict man. Mind you, he was only typical of many fathers of that time, I suppose. Very Victorian. And he had a terrible temper to go with it."

He turned his eyes to me, as if deliberating whether or not to continue. Then he tapped his left leg. "That's how I got like this. He did it."

"How . . . ? Why . . . ?"

"Because of the Temples." A simple statement. He added: "Mind you, I think I deserved it."

". . . I don't understand."

He gave a rueful little smile. "Hasn't Fred Timpson told you the rest of the story yet?"

"About Temple and his wife? He only told me what I told you—that if I wanted to know any more I should ask you about it."

He nodded. Then a little sadly, he said, "There are some things you don't ever really get over . . . Regrets can be so . . . consuming."

"You mean your leg . . . ?"

"Oh, no, that's just—well, a reminder. A reminder that's always with me." He stared down into his glass, then looked up at me again, smiling. "*One* drink's my limit, really, you know. Any more and I start to talk too much."

"Am I asking too many questions?"

"No, no, you're not. Anyway, it's no secret. If it had stayed a secret I wouldn't"—here he touched his leg again,—"have ended up with it like this."

I said nothing, just toyed with my glass. He wanted to talk, I could tell. After a while he added quietly:

"You see, it was my fault. Bronwen . . . Her dying like that."

"But—but how could that be? It seems pretty well known how it happened. Isn't it?"

"Oh, yes, it is. I said to you before that nothing was ever proved, but—as you say—it's well known what happened. And," he nodded, "I was—partly responsible."

I waited. He went on:

"I told you how I used to run errands for them, the Temples. That was fine with my mother and father. But what they didn't know was that some of the messages I carried were between Handyman and Effie. She was our dairymaid."

"Yes, I remember your telling me."

"I'd reckon their—love affair—had been going on for about five or six months before they went off together. You did hear the odd whisper about them, but nobody knew for *sure* that there was anything going on. Except me. I knew, of course, because of all the notes and things. But I didn't tell anybody." He spread his hands in a brief gesture of helplessness. "Well, I couldn't. Effie had been good to me. She'd helped me out when I'd been in a bit of trouble—just minor things—but she stopped my father finding out and—anyway, because of that—her helping me—I agreed to help her and Handyman with their messages to and from each other. And I was glad to do it. Because—as I say—I liked her . . ."

"And you knew they were going away together."

"No, that was kept a secret right up till the last minute. She lived at our house, you see. She didn't come from the village originally." He paused and took a drink. "We'd had a very dry summer that year, and that was the time the weather decided to break. Thunder woke me up—and my dog barking downstairs. There was lightning too, I remember. My dog was afraid, and I knew if I let him keep that racket up I'd have to answer for it later on. So, I went downstairs. And that's when I saw Effie just sneaking out. I remember the way she put her finger to her lips, warning me not to make a noise. I asked her what she was doing, and that's when she told me, that she was going away with Handyman—to America, she said. She seemed so excited, and so nervous at the same time. She asked me not to tell anybody—not for a few days, anyway—after that it didn't matter, she said, 'cause they'd be safely away . . ." The smile that came through his memory was very gentle. "She put her arms around me there in the hall and asked me to wish her luck. And then she kissed me." The smile stayed on his mouth. "I really liked Effie. I really did. I would have done anything for her. I don't suppose she was what you'd call a pretty girl, but she was nice. Ah, she was so nice." He was silent for a few moments as he thought back to the past; I was briefly aware of the chatter going on around us. Then he continued.

"So . . . she went off, out into the rain. Carrying her tin box, and the sunshade my mother had given her at Christmas." He gave a little laugh. "She had her sun-shade *up*—trying to keep off the rain . . . Handyman would meet her with the horse and trap, she said, then they'd be off to Southampton . . .

"She was missed later on, when my father and mother got up. They couldn't imagine what had happened to her. Then when my mother found Effie's things were gone as well they realised she'd left. My father asked, as a matter of course, whether I knew anything about it. I said no. But I was nervous, and he knew, and he was suspicious. He asked me again, but still I said no, I didn't know anything about it. Afterwards I was glad I'd lied because later, when I went out with my father on the milk cart, I saw Effie still there, waiting at the side of the road, under a tree. Waiting for Handyman. She dodged back and hid when she saw us coming. My father didn't see her. When we came back an hour or so later on she was gone; she'd met Handyman and they'd gone off . . . And that, I thought, was the end of it."

He took a drink from his glass, tapped the ash from his pipe, repacked it and lit it. "Oh, no," he said, "that wasn't the end, not by a long chalk. Three days later somebody, wondering why Handyman hadn't turned up with a piece of work he'd promised, went round to see him. And of course, there was no Handyman there. Only Bronwen. And she was dead . . ." His voice grew quieter. "It was a terrible thing. Terrible. I felt so bad about it. But can you imagine how I felt when it came out that she'd actually died only a matter of hours before she was found? I knew, that if I'd told the truth when my father had asked me, that she could probably have been saved. If I'd told the truth somebody would have gone to see her and they would have found her. Maybe in *time*."

I looked at him, the old man who sat across from me, even now, after so many, many years still carrying around the weight of the guilt he had taken upon himself. "No," I said. "No, it wasn't your fault . . ."

"Ah, well . . ." He sighed. "She might have been saved . . ."

"Do you think Effie had anything to do with it—the killing of Mrs. Temple?"

"No."

I was surprised by his positive tone.

"Never," he said. "She'd never have been a party to that. I'll bet she didn't know anything about it. No, that was purely Handyman's business." He lowered his eyes, gazing past me at nothing. "I couldn't bear to think that she'd had anything to do with *that* part of it. Not Effie." He paused, looked back to me. "You don't think it's likely, do you . . . ?"

What did I know about it? "No," I said. After a moment, watching as he puffed at his pipe, I asked, "Is there more?"

"Not much . . . Not really. I didn't keep my secret much longer. A woman in the village—the butcher's wife—was asking me questions about Effie, and so stupid and unthinking I mentioned America. I can see her face now—that flash of—*knowing*; you know what I mean. And then she asked me what *you* asked me: How did I know where they'd gone?"

"You didn't tell her . . ."

"Oh, no, of course not. I think I just—just stood there—saying nothing. I don't remember *what* I said . . . But I didn't tell her. I wouldn't have dared—for being afraid of what might happen, I mean." He shook his head, sighed. "I might as well have told her, though. She guessed something, and *enough*—and it got back to my parents that I knew more about it than I'd let on. I didn't know they knew, though. Not until I went one day to take my father his dinner where he was working in the Big Field. Well, he'd obviously just heard about it. I'll never forget that day. I was going along a footpath leading to a stile. As I got close to it he saw me and came across the field towards me. I was half-way over the stile when he got to me. I remember the—serious—look on his face, and I could tell at once that something was up. I smiled at him. I held out the basket with his dinner in it but he didn't take it. Just looked at me. And then he said he wanted to know the truth. That was *my* turn to say nothing then. He asked me again. He knew, he said, that I'd lied to him, that I knew more than I'd told him. So"—he shrugged—"I told him. I had to. You couldn't stand up to a man like him, and anyway, I was only about ten or so. I told him everything. About the messages I'd carried between Effie and Handyman, and about Effie leaving that morning of the storm. And he was so angry. When I'd finished I just—waited—not looking at him; I daren't. I remember I was sitting astride the top bar of the stile. And then—he hit me."

He smiled at me. I won't forget that smile.

"Oh, Lord, yes," he said, with a little shake of his head, "he hit me, all right. Twice. In the face. The first time really rocked me, but I dropped the basket and held on. Anyway, I had one leg behind the second rung so that helped me. I didn't fall. I did the second time, though. He hit me again and I went over that time for sure. Oh, yes, I went. And so did my leg. In two places."

I sucked in my breath at the picture his narrative conjured up. He went on:

"My memory after that is of coming to and finding myself in my father's arms as he carried me home. And looking up into his face and seeing how he was." He paused. "I'd never seen him cry before."

I was still thinking about Mr. Pitkin, his sad story and his guilt as I walked back to the cottage. I let myself in at the front gate and, as I turned, saw Jean Timpson come round the side of the house.

We stopped, facing each other.

She had been crying, I could see. Her eyes were red-rimmed, and even now I saw her chin quiver and her eyes fill with tears. I attempted a weak smile, but it didn't come off; her face didn't change. Voice soft, breaking, she said:

". . . *Why* . . . ?"

I shrugged, at a loss. "I'm sorry, Jean, really I am. But I did explain in my letter . . ."

"I don't understand . . . It was all right be*fore*. Why not now?"

"I told you." I must be calm, businesslike, show her there was no need to take it personally, to get upset. "Shelagh's here now, and we can manage on our own. It's different now that she's here. We just don't *need* any help."

She looked at the ground, shuffled a pebble aside with her shoe. The tears spilled and ran down.

"Mr. Warwick . . . I—I *likes* to come and help. I—enjoy it." Her glance flicked up to my face, then across to my shoulder. "You don't have to pay me if it's the money that's a problem. I just likes—coming here."

I felt desperate to get away, desperate for her to be gone so that I wouldn't have to look at that misery in her face. I thought of the sob story her father had given, and felt pity rearing its head. But I couldn't give in to it. I had to be realistic; I had to think of the razor blades, the glass. I wouldn't allow myself to be moved by her sadness.

And how, I asked myself, could she come around beseeching, begging like this, after what had happened? Or could it be that she really wasn't aware of what she had done, or of the possible result of her actions?

"It's not the money," I said, shaking my head. "I explained—we just don't need any help."

"You do," she said. "You do."

And my embarrassment became tinged with impatience, irritation. "I'm sorry," my voice sounded distinctly cooler, "but I've told you, and I think I'm best aware of what we need . . . And I really don't see much point in going into all this."

Her crying burst out with renewed strength. She reached into her pocket and, drawing out the money I had left in the envelope, thrust the notes towards me.

"What's this for?" I asked.

"I can't take it."

"Yes, you must." And then: "Please . . ."

"No. No. You weren't satisfied with what I was doing so I don't think you should pay me."

"I can't possibly take it back." I shook my head. "I can't. And we *were* satisfied with what you did for us.

The money is yours. You earned it. And anyway, part of it is only what you spent on us at the shops."

"Well . . . take *some* of it back."

"It's yours. How can I?"

She looked at me for a second longer, saw that I was determined, and then slowly stuffed the notes back into her pocket. I thought, hoped, that that would be the end of it, but no. She turned her head, looking dully off into the distance.

"Is it quite certain?" she asked flatly.

". . . Certain?"

"That you don't want me round no more . . ."

"Please—Jean—don't make it more difficult. You mustn't take all this personally. You're building the whole thing into something out of all proportion. Now you go on back home. Who knows, when Shelagh and I return here to live we might decide at some time that we do need a little assistance. And if so we'll be in touch." Afraid of going too far, of handing out false hopes, I added, "We *might* . . ."

"That means you won't."

Silence between us. And in the silence I heard the sound of horse's hooves on the road. We both turned and together saw Shelagh come into view astride the big chestnut mare. She waved to us, called "Hi!" and pulled the horse up next to the front gate. I walked towards her. "You cut quite an impressive figure," I said.

She laughed. "Oh, yes, fine seat and all that." She spoke like some English county duchess. I nodded in agreement. "An absolutely *splendid* seat." She turned her smile then, directing it past my shoulder to Jean Timpson.

"Hello, Jean. How are you today?"

". . . Fine, thank you, miss . . ."

Shelagh's eyes came back to me; there was a question in them. I shrugged my eyebrows.

"Are you having a good time?" I asked her.

"Fantastic. You don't know what you're missing."

"Maybe."

She looked, obviously concerned, at Jean Timpson again, and then back to me. Then she smiled. "I just thought I'd come and show you; give you a little treat. Give you a little cause for pride."

"You have. Indeed. I'm proud. I'm proud."

"And so you should be."

Glancing round I saw that Jean was looking straight at me. Then she lowered her eyes and came past me. I opened the gate for her and she went through under the arch. It was an awkward moment, for both of us—all silence and averted eyes, while Shelagh looked down not knowing what the hell was going on. As Jean Timpson got near to the horse she looked up at Shelagh as if she might say something. But she didn't. She turned to the right and, footsteps quickening, walked away. In a few seconds she had gone from sight, hidden by the screen of the hedgerow and the oaks.

"How's the horse behaving?" I asked Shelagh after a moment.

From where she sat I could tell that Jean Timpson was still in her view. Shelagh was watching her, frowning slightly, not hearing me. I repeated my question. She turned back to me.

"Oh, lovely. Such a sweet, placid nature." She lowered her voice, added: "What's wrong? What's up with Jean?"

". . . I don't know."

"She looks—upset."

"Oh, she'll be all right." Changing the subject I asked, "Have you had a good ride?"

"Wonderful." She pointed back past the village where the hills rose up. "It was marvellous."

"Rather you than me."

She grinned. "I'd better get back now." Clicking her tongue, she pulled on the reins and turned the mare to face down the hill. "After all, I've got better things to do than stay here talking to you all day."

I grinned back. "The feeling's mutual, I'm sure."

I watched as she dug in with her knees and the mare moved forward. On my side of the hedge I kept pace with them for a few yards and then stopped as they drew ahead. She turned, waved to me. "See you soon."

About ten yards further on I saw her stop. I leaned

over the hedge and saw Jean Timpson moving towards her from the shade of the trees. Shelagh bent down in the saddle. I couldn't hear what was said, but some exchange was made, and then Jean was out of sight again—this time hidden by the broad body of the horse.

And all of a sudden the mare gave a loud, vibrating whinny. I saw the great head rock back, the eyes rolling in fright and shock as it reared. I saw Jean Timpson reaching up, her hands moving. I heard Shelagh's scream, saw her own hands flailing, clutching, and the next moment the horse had leapt away.

I threw my carton of cigarettes to the ground and dashed to the gate. The chestnut mare was moving as if pursued by all the hounds of hell. For some yards it kept a straight course and then, suddenly, with Shelagh desperately clinging on, it veered sharply to the left, leaving the road and flinging itself into the wheatfield.

19

In seconds I was through the gate and running as fast as I could down the road and into the field. Up ahead the horse plunged onwards, and I ran in its wake, following its track in the wheat, and watching as it got further and further away from me with every second, eventually seeing it disappear from my sight into the trees at the far edge of the field. I ran on through the broken wheat, cursing my deformity and my unrhythmic stride. The ground was rough beneath my inadequate sandals; I felt about as nimble as if I were trying to make progress through molasses.

Slowing, at last, I came to a stop and stood gasping for breath, looking about me. Down to my right the fields and hedges fell steeply away towards where the village lay; I could see the road winding by at the foot of the steep slope. There was no sign anywhere though of the horse or its rider. I called out wildly, *"Shelagh!"* and heard nothing in return but the sound of birds crying and my own breathing. And then suddenly, there on the horizon I saw the horse break from cover and come charging out into the open. Right there where the earth met the sky it reared up—the size of a toy in the distance—then whirled and took off down the hill towards the road below.

My heart was thudding from my exertions, and now my rising fear only increased that thudding; I knew that once the horse got well set on its course, with its own weight bearing it on, there would be nothing anyone could do to stop it. I swerved to the right, keeping ahead of it, my fear and desperation keeping me balanced somehow. And seeing the mare taking a semi-circular route I increased my speed, feeling the flesh bouncing on my cheeks as I ran on in the desperate hope of heading her off.

Coming up against the hedge at the end of the wheat-field I didn't hesitate but scrambled through, while the briars tore at my skin and petals of dog roses fell about me like a gentle shower of pink snow. In the ditch beyond I tripped and sprawled, got up and out and ran on again, pounding over coarse grass, leaving the wheat-field further and further behind.

Up ahead I could see the road clearly now; it wasn't more than two hundred yards away. And I was still in front of the horse. Half turning, briefly, it looked now as if it was coming straight at me, and only moments later I heard the thundering of its hooves. Shelagh, I saw as the horse came on, had thrown herself forward over its neck and was frantically clinging on with both hands, while the reins and the stirrups danced, madly, useless.

The horse drew closer still, and I put on a spurt; I had to try to keep level with it—if only for a couple of seconds; the hard surface of the road was just beyond the hedge, too near, too dangerously near.

"David . . . !"

Shelagh screamed at me in terror, her face a white blur. The horse was just ten yards behind me, then five, then two, and then it was there, right beside me. We were running level. I could see its eyes rolling in its head, and the froth from its mouth hung and splashed onto my arm as I leapt sideways, clutching for the bridle.

I didn't have a hope in hell. Even as my fingers touched the bridle the mare swerved violently aside, her flank catching me a crashing blow that sent me reeling, so that the earth spun and I slammed down, rolling over on the rough turf, the breath knocked from my body.

As I staggered to my feet again, dazed, sucking in air, I was just in time to see the mare nearing the hedge at the bottom of the slope. She was moving much too fast to stop. I watched her as she got right up to the hedge, saw her suddenly stretch herself, reaching up; I watched as Shelagh slewed sideways in the saddle, hands clutching at the sky. Higher the horse rose up beneath her—and then Shelagh was gone, pitched headlong out of sight beyond the hedge.

I had one last glimpse of the mare. Free of her rider she managed somehow to clear the hedge. But, propelled onwards, downwards by her own weight and momentum even *she* couldn't stop herself now. A second later, in one single flash of shining chestnut, she had crashed acrosss the tarmac and smashed into the stone wall that ran along the far side of the road. The wall shattered. The mare fell.

"Shelagh . . . !"

I leapt the ditch and scrambled through the hedge. Shelagh lay partly on the grass verge, partly in the road, prone, her right arm flung out and forward and her hair spread, hiding her face from view. I knelt beside her and brushed the hair from her forehead where I saw an ugly graze etching itself in blood against the pallor of her skin. Ripping off my shirt I rolled it into a pad and then gently, so gently, eased up her head a fraction and placed the makeshift cushion beneath her cheek. Hearing the sound of an approaching car I ran out into the road, arms waving, seeing it as it rounded the bend and

yelling for it to stop, stop, stop . . . And then Bill
Carmichael, the man from the garage, was getting out
of the car, running past me. I watched him kneel beside
Shelagh's body and I shouted at him, my voice shrill,
"Do something! For Christ's sake, do something!" I
was going in circles, quite useless in my panic.

"Take it easy," he said, and then he was straightening
up, running back to his car and reappearing with a rug
which he softly spread over her. "Stay here." He stood
up again. "I'll go and phone for an ambulance."

As he drove swiftly back towards the village my eyes
took in, briefly, the sight of the chestnut mare where
she lay just a few yards away beneath the wall. The animal's head lay in a widening pool of blood, her neck
bent at a crazy angle, eyes staring sightlessly past me in
the direction of the fields. She was quite dead.

Shelagh, though, was alive. She was alive. I laid my
hand softly on her back and felt the gentle swell of her
breathing beneath the chequered rug.

"She'll be all right."

The young, red-haired doctor looked down at me as I
sat hunched in my chair in the hospital waiting-room. I
nodded my gratitude for his words.

"She was lucky," he went on. "God knows what
would have happened if she hadn't come off when she
did. That's what saved her, being thrown when the
horse took the hedge. If *she'd* gone into the wall, too
. . . well . . . " he let his hands fall; they told the rest of
the story. My fingers trembled as I fiddled with the buttons of my shirt. There were little traces of blood on it;
Shelagh's blood.

"She's concussed, certainly," the doctor went on,
"but we won't know any more than that until we've had
a chance to examine her." Briefly he touched my shoulder. "But don't worry. She's in good hands." Glancing
over to where Bill Carmichael hovered by the door, he
added: "What are you going to do now—? Get your
friend to drive you home again? It would probably be
the best thing. There's nothing you can do here. She's
only just regained consciousness."

"I'll stay—if that's all right. I must. At least till I've seen her."

"That might be a little while yet."

"It doesn't matter how long."

When he had gone Bill Carmichael came over to me. "Is there anything I can do?" he asked.

I shook my head. "No, Bill, thank you. You've been so kind."

"It was nothing."

"Thank God you came by when you did. I was like a chicken with its head cut off." Smiling, I added, "You're making a habit of it."

"A habit?"

"Calling the ambulance. First my brother and now Shelagh."

"Like you said—Thank God I was there." He shook his head. "I don't understand Mrs. Stoner—letting her go out on a horse that wasn't safe."

"It wasn't the horse," I said, "*or* Shelagh." Carmichael looked at me and I added: "She's a very good rider. She grew up with horses. And anyway, she'd told me, just before it happened, how well-behaved the horse was . . ." I had a flashing image of the mare rearing up, of Jean Timpson standing there, so close, so close. "It wasn't the horse," I said again. "Or Shelagh . . ."

His look continued blank, not understanding. After a moment he said, "Look, when you decide you want to go home just give us a call and somebody'll come and fetch you." He handed me a card with a number and an oily thumbprint on it.

After he was gone I continued to sit there. Other visitors came and went. At last, nearly two hours later, a young nurse came over to me and said yes, I could go in and see Shelagh for a minute. "But *only* for a minute," she emphasised as she led me into the corridor.

At last I stood looking down over Shelagh's bed, looking down into her eyes. There was a white bandage around her head. She gave me a weak smile that came and went like a faulty neon sign.

"The doctor says you're going to be okay," I said,

pushing the words past the lump in my throat. "You've had a hell of a bump and a bad shock, but you'll be okay."

Her eyes closed briefly in acknowledgement.

"You've got to be okay, anyway," I said. "I've got a wedding coming up on Saturday and I'd like you to be there."

Drowsily she smiled at me. I whispered, bending closer:

"Oh, Shelagh, you're all that matters to me. Only you . . . Always." It was true. I felt it so strongly; not to be denied, ever. I bent closer to her bruised, pale face. "I love you so much . . ."

Her eyelids were flickering; she was growing sleepy. At my elbow the nurse appeared, whispering to me that I must go, but adding that I could come back in the morning.

When I looked down at Shelagh again I saw that she was asleep. I wanted to kiss her cheek; I moved to do so but the nurse's gentle but firm hand restrained me and, feeling slightly cheated, I turned and tiptoed away.

In the corridor the doctor stopped me and told me that Shelagh's x-rays had shown up a fine hairline skull fracture. When he saw panic in my face he added quickly:

"It's nothing to be alarmed about. She'll be as right as rain in no time at all."

I said stupidly, "We're supposed to be getting married on Saturday . . ."

He smiled. "Well—we'll have to see how it goes. You might make it okay."

Back in the waiting-room I phoned Bill Carmichael and in just over twenty-five minutes he was there. As we drove away he asked me whether I'd been in touch with Mrs. Stoner at the stables.

"About the horse, you mean . . ." I shook my head. "I haven't even thought about it."

"If you like I'll give her a call—and tell her . . ."

"Thank you. I'd be grateful."

"She's probably learned about it by now, anyway,"

he said. He paused. "Strange that that horse should behave like that . . ."

"Yes," I said, then: "What do you know about Jean
Timpson?"

He looked a bit puzzled at the suddenness of my
question. "Well . . . not that much, really . . ."

"How much?"

"Well . . . things have been said . . ." He kept his
eyes on the road ahead. "But I don't concern myself
with it."

"It's not just idle curiosity," I said. "I really do want
to know . . ."

After a pause, he said, "I've known her since we
were at school. I don't really remember much about her
there, though. She was always so shy, so quiet; never
the kind you'd really notice. A couple of years younger
than me, I think . . . Later, when she left school, she
went to work at the stables and——"

"Yes," I cut in. "Shelagh mentioned that. So she
knows about horses."

"Jean? Oh, yeh, she ought to. She was at the stables
quite a few years. Probably still be there if that chap
hadn't turned up."

"Who was that?"

"I don't remember his name. He wasn't from the village. Just sort of came here and stopped for a while,
then went off again." He gave me a half-glance. "He
knew your sister-in-law. When she came here to live he
came back and stayed with her."

"Alan De Freyne."

"Yes, that was his name. A bit of a swine, leading
Jean on like that. And he *did*. Everybody knew that. He
didn't care for her at all, not really. Just in it for what
he could get."

"From Jean Timpson . . . it's hard to imagine."

"Oh, you must understand—this was a few years
back. She'd only be about twenty-five, twenty-six then.
She was a really nice-looking girl. Very pretty."

"And what happened?"

"Well, he suddenly left, and then, only about a

month or so afterwards, Jean left as well. To get away from it all, I expect. Her dad packed her off."

I remembered the name of the place she had mentioned. "Marshton Ridge," I said.

"Is that where it was? I know she'd gone to stay with relatives somewhere."

"With her aunt. She had a baby there."

"Oh, yeh, everybody knows that. I think it was born dead or she lost it soon after it was born. She didn't come back here for quite a time then. She got a job as a nursemaid with some family, looking after their boy . . ."

"And there was an accident, right? So her father said."

"Yes. It was in the last week of her job."

"She was leaving them?"

"No, the family was leaving England. Selling up and going abroad. Then, just a couple of days before they were due to go the little boy was dead. Drowned. A pool in the garden, I think." He clicked his tongue. "Really sad."

He drove in silence then, and I realised he wasn't about to add anything else. "What happened," I asked, "then?"

"Oh—she went away for a time—somewhere else— and then after a time she came back to live with her dad again." He paused. "I remember seeing her not long after she got back to Hillingham. There was quite a difference in her. Mind you, it had been over ten years since she'd left."

"Where did she go?"

"Marshton Ridge, didn't you say?"

"No, you said she went somewhere else *after* that— and before she came back to Hillingham . . ."

"About two years, I think."

"Where to?"

He didn't answer. I said again,

"Where to?"

"Elmacre, I believe."

"I never heard of it."

". . . It's a mental home."

An hour after he'd dropped me off at the cottage I phoned the hospital and asked after Shelagh's progress. I didn't care if I was being a nuisance; I wanted to be reassured. They said she was as comfortable as could be expected.

After that I felt lost. After her presence there in the cottage my sudden aloneness was difficult to cope with, and the company of Girlie couldn't do anything to make up for my sense of loss. Aimlessly I wandered about the house, unable to settle to anything. On the carpet the jigsaw lay where I had left it, still unfinished. I lit a cigarette, poured myself a drink and sank into my armchair. On the shelf the clock ticked into the silence, underlining the slowness of the passing of time.

So restless, I got up, left my glass on the coffee-table and went out into the garden where I ambled, slowly, without direction or purpose. I crossed over the lawn into the orchard, leisurely strolled its perimeter and ended up back at the gate. To my left I saw the remains of the old sundial, broken by the tree on the day of the storm. Poor Bronwen, I reflected, she must have thought the world was coming to an end—what with the storm, then Handyman attacking her and going off. And for her, of course, the world *did* come to an end; that day, the day of the storm, had marked the beginning of that end; three days later she was dead . . .

Pressing aside the weeds, grass and briars with my feet (my hands too; a few more scratches wouldn't make any difference), I managed to get a grip on the heavy stone face of the dial. I tried to lift it back to its original place on top of the pedestal but it was too heavy, and even so I could see that with the column so badly shattered it wouldn't have stayed in place anyway. Perhaps in time I might be able to get it repaired . . . it was a pleasant thought.

As I straightened up my eye was caught by something lying half-buried deep down in amongst the tangle of the briar's woody stems. Carefully I reached down and drew out a flattish piece of metal, quite black, round, about an inch-and-a-half in diameter.

"What have you found?"

Reese's voice, coming so suddenly out of the stillness into my concentration, made me jump.

"My God, don't *do* that," I said, smiling. "You're a doctor; you should know better."

"True, true." He laughed. Then he said, "I just dropped in to see how you are. Bill Carmichael told me what had happened."

I nodded. "Shelagh's going to be all right, thank God."

"Good." He paused. "And how about you? Bill said you were pretty shaken yourself."

"Oh, I'm okay now, thanks. But I appreciate your concern." I began to walk back towards the house. He fell into step beside me. "Have you got time for a drink?" I asked.

"Maybe. A small one."

Inside the house I poured him a scotch and topped up my own glass. He sat in the chair opposite my own. "You're quite sure," he said, "that you're right . . ."

"Quite sure." I hesitated and then burst out: "Why didn't you tell me about Jean Timpson? Why didn't you warn me?"

He stared at me in surprise. "Warn you? What about?"

"About her—state. The way she is. *She—she tried to kill Shelagh.*"

He said nothing, just kept staring at me in disbelief.

"You think I'm making it up," I said, my voice rising, "but I'm not! She's so—jealous. She wanted Shelagh gone—so desperately. And I realise, today, now, that there's nothing she wouldn't do to get rid of her. What happened this afternoon—that wasn't her first attempt to—to hurt her. She's tried be*fore!*"

He continued to look at me quite steadily, still with that rather bemused expression on his face, his brows raised slightly. I avoided his gaze. I saw that the knuckles of my fists were white.

"I don't think you know what you're talking about." he said softly, at last. "You're over-reacting a bit, aren't you? You've had a bad shock and——"

I didn't give him a chance to finish. I slammed my glass down so violently that the scotch slopped over the rim. "Don't use your unctious bedside manner on me," I said through clenched lips. "Save it for those who need it. I'm not a child! I know what's been happening here. That woman—she even put glass in Shelagh's food!"

He got up then. "Jean? You can't be serious . . ."

I snorted my disdain. "I thought she might be a bit *odd*. But even I didn't guess *how* odd." I looked at him, waiting for my words to sink in. "Don't you understand?—*she* made Shelagh's horse bolt."

"I think perhaps you need a sedative," he said, so gently, so reasonably that I wanted to hit him.

"Please go," I said shortly. "I'm sure you're doing your best—what you think is best, but it's not helping me in the least." He still stood there. "Please," I said, "go."

He took up his bag, opened his mouth to speak—probably more words of comfort—and then stopped, his glance moving past my shoulder, beyond the window.

"Here she is now."

I turned, just in time to see Jean Timpson go by on her way round to the back of the house. I stood for some seconds, gripping the back of the chair, feeling my anger growing inside me, then, when her knock came on the kitchen door I almost ran from the room.

Flinging open the back door I confronted her. She looked up at me and seemed almost visibly to shrink from my stony-silent glare. The fingers of one hand moved nervously to her cheek, fluttered down again. Her other hand held a bunch of pink roses.

"I—I just wanted to ask how Miss—Miss Shelagh is . . ." she faltered, her voice almost fading away. "I—I heard about her . . . her fall . . ."

I still said nothing, just stood there, feeling my mouth working; not even attempting to control the rage that welled higher and higher in me. She would offer me her flowers any second.

She licked her lower lip. Her glance flicked away and

came back to rest on my shoulder. "I just wanted to say," she whispered, "that if there's anything I can do . . ." Her words tailed off. Then, with an obvious effort, bathed as she was in my granite stare, she mumbled:

"When you see her next would you . . . would you . . . give her these, please . . ."

And then the little bunch of pink roses was lifted up to me. And I snatched them from her hand and hurled them down onto the step.

"You've done enough!" I said. "Haven't you? Haven't you done *enough*?

She flinched, stepped backwards, and I lashed out, kicking the flowers off the step.

"Keep your roses! Keep them! She doesn't want them!"

Her hands were at her mouth. Her eyes, wide with horror and shock, glanced down at the flowers that lay between us, then, frowning, as if comprehending nothing, she looked up into my eyes, reading the relentless fury there. I advanced on her, feeling the rose-stems beneath my sandal, my hands clenching and unclenching as I raised them.

"*Get out of here.*" I ground the words out. "Get out of my sight. I don't ever want to set eyes on you again. I don't want to hear your voice or even your name."

"Oh," she said, "Oh . . ." and the sound was like the frightened bewildered voice of a child. The shadow of a small, grotesque smile pulled at the corners of her mouth, as if her only defence, her only hope for sanity lay in the belief that it was all some monstrous joke. And then, suddenly, the smile was gone and she was pleading, "Oh, please . . . no, no, *please* . . ." backing up from the path onto the edge of the lawn, her heel catching, so that her body jerked ungracefully as she recovered her balance. Behind me I heard the sound of a step and then Reese's voice telling me to calm down and stop being a fool. I ignored him. All I could think of was Shelagh: I saw her there astride the horse, so happy; saw Jean Timpson reaching up, saw Shelagh's terrified face as the horse raced by me, saw Shelagh lying in the road, still as death.

Now I shook off Reese's restraining hand, and Jean Timpson edged further back onto the grass.

"You tried to kill Shelagh," I said to her, and then, unstoppable, added: "You're evil. *You're insane.*"

Still retreating, she shook her head mechanically from side to side. "Oh, God," she breathed. "Oh, God . . ." And I saw the tears almost springing from her eyes. She gave a little animal whimper and with a last stricken look at my face, awkwardly turned and ran off across the grass. I stood there, shaking, watching without pity the indignity of her flight.

She ran through the orchard gate. Reese grabbed my arm again and said:

"Are you satisfied?"

I didn't answer. I shook his hand away.

"Go after her," he said.

No. I would have every ounce of my pound of flesh.

"Go after her yourself," I said.

I saw distaste in the curl of his lip. I felt the tide of my anger turning, ebbing away. Then Reese was gone from my side, running over the grass. I waited a couple of seconds and hurried in pursuit.

There was no sign of her in the orchard and Reese, up ahead of me, was hovering distractedly, not knowing which way to go. When I realised all of a sudden where she must be heading I ran faster, making for the gap in the hedge. "This way!" I shouted.

Scrambling through the gap ahead of him I dashed through the thicket, running in a straight line down the steep open track towards the edge of the pond.

There was no sign of her in the water, but I knew she was there.

❧ ❧ ❧

20

I paused only long enough to rip off my sandals, then, running down the steep, slippery bank I took a deep breath and plunged in.

One place where my limp had never hampered me was in the water. I was a strong swimmer; and now I would need all the strength I could muster.

My shallow dive—shallow for my own safety's sake—brought no results, and I surfaced as fast as I could and dived again, kicking hard, diving deep. I could hardly see anything; the water was cloudy and becoming cloudier all the time; mud was being stirred up—and not by me, so I knew she was down there somewhere, and not too far away. Holding my breath till I felt as if my lungs were bursting, I forced myself deeper still, my hands searching desperately about me, trying to make contact.

And they did. I didn't see anything, but I touched some hard, resisting object and then, as my fingers left it they brushed, just briefly, the softness of clothing, the softness of her arm.

So I knew where she was. Kicking with all my power I reached up, soaring to the surface, then, taking a great gasping lungful of air I dived down again.

I found her at once this time—but only by touch; the mud had been stirred up so much it was impossible for me even to keep my eyes open. Getting my hands under her arms I tried to drag her up with me, but although she didn't forcibly resist me I couldn't move her. I let go her arms and pushed deeper, frantically groping about to find just how she was caught.

It was by her foot—trapped between what felt to be

the spokes of some old half-buried wheel. I took hold of her ankle; a slight twist, a slight push, and then she was free. And in almost a continuation of the same movement I reached higher, grasped her firmly by her upper arms and kicked upwards.

As we broke the surface Reese was right there just a yard or so away. Without a word his hands came out towards us, fingers gripping, holding tight. Together, with Jean Timpson held securely between us, we struck out for the bank.

We laid her down in the soft grass at the water's edge. She didn't fight at all, or struggle. I watched as Reese knelt over her, his hands rhythmically working—pushing, pressing, on and on, and with every second my panic grew and grew. I could do nothing but crouch there, watching and praying . . .

And then the water was coming out of her mouth; with each push down he was forcing the water from her body. Yet still she didn't move.

I watched as he turned her roughly over onto her back, pinched her nostrils between his finger and thumb, took a deep, deep gulp of air and closed his mouth over hers. He was pushing the air into her now. Again. Again. Again. It's useless, I wanted to say, it's useless, she's dead. But he kept on.

And then suddenly she gave a shudder, her hands jerking at her sides, reaching up and out. He released her and her head moved, writhing in the grass; her mouth opened and she gasped, sucking in air.

When he looked across at me his face showed strain—but even stronger was his look of relief. He gave the slightest nod and said softly:

"She'll be all right now."

After a while he rose and lifted her up in his arms. Through the sound of her dry sobbing I heard her little murmurs of protest.

"Hush, hush," Reese said, soothing, gentle. "It's over now. There's nothing to worry about now . . ." To me he said after a moment's thought: "Let's get dry and then I'll drive her back to my place. I don't think she'd better go home today." He looked into Jean Timpson's face. "Do you think so?" he asked her. She didn't answer, but he said, "No," as if she had.

In the cottage she stood dumbly while I gave her towels, and some of Helen's clothes to change into. In her dull eyes pain and fear lingered like a bruise. I couldn't look at her; I had to turn away.

I gave Reese a shirt and a pair of Colin's trousers, then went upstairs and pulled off my own wet things. Afterwards, in dry gear once more, I went back down to the kitchen where Reese sat. When Jean Timpson was ready we drove to his house.

In his front room I waited while he and his wife put her to bed. When he came to me some minutes later I saw that he'd got into his own clothes. He handed me my shirt and Colin's trousers.

"Is she all right?" I asked him.

"Yes." He nodded. "And fretting in case her father finds out. But that's a good sign—hopeful. I've told her there's no need to worry. I shall take her back home tomorrow—if she's all right. I'll tell her father something—then he needn't know anything about it. No point in making it worse."

"Will she—try to do it again, do you think?"

"Let's hope not."

He moved back towards the door. "Come on," he said, "I'll drive you back."

"I can walk."

He gave me a look that said this was no time for me to be over-sensitive, then said, "I've got to call in and see her dad anyway. Come on. Carol will stay with her."

"Oh, God . . ." I shook my head. "When I think what might have happened . . . I'm so glad you were there."

"Yes," he said, "so am I."

I made my way slowly up the hill towards the cottage, leaving behind me Reese going on his way to see Mr. Timpson.

"What will you say to him?" I had asked.

"I'll say that Carol and I have unexpectedly been called out—that we need a baby-sitter."

"Will he believe that?"

"Why not? He'll be glad to believe it."

"Because he'll think she's being entrusted with the care of children . . ."

He gave me a quizzical look. "Who have you been talking to?"

"Bill Carmichael. He told me something of her story." I added, "Albeit reluctantly."

"Hm," he said, "well, I hope it was the *right* story."

"Her father talked to me as well," I said. "It's certainly a *sad* story, anyway."

He nodded. "It is—hers. It must have been hell—to live with the thought that people can believe you to be capable of something so—awful."

"You mean the boy—drowning."

"Yes. And as if she hadn't gone through enough before that. With her own baby, and with De Freyne."

"De Freyne . . . he keeps cropping up."

"He was in Hillingham long before your sister-in-law was here. That's how she got to know about the place, I believe, because of him. They were related, weren't they?—cousins or something?"

"I don't know. In fact the longer I stay here the more I realise how very little I know of Helen."

". . . Anyway, he was here first of all—working at the stables. That's where he got to know Jean."

Silence. Then I said, suddenly realising:

"He was the father of her child."

"Yes. There was hell to pay when Timpson found out."

"With Jean?"

"No, with De Freyne. Well, Timpson knew that De Freyne had only been leading her on. He had, too. I think she thought he might marry her, but *he* didn't have any such ideas. He just wanted a good time. He was younger then."

"He doesn't sound a very pleasant character."

"Well, *that* didn't make him very popular, or what happened afterwards with her father."

"What happened? He kicked up a fuss?—Timpson?"

"I'll say. I was called up to the stables one afternoon. It appeared that Mr. Timpson, when he found out, had gone up there to see De Freyne. There was a bit of a scene and poor old Timpson ended up getting knocked flat. That's why they sent for me. He was in a pretty bad state, but there—you wouldn't expect much else, would you? I mean, Timpson was getting on and De Freyne was young and strong."

"De Freyne seemed to make a habit of getting into fights," I said. "How did it happen that time? Who started it?"

"According to what I was told later, Timpson started berating De Freyne for leading Jean up the garden path, with promises of marriage and so on. Then, apparently, De Freyne said a bit too much in return, and Timpson went for him."

"Good for him."

"I persuaded him to let me drive him home. But, my God, he was in a rage. He was white with anger. He's always been so protective where Jean is concerned. Just couldn't bear the thought that somebody had made such a fool of her. Even then, just before he got into my car I had to pacify him or he'd have gone for De Freyne again. And the threats he called out to him—what he wasn't going to do to him if he stayed around." He made a wry face. "Funny, really, to see Timpson making dire threats to someone much younger and so much bigger."

"Was that the end of it?"

"Yes. De Freyne went. He left the next week or so."

"But later came back."

"Years later, yes. After your sister-in-law had bought the cottage. I think she must have visited him while he was staying here before, and liked the place. So when your cottage came on the market she stepped in and bought it. You know how you discover things . . . places . . . Anyway, as I say, he came back. I had quite a surprise to see him riding through the square one day as large as life."

"Riding? He went back to work at the stables?"

"No, he was riding his bike. Unmistakably his—all painted with fluorescent colours, with his initials everywhere. Afraid of getting it stolen, I suppose." He laughed. "In a place like this, too. Still, rather typical of him."

"Was there any further trouble with him and Timpson?"

"When De Freyne got back? No, I don't think so. It was all very much in the past then."

I thought of Jean Timpson's reaction when I had asked if she knew of De Freyne's whereabouts. And it had been obvious that for *her*, certainly, it wasn't all very much in the past . . .

"How?" I asked, "could he have such colossal nerve—to come back to a place where he'd caused so much trouble?"

"Yes . . . It's not easy to understand some people, is it?"

"It must have been a pretty unhappy situation for Jean Timpson—to have him back here, practically under her nose."

"It was, I think. At that time I believe she'd just started to work for your sister-in-law—before she was your sister-in-law, I mean—but when De Freyne showed up, and stayed, Jean left. She didn't go back till he'd gone."

"He was a painter also," I said, remembering. "I suppose he was working there at the cottage—at his painting."

"I don't know. Probably."

"Maybe he was a freeloader."

"A what?"

"A sponger."

"*Ah* . . ." He nodded. "Anyway, he wasn't there that long. Not before your brother came on the scene. And certainly not for very long afterwards."

"*Was* he—Helen's lover, do you think . . . ?" That, I thought, could account for the ill-feeling between him and Colin; which in turn could account for their fight, and then De Freyne's sudden departure.

"I told you before," Reese said. "All I know is that

he was there." He clearly didn't see any point in going on with it. He had his own question to ask. Which he did:

"Did you mean what you told me earlier on?"

"What was that . . . ?"

"About Jean. You made some—some rather wild accusations."

I avoided his gaze. "I was in a rather wild state," I mumbled.

"Yes . . ." And then he smiled suddenly, reached out and shook my hand. "Go on home and get some rest. It's been a rough day, with one thing and another, hasn't it?"

"You could say that." I smiled at his understatement.

He turned, ready to go on his way. "Anyway, Shelagh—Jean—they'll both be all right. I don't think you need have any further worries."

On the coffee-table I found my drink where I had so angrily placed it just before Jean Timpson's visit. I topped it up and added more ice. I needed a drink. Badly.

I sat down in my armchair and I thought about Shelagh. And then I thought about Jean Timpson.

I had driven her to try to kill herself. The sound of the words I had hurled at her came back to me, re-echoing in my brain. When I lifted my glass I saw all the snags in my flesh, over my wrist and hand; from my scramble through the hedgerows; from the roses Jean Timpson had brought, the roses I had snatched from her hand and dashed to the ground. I must have been mad to have attacked her in such a way.

But even so, that thought, that realisation didn't mean that I had been wrong in the reasoning that had led to my outburst. My conclusions had been the only ones possible for me to reach. Jean Timpson had a sad, sad story behind her, but I couldn't allow that to affect my interpretation of the evidence I had . . .

When my drink was finished I poured myself another. Although I hadn't eaten since breakfast I didn't in the least feel like facing food. I was totally disorientated. I was drinking too much, too, that was clear. Looking out I saw that the day had begun to die, the shadows were lengthening on the lawn. Could so much have happened in a single day?

Near my left hand was the little knight on his charger. I picked it up, turned it over in my scratched fingers. It was a beautiful piece of work. But there, everything I had seen of Helen's had been exquisite.

The drink and the events of the day fostered my melancholy and I reflected how even the sorrow of their deaths—Colin's and Helen's—was no longer a clean sorrow. Not now. I didn't now even have the comforting thought that while they had been together they had been happy. I had thought so once. But now it was different. There had been the phone call . . . and also the gossip that he had become involved with Elizabeth Barton . . . And what about the missing photographs . . . ?

I wanted Shelagh with me. Without her, alone, my inclination was to curl up in a foetal position and take, in sleep, refuge from all the problems, the questions that gyrated in my head. I wouldn't sleep, though. I couldn't. Those same problems and questions would see to that.

I had told Shelagh that I was through with all the probing, all the wondering. But how could I be? My brother had been accused of murder for gain, and while that calumny hovered over his head I knew I would find no real rest. Yet how I could set about disproving it was beyond me. There was a story there somewhere—and probably a simple story—if I could only find it; if I could only get to the beginning of it, and unravel it, thread by thread.

I must, I told myself, try to find out more about Helen, about her relationship with Colin. And I must find out, too, just how Elizabeth Barton fitted into the story. Yes, I *would* see her again. And this time I wouldn't be put off. And De Freyne, too; I had to see him as well—even if only to eliminate him from the puzzle. But how would I find him? He seemed to be something of a drifter. All I knew was that a year ago, after a quarrel with my brother, he had left the cottage for London. And since that time there had been no word or sign of him . . .

When my glass was empty I set it down and went out into the garden. I wandered under the arch into the thicket and made my way to the little clearing where the summer-house had been. I sat on the stone bench for a while and smoked a cigarette. Here, next to the remains of the original foundations was Colin's marked out plot for the summer-house he had planned to build for Helen. So why had he stopped? Was it time that had run out on him? Or was it indeed his love for Helen . . . ? No, not the latter. Such conjecture was dangerous, and faithless to his memory. Think about something else, I admonished myself—or, rather, *do* something.

And the idea came to me: just the other night I had sat here with Shelagh, at her side on this bench. "You shall have your summer-house," I had told her. I thought of her lying there in her hospital bed, bruised and shaken. And she *would have* her summer-house.

Yes. Tomorrow I would see some local builder and present him with Colin's plans, and in the meantime, now, I could clear the area and remake Colin's beginning.

In spite of the fading light I fetched tools from the shed and set to work. I found that the earth was loosely packed; Colin's digging had obviously been thorough. I was glad; it made my work, now, much easier.

As I worked I was aware of the sounds of approaching night all around me. Leaves rustled with a different sound, crickets chirped and somewhere, deeper in the thicket, a nightingale sang.

It was getting more and more difficult to see clearly what I was doing now. But I kept on. And through it all my thoughts went time and time again to dwell on Colin and Helen. I couldn't get away from them. Would I ever?

The hard, resisting object against which I slammed my spade jarred my arm up to my shoulder. I struck down again, a little to the side, but it was still there, beneath the surface. I crouched, peering down in the gloom. Taking a stick I poked about until at last I had cleared away enough of the soil to see what lay buried there.

A skull it was I'd struck.

21

❧ ❧ ❧

Mouth instantly dry, my lips opened, whispered, "Oh, Jesus Christ . . ." and I straightened up, feeling myself go cold, feeling the sweat suddenly chill on my panting body. I trembled.

Taking a deep breath I forced myself to crouch low again and picked up the stick where I had let it fall. Raking away with it, hands shaking, I uncovered the grotesque head still with traces of skin stretched tight across the bone. There were bits of hair, too; it adhered disgustingly to my fingers and I shuddered, shaking it free. I unearthed more of the body and felt the texture of decayed clothing. One hand, disturbed by my work, shifted and stuck up through the soil, fingers curled, beckoning. And then my own fingers brushed and held a squarish object which, when I'd rubbed the soil from it, turned out to be a bicycle lamp. It was pitted with rust, but even in the dim light I could still make out the bold initials emblazoned on the patterned paintwork: ADF.

De Freyne, De Freyne, De Freyne, my mind was shouting. Dropping the lamp—as if it were red-hot—back into the trough of earth I covered it up again.

I stood up, turned away. All around me the woodland seemed to have undergone a change; I wasn't aware of it till now. I knew it must only be the result of my imagination, and I told myself as much, but I reacted as if it were real. It was as if my senses were suddenly tuned only to that which was dark, unknowable, shutting out the sweetness of the coming night. Was that nightingale still singing? I don't know; I wasn't aware of it. I was aware only of malevolence and menace—in every pale-grey shadow; heard whispered voices in the rustling leaves, and when the breeze was stilled even the silence turned to shriek.

I mustn't be afraid, I told myself. There was nothing to be afraid of . . . I began to spade the earth back into the shallow grave, covering everything that was there. And I couldn't pause until the last scattering of soil had been thrown down, patted down—until there was nothing left to see but a mound of newly-turned earth. Only then, leaving the spade and fork behind me did I walk away—back consciously straight, head up— back towards the house, the kitchen.

At the table I sat and rested my head in my dirt-smeared hands, hearing nothing but the drip of the cold water tap, and the moths as they moved to the light, driven, their flight paths as inescapable as destiny. I found myself wincing as, without rest, they flung themselves against the glass.

I had to have a drink. I poured myself a large scotch. Then another, and another. And I continued to sit there while the cigarette-butts and the grey scum of ash filled and overflowed the ash-tray. It began to rain. I went to the door and stood looking out, seeing in the light from the doorway the raindrops pelting down, bouncing up from the flags of the pathway. No stars were visible, nor the moon—only the darkness where the rainclouds hung low. Against my ankles Girlie brushed her smoothness, pushed her nose out into the damp air and withdrew it again, going back to her basket beneath the window. She curled up, slept. I, too, I told myself, must sleep . . .

But not yet . . .

Closing the door on the rain I carried my glass and the bottle of scotch into the living-room. Sleep could wait. I sat in my armchair and thought again of my discovery. Who, I asked myself, had killed De Freyne? And why?

He had not been popular, that much was certain. And there were those who'd had cause to positively hate him . . . Jean Timpson and her father, for instance . . .

Alan De Freyne had been the cause of great unhappiness for Jean Timpson. She'd even refused, when he'd returned to the cottage, to continue with her work here; and she'd only agreed to come back once he was gone . . . Did she know then that he had gone for good . . . ?

But was Jean Timpson physically capable of such an act—albeit she might have wished him dead? Of course she could have lured him somehow to the thicket and killed him there, on the spot. Her task would have been relatively easy then. And the clearing in the thicket was well away from the house so there wasn't much chance of discovery while she was burying his body . . . Then was it she . . . ? Bill Carmichael had told him that she had spent time in a mental home, and I already had ample evidence of the strange workings of her mind where Shelagh was concerned. I had only to think of the razor-blades, the splinter of glass and the business with the horse . . .

My thoughts took me further, still further . . . If Jean Timpson had killed De Freyne, and if she had actually tried to kill Shelagh, then was it not possible—likely, even—that she might have been directly concerned in Helen's death . . . ? Perhaps in one respect the anonymous telephone-caller had been correct—Helen's death had *not* been an accident. It could be. Jean Timpson had had opportunity there; there was only her word for it that she had been *inside* the house at the time of Helen's fall . . .

But there, on the other hand, it was also possible that the old man Timpson had killed De Freyne. He had fought with him all those years ago. Threats had been issued. And it was possible that those threats hadn't been as empty as people had believed. Had *he* somehow got De Freyne into the thicket, killed him and hidden his body there . . . ?

My mind was full, crowded with images, words, thoughts and memories. I closed my eyes, leaned back against the soft cushions and gave myself up to the turmoil inside me. It was as if my brain was a receptacle, slowly revolving, in which those images, fragmented thoughts turned over, one upon the other, like coloured pebbles in a stone-polisher's drum.

There was one other possibility. Apart from Jean Timpson and her father. And that was that Colin had killed De Freyne. But that was a possibility I couldn't, wouldn't consider, not for more than a second.

I got up and moved over to the sofa, kicked off my shoes and put my feet up. My head was spinning, and still the thoughts went on, turning over and over.

I awoke with the sunlight streaming in on me. It took me a second or two to realise that I was still downstairs, still on the sofa.

"I've been waiting for you," Shelagh said.

I leaned down, kissed her gently on the mouth, and asked myself why did I concern myself so much with the dead. She had escaped it—death, and that was enough to keep me going through anything.

She was still decked out in the bandage and sticking plaster, but her bright, warm smile was new, and so welcome after the image I'd kept of her since the previous day. I put my armful of roses on the bedside locker and took her hand.

"You look just fine," I said. I sat down on the chair beside her bed.

"I *am* fine. And I'll feel even better when they let me out of here." She paused. "Supposing they don't let me out by Saturday—what happens?"

"The licence is valid for three months, so we can make a new appointment any time."

She sighed, smiled, lying back on the pillow while I held her hand and looked at her. Into the restful silence a nurse came, took up the roses—"Let's find something to put these in . . ." and went away. She returned a few minutes later with them arranged in a tall vase which she placed carefully on the locker. After giving the flowers a few last little touches of artistry she gave us a smile and a nod and went as quietly as she had come.

"They're beautiful, the roses," Shelagh said. "And the scent is so sweet."

I didn't want to get my thoughts sidetracked by other things, but with her words I just started thinking of the roses I had found on the pillow—and then of course came other thoughts—of the glass, the razor-blades, the horse rearing up and taking off on its death-headed flight across the fields. And so to the body of De Freyne . . . And *Yes,* my mind said, *it had to be Jean Timpson* . . .

"What are you thinking about?" Shelagh asked.

". . . You . . ."

I stopped at the cemetery on my way home. All peace and tranquillity under the one o'clock sun. And that same peace was there at their graveside. I was aware of it, the peace, and wished I could have some of it inside my head.

I realised suddenly that I would have to sell the cottage. I knew I could never be content there now. Not while that body lay out in the thicket. Not while Jean Timpson lived so close by, a constant reminder of all that had happened . . .

It was the only answer. I'd never be free of it all until Shelagh and I were gone, away from it all. And until that time came I must shut it out of my mind. Everything. The phone call, De Freyne, Elizabeth Barton, Jean Timpson . . . Yes, *her* most of all. But there was no need for me ever to set eyes on her again—and with luck I never would . . .

At the hospital that evening Shelagh told me that Bill Carmichael had been to see her. So had Mrs. Stoner from the stables.

"I feel so bad about that beautiful horse," Shelagh said. There were tears in her eyes. "Mrs. Stoner was so good about it. Me—I'd want to kill me."

"Don't talk like that." I followed up my words with a quick smile, trying to dilute the sharpness of my tone.

When it was time for me to go I said, "I'll be back in the morning. Is there anything I can bring you?"

"You could bring me a good book."

"Right. I'll bring you a good book. Your usual taste, and nothing to get you too excited; just sex, lust, rape, mayhem——"

"And murder," she finished for me. *Murder* . . . the word had stuck in *my* throat . . .

I kissed her and turned to go. From behind me her voice called softly:

"You could bring me some more flowers, too, if you like."

I followed her eyes to the vase of roses on the locker. Already they were wilting, dying . . .

In the corridor the young red-haired, white-coated doctor came to me and told me he thought Shelagh would be fit enough to leave in time for our wedding.

"Can I tell her?"

"Wait till we're sure—on Friday. Then there won't be any chance that she'll be disappointed."

Tomorrow, I decided, I would go and see Mr. Jennersen at the bank; get him to set about selling the cottage for me when Shelagh and I had returned to New York. I knew it was the only thing to be done, yet I dreaded the step. I sat in the living-room with my scotch-on-the-rocks and found it almost impossible to imagine that the day would soon come when I would leave this place forever. I loved the cottage. The warmth I had felt on that day was still here. It was all around me . . . But it couldn't change what had happened. That body in the thicket was still there, and nothing could change my knowledge of that . . .

When my drink was finished I poured myself another one. I seemed to be going through the scotch at an alarming rate; but I preferred not to think about that. Before me on the carpet the large tray still held the unfinished jigsaw puzzle. I scooped up the pieces and dropped them back into the box. I'd never finish it now. I replaced the lid and knelt there for a moment looking at the idiotic delight on the woman's face as she sat on her swing, cavorting, and then I got up, went upstairs and put the box back in the cupboard where I had found it.

On the shelf next to it were several fairly large leatherbound volumes. I took them down. They appeared much used, the covers thumbed and ink-stained. Helen's sketch-books. Each one was crammed with sketches; ideas in pencil, ink, colour and tone; drawings of faces; figure studies. I flicked through the pages; the books seemed to go back years, beyond her days as an art student.

Raising my eyes I saw before me again her paintings on the walls. I felt myself drawn closer. There seemed to be something different about them. But was it possible . . . ?

The painting of the back garden looked somehow changed, strange. Those roses that grew against the white-washed wall—surely, before, they had all been only in bud . . . No, no, it couldn't be; here, now, some of the flowers were open.

I stared at the picture, seeing clearly, but not taking it in. I was sane, I was relatively sober—and yet one or two of the roses painted there were open, open . . .

And there was something else. That shadow cast by the birch-tree. It was not a shadow at all. How had I ever taken it to be one? Clearly it was a figure. The figure of a woman.

But I *must* be wrong about *that* . . . I could so readily recall the purple shadow of the birch. I was certain I'd never before seen this woman, mysterious, indistinct, as she leaned over the flower border, a bunch of flowers in her arms . . . A woman in a purple dress, holding roses, where once there had been only the shadow of a tree . . .

I forced myself to look away; it was madness to give in to the tricks my mind was playing on my eyes . . . I looked at the next picture.

This was the one where I had seen the romanticised figures of Colin and Helen. And they looked the same. And yet, perhaps . . . yes, surely, the colours of the flowers were different; they had been pinks and blues before; I recalled examining the little touches of pigment, awed by Helen's talent. Why, then, were some of the flowers now white? And why, where once they had appeared to be quite unspecific, did they now seem to be, quite clearly, roses?

And now my eye was drawn back to the girl in the picture, with the bird flying over her head—the bluebird, mythical bird, symbol of happiness. And here again it seemed I had been mistaken . . . The bird that now hovered over the girl's hair was black and white. A magpie? Yes, a magpie. The magpie, too, was surely a symbol of something, wasn't it? And then I realised just *what* it symbolised—and gave an involuntary shudder. The magpie was a symbol of doom.

My hand trembling, I reached out, touched the paint on the magpie's wing. The paint was still wet.

I stared at the girl with her bright smile. Her hair was not black. It *had* been, *before*. Not now. Now, beneath the open wings of the bird her hair flew coppercoloured.

It wasn't Helen.

It was Shelagh.

The chill was inside me. It wasn't in the house. The chill was inside *me*; and all the scotch I drank did nothing to bring back the warmth. I thought about it. There was no sudden coldness, no feeling of antipathy in the house. Where I sat in the living-room, the scotch-bottle at my side, I felt only that accustomed welcome and comfort surrounding me. The coldness, the chill was inside *me*.

I don't know how long I sat there, but it was a long time. When at last I got up I misjudged the distance to the table and my empty glass ended up on the floor. Too much alcohol, and the co-ordination was one of the first things to go.

I was aware of Girlie weaving seductively around my ankles, and I stooped and stroked her soft fur for a moment. Then I went upstairs.

I was dead-tired. It had been a day beyond imagining and my brain, inadequate to cope with it all, felt numbed—from the happenings, the drink and from the frantic clutching for answers.

I flicked off the landing light, went in and lay wearily on the bed. As I sank back my mind told me that everything would be as usual in the morning . . . And then my cheek brushed against something on the pillow and in the same instant the perfume of a rose came to my nostrils.

I jumped as if I'd been stung. Reaching out for the bedside lamp I found it to be in a slightly different position, and when I turned it on I saw that it was a different lamp. I was in Colin and Helen's room. Why, how had I come in here . . . ?

I lifted my head and looked again at the painting immediately above me. Of course the girl in the picture was Shelagh, there was no possible doubt—just as there was no doubt that the bird was a magpie. Not only could I see that, very clearly, but to my dazzled eyes it looked as if the bird was a little closer to the top of her head.

Beneath my taut body Helen's patchwork quilt was a kaleidoscope of blues and browns. The rose had slipped down from the pillow and now stood out sharply against the muted tones, a soft, creamy white, just tinged with the faintest blush of pink. I moved my head away from the sweet, sweet smell—and Helen's sketch-books fell to the floor.

Leaning over the edge of the bed, head hanging down, I glanced at the books where they lay in an untidy heap on the carpet. The top one had fallen open, showing the flyleaf with Helen's name written on it. Helen's full name.

Rose Helen Cartwright.

Rose Helen . . .

Rose . . .

I hadn't known her first name before.

I felt, once again, and so strongly now, that familiar embracing warmth; it was as if there was another presence in the room, someone who was there watching me, someone who had been there in the cottage since the moment of my arrival. And that presence was so strong that I felt I need only stretch out my hands in order to make contact . . .

Helen's first name was Rose . . . I saw again the rose lying on the quilt, saw the roses in the paintings.

Roses, roses, roses . . .

One part of my mind kept insisting that such things couldn't happen, didn't happen; I knew they didn't. And the other part of my mind watched as the pieces, like those in the jigsaw, slotted into place.

Roses, roses, roses . . .

It seemed to me as if the whole house was hushed. I heard only silence. Felt it. There was no sound of any breeze from the open window, no leaves tapped against the pane. I was enveloped in a great stillness that was drenched in the scent of roses; a stillness so complete that it seemed almost tangible.

"All right," I said into that stillness. "All right, Rose . . . Helen . . . I know you're there . . ."

And then it seemed I heard a sigh, gentle, plaintive, that whispered in the room for a moment and was gone.

PART THREE

They say the dead die not, but remain
Near to the rich heirs of their grief and mirth.
"Clouds"—Rupert Brooke

22

That presence I had sensed was even stronger now, and with the realisation came the surprising knowledge that I was no longer afraid. I had been, I could see, but now no longer. I was afraid for Shelagh, oh, yes—but at the moment she was safe and could come to no harm—but for myself I was not afraid; that sensation of warmth and welcome that enveloped me was totally benevolent.

I heard myself laugh softly into the seductive silence and thought vaguely that I must be more than slightly drunk. I saw the rose in my hand; it was giving up that scent that I had come to know so well. I held it to my cheek, happily, feeling the softness of the petals like a caress, while all the while the warmth drew closer, came closer, embracing me, and it seemed for a moment as if the whole room spun—a whirl of roses, so that I drifted in rose-petals, wallowed in the scent of them.

The cat was there on the bed. She nudged gently at me and I took her onto my lap where she purred and gazed at me with soft adoring eyes. I sank back once more on Rose Helen's patchwork quilt, my arm across my chest, the rose still in my hand.

Everything was changed now. I had been amazed before at the strange happenings, but they were as nothing compared with what I now knew to be the truth. I had, of course, been looking for *natural* explanations that would account for the bewildering incidents. Anything beyond my knowledge of what was accepted and known had never for a moment entered my mind. There was only one thing I now knew for an absolute certainty— and that was just *how little* we knew of what went on outside the limits of our own lives.

Certain things I *was* sure of, though, even in my ignorance. One being that I had so wrongly accused Jean Timpson. She had not been responsible for the odd things that had happened. It had been Helen. Helen it was who had put the glass in the ice-cream, my razor blades in the hand-cream jar, who had made Shelagh's horse take flight in terror. She it was who had left the roses on my pillow, who had touched up the paintings. Yet how, I asked myself, could a *ghost* do such positively physical things? I had read of poltergeists, spirits who had the power to throw objects about and generally kick up a racket, but, as far as I recalled, they were reckoned to be relatively harmless agencies. So how did Helen's malevolent, physical powers fit in with the powers of *those* phantoms? But in asking such a question I was making the mistake I had made before—looking for answers within the boundaries of my own knowledge; I was trying to take those supernatural events I had witnessed and fit them into understandable, manmade, earth-made rules, when by their very nature they defied such categorisation. They were *not natural*. They were *super*natural—and as such could not be explained by our everyday laws and logic. Once explanations— *understandable* explanations could be found, then they would no longer be supernatural but natural. No, there was nothing I could do but accept. I would accept. I *must*.

Soon, I slept . . .

With the morning sun bright upon me I lay for some moments trying to orientate myself, and wondering how I had come to sleep in Colin and Helen's room, and fully dressed, too. I felt scratchy, dirty and uncomfortable, my head heavy. Gradually the strange events of the night before came back to me, piercing the armour of my half-sleeping state and bringing me fully awake, leaving me stranded again in the realms of reality. And reality now was different from anything I had dreamed of before . . . I was afraid to look at the pictures on the wall. I knew, though, that I hadn't been dreaming. I didn't even need to look at the pictures for confirmation. No. I had only to turn my head a little on the pillow and see if the rose was still there.

It was. Not just one rose, though. Not now. Now there were three.

I got no answer to my persistent knocking on the Timpsons' front door so I got back in the car and drove down to the village. It was just after nine o'clock. Reese, when I arrived on his doorstep, didn't appear actually overjoyed to see me. I asked if he knew where Jean Timpson was.

"She's still here," he said after a moment. "She's going home this morning."

"I'd like to see her," I said, then added quickly, seeing his frown, "I haven't come to upset her. Please believe me."

He gestured for me to come in. When I was inside he said softly: "She's just finishing breakfast. I was about to drive her back."

"How is she?"

"None the worse, now." He gave me an axious look. "And I'd like it to stay that way."

"Don't worry."

"She's still under a bit of shock, but that's understandable." He gave me a grave smile. "She'll be all right."

"I thought she'd be back home by now. I just called at her house. When I couldn't find anyone in I began to get a bit anxious."

We stood in silence. I realised he'd be happier if I just left.

"I'd like to see her," I said. "I would."

He hesitated, nodded doubtfully, then showed me into the waiting-room where I stood nervously beside the table with the same old magazines on it. When he came back a few minutes later he shook his head and said apologetically:

"She doesn't want to see you."

"I *must* talk to her."

"She doesn't want to see you. She says she can't."

"Look," I said, "certain things—have been happening. I can't explain any of it now, but—well, after what I'd been told about her, I thought . . ." I was floundering . . . "Those half-stories you warned me against. You said they could destroy. You were right. They almost did . . ."

He nodded, silent, giving nothing away.

"And then," I went on, "when Bill Carmichael told me she'd been in a mental home——"

"She was a voluntary patient." Reese said. "She had a breakdown. And I'm not in the least surprised that she did. She really loved that little boy she was caring for. And she blamed herself for his death. Though it wasn't her fault—that became quite clear afterwards. It was just one of those tragic accidents that sometimes happen. He got out of her sight for only a few minutes and—well, it doesn't take long." He paused. "She went to pieces, and even now she's never forgiven herself. I doubt that she ever will."

"And after her own baby died," I said. "I can imagine how she must have felt."

"Can you?"

For a second longer I stood here, only a second, and then I determinedly stepped past him through the hall and opened the door into the room beyond. Apart from a little half-hearted gesture of protest he made no attempt to stop me. I found myself in a large, sunny kitchen where the doctor's wife and Jean Timpson looked up at me in surprise from their places at the breakfast-table.

The words I had all ready to speak somehow refused to come to the surface and I just stood there, dumb, looking stupidly from one to the other. At my shoulder, after a moment, came Reese's voice:

"Mr. Warwick *insists* on seeing you, Jean . . ."

I watched while she shook her head distractedly and gripped the tablecloth. She turned away. Mrs. Reese got up, looked anxiously at the woman beside her, then at me, and then moved across the room, going by me to the door. An instant later the click of the latch told me that Jean Timpson and I were alone together.

There was a long silence. Jean Timpson sat there, her

face still averted. I could hear the sound of her breathing. I didn't know where to begin. At last I said:

"How are you, Jean . . . ?"

She didn't answer; just gave a little half-nod.

"Jean . . . I've come to ask you to forgive me."

She briefly turned towards me then, though avoiding my gaze, and in her eyes I caught the glisten of unshed tears. She looked away again.

"I made a mistake," I said. "A terrible, terrible mistake. And I'm sorry."

I waited. Still she said nothing. She looked numb, out of her depth. All in a rush I went on:

"I accused you of dreadful, unthinkable things. And I was so wrong. I've caused you so much misery. I'm sorry. Please—please, forgive me."

Still no word from her.

"Believe me," I said, "if I had known what I know now . . . Anyway, perhaps one day I can explain it all, but for now . . ." I took a step towards her. "Can you forgive me . . . ?"

Her downcast eyes were unreadable.

"*Please* . . ."

Then she nodded. "Of course . . ."

Of course. She was so trusting, so desperate for trust, for love. I felt wretched and even more ashamed.

"I'd—we'd like you to come back," I said, "if you will. Shelagh and I will be returning to the States soon, but till then—well, we'd both be glad if you'd come back and—and help out—like before . . ."

Her moist eyes flicked briefly up to mine and then down again to make a study of her bitten fingernails.

"Shelagh'll need somebody around," I said. She won't feel up to doing very much . . ." I paused, hopefully waiting. "Will you?"

A tentative nod of her head, then another. She said, ". . . Ah . . . I'd be glad to—if you really want me."

"We do."

". . . Thank you."

Her thanks after what I had done made me cringe. "*Don't*—don't thank me," I said. "Just . . . come back."

She smiled then. The tears clearly in her eyes. But they were, I knew, tears of relief.

"Doctor Reese says you're going home soon," I said.

"Yes."

"Would you like to go now?"

A shrug. "All right . . ."

"Come on then. Let me drive you."

When I followed her into the house her father was there. He smiled at me, but there was a definite wariness behind the smile and I said quickly, making an effort to sound off-hand and cheerful:

"I was wrong. I'm afraid we can't let Jean go after all." I loathed myself so much it made me want to throw up.

His wary look went, though. He asked her how the job had been looking after the doctor's children and she replied, "Oh, fine, fine," without looking at him. He seemed pleased and satisfied with that and, turning to me, asked me how Shelagh was going on. I told him she was okay and that I was just on my way to visit her. When he had gone I said to Jean:

"Shelagh and I are going to be married soon. We think it'll be on Saturday . . ."

"Oh, that's nice," she said, smiling. "I'm glad. Really glad."

"We'd like you to be there, too, if you will."

The smile she gave then was the warmest I had ever seen on her face. Her eyes shone. "Oh, ah," she said, "I'd like that. I'd like that fine."

I went away from her feeling so much relief. At least *her* part in the story of horror was over . . .

And how wrong I was about that.

Shelagh was sitting up when, armed with paperbacks and anemones, I hurried to her bedside. As the nurse took away the flowers to put them in water Shelagh asked, "What happened—did you run out of roses?"

"I thought anemones were more original . . ." I'd give her no more roses—not while we were based at the cottage; not while they were a symbol of Helen's love for me, and of her hatred for Shelagh. I thought again of the girl in the painting—the girl who had become Shelagh, with the magpie hovering above her head. Where I was concerned Helen's lingering presence showed only tenderness and caring. Not so with Shelagh. With Shelagh it was another story entirely.

I wanted so much to share my knowledge. I could make a joke of it, perhaps. *What would you say if I told you the cottage was haunted—by Helen . . . ?* But it wasn't a joke. Unless the joke was on me and I was going round the bend. No. I knew it was all real. Too real . . .

"When you come out," I said, "we'll go away somewhere. After our wedding. We'll go away. Anywhere you like . . ."

She looked puzzled, then amused. "You mean for a honeymoon or something?"

". . . Call it that if you like. Yes, why not."

"Oh, no . . ." she shook her head, "I'd like to stay at the cottage till we have to go back to New York. I mean, we haven't been there five minutes. I love it. Why should we want to move?"

I shrugged. "It's—it's not really so—ideal. I'm thinking of selling it."

"Are you serious? Sell our beautiful cottage?"

I could understand her surprise; I'd done nothing but eulogise about it till now.

"It's just a thought," I mumbled. "Just an idea. We can talk about it later."

She gave a wry little smile. "Some idea. Are all your ideas that good?"

At the cottage on my return I found Jean Timpson there. She was preparing my lunch. She told me she had brought back Helen's clothes, that she'd hung them up in the bedroom. I stayed for a few minutes chatting to her—or trying to; chatting, in the constrained atmosphere that was there between us, was hardly what we did. I was relieved when enough time had passed to enable me to make my escape to another part of the house. After what had passed between us over the past couple of days I somehow doubted that we could ever really be at ease in one another's company.

In the hospital ward that evening I made no further mention of selling up and leaving the cottage. Shelagh didn't bring up the subject either. We talked of other things, general things, our voices soft in the hush that always seems to go with hospitals. The atmosphere there was one that spoke of practicality, rationality and method, and it didn't prepare me for the atmosphere that greeted me when I returned to the cottage. There it was—even stronger by contrast with what I had left behind—that powerful, soft, insinuating warmth. It was everywhere . . .

But now, now, I could arm myself against it. In the past I had allowed myself to be taken in, to be seduced by its cloying sweetness. But now I knew that it didn't come from the house itself but from that unseen occupant within, and I could, I felt, be on my guard. And I would be.

I stood in the living-room while Girlie wove between my ankles, and I could feel my heartbeat almost quicken as if I were preparing for some physical onslaught where I would need all my wits and my strength. I heard relief in the sigh I gave and the hollow bravery in my whistling as I prepared for myself a scotch-and-water.

Jean Timpson had left for the day. There was a note from her on the kitchen-table, telling me that my dinner was in the oven. I opened it and saw the casserole she had put there. Perhaps I would eat some of it later on. In the meantime I carried my drink into the living-room and sat there with Miss Merridew smiling her vacant smile upon me and the light of the low sun glowing on Sad Margaret's sad sampler.

I did eat later; with a tray on my knees, gawking at the television screen while John Wayne and Maureen O'Hara yelled at each other in glorious Technicolor. I couldn't concentrate on the film, though, and in the end I switched off and went upstairs.

It was into Colin and Helen's room that I went.

Everything seemed to be just as I had left it. My eyes flicked at once to the paintings on the wall—and there was Shelagh—so clearly, so definitely Shelagh—all smilingly unaware while the magpie fluttered above her head.

I said suddenly, loudly into the stillness, riding on a flood of bravery:

"We're leaving." Then louder: "You hear that? We're leaving."

And I heard the sounds of the words going on in my head like a stuck needle on a gramophone record: *leaving, leaving, leaving, leaving*—loud against the silence that was suddenly deeper.

"We're leaving," I said again. "We're going, Shelagh and I. We're going and we're not coming back."

And I felt the silence closing in. The air in the room became cool, cooler, icy cool. For long, long seconds I stood still in the cool quiet, and nothing moved. And then, as when the sun appears from behind a cloud, the coldness passed and I was bathed in warmth. And the warmth grew, and grew. Outside in the night air I saw bats wheeling against the moonlit sky, an owl hooted, crickets chirped. I stood there while the warmth drew nearer; felt it wrapping me, holding, pressing. I felt the caress of fingers against my hot skin; fingers touching my clothes, running over my body, gentle but aggressive, exploring me with an intimacy I had never before experienced.

I could do nothing but submit. I was powerless to stop it. Through my veins the blood surged with such pressure that my cheeks felt as if they were on fire. I was bathed in a hot glow, and my inner heat reached out and responded, hypersensitive, to the touch on my skin. My head swam. I felt as if I was being undressed. There was the softness of lips against my mouth, kisses soft, all-possessive on my cheek, my forehead, my throat and on my bare chest. Reaching up one drugged hand I realised that my shirt was open to my navel; and all the time my heart beat faster, faster, the blood racing frantic through my veins. Dimly I was aware that I had an erection, but I was unsurprised by it; I was just accepting, accepting it all. No, not accepting; *wanting* . . .

Sweat ran down from my armpits and I felt its wetness on my hands. The thought came to me through the fog of my ecstasy that perhaps I was going mad; what was happening to me *couldn't* be happening. None of it, nothing, not one thing could possibly be anything but the product of my mind!—and still the touching, the caressing continued. The thought wavered through my brain that if I was *not* mad that I was being *driven* to that state, and I made a last desperate clutch for rationality, a final desperate attempt to hang on to reality, and I flung out my arms, wide, and shouted with all my force into the sweet-fogged-rose-scented room:

"*No* . . . *!*"

And with the sound the heat retreated, from within me and from without. I shouted again:

"I'm going, Helen! I'm leaving! I'm *leaving!*"

The sound of my voice, so brave in the face of that unseen, adoring spirit, restored me, and I felt my body begin to relax again.

Until I heard the sound.

Her laugh. I heard her laugh.

It was not the laughter I had heard in those movie bloodcurdlers—that maniacal sound that wells up, product of engineering married to an actress's vocal prowess. No. This was a gentle little sound, almost childlike, little more than a giggle; rippling, breaking on its treble note. And it was the most terrifying sound I had ever heard.

My feet might have been nailed to the floor. I saw my hand, fixed in the act of reaching out for the light-switch. I was frozen with fear.

I gasped for breath. I was afraid now for *myself*.

And then with a rush the warmth came back. And this time I had no defence. The blood surged to my loins and to my head, swift, tidal, engulfing me like some great voracious mouth. All the red through my clenched eyelids became just black. There was a moment of total blackness. And then there was nothing at all.

What was I doing lying on the carpet?

Something nudged me in the quiet room and my hand came up and touched the silkiness of Girlie's fur. I pushed her away.

The smell of roses was so strong.

I got to my feet—like watching the actions of someone else; ran my fingers over my body, tentative, touching briefly and flinching away, away from the wetness of my orgasm.

I picked up the roses that lay strewn around my feet and threw them through the wide-opened window into the night.

23

❧ ❧ ❧

"Are you all right?"

Shelagh's question, even coming after the rather searching look she gave me, still took me by surprise; I had thought my cover-up job was working pretty well.

"Yes. Why—don't I look it?"

"You look tired. And a bit—strained."

"I'm okay. Anyway, you're the one who's in hospital."

"Only till tomorrow morning, though." The doctor had given her the good news. Now she grinned. "My God, you can't imagine how relieved I am." Her expression gave way to a more serious one. I felt her contemplating me again.

"All right," I said, "what is it now?"

". . . I've been thinking."

I waited. "Is that it? Or is there more to come?"

"About your father."

"What about him?"

"Why don't you ask him to the wedding?"

I shook my head.

"Why not?" she said.

I shrugged. "I *could* ask him—if you really want me to."

"Don't you want to?"

No, I didn't. Why? Was I afraid? Did I fear his possible (likely?) refusal? Or was I afraid, if he did come, that he would somehow disapprove—and *show* that disapproval? But what could he disapprove *of*?—Shelagh? No one could disapprove of Shelagh. Disapprove of me? I was used to that.

"I'll think about it," I said.

"Which means you hate the idea."

"Why do you want him there?"

"Well—he will be my father-in-law, and we've never met . . ."

I might have added to that that he was *my father*— which relationship hadn't done anything to foster any closeness between us. I nodded. "All right. I'll try to get in touch with him. Maybe I'll go and see him."

"Good." Her eyes were steady on mine. She smiled and handed me a piece of paper with a list of items pencilled on it. Her "coming-out" clothes and things, she told me; if I'd pack them into her red overnight case and bring it in with me when I visited her that evening . . . I put the list in my pocket.

"You won't forget, will you?" she said.

"As if I would."

"As if." She smiled again, eyed me through lowered lashes. "It's just that you seem rather—preoccupied. And that was before I ever mentioned your father."

She was right. Of course I was preoccupied. And it had nothing to do with my father. All through my waking hours I was plagued with questions. And not only during the days; even my nights now were not free from the needle-pointed fantasies that insinuated themselves into my dreams. My mind was in a constant turmoil as I wrestled to accept, and come to terms with what I found to be so totally unacceptable. But I had no choice. Even now, sitting at Shelagh's bedside, half my brain seemed bent on reliving and examining the incredible events that had taken place since my arrival in Hillingham. No, no past tense; those events were happening *still, now*. Even now as I held Shelagh's hand and looked into her blue eyes I knew that someone else was waiting for me. *Helen* . . . Her name kept going through my head as I recalled the power of her presence there in the cottage. Yes . . . last night had proved to me just how powerful she could be, and how warm her embrace and how tenacious her loving . . .

Other hospital visitors were moving past us, away, out of the ward. My time had come to an end again. I kissed Shelagh softly on the lips, then said: "I'll be back later on."

"All of you?" She was holding on to my sleeve.

"Mm?"

"Like I said, you've only been *half* here this morning."

I was apprehensive about returning to the cottage—until I remembered that Jean Timpson would be there. And I was so glad when I went in and saw her there, standing over the stove. Poor lost, insecure Jean Timpson; with her there I felt safer; she was a shield between us, me and the other one.

Recalling my promise to Shelagh I telephoned my father and said I'd be coming up to see him. When he asked me "What about?" I just hedged and said it would wait till I got there.

In the polished, clean-dusted living-room I sat down and lit a cigarette, noticing how the sun glanced off Margaret Lane's sampler, blotting out her embroidered sadness. It was difficult to believe, in this time of bright day, what dark spirit crept within these comfortable walls; a spirit that seemed to grow stronger with each passing night. Here, in the sunlight though, nothing seemed to be amiss; Miss Merridew still sat, happily surrounded by her cats, and Temple and his pretty wife still gazed out into the room, she with her gentle, self-conscious smile and he stern-faced—no doubt dreaming of the dairymaid and far away places. Everything was as it should be, it seemed—yet I knew that nothing was.

After lunch I went to get Shelagh's overnight case from the cellar, but the light still wasn't working. "Can you manage with a torch?" Jean Timpson asked me.

"That's not working either."

"I got new bulbs and batteries . . ."

While she fiddled with the torch and screwed in a new bulb the telephone began to ring.

"Oh," she said as I moved towards it, "there was a phone call while you were out."

I stopped, about to lift the receiver. "Who was it?"

"I don't know. When I answered they hung up."

I lifted the phone and gave the cottage number. The voice on the other end—the same voice as before—said: "So you're back."

"Who's speaking?" I said.

"You know bloody well who it is, Warwick, so don't play the innocent with me."

"I don't know who you are."

"It'll come to you in time. And I'll keep this up till you remember. Until you crack."

"I don't know what you're talking about."

"I'm going to make your life a bloody misery. Just as you made hers."

That's when I hung up.

I wiped my sweating palms on my trousers and, without looking at Jean Timpson, took the torch she held out to me. I could sense the puzzled look on her face, but I wasn't about to enlighten her. At the bottom of the cellar steps I located Shelagh's cases. My torch also lit up Bronwen's Welsh dresser. It was such a beautiful, impressive piece. In a way I could understand Pitkin coveting it.

Over to my right above the level of my shoulders the torch beam lit a stack of canvases leaning against the wall. I hadn't looked closely at them before. I moved nearer, squeezing between the junk and the old bits of furniture and shone my light directly on them. The back of the nearest canvas seemed to be covered with dark marks, like splashes of black paint, but peering closer I saw that the marks were *not* marks; they were slashes in the fabric. The canvas had been rent almost from corner to corner, not just once, but several times.

I took hold of the wooden stretcher and turned the canvas around to face me.

It was a portrait of Helen. Or, rather, it *had been* a portrait of Helen.

A self-portrait. She had painted herself standing at her easel, a paintbrush in her hand. Whoever had mutilated the painting had been thorough and in no two minds. The slashes went right across her chest, neck and head, almost obliterating the look of steady concentration on her face. One eye had been totally wiped out, but the other one survived and peacefully returned a gaze of calm in return for my own staring shocked horror.

I turned towards me the second canvas, then the third. They were also of Helen. And both self-portraits, and both of them as badly disfigured as the first.

Quickly I pushed them back to face the wall again. I couldn't look at them. But the ruined paintings started me off on a search, and I didn't stop until I'd found what I was looking for. In the old carved-wood chest I found a large envelope. I opened it, shook out its contents.

And there they were. Helen's photographs.

I stared down at them as they lay spread out before me on the old books and clothes. Each photograph had been treated in the same vicious manner as had her self-portraits; there wasn't one that hadn't been defaced.

Had Colin done this? But why? Why had he abused her image—painted and photographed—in such a way? And what could have made him carry out such a terrible act? I could only wonder at the passion that must have driven him. And wonder what Helen had done to him that he should set out to destroy, to totally abscind her image and her memory in such a way . . . Had the anonymous caller been speaking the truth? Had Colin killed Helen? It might be as simple as that . . . I had always thought of Colin as a kind, caring person. Had I been wrong? Had he killed her? And what about his own death? Remorse? Perhaps I had never known him at all.

But my mind refused to accept such an answer. There were still many things I didn't know; there was a possibility that a little more knowledge might lead me to a new conclusion.

I switched on the torch and made my way back up the steps. I'd set about finding the answer to one question right now. It was time. And I wouldn't be fazed, even should the answer I received be one I didn't want. I had to have the truth now. I had reached the point where too much had happened, where I had learned far too much for any degree of peace of mind. If Colin had killed, then I must know it. I had to know too the reason for Helen's unhappiness. The man on the phone said Colin had made her life a bloody misery. Was it true? And what kind of woman, living, had Helen been, that even in death she would not rest but seemed bent on destroying?—destroying Shelagh . . . Did she, Helen, really love me?—or was it because I was so like Colin and she was seeking revenge through me . . . ?

It was the not knowing that was impossible to live with. Perhaps before I could have been happy in my ignorance; I could have learned to live with the memory of the tragedies that had taken place—but now it had gone far beyond that stage. If the mystery, even though unsolved, had somehow come to an end I could perhaps have learned to live with that too. But it had not ended. How could it end, I asked myself, when Helen's spirit, in malevolence, was still roaming the house?

The girl of twelve or thirteen who answered the door to my ringing had blonde hair held at the sides in bunches. She smiled up at me.

"Is Mrs. Barton in, please?" I asked.

"Just a minute . . ." She turned back into the hall and called out, "Aunt Liz . . . Aunt Liz . . . There's someone to see you . . ."

A minute went by and then above my head a window opened. I looked up and stared into the eyes of Elizabeth Barton. For moments our glances were locked. I moved to speak, but she cut in quickly:

"Please . . . go away."

"I'm sorry to bother you," I said, "but could I talk to you for a minute . . .?"

". . . There's nothing to talk about."

And then her head had gone back inside and the window came down. The next thing was the little girl standing before me again, her hand on the door.

"I'm sorry. Auntie says she can't see you now . . ."

"It's very important. Please tell her."

She hesitated, looking back over her shoulder. Then, gathering her courage, she said:

". . . I'm sorry . . ."

". . . Okay." I smiled at her; what else could I do. "Thanks, anyway."

I should have found some other way of getting to see her, I told myself as I crossed the street. She'd made it clear before that she didn't want to talk to me, so I had no reason to think I'd do any better on a second attempt. But somehow I would have to find a way. Her avoidance of me made me all the more determined.

A few yards along past a telephone kiosk I turned a corner and stopped at a small café where I bought a cup of coffee I didn't want and let it grow cold before me while I sat thinking over everything. I sat there for half-an-hour, then, unable to ignore any longer the glacial glances I was getting from the woman behind the counter (was I taking up valuable space?), went outside. I had told my father to expect me around four o'clock. I was already late.

Taking change from my pocket I went back around the corner to the phone box and started to dial his number. I had only got through the first three or four digits when I saw Elizabeth Barton and the girl appear on the opposite pavement. The girl held a tennis racquet. For a second they stood there while the woman looked about her. She didn't see me. They began to walk away up the street. Only briefly did I hesitate before I replaced the receiver, left the kiosk and started off cautiously behind them. My father, for the moment, didn't get another thought.

Up ahead of me they turned a corner and I quickened my steps so as not to lose them. I saw that we were heading towards a park. I relaxed a little then, and kept safely behind while they crossed at the lights and entered through the gates.

The park was teeming with people, all taking advantage of the warm sunshine. They lounged on the paper-scattered grass, licked ice-creams, laughed, talked, kissed, or wandered among the trees, away from the crowds, doing the little they could to get back to nature, yet at the same time shielding themselves from it with their tinny transistor radios and cassette players. For a moment or two there I panicked, losing sight of the woman and the child, but then I saw them again, separate, the girl running on ahead, the woman keeping to her leisurely, steady pace.

Approaching some tennis courts the girl came back to the woman, spoke briefly to her and then dashed off to where another girl, also holding a racquet, waited near a park bench. Elizabeth Barton called out some words I didn't catch and then moved on some forty yards to a fairly isolated spot and sat down. For a while she watched, and I watched too, as the girls went onto a vacant court and started to play. Turning my attention back to the woman I saw her take a book from her bag and begin to read. In the cool shadow of the trees I stood, getting up my nerve to take the heaven-sent opportunity that was offered me. After a while I went over to her across the grass, stood looking down at her.

". . . Mrs. Barton . . ."

Even as I spoke she was turning to me, aware of someone's presence at her side. And as her head came up and she heard my words I saw the fear and distress flash into her eyes.

She gave a very slight gasp, then averted her gaze. She said softly, but with intensity:

"Do you want me to start shouting for a policeman?"

I said nothing. She added quickly:

"I will if you don't stop bothering me." Her voice

rose slightly. "Please—leave me alone. I've got nothing to say to you. Nothing." With her clenched fist she hit at the dry grass.

I didn't know what to say. I couldn't give up and just go away—as I wanted to, but neither did I want to add to that anguish I saw there in her eyes.

"Please," I said, "I've got to know . . ."

She gave me another look, full of anger, full of hurt, then got purposefully to her feet. Her hands were clenched, her whole body tense. She looked wildly about her, and I braced myself.

24

∾ ∾ ∾

She didn't yell. She turned back to me. Her breath came out in a deep sigh. I saw her shoulders sag and the tears well up in her eyes. I stayed quite still. Her glance moved away from me. For long, long moments there was no movement, no sound from either one of us. Then slowly, tiredly she sank down on the grass again.

Looking at her I could understand why there had been rumours. The paleness of her skin, the dark smudges beneath her eyes couldn't take away from the considerable beauty that was hers. She really was beautiful. Her honey blonde hair fell in loose, casual waves. Her green eyes, so sad when she lifted them to me, were enormous.

"I'm sorry," she breathed, "but you don't know what it's been like." She paused. "What is it . . . that you want to know . . . ?"

I sat down, just a couple of feet away. "About my brother," I said.

"Of course . . ." Then her eyes roamed my face in a kind of wonder. "Seeing you—it brings it all back.

You're *so* like him . . ." A hand lifted, fingers fluttering, brushing her cheek. Her eyes blinked nervously. She said, "I'd decided never to talk about it. But you can't stop yourself *thinking*, can you? And I do. All the time." She shook her head. "I can't get over how like him you are. When I saw you first it was the most terrible shock. I knew he had a twin brother, but I never thought about you, and then when I saw you it—it was as if he'd—come back . . ."

I waited. She said suddenly:

"Have you got a cigarette, please?"

I gave her one, took one myself, lit them. Then I said:

"I had to find you—to talk to you—to find out what happened."

"He was a good man—Colin . . ."

"Yes . . ." I paused. "And Helen?"

"It was harder to know her. She was a more—private person."

"Did you know them long?"

"I met Helen first. Not long after she moved there. And we became good friends—I thought, in spite of her more—private self. Colin . . . well, he was much easier to get to know." She nodded. "I really liked them both. When I left the village for London in the early spring we—we kept in touch."

"Sometimes you went back."

"Yes. Quite often—at first."

I could read nothing in her expression. "Why did your visits—end?" I asked.

She gave a little shrug, plucked at a blade of grass. "There were certain—difficulties." She added quickly: "Mine, not theirs."

I didn't understand. After a moment I said: "You were there on the night Helen died . . ."

She puffed at her cigarette, and all the time her free hand never stopped working; she tugged at her skirt, the grass; fingers turning, twisting, weaving. "He phoned me," she said, "from a public phone box and asked me to go down and see them. It was quite late, but he was

insistent that I go straightaway. I was surprised—
hearing him."

"Surprised? How?"

"He sounded so—well, distraught—upset. All he
would say was that he was worried about Helen . . ."

"So you went."

"I got into the car and drove down there at once.
Helen was in bed when I got there—apparently she
hadn't been well for some days. Jean Timpson was
there too; she'd been helping to look after her . . ."
She came to a halt. Gently I prompted her.

"Yes . . . ?"

"I went in to see Helen, but she was asleep. Even so I
could see that something was wrong."

"How? In what way?"

"Just the way she lay there. Tossing and turning in
her sleep. Colin said he didn't know what to do. Then
he said he wanted to talk to me—but not there inside
the house. So we went outside, through the garden and
into the orchard—right away from the house."

"And what happened? What did he say?"

"He said very little. I remember it came on to rain
but he didn't seem to be aware of it. We just stood out
there in the rain. There were lots of long pauses . . .
awkward . . . I knew he was desperate to talk, but he
just didn't seem able to—or else he couldn't find the
right words—I don't know. He asked me if I'd noticed
anything about Helen."

"Noticed what?"

"Anything—odd about her, he said. Anything—
strange. Not just then—that night—but before—over
the past weeks . . ."

"What did he mean?"

"That's what I asked him. He said she was so jumpy
and nervy. Hysterical sometimes, he said. He said he
thought . . . thought that she was losing her mind.
Well, I said perhaps she was a bit overwrought. Perhaps
she'd been working too hard. I had noticed a gradual
change in her but I had thought it was probably something to do with her pregnancy. I wasn't aware that she
was *that* bad . . ." She stopped, then went on: "Any-

way, he suddenly turned to me and said, 'There's something I want to show you,' and he took my arm and led me out of the orchard into that little copse that runs by it. He took me to the spot where a summer-house used to be. It was quite dark, but even so I could see he'd been working there."

"Working?"

"He'd promised to build her a summer-house—right next to the site of the original one. I could see he'd started. The ground had been marked out and he'd been digging. It was still raining but he said to me, 'Stay here,' and turned back towards the house." She paused. "He said a strange thing. Just before he actually ran off he asked me whether I was afraid . . ."

"Afraid?"

"I don't know what he meant. But I said no, and he ran off. I waited there by the little stone seat . . . and it was only minutes later that I heard Helen screaming out."

"Colin wasn't with you at that time . . ."

"No, I told you—he'd gone back to the house. I ran back as well then—and found him holding her in his arms at the bottom of the sunken garden." Her eyes closed as if there were pictures in her mind she would shut out. When she opened them again she said: "It was awful. There was . . . blood coming from her mouth and . . . oh, there was so much blood. And she was still conscious. She kept talking—wild, rambling words. But she was dying. I knew it." She shook her head several times. "God, it was terrible."

"Was there nothing anyone could do?"

"Nothing. Jean came out, I remember. She said, later, that she'd been taking a bath, I think. I remember Colin saying something about the kitten—Helen's kitten; apparently she'd tried to get it down from the roof. Colin was in a dreadful state. We all were; it's not easy to remember what was said at the time. Or later."

"Later?"

"At the inquest."

"Oh, yes." I nodded. "I'd forgotten that."

"Of course, it was all explained then. Though I know

there were some people who didn't believe us. Either of us. But it was the truth."

". . . What did he say—at the inquest?"

"He just told them what had happened. The truth. He'd just gone into the house, he said, to get a torch, and while he was in there he heard her outside, screaming. And then—then she fell."

"Trying to get her kitten down from the roof . . ."

"Yes. She told him that herself, just before she died. The kitten was up on the roof, she said, and couldn't get down . . ."

I hesitated, then asked abruptly: "Did you see the kitten?"

"No." She looked at me sharply. "Why do you ask that? The fact that I didn't see it doesn't mean anything. Dear God, remember what had *happened*! To start looking around for some kitten wasn't the first thing on our minds."

"No . . ."

"It was like a nightmare. The phone wasn't working so I had to drive down to the village to get the doctor. When I got back with him it was all over. Colin and Jean had wrapped her in a blanket and taken her inside out of the rain. But she was quite dead." She gave a kind of dry little sob, her breath catching in her throat. I looked into her eyes but I could see no tears.

"I stayed with him that night," she went on. "He wasn't fit to be left alone. He took some tablets the doctor left him, but they didn't help. He didn't sleep at all, I know. Neither did I—hardly. We sat up most of the night; not saying anything really, just—sitting there, and when we *did* go to bed I could hear him, moaning, crying out in anguish in the next room." She sighed. "And that was it. There were the police, questions, the inquest, the funeral. That was it."

"Did he talk at all—to you—about that night?"

"No. As I said, I heard him raving and going on in his room—all sorts of things—but nothing made any sense to me. I went back to London the next day. I had to. I only saw him—twice more; at the inquest and at the funeral. After that I didn't—didn't see him again."

She stubbed out her cigarette, eyes cast down. "Now you know it all. That was it."

She continued to grind the cigarette-end into the dry grass. Against the silence between us now the shouts, murmurs of the other people seemed a sudden thing, a wave; and I became aware, just briefly, of all those other lives going on around us. Over on the tennis court the two girls laughed and squealed in anguish as they served and backhanded into the net. I watched them for a moment, half-seeing; half my mind acknowledging that for all their energy and go they wouldn't ever give Chris Evert any sleepless nights. I turned back to the woman.

"But that *wasn't* it, was it?"

"What do you mean?" She didn't look at me.

"You did see him again. You were there too on the night *he* was killed."

". . . You know that."

"Yes."

"You know a good bit more than anyone else." She still didn't look up.

"Jean Timpson saw your car that night, where you'd parked it behind the trees. She heard the crash of Colin's car—and saw yours was still there—later, much later. Why didn't you tell the police?"

"I couldn't. I'd already been—involved to an extent in Helen's death. I didn't want to be involved again. Anyway, they wouldn't have believed me."

"Why not?"

"They wouldn't. I know that."

"But you *were* involved."

"They didn't know that." She looked at me suddenly, and the question was there so plainly in her anxious eyes.

"No," I said, "they still don't know. Jean never mentioned it to anyone. Only me, I think."

She gave a little sigh—relief, then said, almost in a whisper:

"But mostly it was . . . because I was afraid. Oh, God, I was so afraid."

"Of the police?"

"No. Of *her. Helen.*"

Her look told me she feared to go on—that I would think she was mad.

"It's all right," I said, "I know about Helen."

". . . You know . . ."

I nodded. "She's been there all the time since I got to the house." I added, before I could stop myself: "She's cruel. She's evil."

"Yes. *I* know that now."

"But why should *you* be afraid of her? She was your friend."

"That was *before*—when—when . . ." Her voice tailed off and I finished the words for her.

"When she was alive."

Across the grass a ball rolled and came to rest against my shoe. I picked it up, threw it to the little boy who came in hot pursuit. When he had gone away again I said to her:

"That night when Colin died . . . Tell me about it."

She hesitated as if making up her mind whether or not to speak—or perhaps she was just getting the courage—then took a deep breath and began. She spoke for the most part haltingly, and then sometimes very rapidly—as if the flow of her memories gathered momentum over which she had no control.

"Somehow," she said, "once Helen was dead I never thought I'd hear from him again. There are certain things that happen in your life when you think that a—a certain point has been reached, and for the sake of the—survivors it's best not to meet again. That's how it was with me. I—I wanted to see Colin, but I felt too much had happened. With Helen dying like that—so violently—it all seemed somehow so—final. I thought he and I would never meet again . . . But then he came to see me late one afternoon. Soon after the funeral. He'd come up to stay with his—with your father for a few days, he said. He said he wanted me to help him. That I *must* help him."

"How?"

"He wanted to go back to the cottage—and he wanted me to go with him."

". . . Is that all?"

She nodded. "He wouldn't go alone."

"Why not?"

"Because," she said very simply, very quietly, "he was afraid." She looked at my face as I waited, then said emphatically, "Oh, yes, he was afraid, I could see. On the surface he appeared almost—calm, but I knew him, and I could see what was happening underneath. He was so tense. He was terrified at the thought of going back alone."

"But he'd have to be there alone at *some* time," I said. "He didn't expect you to *stay* there with him, did he?"

She shook her head. "Oh, no, he didn't want to go back to *stay*. He said he would never live there again; never spend another night there. But he had to go back because—well, he'd left in a hurry, he said and—well, everything he owned was in that place. He'd left his car there, and there were other things he needed: money, papers and various things. He said he'd pack what he needed, then sell the place and never go near it again."

"But why did he come to *you?*"

"I think—because he knew I would *believe*. Yes . . ." She looked at me searchingly, then looked away again. "I always have. I know—that things exist beyond our reasoning. They *do* exist. We may not understand them but that doesn't mean they can't *be*. You find people so ready to—to scoff at anything they can't figure out, can't reason, and those same people will turn straight round and tell you that they believe in God. Is *He* understandable? Is that belief backed up by reasoning, scientific logic? We live with mysteries all day long, all our lives, but because they're *familiar* mysteries we accept them. Well, you'd have to—or go mad. Who understands *life*? Yet we live it. We hang on to it. We accept it just as we accept the inevitability of death. Life and death: the only two absolute certainties we're aware of, but we can't even *begin* to understand them." She became quite animated here, forcing her words home with little jerky movements of her hands. "And there are other things, I know. Things that perhaps only—

only *touch* us—and only touch *some* of us. But they're there. Perhaps they are not quite life, not quite death—perhaps they're something quite—quite beyond the powers of our—our earthbound conception altogether—and of course we don't understand them. But I know they're there." She paused. "And if I was never sure before, then I'm certain now."

She took a cigarette from the pack that lay beside me. I flicked my lighter, watched as she drew on the wavering flame.

"I wish I hadn't seen you," she said. "I'd made up my mind that it was all finished—once I could get over all the—remembering. I never wanted to think about it again. But *you* had to come here."

Into the silence that fell I said, "You loved my brother." It wasn't a question.

After a second she nodded her answer, yes. "I never told anyone before," she said. "No one knew. I never even told *him*." The smile she gave was rueful. "He didn't love *me*, though. He only loved Helen. I'm sure he never dreamt how I felt." She nodded again, slowly. "Yes, I loved him. He was—a good man."

I thought suddenly of the defaced photographs, the slashed paintings.

"Are you sure he loved her?" I asked.

"Oh, yes." She looked at me in surprise. "Yes, he did. I know that. And she loved him—at least, that's how it always looked to me . . ." She seemed lost in thought for a moment, then she added: "I always thought she did—love him. That's why I couldn't believe—at first—she could do to him what she did. Mind you, I don't know what they were like—at the end . . . not really. He hardly spoke of her at first when he came round to see me on that last day. And when he did he never once called her by name. He said very little, actually. Just asked me—*begged* me—to drive him down to the cottage. And when I asked him why, that's when he told me, told me that he was . . . that he was afraid. I can remember his words, so clearly. He said she was there, still there. 'She's waiting for me,' he said, 'and I'm afraid to be alone with her . . .' He began to get almost incoherent then—just rambling on and on. I tried to calm him. Certain things could be done, I told him. He didn't have to give up living in his house. But I couldn't get through to him. He wouldn't have any part of it."

"What did you mean? What could have been done?"

She didn't answer at once, just drew hard on her cigarette and watched as the smoke drifted, melted away. Then she said:

"There's—there's someone I know—a priest in the High Church. He has some experience of such a thing, I know. We talked on several occasions—not about Helen, of course—I didn't know about her then—but before . . . other situations . . ."

". . . You mean—exorcism?"

"Yes. He could have helped, I'm certain. *He* believed. And he *would* have helped. But no. Colin said no. All he wanted was to go down there, get his belongings and get out."

"So you went."

"That same day. I didn't park in his driveway. Although it goes a long way back from the road it's very straight, and my car could have been seen by anyone passing by and—well, there'd been enough talk already. And apart from that, Colin had his own car there."

"So you parked in that little clearing almost opposite the house."

"Behind the trees. Yes, it seemed the best thing." She paused. "I let him out first and then I parked. When I went up the drive a couple of minutes later I found him sitting in his own car. He was afraid to go into the house. In the end I went in first and he followed. Then I helped him get his things together."

"I saw his suitcases," I said, "all packed. I couldn't figure it out."

"We'd almost finished," she said. "It was quite late by then. I'd done about as much as I could do and was just waiting while he finished sorting out some odd papers and things. You should have seen him then. With the darkness he had got more and more—edgy. He was

working feverishly—almost in a panic, so anxious—
desperate—to be gone."

She stopped then. I said nothing, just waited for her
to continue. It was easy to see she didn't want to. I said
at last.

"What happened? Something happened. Please . . .
tell me . . ."

Carefully she stubbed out her cigarette and then her
hands came together again, fingers gripping hard, the
knuckles whitening.

". . . The lights all . . . went out." She barely
breathed the words and I leaned closer to her. Her eyes
were screwed up, tight as her fists. "All the lights. Just
suddenly went out . . . For a little while we were in
almost complete darkness—there was only the moonlight coming through the window. I remember Colin
giving a kind of—cry. I called out to him not to worry,
that there was nothing to worry about. I could tell he
was absolutely terrified. As I was. Then I remembered
the candlesticks on the sideboard and I edged across
and lit one of them. I could see him then—still kneeling
in front of his suitcase, almost—transfixed. I started to
carry the light over to him. I was saying something—I
don't know what—trying to calm him—making out it
was all going to be all right, I suppose—going on about
a power cut or a fuse, when he suddenly said to me to
be quiet. 'Listen!' he said to me. 'Listen . . . !' So I
just . . . stayed where I was. I didn't move . . .

"And that's when I heard her. Breathing."

25

❧ ❧ ❧

I walked back onto the asphalt path, leaving her still sitting there on the grass, the tears running from her eyes, wet on her cheeks.

Amongst the other sojourners in the park I wandered. I felt dazed, disorientated. Of their own accord, it seemed, my uneven steps led me out, through the gates and onto the pavement again. From there, just because I had planned to, I set off for my father's house, flagging down a taxi and, as I opened the door, giving my father's address.

I think it was the driver and his aggrieved look that brought me closer back to reality. He managed to both smile and frown at the same time as he whined.

"Oh, guvnor, I was goin' 'ome—in the opposite direction."

He obviously wanted—perhaps expected—me to close the door again and send him on home with my blessing.

"Is your sign on?" I asked shortly. I still held the door open.

"Well, yes, but . . ."

"What does it say?"

"Well—For hire . . ."

"Thank you, that's good enough for me." I got in, slammed the door, slid back the glass partition between us and repeated the address I'd given. "And if that still doesn't suit you," I said, "you can make it the nearest police station."

"That's all right, sir," he said grudgingly, " 'ampstead'll do fine."

When we got there I counted the exact fare into his outstretched hand. No tip. Just a smile.

"You'll learn," I said.

As my father opened the door to me all he said was: "I expected you earlier."

I followed him through into the lounge, took off my jacket and sat down while he continued on into the kitchen. "I'm just making some tea," he said through the open doorway, and I said that would be nice, thanks. We kept up a desultory exchange as he busied himself—the predictable, polite questions and answers: Yes, he was getting on all right; yes, the garden *was* looking good, and no, there wasn't anything he needed. The talk dwindled, died, and I thought again of Elizabeth Barton as she had sat there in the park, clenching and unclenching her hands. I recalled the feel of my own hands—stiff, wet with sweat when she had spoken of the breathing. I had wanted to say: *Yes, I too. I've heard her too* . . . But I stayed silent.

"I'm not making it up," she said. "I really heard her. It was—frightening. I could see Colin there, more clearly in the candlelight . . . and I shall never forget that look on his face. He was—tormented. His eyes were wide open, staring. He was rigid. With fear. He suddenly shouted out, 'No! NO! Leave me *alone* . . . !' —just kneeling there, bolt upright . . . And *she* just— laughed."

Hands lifting, she covered her mouth, her breath beginning to come in dry, rasping sobs. The tears sprang into her eyes and ran down onto her fingers. "That laughter," she said, "—I can't describe it. It was so vile, so cruel, so—so smug. He went as pale as death, Colin, when she laughed, and he shouted out: 'I'm going! I'm leaving!' Yet he still knelt there. It was as if he wanted to get up, but couldn't. His eyes were rolling back in his head; he looked as if he was in agony. 'I hate you,' he kept shouting. 'You murderous bitch, I hate you!'" Her hands stayed at her face for moments longer, fingers pressing into her cheeks, then she let them fall.

"I couldn't do anything," she continued after a moment. "Nothing at all. I could only—watch. His mouth was opening and closing with no words coming out. And then he started to gasp and clutch at his chest, and then to shout things like 'No! No! Don't! Keep away. *Don't* . . . !' He managed to get up, but it was as if he was *fighting* to do so. I watched him struggle to his feet, hands flailing, lashing out, clutching at his chest again. He turned towards the door . . . And that's when my candle flickered and went out. But I could—could still hear him. Oh, God, yes. I heard him as he cried out— a terrible, strangled kind of sound. And then he ran outside."

She sat staring ahead, the tears running down. "That's all," she said at last. "After a few seconds I heard the sound of his car. I heard it, starting up very fast. Then came the sound of the crash. He must have been going at such a speed. I was like—well, as if I was frozen there, but then I got up and went out to him. I could see at once that he—he was dead. I knew there was nothing I could do. I—I went back, into the house, to get my bag, my keys . . . and I just . . . sat. Alone." She shook her head. "No, not alone. *She* was still there. Helen was still there. There were no more sounds, but she was still there. Quiet . . . quiet . . . but *there* . . ." Across her cheeks she brushed her hands, wiping away the tears. "After a time I left."

And soon after those words I had left *her*, Elizabeth Barton; walked past the tennis court where the girls pressed on with their game; and so to my father . . .

He was pouring tea into the cups. Now he looked up at me and asked:

"So to what do I owe this visit?"

Back to us then—him and me.

"I'm getting married tomorrow." Now, when the time came I just blurted it out. No subtlety at all. He looked at me blankly for some seconds, then said:

"You haven't wasted any time. You haven't been back five minutes."

I laughed, too loudly—it sounded false, forced. "Oh, I didn't meet her *here*. I've known her a long time." I added lamely: "Her name's Shelagh."

"I thought you came back to England on your own."

"I did. She just arrived a few days back. She's in the hospital right now. She had an accident. But the doctor says she can come out tomorrow . . ."

"Good," he said. "Good."

"I've—I've come to see whether—well, whether you'd like to come to the wedding. I mean—we'd like you to be there . . ."

He was hesitating. I'd put him on the spot, I could see. Not for long, though.

"Well . . . I don't get out much, as you know," he said. "What a pity you didn't mention it earlier."

He wasn't my father for nothing.

So that was that. I could feel the blood rushing to my cheeks, anger and humiliation burning inside me. I wouldn't ask him again and give him another chance to cut me down. I wanted to get up at once, leave abruptly, but I lacked the courage for that. Instead I let the seconds tick by while I stared into my cup and tried to tell myself it didn't matter.

After the longest ten minutes I got up to go. I made some excuse about having to hurry back—but it was superfluous, anyway; he wasn't about to press me to stay. And still I couldn't figure out whether his feelings for me were of indifference or positive dislike . . .

As I put on my jacket my eyes took in again the photographs: Colin; my mother on the gate, my father at her side, proud and protective. He looked happy too, and relaxed; I'd never known him during that period of his life. I picked the photograph up, looked more closely at his young, hopeful face. I couldn't see that I resembled him, and I was glad.

As I moved to replace the framed picture on the sideboard I propped up again the envelope that had fallen over on its face. And saw that the envelope was addressed to me.

It was an air mail envelope, written in Colin's hand.

Looking quickly back, questioning, to my father, I saw that his eyes were on the envelope. Then his eyes lifted to mine, flicked away again and he began to speak, quickly, with an attempt at casualness, trying to cover embarrassment.

"Oh, yes . . . Colin wrote that to you—while he was staying here . . ."

I picked up the envelope. "I wonder why he didn't post it . . ." It was unstamped.

"He—He asked me to. I said I would. I was going to and then—then *that* happened—just a few hours later—and—and there didn't seem much point in it any more . . ." He wouldn't look at me.

"No, maybe not . . . Even so, you could have given it to me when I was here before . . ."

He shrugged. "I was going to. I forgot." A slight pause. "Anyway, it's not that important, is it?—*now?*"

I stared at him, then looked back at the envelope, moved to open it. Stopped.

"It's already been opened," I said.

My father's silence drew my gaze back to him. He was still avoiding my eyes.

"*You* opened it," I said, not quite believing.

He said nothing.

"*You* opened it," I repeated. "Colin wrote to me and you opened the letter, and read it."

"Colin's dead," he said shortly. I could hear the anger in his voice. I drew the letter out, opened it up and saw the date, *Tuesday, 16th May.* Colin had written it on the day of his death. "You should have let me have this," I said.

My father said sharply, guilt turning more and more to hostility: "Anyway . . . What does it matter about some letter."

"It matters," I said. My hands were trembling. "He wrote it to *me*. Not to you. He wrote it to *me*."

I turned away from him, refolded Colin's scrawled pages and put them back in the envelope. And as I did so my father—as if the bitterness had been building up inside him—said, "*Yes!*"

I stared at him.

"*Yes!*" he said again, his head jerking as he flung the word at me. "Yes. To *you!* He didn't write to *me*. But to *you*."

So that's what hurt so much. Now it was clear. I could understand it now.

"He had no *need* to write to you," I said, "not when he was staying here in the same house with you. He could *talk* to *you*—in person."

"*Talk*." The word was dismissed with a wave of the hand. "He didn't talk to me at all. He told me nothing. Nothing that mattered, anyway. He told me nothing of what he was going through, and it was obvious to anyone that he was going through a—a bad time. No. *You* were the one he chose for that."

He hated me in that moment. It was so clear. It wasn't indifference. His feelings for me were very positive. Colin hadn't confided in him—but on his last day on earth Colin had written me a letter. And that my father couldn't forgive; he couldn't forgive *me* for it.

We stood in silence while inside me a lifetime's simmering resentment came up to the boil. Trying to keep my voice low, even, I said at last:

"If I'd been perfectly normal you could have accepted everything, couldn't you—in time?"

He was taken aback, I could see. He stared at me.

"I don't know what you're talking about," he said shortly.

But I wasn't about to be put off. Not now, not after all this time.

"It wasn't *my* fault that she—that she died—my mother. I didn't ask to be born."

I'd said it at last, and it had been easier, so much easier than I would have dreamed. I went on.

"If *both* your sons had been perfect you could probably have accepted it, couldn't you?—her death? We, Colin and I, would have been equal; no deformity, no—label—to separate us. We would have been identical in every way, and the fact that she had died giving birth to one of us—*me,* the second—wouldn't have reflected on me, would it? But no. She died giving birth to something which, in your eyes, wasn't worth the sacrifice, wasn't worth being born—a cripple. With the birth of Colin you had just what you wanted; you had a son and you had your wife. And then hours later *I* come along. She dies, and what have you got instead?—a sickly baby who has a congenital dislocation of the hip."

"I didn't treat you any differently from your brother," he said. "At the beginning we didn't even know that you *had* that—that trouble . . ."

"No. At the beginning you didn't know I was any different. Not till the time came for me to start moving around. And then you had all that—that boring stuff to cope with; taking me on those endless visits to the doctors . . ." As I went on the realisation came to me, dawning slowly but surely, that I didn't *want* his love. Not now. Not even if it was offered to me. And the knowledge was like an unexpected gift. I held on to it, and it gave me strength, and the courage to continue.

"How did you look upon me?" I asked. "I'll tell you. You viewed me as someone who had killed her, didn't you? And all the time I stayed around I was a constant reminder of what you'd lost—what you felt I was responsible for your losing. And it wasn't even as if I were a worthy consolation prize, was it?—in those splints for months on end—having to be *looked after* all the time. God, that must have rankled: having to give me so much attention when you couldn't stand the sight of me. No wonder you packed me off out of your way as soon as you could." I felt my anger merging with self-pity as I added bitterly:

"And what about Aunt Marianne? I hope you made it worth her while. She certainly didn't do it for *love*."

I swallowed, cleared my tight throat. My voice was calmer when I continued.

"I'll tell you something: for years, from the day I was old enough to realise, I've tried to—to make you—*care*. I wanted you to love me. Oh, God, I did. All my life, since I can remember you've been my one constant ache, a single, unbreaking thread of unhappiness. *This*"—I slapped my leg—"I could deal with. I learned to live with it. It hardly ever bothers me now. But your—rejection . . . that was something else. I never got used to that. That was something I *never* learned to cope with." Carefully I put Colin's letter into my inside pocket, moved to the door. My father made no effort to say anything. I turned back to face him.

"No, I never learned to cope with that. Until now.

Today. Now, at last, I finally have. I've realised that my love, my caring are too bloody precious to be thrown away on someone such as you. I've realised today something that *you've* known all along: all that guff about—kinship, blood-of-my-blood—it doesn't mean a thing. Not a thing. I know now that I loved Colin because he was *himself*—and not just because he was my brother. And I realise too that it no longer matters that you are my father. *Father!*—the word's a joke. I realise that for you I feel absolutely nothing. *Nothing*." I opened the door, stood with my fingers gripping the handle. I added, more quietly:

"If you had wanted my love you could have had it; earned it. But you didn't. And now it doesn't matter any more. I'm glad you won't be at my wedding. Shelagh wanted you to be there—but she doesn't know you. I do. And I know that without you it'll be a better day. I'll be happier, and she'll be happy too. And her happiness is the only thing I care about." I shook my head, slowly; it was as if I was seeing him, really seeing him, for the first time. "You were supposed to have loved my mother, loved Colin. But I have to ask myself: what kind of love was it?"

All the time I had been speaking he had sat there in his armchair, looking at nothing. Now, with the mention of his love for my mother he got up, faced me.

"Don't talk about her," he said. "Don't talk about either of them—not where they concern me." His tone was slightly outraged, as if I'd trodden on forbidden ground. I wasn't bothered. "You deserve to grieve," I said. "It makes me glad."

He just looked at me, frowning.

"Do you know," I said, "that for all your *great love,* when you die you'll die a frustrated, embittered old man. And more than that—you'll die alone. Completely and utterly alone."

Before I pulled the door closed behind me I added, very softly, without passion:

"And that certainty doesn't touch me, move me at all."

In the taxi on the way to the staion, and in the train going back to Reading I sat numbed. Reaction setting in. But, I told myself, what had happened was *positive*. I had finally acknowledged that my father and I would always be apart. We had been apart before, and now I knew it would never change. Couldn't change. I knew now there would never come that moment (had I wanted it?—I suppose so) when he would come to me and say, "David, my son, forgive me." No, that was for the movies. Strictly *B* movies.

But there was something else I knew. And that was important too.

I knew now that there was no truth in the assertion that Colin had been in love with Elizabeth Barton. And if those who had spread such a rumour were wrong about that then they could be wrong about other things . . .

On the train I took out Colin's letter and read it. Below my father's address—and that fatal date—he had written:

David,
    As you can see I'm staying at Dad's. I came here so quickly, without any preparation—a very quick exit. Well, I had to go somewhere. I couldn't stay there—not on my own. I wish I could talk to you. It's so difficult; the phone at the cottage is kaput, and anyway, with the time difference I hate the idea that I might be dragging you out of bed or something— just to have you listen to my ravings.
    Dave, I just don't know what to do any more. I've got to go back there to get my things, but I can't face the prospect of going back alone. If she weren't there—well, everything would be O.K. I could cope somehow with it all—with everything that's happened. But she is. She is there. It doesn't matter that I keep telling myself she's dead, that she can't hurt me, because I know she could if she wanted to. I'm afraid of her. I know what she's done already, in the past—things nobody else knows about, and I know what she's capable of doing—even now. She told me

she loved me—still *loves me, but it's an evil, posses-
sive love; I know* she'll stop at nothing to keep *what
she loves, what she wants. God save me from such a
love. Oh, Dave! Jesus Christ, I must sound like a
madman. And I'm asking myself whether any of this
makes sense to you. How can it? You don't know the
story. I'm not mad, Dave, though over the past
weeks, months I've really felt I was being driven in
that direction. I wish you were here. I know we've
never been together that much, but I do know also, at
this time, that you're about the only person I can rely
on—who I could turn to. Somehow I've never ever
had to explain things to you . . . She wants me to
stay there . . . But how could I? Not after what's
happened. No. And once I've been back there and
packed what I need I shall never go there again. I
just want the courage to do that and then I shall be
O.K. Yes. I must go today. I've decided. There's no
sense in putting it off. When I've finished this I'll go.
Not alone—if I can help it—but I'll go.*

I don't know how long I shall be staying here with
Dad. Not too long. Just as soon as I get on my feet
again I must start to look for a flat somewhere. I
need a rest. I'll sell the cottage. Or it can stand and
rot. I don't care. Dad would like me to stay here, but
that wouldn't work. Anyway, you can write to me
here for the time being. You know—I'm trembling.
Even now, just at the thought of setting foot in that
place again. Stupid, isn't it. I really must get a grip.

Now the thought occurs to me that perhaps it's
really the embodiment of emotion that lives on. Could
it be, do you think? Whether it's a great love, great
hatred, or great sadness—perhaps it's that strong feeling that keeps the spirit here, earthbound. All the
"ghosts" one ever reads of—they all seem to have one
thing in common—some strong, restless emotion.
Well, it seems to be the case here—though I'm not
sure what the particular emotion is. I said she loves
me—but it's a kind of love I want nothing of. She's
consumed with jealousy and I know she would hate
whoever I loved. My God, here I am, writing to you

about her as if she were some living, breathing person; presuming your acceptance of such an unbelievable situation. All I can say, Dave, is believe me. Please. *Of course, I knew nothing about all this at the beginning, and I'm sure that if anyone had hinted at such happenings I would have laughed. Of course I would. How could I ever have dreamt what was going on? Later, of course, I knew that something was, but at the time—well, it isn't anything that would cross one's mind—even to wonder about it; it's so apart from everything we accept as the norm, the acceptable. Knowing nothing at all of her history there was nothing to make me suspicious. It was the summer-house that made it all clear to me—getting to work on that. Or made it* clearer, *at any rate. I knew then what she was, and that it wasn't safe to be under the same roof with her.*

I wish you were here. Come, please. Bring Shelagh with you. But if she can't come, then come alone. I feel I need some support—and I must have it if I'm not to be a candidate for the bin.

My God, how depressing this all is. But how else can I write at this time? Anyway, I console myself that by tomorrow everything will be settled and it will all be in the past. It will only remain for me then to pick myself up and pull myself together . . . I know I'm taking the right course in getting out of that place. Well, it's the only course. If I'm to survive. One thing's for sure, I'm not staying there to let her do to me what she did to him.

I've just read through what I've written, and I sound such a mess. God help me. Maybe I won't send this after all. We'll see.

I must stop. Dad is hovering about. He just came in and asked me who I am writing to . . . He seems concerned—I think it's that—that I should seek privacy in order to write to you . . . Ah, well.

Please, Dave, write to me soon. Or better still, come and see me.

Colin.

So that was it. Soon after writing the letter he must have gone to see Elizabeth Barton to ask for her help . . .

I folded the letter and put it back in my pocket. It didn't really tell me much that I hadn't already guessed at. Or did it? My doubts returned. What had Colin written? I took out the letter and found again the line that presented me with a different answer: *One thing's for sure, I'm not staying there to let her do to me what she did to him.* What had Helen done? And to whom? And what was that about the summer-house? What did that mean? *Did he mean De Freyne . . . ?*

Later I took out the letter and read it yet again. But nothing was made clearer—only the tortured state of his mind. I remembered that my father had read it, and vaguely I wondered how he had reacted. What had been his feelings when his son's last written words had made him, his father, seem like some stranger . . . ?

When I got off the train I got the car from the car park and made my way straight to the hospital without going through the village. I'd only been with Shelagh for a second or two when she asked (again) what was on my mind. "Nothing," I told her. "Why?"

"You forgot to bring my suitcase."

In Helen's studio I found some turpentine and some cotton-wool and went up to the main bedroom where I set about cleaning the newly-added paint from the pictures. I didn't want Shelagh to see them as they were. To my relief I found the job was surprisingly easy—the paint hadn't had long enough to dry. Within ten minutes I had finished, wiping away the crude daubs until the roses had gone, until the birch shadow was back, until the girl's hair was once again its original colour, until the magpie had disappeared and the bluebird could be seen again, as bright and romantic as ever.

It came on to rain as I washed my hands. So many showers recently. I found later, in my bedroom, that the rain had come through the ceiling, dripping down onto the turned-back covers of my bed. Already it had made a large wet patch. I gazed at it for some seconds then flicked off the light and went across the landing to Colin and Helen's room. No ceiling leaks there, just the paintings as Helen had first painted them, the large, comfortable-looking bed and, now, the single white rose on the pillow.

In the bathroom I brushed my teeth, washed my face, then returned to the bedroom to prepare for sleep.

I sensed the very moment she came into the room. I saw nothing, heard nothing—but I knew when she was suddenly there.

For some seconds I remained absolutely still, not moving a muscle, arrested in the act of slipping off my shoes. I could feel the louder, faster pounding of my heart, hear the quickened rate of my breathing.

I continued, fingers trembling as I dropped the second shoe on the carpet. If she wanted to stay there watching me then there was nothing I could do about it.

And she *was* watching, I could tell. I knew. She was watching me as I got undressed. I realised suddenly that I was not hurrying my actions. Rather I was slowing them down. I felt no modesty or shyness at all. I saw my shaking fingers undo my belt and peel off my trousers. I found something so unbelievably exciting in the knowledge that a strange woman, unseen by me, was watching my every movement, watching as I draped my trousers over a chair, watching as I slowly, languidly took off my socks, my shirt. Standing before the dressing-table mirror I pulled my undershirt up over my head. And then she was watching me as I stood only in my underpants.

I was shivering, but it was not from cold. Anticipation? Fear? Excitement? One part of me, my sense, was yelling out that I must be mad to give such a show of encouragement, while the other part of me—my sensibility—was revelling, glorying in my near-nakedness.

I waited a moment longer, then hooked my thumbs under the waistband of my underpants and slipped them off. I straightened up, my sex a figurehead, proud, denying any shame my brain told me I should feel.

I studied myself in the glass—all the time feeling her eyes upon me. It was as if I was seeing myself for the first time. And I was not just a walking limp. No, my body was fine, good. From this angle my deformity could barely be discerned. One would hardly know it was there. It wasn't there. I was perfect. Perfect.

I wouldn't speak to her, to the woman who eyed me so rapaciously. I wouldn't make it easy. By such a decision I could cop out of responsibility; I could still *pretend* I was alone if I didn't acknowledge otherwise.

I walked slowly, perfectly on my perfect legs, to the bed, put out the light, then lay down and drew the sheet up to my waist.

And waited.

I knew she would come to me. Feared she would. Hoped she would. I closed my eyes and waited for her touch.

By the time it came I'd begun to think (with relief?—with disappointment?) that I'd been mistaken, that I was, in fact, alone.

No, I was not. She was with me.

It started like a whisper, her touch, and at first I wasn't even sure it was there. But a moment later I was. Her fingertips brushed my shoulder, my nipple, then moved to the line of hair that ran down to my navel. *Yes!* I wanted to say. *Yes! Yes!* I was not me. I was someone else. *Yes. Yes.* I felt a slight weight moved from my thighs and realised that she had fully drawn back the covers, leaving me completely exposed again. A wetness, her tongue, caressed my calf, my knee, and moved up my thigh. She kissed, kissed, while her hands roamed, sweetly exploring my spreadeagled body. Her fingers moved down, encircled me, and then her mouth, warm, wet, open, was there. My back arched. I thrust forward, joining deeper. I reached out for her, grasping, clutching, and together we began our moist, sliding, hot, fevered battle; a battle that raged long into the night. A battle where we were both the victors and where ecstasy was the weapon and the reward.

❧ ❧ ❧

26

After I had bathed and dressed the next morning I packed Shelagh's little red case and set off in the car.

At the bottom of the hill I turned left and drove up the lane to Timpson's house. There was no one in so I left a note telling him that the roof was leaking and asking if he could arrange for somebody to come and fix it. Then I continued on to the hospital.

Shelagh was waiting impatiently, sitting in her dressing-gown when I got there. I embraced her, kissed her, and then retired to the waiting-room while she got dressed.

I was preoccupied as we drove back to the cottage. I still couldn't get over what had happened last night (*had that really been me?*)—and also I was faced with the unpleasant fact that I was taking Shelagh back to a place where a lingering spirit had tried to do her harm. That same spirit that had come to me in the dark; that woman in whose embrace I had touched a passion that I had never before experienced. Briefly, on my skin, I felt again the touches she had touched, the kisses she had kissed, felt again the contact, slipping, of writhing, twisting limbs; I remembered, so vividly, my blind, consuming wanting, the obscenities I had uttered, softly at first, and then, with her encouragement (*"Yes! Good! Good!"*) and my own swiftly increasing abandon, loudly-shouted, defiant, joyful. Nothing held back. Nothing at all . . . Nothing . . .

I mustn't think about it. I must not. And it must never happen again. Nor would it, ever. I was determined . . .

I must think, instead, on how to ensure Shelagh's

safety. I had toyed with the idea of booking us a room in a hotel, but how could I do that without provoking from Shelagh all kinds of questions? And the last thing I wanted was to tell her what I knew. Would she have believed me, anyway? I doubted it. So, there we were, heading back to Hillingham, back to Gerrard's Hill. But, I had decided, it wouldn't be for long. Just three nights. On Tuesday we would return to New York. It couldn't be before then; I would need the Monday to fix with the bank for the sale of the cottage . . . So just three nights and three days. It wasn't that long. And during that time I would make sure that Shelagh was safe. I would watch her . . . watch her . . . watch her . . .

Arriving at the cottage I saw that Jean Timpson was all ready for the wedding. Beneath her apron her violet-coloured linen suit smacked of Sunday-best. She brought us tea into the living-room and joined us as we drank it. Afterwards Shelagh looked at her watch and I said, "How much time have we got?"

"You make it sound like a death sentence," she said, and I inwardly shuddered.

Soon after ten o'clock the three of us walked under the flowered arch towards the car. Shelagh had changed into a long, summery-looking dress of pale lemon, with white lace fringing the sleeves. She looked beautiful.

"Wait!" she cried as we started to pile into the car. "I must have a bouquet. And you must have bouton-nieres."

"Buttonholes." I translated for Jean Timpson who at once said, "I'll do it," all shy smiles and eager to be of help, and hurried back into the house for scissors. A few minutes later she came to Shelagh holding out a beautiful bouquet of yellow and white roses. She had brought pins too and handed one to me along with a perfect specimen of a delicate white rose. A second bloom she pinned to the jacket of her suit. "That's it," Shelagh said, smiling, looking at us. "Now we can go." I hesitated for a moment, uneasy about the white roses— symbols of *her*, who waited, unseen, in the house. Then

I mentally shrugged off my misgivings. I wouldn't let anything get in the way of today's promise of happiness.

The ceremony seemed to be over in no time at all and I could understand somehow why couples went for the big church-weddings with all the dressing-up, the service, the ritual, the choir-boys and the confetti; I felt somehow that such a change in one's life-pattern—from unresponsible singleness to a till-death-us-do-part alliance *needed* to be marked by some remarkable, dynamic occasion. Did Shelagh feel that too? Did she feel let down at all? She didn't show it. She looked so happy. And the only shadow that came over her smile was as we were getting into the car again to return to Hillingham. She was looking at her bouquet, and I heard her sigh. "What's up?" I asked, but even as I spoke I saw the reason. My heart gave a thud and turned over. Dimly, while I gazed at the withered white roses I heard her say: "They're dead—and in so short a time."

The yellow roses, I noted, looked as fresh as ever, though. As did the white roses worn by Jean Timpson and me . . .

On Gerrard's Hill I pulled up the car outside the cottage and Jean Timpson and I got out. As I stood there with one hand on the car door a crowd of youths dressed in metal-studded black leather came thundering down the hill on motorbikes. They saw our rose buttonholes and hooted derision at us. I wasn't bothered by it though. Anything that came from *their* empty brains couldn't do anything to pierce the armour of the happiness I was feeling. Their scornful, mindless insults went right over my head. Other things would bother me, but not *those* drop-outs. Jean Timpson was affected differently though. She stood watching as their emblazoned leather backs roared on down the hill and shook her head in disgust. "Louts," she muttered. "Not from round here. From London or Reading, I expect. Out on a *pleasure-trip*."

"Forget them," I said, "They're not important." Shelagh, I saw, had moved across into the driver's seat. "Are you going somewhere?" I asked her.

"Down to the village." She put up a hand as I moved to get in beside her. "No, please. I want to go on my own."

And there was nothing I could do about it. I didn't want to let her out of my sight, but there was nothing I could do. She gunned the motor and took off down the hill while I watched until the car was out of my view . . .

I needn't have worried. Fifteen minutes later she was safely back again. She held a package under her arm.

"What have you got there?" I asked her.

"A surprise."

"For me?"

"Maybe."

"Isn't this wonderful," she said as she sat at the piano making Beethoven turn in his grave.

"You mean your playing?"

"Well, yes, that too—but really I mean being able to make as much noise as you like without anyone being able to hear."

"*I* can hear."

She ignored this for a moment, then said patiently: "I mean outsiders."

"They're very lucky," I agreed.

She flicked a suspicious glance at me. "I mean it's not like in some city apartment where you'd have them hammering on the walls yelling at you to be quiet." To prove her point she struck a succession of heavy chords (which Beethoven had surely never written) and then looked at me askance as I sat wincing in my armchair. "Don't look like that," she said, and she played on, my wife the pianist, abandoning *Für Elise* for a song, adding the words as she read them from the old piece of sheet-music before her:

> *Sweetheart, sweetheart, sweetheart,*
> *Will you love me ever . . . ?*

We had spent a relaxed, happy afternoon. At Shelagh's insistence I had got out the croquet set and together we had set up the hoops. I couldn't find the colour-banded finishing-post though, but we made do and hammered into the turf a sharp-pointed dibber from the shed's array of gardening tools. I tried to get Jean Timpson to come and join us, but shyly—though she was grateful, I could tell—she declined, and left Shelagh and me to fight it out between us. We did so aided by gin-and-tonics (a small one for me; I'd been drinking too much of late) and plenty of curses at the treatment we received at each other's hands. When at last the game was over—Shelagh won, albeit she bent the rules if not actually broke them—I put the bits and pieces away again and we retired to the house where we sat in the living-room playing records.

Jean Timpson had surpassed herself preparing our dinner and we ate leisurely, relishing it. Then, coffee served and the washing-up done, Jean whispered to us a happy goodnight and went on her way home.

Now, while Shelagh sat at the piano the clock struck eleven, making an even greater discord of her song. I yawned. She broke off her playing and singing and turned to me.

· "David, do you really want to sell this place?" It had obviously been on her mind.

"Well . . ." I floundered. "It's . . . It's not for us . . ."

"Why not?" ·

". . . There are other places. We'll find somewhere else. Somewhere just as nice."

After a moment she murmured sympathetically: "I know why."

I looked at her. Did she? How could she know?

"It's because of its—associations, isn't it?" she said. "Colin—and all that horrible business."

I felt relief. "Yes . . ." I nodded. "Something like that . . ." I couldn't tell her the truth. I couldn't tell her that this beautiful old house harboured a restless, malefic spirit—a spirit from which, even at this moment, I must protect her . . . *Although Helen is dead, still she lives on*, I would have to say. *She wants you gone. She hates you.* Yes, I could say all that—and then Shelagh would be certain that I was cracking up.

"Have you any idea," I asked her, "how the horse came to bolt like that?"

She looked suddenly sad at the memory of the dead mare. "I've no idea. Something scared her, I guess." She shook her head. "I don't know—it's a mystery to me . . ."

After a while I said: "I didn't go to Colin's grave today."

". . . Well, you haven't had time, have you." She added softly, "You feel bad about it?"

"I must go tomorrow. First thing."

"Yes . . ." She smiled. "Anyway, cheer up. It's your wedding-day."

I got up and went over to her, knelt by her, my arms around her waist. With her fingers she gently traced the livid scar on my suntanned arm. "Does it hurt now?" "No, no, not at all." She touched my hair. Dear, dear Shelagh; so much love, so much tenderness.

"I do understand how you feel, you know," she murmured. "But it's over, isn't it?—with Colin and Helen . . . all that—horror . . ."

"Over . . . yes," I said. *Over*—how I wished it were. It wasn't over at all. And the horror was greater than Shelagh could ever dream of. At that moment in the thicket, beneath the earth I had hurriedly replaced there lay the remains of a human body. And if Colin's letter was to be believed, I told myself, it was proof that Helen would stop at nothing to get and keep what she wanted . . .

"I'm tired," Shelagh said, cutting into my thoughts. "Let's go to bed."

"Are you okay . . . ?"

She put a hand up to her head. "A bit of a headache, that's all."

"Poor baby."

I left her for a moment while I went upstairs. Timpson hadn't been in touch about the leak in the ceiling so Shelagh and I would use the main bedroom. It was all right. There was no rose there. The pillows lay as

smooth and undisturbed as I had left them that morning
(after I had found fresh linen and remade the bed).
Later, seeing her safely in the bed, with a promise to
yell if she needed anything, I left her alone and went
back downstairs.

In the living-room I poured myself a drink, sat sipping it for a while then crept up the stairs again and
looked in on Shelagh. In the light from the landing I
could see that she was fast asleep. I left the door open
and returned to my chair and my scotch, and sat there
while all the same old questions re-invaded my mind; I
couldn't do anything to stop them. From the kitchen
Girlie came and got up into my lap. Mechanically I
stroked her soft fur. I closed my eyes . . .

I couldn't have been asleep for more than a few minutes when I came back to consciousness.

I had been awakened by the sound of Shelagh's
screams as they rang through the house.

Tearing up the stairs I flung wide the bedroom door.
The light by the bed was on and I saw her as she sat
pushing herself back into the pillows, clutching the
sheets to her, her mouth wide in terror.

I could see why. One look was enough.

There on one of the corner-posts at the foot of the
bed sat an enormous rat.

27

❧ ❧ ❧

The spider on the stone, as it sits motionless in the crev-
ice of the *L* makes me think at once of the rat—simply
because both creatures are able to generate in so many
people—rationally or irrationally—a high degree of
fear. So many people feel threatened by various creatures—insects mostly, I suppose: moths, ants, spiders—

though a spider, having eight legs, is not, by definition, an insect, I believe. Anyway, whatever—moths, ants, spiders have never bothered me.

The rat, though, was a different matter.

I can recall, even now, my feelings of cold horror as I saw it sitting there as if carved from stone, its tiny pinhead eyes staring unblinking into Shelagh's terrified face.

For a long moment I too was still as stone, and then, reaching out my trembling hand, I picked up a book and hurled it with all my force.

I missed. In a clatter of tumbling pages the book hit the carpet. The rat continued to look at me for a second and then, in a smooth flash of sheened brown, leapt down, pattered briefly on the floor and disappeared beneath the bed. Getting down on my hands and knees I peered underneath. There was no sign of it.

"It's gone," I said to Shelagh, holding her shivering body close. "It's gone . . ."

Nothing I could say, though, no amount of comforting words could induce her to stay in the room any longer, and in the end I took her downstairs where I made up a bed for her on the living-room sofa. At my insistence she took one of my almost-forgotten sleeping-pills and when she was at last settled I sat on the edge of the makeshift bed looking down at her. The tears of fear and hysteria were gone now from her eyes but even so her hand in mine didn't relax for a long time. Gradually, at last, her breathing became more even, and she slept.

In the gentle, dim light I watched over her, sitting in my armchair at her side, unresting, covered with a rug, my feet up on the footstool. I whispered into the greyness:

"Well, Helen, you didn't want us to be together, and you got what you wanted." I paused then added: "But it won't always be like this."

Then, tensed, I waited for some kind of reaction. What?—breathing? laughter? There was nothing. Only the silence.

Jean Timpson arrived early the next morning and I told her what had happened. She gave me an odd sideways look. Once, she recalled, they had been plagued by mice at the cottage, but rats?—never.

I sat in the kitchen while she set about preparing my breakfast. Shelagh, in the living-room, was still asleep. "Let her sleep," I said. "She needs the rest."

After I had eaten I went into the garden and cut a large bunch of cornflowers. Before I set off for the cemetery I had a word with Jean Timpson and she gave me her promise to watch over Shelagh, then, feeling much relieved on that score I started off down the hill. I didn't bother with the car; the walk would do me good. Shelagh would be all right with the older woman, I was certain. I was convinced now of Jean Timpson's complete honesty and trustworthiness.

One other thing I was convinced of: that Shelagh and I must leave the cottage *today*. Last night's terrifying happening made that clear enough . . .

As I approached the cemetery I was surprised to see several cars parked alongside the wall; it was an unusual sight; the area generally presented a picture of perfect peace and quiet. There were people milling around the gates. A wedding, I thought, or a funeral . . . But then I realised that it was Sunday. Yet the people there didn't look as if they were dressed for church; didn't look as if they were there for a church service. Across the heads of the onlookers I saw, there beyond the wall, a knot of official-looking men, a couple of policemen among them. They were gathered around a small area over to the left of the gates. They were standing at the site of Colin and Helen's grave.

I hurried to the gates and pushed my way through the crowd of rubber-necks—only to be stopped on the other side by a young village constable who told me he was sorry, but that I couldn't go in. "What's happening?" I asked. I looked again towards the nucleus of men by the graveside and saw Reese standing there. At the same moment he turned, saw me and came over to my side.

"It's all right," he told the constable, and, taking my

arm, led me away to another part of the cemetery, far away from the men around the grave. We stopped, facing each other and I could tell at once from his set face that something was wrong—very, very wrong. He looked down at the flowers I held, sighed and said:

"Go on back home, David."

I stared at him. He asked:

"Did you walk or come by car?"

"I walked."

He nodded. "Come on, I'll drive you back."

"I just *got* here."

He shook his head. "You mustn't stay—really."

"What the hell's happening?"

He didn't answer and I made to step by him, heading for the grave. Through the legs of the grouped men I could see earth piled up. He reached out, grabbed my arm.

"Don't go over there."

"What's up? *Tell* me."

Very reluctantly he said, looking steadily into my face:

"Someone . . . opened their grave last night."

My mouth went dry. I just stared. He added then:

"They—they broke open your brother's coffin . . ." His voice was shaking.

"Go on," I said.

He put up a gentle hand, to comfort, on my shoulder. I shrugged it off. "*Tell* me. Don't just stand there."

He shook his head. "Not here . . ." His hand moved again, took my arm, and I let him lead me away, out through the gates, past the gawking, muttering villagers, to where his car stood at the roadside. We got in. I was still clutching the flowers in my sweat-damp hands. He reached forward with the ignition key but stopped, leaving it unturned.

"The police are pretty sure who did it," he said. "A crowd of young kids—hooligans—they were in the village last night on their motorbikes. Going from pub to pub, all in their leather gear, and generally creating a nuisance. The police are pretty sure they were responsible. Though why they'd want to do such a thing I can't

imagine. There's no explaining the way some people get
their kicks. Trouble is, nobody knows where they were
from. Somewhere in London, it's thought, going by the
accents . . ." He paused. "It makes me *sick* . . ."

"Did they—do anything else? Apart from—from ripping open the grave, did they do anything else . . . ?"

He sighed, closed his eyes.

"You might as well tell me." I said. "I've got to
know."

A fly buzzed through the open window, hit the wind-
screen, *pit, pit, pit,* then flew out the way it had come
in, leaving us in our own silence again. Reese said:

"They—whoever . . . they didn't only open the
grave . . . They opened up your brother's coffin . . .
and then they . . ." His voice tailed off. He added, all
in a rush:

"They cut open his body. His chest."

His eyes moved from mine, his voice falling to the
faintest whisper.

"And tore out his heart."

Inside Reese's house I drank the brandy he gave me.
When I got up to go I found I was still carrying the
flowers. I put them on the table. "Please," I said, "get
rid of these for me. I don't want to take them back to
the cottage and then have to explain *why*."

"They'll know, sooner or later," he said. "A thing
like this won't be kept quiet for long."

I nodded. "Doubtless."

Of course I didn't mention anything when I got back
to the cottage. And, with luck, I thought, Shelagh would
never hear about it, and if Jean Timpson did—which
wasn't unlikely—I didn't really believe she'd pass on
any such information to Shelagh. The more I could protect Shelagh from the horrors that surrounded us, the
less unhappy I would be. So I kept quiet.

Shelagh was quiet, too. Very subdued. She hadn't in
any way got over the happening of the night before and
that, while she still hadn't fully recovered from her fall,
had taken an even greater toll of her vitality.

"But I'll be all right," she told me. "It's just that it's not that easy for me to—to shake off just like that."

We were sitting in the living-room, drinking coffee. "We could go out somewhere this evening," I said. "Out for dinner somewhere . . ."

She nodded. "Good. I'd like that."

She had agreed so readily; I knew she no longer felt the same way about the cottage. How could she—after last night?

"Why don't we *stay* out tonight?" I said.

"*Stay* out?"

"At a hotel somewhere. In London maybe. Just for the night . . ." I had more in my mind than this, but at the moment I felt it was safest to say as little as possible. "It's still early," I said. "I'll bet we can get tickets for a concert or something, then have supper and spend the night at a hotel."

"And come back tomorrow . . ."

"Yes . . ."

"You really do have sudden brainwaves, don't you?" But she wasn't making any objections.

"Come on," I said, "let's get ready."

As I got up I saw Timpson go past the house on his way round to the kitchen door. I went out to him. He had brought tiles for the roof. I told him where the leak was and left him to it.

I was standing before the bathroom mirror rinsing the lather from my face when Shelagh knocked at the door. I called out for her to come in and she entered carrying a gaily wrapped package tied with ribbons. I rubbed clear the steamed-over glass before me and smiled at her reflection as I dried my face. "You look so pretty," I said.

"So do you."

She came to me over the soft carpet, looked up at me and touched my chin. "I'm too late," she said. "I thought part of this"—she indicated the package— "might be useful . . ."

"Useful for what?" I asked, but without waiting for an answer put my arms around her and drew her to me, holding her tight, tighter. There was only a towel around my waist between me and nakedness and I pressed my growing hardness against her as I kissed her. Our mouths separated. We grinned at each other. "Keep going," I said, "and it's going to be a long time before we get out of here."

Laughing, she broke away from me. "I didn't come in here to seduce you. Only to give you this." She held up the package. "I should have given it to you yesterday."

I took the package from her. "Right now I'd much rather have you."

She backed away. "Not now. I'm getting steamed up in here."

"So am I."

"That's not what I meant."

The ribbon was coming adrift from the wrapping. She saw it, clicked her tongue and said, "Damn, and I thought I did that so carefully too."

"I didn't get you anything," I said. "I'm sorry. I will later, though, don't worry."

She smiled. "I won't." She moved towards the door. "Come back," I said, but she shook her head, said a girl wasn't safe, and went out.

I was still smiling as I tore off the paper and took the lid off the box. The inner soft-tissue wrapping was of white, patterned here and there with little flecks of red. My hand dipped down amongst the tissues, and my fingertips touched—not the cool hardness of the china I had expected to find, but something else—some soft-textured, rubbery thing . . .

Even as my fingers withdrew the object, before I looked at it, I knew what it was. My eyes only confirmed my dread.

I was holding in my hand a human heart.

28

❧ ❧ ❧

I stood clutching the edge of the wash-basin, my eyes
shut tight, trying to blot out the image of what I had
seen, while in my head the black and red haze swirled,
converged, spread and fused again. There was a whisper
of breathing behind me and for a second I thought it
might be Shelagh. But I knew it wasn't. And I was
afraid to look around. The *thing* lay before me in the
wash-basin where I had let it fall. And still I kept my
eyes closed while nausea rose up in me and I groped my
way to vomit into the toilet bowl.

Shelagh, all unaware, at the piano, didn't hear me
creep down the stairs; didn't see me, in my towelling
robe, go outside and into the toolshed for the trowel.

Timpson saw me, though. I'd forgotten he was there
and when he called out to me I jumped as if I'd been
stung. I stood shaking as he climbed down the ladder
and came towards me. He had, he said, noticed that
some of the slates on the garage roof needed replacing
as well. "Fine," I said, "do whatever you can." He began to go on about the technicalities of the work while I
stood there nodding my head like some rear-car-
window mascot. I don't know what he must have
thought of me. I was like a zombie. All I could think of
was how much I wanted him to stop, to go away. In one
hand I held the trowel. In the other I held, wrapped in
Kleenex, Colin's heart.

At long last he moved back to the ladder, then I
walked on till I was in a part of the garden where I was
hidden from his sight. There I knelt and scooped out
earth from one of the flower borders. When the hole

was deep enough I held my breath and forced my trembling fingers to pick up the dreadful object that lay beside me. I dropped it into the hole. Even after I had covered it up I could somehow still feel it in my hand, dry and spongy, too disgusting to contemplate.

I patted down the soil, stood up and looked around me. It was all right; no one had seen. I put the trowel back in the toolshed and returned to the house.

In the kitchen I washed my hands and dried them with paper towels, rubbing away at them long after they were clean and dry. It was when I lifted the lid of the trash bin to dump the sodden paper that I saw what was left of Shelagh's wedding gift to me.

I didn't realise what it was at first. Just bits of broken china, I thought. But then I recognised the colours of the shaving-mug, the curving neck of the amorous swan, Leda's head . . .

My fingers trembled as I stooped and picked out the pieces.

In the living-room Shelagh looked at the fragments of china I held in my hands.

"I never thought I was marrying such a klutz," she said. The disappointment that came through her smile was heartbreaking. Then she shrugged. "Ah, well, never mind, so what's a priceless antique here or there . . . ?"

In the Royal Albert Hall that evening as the rich romatic sounds of Pachelbel's *Canon in D Major* swept over us I was aware of Shelagh's complete stillness at my side. I turned slowly, stealing a glance at her, saw her quite rapt; and I realised that for all my own fears she, at this moment, was happy. She knew nothing of what was happening; safe in her blissful ignorance she didn't know how close she had been to death, of the hatred that even now awaited her in the cottage. And if I possibly could, I would keep her in that ignorance. Always . . .

Without drawing any comment from her I had got us away from the cottage as quickly as I could; leaving with Timpson a message for Jean that we would be returning tomorrow afternoon—and this was what Shelagh also believed. I hadn't yet mentioned to Shelagh my intention that we should return to New York on Tuesday; there would be time for that soon—the right time. Now, passionately, I looked forward to that return.

Apart from my nagging fear of Helen—which was always with me now—I found I was also affected by anger and resentment. Yes, it was as simple as that: I was filled with anger at her. For all she had done, for the evil she had perpetrated, for the misery and terror she had caused. Angry, too, that I was being forced to run from her, that she had driven us away from the house—*my* house.

From my resentment an idea began to take shape in my mind; a plan, and once lodged there it took root and grew, refusing to be budged by an external influence. And I found I had a purpose. Bruch's violin concerto had begun, but as beautiful as it was it never, for more than moments at a time, got between me and that growing purpose . . .

I hugged my plan, my hope to me, and it gave me strength; and that strength, plus the relief at being away from the cottage, helped me, bringing me a feeling of elation. I realised, too, that away from the cloying warmth of that welcome that always greeted me in the cottage I could think more clearly. That love, that warmth, so positive, reaching out, so totally embracing had been, I felt, like a drug to my reason and my senses . . .

"How do you feel?" I asked.

We had booked into a hotel just off Baker Street and now, after supper, in the security of our room I held Shelagh to me. She smiled at me.

"Oh, I feel good now. Very good."

"No pain? No headaches?"

"No pain, no headaches. Just . . . good."

I had drawn back the curtains and the light from the star-filled sky lit the room with shadowed greyness, softening its impersonal lines, mellowing its austerity. I drew her closer still to me, brushing back her hair as it fell across her cheek.

"I've been thinking," I said, ". . . let's go home on Tuesday . . ."

". . . Okay . . ."

"I think it's the best thing. I'll go and see Mr. Jennersen at the bank. Get him to see about selling the cottage."

"You've really decided then."

"Yes . . ."

"Okay. If that's what you want."

"We'll come back another time. One day when it's a happier time. If you want."

She nodded against me in the crook of my arm. "Yes. We'll find our own place, our own cottage. Some place of our own, where we'll be . . . on our own."

". . . What do you mean?"

"We never were *alone* there, were we? How could we be?—all those memories. It's a beautiful, beautiful place but . . . I never really felt it was ours. For me it was always so . . . so full of ghosts."

I turned, studying her in the dim light. Her eyes were shut and she looked peaceful. There had been no fear in her words—only sadness.

"Yes . . ." I wrapped my arms closer round her. I felt I could never be close enough. "I don't care where we go, as long as I'm with you—and you're happy."

"I just want us to be together," she said softly, her words muffled against my cheek. "I love you so much, Dave."

"Good, I'm *glad*." Softly I kissed her.

Long after I had drawn the curtains together again, shutting out the sky; after I had sunk back beside her on the bed, the thoughts of tomorrow came crowding back into my mind. Tomorrow, and what I had determined to do. And without Shelagh's knowledge.

Her breathing was soft, regular beside me. I whispered:

"Are you asleep . . . ?"

She stirred against me. "Almost . . ." Her voice came sleepy. "Why . . . ?"

"I think I shall have to go and see my father before we go back to New York." I waited for her response.

There was none. "I thought maybe I'd go and see him tomorrow morning. It'll be about the only chance I'll have . . ."

"Okay . . ."

"Just to settle up a few things," I added, continuing the lie.

"You must do what you have to do, darling . . ."

"Yes . . . Will you be all right on your own for a few hours . . . ?"

"Don't you want me to go with you?"

I had given her a plausible excuse for my father not coming to our wedding—and she hadn't questioned it. Now I tightened, gently, my arm around her waist. "Darling, I'm not going to see him for pleasure. It's purely business . . ."

Her fingers pressed my arm. "I'll find something to do. Don't worry about me." After a moment she added:

"Dave, don't be so concerned. You think my feelings are going to be hurt because your father isn't ready to welcome me with open arms . . . ? It doesn't matter that much, darling, really it doesn't."

I kissed the back of her neck.

"Will you be back in time for lunch?" she murmured.

"I don't know. We'll talk about it in the morning. Go to sleep now."

I left her sitting reading in the hotel lounge when I went off the next morning. After breakfast we had cashed some travellers' cheques and then booked seats on a flight back to New York leaving the following day. Back at the hotel again I had made arrangements (with luck there'd been a cancellation) to keep our rooms on until tomorrow.

'I thought we were going back to the cottage," Shelagh said.

"Not to stay. I don't think so. No. We'll just do what we have to do and then come on back here. As a matter of fact you might as well stay here while I go there. I can pack up our gear. It won't take me long. Stay and see a bit of London while you've got the chance."

"I'd rather be with you. It wouldn't be any fun on my own."

"Anyway . . . we don't have to decide now . . ."

One thing I had already decided: we would never spend another night at the cottage—and that's why I'd booked the hotel room for an extra night. But the question of whether or not we were *able to, in safety,* had become a matter of principle to me. And to uphold that principle was part of my purpose; its success depending on whether or not I could contact Elizabeth Barton's priest friend, and on whether or not he would be willing and able to help . . .

I left the car in the car park and took a taxi to the address at Turnham Green where I had first seen Elizabeth Barton. Her sister answered the door. Her manner showed that Elizabeth had confided in her, I thought; she greeted me with sympathetic warmth, but then, to my disappointment, added that Elizabeth was out.

"She's gone back to work. I didn't want her to, but she insisted that she felt well enough . . ."

Well, that was it. Forget it, I told myself. Let it be. I thanked the woman, was just turning away and she said,

"But why don't you phone her at her office. Come in. You can phone her from here . . ."

And so, fifteen minutes later I was in another taxi, armed with the address of the Reverend Ian Rogers and heading for his flat in Kensington.

He answered at once my ring at the door; he'd been waiting for me. Inside he introduced me to his pretty young wife and then led me into a pleasantly furnished lounge where he gestured for me to be seated.

Elizabeth Barton, he said, had told him something of the matter . . . As he spoke I studied him; he was a young man, probably not more than a couple of years older than I. Watching him I saw an economy about all his movements that smacked of calm and inner strength. Over the years I had come to associate a certain weakness exhibited in the manner of so many men-of-the-cloth, a certain fragility that spoke of their religion being a resort, a haven, a way out from the harshness of life. Here, though, studying Rogers, I was aware of no such feelings. His position as a man of God was, I instinctively felt, one occupied from strength, and certainty in his beliefs.

I told him the whole story, everything—even to the remains of the body I had found buried in the thicket, and he sat for the most part in silence, listening intently, only occasionally interrupting to ask some relevant question for clarification. When I had finished he sat in silence for some moments then said:

"And you want me to get rid of her."

". . . Yes."

He sighed. "It isn't a job I relish. I've had a couple such experiences in the past and the prospect of any similar task quite . . . disturbs me." He gave a bitter smile. "I don't mind admitting it."

"Then why did you agree to see me?" I asked. I tried to keep the edge out of my voice.

"I didn't know how—how *real* it was. I thought perhaps that it was all—well, in your mind . . ."

"And in Elizabeth Barton's mind?"

"Well . . . she's been under a considerable strain just lately."

"Yes. And now you know why."

He nodded. Then, after a second said:

"You know, such a—business—isn't very pleasant."

The hope that had kept me buoyant was all gone by now. I would be gone too. I moved to get up, but he stopped me, saying:

"But there, I don't consider I'm here only to do what is pleasant. The work to be done in God's name *isn't* always pleasant, easy. It's not all glory and trumpets and celestial choirs and converts, believe me." He smiled again, a brighter smile this time. "In fact it's not all it's cracked up to be." He paused, nodded. "I'll do whatever I can to help you."

"Thank you . . ."

"You're staying in London right now?"

"Yes. I left my wife at the hotel."

"Good. Keep her away from the house until it's all over."

"Oh, yes, I intend to." I hadn't told him *quite* everything; I hadn't told him that we were returning to New York the next day. As far as he was concerned I wanted the cottage safe for Shelagh and me to live in.

"How long will it take us to get there?" he asked.

"You can go now?"

"Let's get it over with."

"About an hour, by car." I added, "I came by taxi. My car's still parked by the hotel. I don't know my way around London that well."

"That's all right. We'll go in mine. Just give me a couple of minutes to get a few things together." He got up and moved to the door. "You're lucky, I've got no appointments today that can't be put off."

He came back after a while carrying his jacket and briefcase. As I rose to join him he said:

"Elizabeth told me you've been living in the States up till now."

"Yes."

"So you don't intend going back."

I couldn't lie to him. Not now.

"Yes, we do. We're going back tomorrow . . ."

"For good?"

"I'm not sure. We're not coming back to the cottage, though. I'm going to sell it."

"Then—then why is it so important that you—you rid the place of your sister-in-law's . . . spirit . . . ? If you're going so soon it can't make any difference to you one way or the other, can it?"

". . . Other people will go there, live there. They must be . . . safe."

And I was lying to him there, all right. Why should I be concerned with other people? I was after vengeance. *Vengeance is mine,* God said, but it would be mine, too.

She had destroyed, and I would destroy *her*.

29

❧ ❧ ❧

"Does your wife know where you are?" Rogers asked as he manoeuvred the car onto the motorway.

"She thinks I'm going to see my father." I paused, then asked:

"Will this thing . . . take long?"

"Let's hope not."

We sat in silence for a while. He said, "Go ahead and smoke if you want to," and I took grateful refuge in a cigarette; a few more seconds, minutes killed. I felt as if I were in some kind of dream. How, when, could I ever have imagined that I might be setting out on such a mission . . . ?

"Why?" I said.

"Mmm? Why what?"

"Why does a ghost—stay . . . ?"

"I believe," he said after a moment, "and so do many others—that a ghost—or spirit—lingers on in a place simply because the soul isn't really aware of the body's death. The body, the flesh has gone, but the soul, not knowing, stays . . ."

I darted a sideways, incredulous glance at him, but he didn't react. He wasn't joking. He kept his eyes steadily on the road and calmly continued:

"The soul doesn't stay intentionally just for the purpose of—of haunting a place. It just—continues to live there. I suppose in a way it's—lost—but isn't aware of it. And it's not necessarily evil—a ghost—any more than is the soul of a *living* person . . ."

"*She* is," I said. "*She* is evil."

"If such is the case"—he gave a half-shrug—"then in life she probably had that same evil within her."

"Yes . . ." And I thought about De Freyne. Had *she* killed him as I had inferred from Colin's letter . . . ? One thing I *was* sure of, though: "I *do know*," I said, "that after she died she somehow managed to kill my brother rather than let him leave."

"Love can take some strange forms."

"Yes, and now she's turned that same love on me." I stubbed out my cigarette. "She's *totally* evil."

When we were within a few miles of Hillingham I said:

"Please, from now on don't say anything about it. Just do what you have to do. Just—go in there and do what's needed without discussing it with me . . ."

He turned his eyes from the road and gave me a brief questioning glance.

"She'd hear us," I said. "She'd listen. And she's not just confined to the house. She moves around. Yesterday she got as far as the cemetery." Thoughts of Colin's mutilated body came into my mind. *Don't think about it. Don't.* "As soon as we get close," I said, "she'll be there. She'll be listening to us and watching our every movement."

"Don't be afraid," he said, and smiled. He wore his casual bravery like a cloak and I felt sure that inside he, too, was not unafraid. He must have sensed my doubt. He gestured to his briefcase which lay on the back seat. "Believe me, I'm prepared for any emergency." He looked at his watch. "And I'll get it all over with as soon as I can. You want to get back to your wife, and I want to get back to mine." He paused, showing his uncertainty. "But mostly I just want to get it over with."

Just after we got off the motorway he stopped the car at the edge of a little country road where the trees grew thickly on either side and the sun came through the leaves in moving, dappled patches. He shifted the gear lever to neutral, turned to face me.

"When we get there I'll go in alone. You stay outside."

The relief I felt at his words was like oxygen to a

suffocating man. Even so I protested. "Shouldn't I go in with you? You won't know your way around . . ."

"You can tell me that, and what I don't know I'll find out." He shook his head. "No, it's better that I go in alone. You're—involved. Too involved. It might make things more difficult."

"Okay." I shrugged, my gesture not giving away the great gladness I felt; while *she* was inside the cottage I never wanted to go in there again.

I watched him as he opened his bag, his hand moving inside, expertly checking, sorting. His fingers moved aside velvet wrapping and I glimpsed a crucifix, a glass vial. The sight of the objects made my heart pound. "Are those things necessary?" I asked. "I mean—we're not dealing with witches, are we—or the devil?"

He snapped the case shut. "I'm sure we're not— though I don't see how you can pigeon-hole things so easily. Anyway, as I said, I have to be prepared."

He drove the car up the drive and parked it outside the garage. Wordlessly we got out and climbed the side steps to enter the garden by the lawn. I saw, with relief, that no one else was about. Timpson, it appeared, had finished his work on the house roof and had begun fixing slates on the roof of the garage; the ladder was propped against it and I could see the new slates on the flat bit above the window. I had no idea where Timpson was—or Jean for that matter, and I dreaded the possibility of them returning at the wrong moment. Anyway, there was nothing I could do about it, not right then.

Rogers, walking at my side, stopped and just stood looking. I halted a few feet further on, watching his face. In his sports-jacket and open-necked shirt he looked more like a rugby-player than a priest. He gave a close-mouthed smile, shook his head. "It all looks so peaceful. And so beautiful."

I turned, looked at the cottage, my cottage. It did look peaceful. Who could ever have believed that such a setting—all of peace—on the surface—could possibly harbour such malevolence? All around, under the late morning sun the poppies, brilliantly red, gently nodded and trembled in the light breeze that brushed the hillside. And there were the roses, too—so pink, so yellow, so white, so white, so white . . . Their perfume was all around us, as positive as the birdsong.

I turned back to him. Was he going to stand there forever? Prompting him to move I gave him a brief description of the layout of the cottage, and still he stood there. Then, at last, with a smile he said, quite breezily:

"Well, better get on, I suppose."

I watched as he moved towards the back door. In the doorway he turned.

"Her name—it's Helen, you said, right?"

"Yes." I frowned. "Yes." I wanted to add: *Don't you realise that she's listening to us, watching us right now! Don't say anything else. Just get on with it . . .*

He saw my frown and read it correctly. He said: "It's all right," and I felt anger and impatience surge in me. Did he know what he was dealing with? He waved a nonchalant hand. "You just relax. I'll call you when it's—when I'm finished."

I nodded. He gave me a last smile that was meant to be encouraging, then went in and closed the door.

I was afraid that if I stayed close to the cottage I might hear him, hear his voice, hear some kind of incantations, calls upon Helen's spirit to be gone. I was afraid of having further knowledge of her presence there, endorsement of what I already knew and feared so much; afraid of acknowledgement of that unreal reality, so at odds with the mellow beauty of the morning. Simply, I was afraid.

I turned, walked slowly away over the grass. The scar on my arm itched and I rubbed at it, forcing myself not to scratch it. The birds went on singing. Bees hummed amongst the roses, living up to their reputation for industry, and a solitary wasp zinged past my nose and disappeared into the little studio. Through the dusty window I saw Helen's self-portrait with the great daubs of paint over the face. I tore my eyes away and let my feet lead me down and out under the arch into the thicket. Following the rough path I made my way among the trees and brambles and the masses of rhododendrons. A flash of red before my eyes gave me my first sight ever of a red squirrel; poor red squirrel, so sadly depleted by his grey cousin from over the water. Seeing me, he stopped, frozen, on the bough. I stopped as well. Sometimes, I had once read, they died of fright. Not this one, though; in another second he had gone, leaping away into the trees. I walked on again, the gentleness and innocence of the creature lingering about me like a little fog. A bird sang, closer than the others, and with a distant kind of pleasure I recognised the yellow plumage and the song of a wood warbler—thanks to Helen's bird book; and so back to Helen again; not that she was ever very far away from my mind. Forget her, I told myself, concentrate on the peace.

But it wasn't *my* peace, I knew, no matter how attractive it might be, no matter how it touched me. And never could be; not *this* peace, here . . . And when I reached the clearing ahead of me I knew, irrevocably, that it was so.

Coward to the last I skirted the clearing, avoiding even a glance at the rough grave that lay to the side of the summer-house. I had told no one of it except for Ian Rogers; I would tell no one else. Ever. After tomorrow I would be away from it for always, and those bones there—as far as I was concerned—would lie undisturbed, rotting, until they became the earth from which they had sprung.

Beyond the clearing I walked slowly on down to the pond's bank. The marsh marigolds still sun-dotted the water's edge, and I thought again of how Reese and I had dragged Jean Timpson out and laid her on the grass. Now I sat down on that same grass, lit a cigarette. I had no idea how long the Reverend would be; I tried to prepare myself for a long wait.

I wondered what Shelagh was doing now in London; probably in the National Gallery; I pictured her— wandering through the Rembrandt Room . . . Shelagh. She'd been so lucky; in any one of her "accidents" she could have fared much worse. But her luck wouldn't have held out much longer, I knew that; how could she, so gentle, so good,—yes, *good*—ever be anything of a match for that other who was so powerful in her wickedness?

My thoughts went on . . .

I had been sitting there for so long, I suddenly realised. Rogers would have done his work by now, would have been shouting himself hoarse and getting no response from me. Quickly I got to my feet and hurried up the wide track through the thicket that led to the gap in the orchard hedge. When I eventually got to the lawn I expected to see him there, waiting for me, ready and impatient to get going. There was no sign of him.

I stood hovering, not knowing what to do. He had said not to go in, to leave it all to him, yet surely he must be through by now. Hesitantly I called to him.

". . . Reverend Rogers . . ."

There was no answer, and the silence that surrounded me seemed somehow deeper than it had been before. I could no longer hear the buzzing of the bees. No birds sang.

The back door was still closed. I went towards it, stood for a moment with my fingers around the handle, then drew my hand away. Looking in at the kitchen window everything appeared to be just as it had before. In Colin's study the same. Because of the sunken garden I couldn't see into the living-room, so I continued on and walked round to the front of the house.

I could see in then all right.

The room was a shambles, and there, sprawled, supine, Rogers lay with his head up against the wall.

30

   ❧ ❧ ❧

My knees felt weak and loose-jointed as I ran back round to the door at the rear. I reached for the handle. And stopped dead.

As my fingers got to within an inch of it the handle turned. And now the door swung slowly open.

Come in, she was saying. *Come in* . . .

For a long time—it seemed an eternity—I didn't move. I couldn't. I was terrified.

But I had to go in. I had to. I couldn't leave Rogers lying in there, alone.

But he wasn't alone in the house, was he? She was there . . .

Still I stayed, like some statue; aware of my hoarse breathing as I panted through stiff lips, the pounding of my heart; aware of *her,* waiting for me. *Come in* . . . *Come in* . . .

Then I told myself—reason, some clearer thought returning—that she had never tried to harm me; her hatred was not directed against me; the evil she had done since my arrival had been done only in order to have me there with her alone. *She loves me* . . . *She won't hurt me* . . . I kept repeating the words to myself.

Yet she had killed Colin. And she had loved him.

But, I reminded myself, she had killed him when he had been packing up to leave—to leave her forever; when she no longer had any hope that he would stay. She had waited until that last possible moment and then, when all hope had gone, she had killed him, killed him rather than let him go. He had tried to make his escape, but he had made the mistake of leaving it too late. He had run outside but she had been with him and she had taken control of the car and slammed it into the beech-tree. No—his mistake wasn't that he had left it too late, that he had stayed too long; his mistake was that he had come back. And she knew why he had come back. After all, she could hear, she could see.

Come in, the open door was saying. *Come in . . .* Oh, yes, she could hear, she could see all right. She knew why Rogers had gone in there. She had been threatened. And she would know that the threat had really come from me . . .

The door opened a fraction wider.

Come in . . . come in . . .

Perhaps she wanted me there just to kill *me.* As she had killed Colin . . .

Another two inches the door swung back. The gap was widening, widening . . .

Come in . . . Please come in . . .

And then I realised that if she wanted only to kill me she could find some way of doing it now, out here . . . She didn't have to get me inside the house to do it. No, she didn't want to kill me.

Come in . . . come in . . .

She just wanted me in there.

I stepped forward and passed through the wide-open doorway.

I could feel her watching me as I went through into the living-room. The ticking of the clock was deafening in the silence, and although there were no roses there the scent of them was all around me, thick and heady.

I hurried to Rogers' side, my eyes taking in the chaos that had resulted from whatever confrontation had taken place there. A confrontation that Rogers, poor novice that he was, had so completely lost; he hadn't been as prepared as he'd thought, in spite of his assertions.

I knelt beside him. He looked as if he'd been struck. There was a mark, a great livid bruise right in the centre of his forehead. The blow had felled him and he had fallen back against the wall. A small table had been

toppled and now lay on its side. Pink and blue cornflowers lay in a wet patch of carpet amongst the bits of
a shattered china vase. The white knight on his charger
lay unbroken. Beside Margaret Lane's sad sampler the
heavy antique sword lay where Rogers' powerful body
had knocked it from its fastenings.

But he was alive.

I spoke his name. He didn't answer or open his eyes,
but gave a slight groan, his head moving, leaving on the
wall a faint smear of blood. Oh, Christ, don't let him
die, don't let him die . . .

I put my hands under his arms and tried to lift him,
but it was impossible. He was out completely cold, a
dead weight. I must phone Reese, get him to come
round . . . I took a cushion from the sofa and put it
behind Rogers' head in an effort to make him a little
less uncomfortable. The sword was jammed awkwardly
underneath his sprawled body and I eased him up a
fraction in order to draw it out. As I straightened up I
saw his briefcase lying there; saw the crucifix—he
hadn't even had a chance to get it out; I saw the little
vial of holy water.

And as I looked at it I saw it crushed.

It appeared to be trodden upon by an unseen foot.
One moment it lay whole and perfect and the next moment it was just a little oblong shape of crushed glass
with the water staining the carpet.

"*Helen* . . ." I whispered it.

I felt her hand on my shoulder.

I shuddered. My heart thudded and lurched. I stood
up, brushing frantically at the unseen touch. I felt her
hand move from my shoulder to my throat, and I
thought, She *could* kill me . . . She could kill me for
trying to destroy her. Fingers fluttered on my neck for a
moment, then settled again, tighter, tighter. I felt
thumbs digging in, pressing, pressing hard, harder, felt
the shape of her hands as they encircled my throat. She
was strangling me.

I choked, gasped, struggling for breath, trying to
move out of her grasp, desperately jerking my head
from side to side. But she held on. I was getting no air

at all. Black and blood-red shapes swarmed before my staring eyes and I sank to my knees on the carpet amongst the broken china and the cornflowers.

And still her iron grip was there. My head, my lungs felt as if they would burst; I felt I would never breathe again.

And then, just as I was sure I was about to die, all at once the pressure eased and her fingers loosed their grip. Her hands released me, moving from me with a gentle, caressing brush of my cheek. I knelt there on the floor with my head hanging, sucking gulps of air down into my lungs.

For a time I didn't move. When my thoughts were able to get past the sheer relief at being alive, of the burning in my throat and the hammering in my head I asked myself *why* she had stopped. And I realised that she'd had no intention of killing me. She hadn't meant to kill me at all. She had been punishing me for trying to harm her. And warning me also? Warning me not to try to leave her? Yes, perhaps. If so it was a warning I must heed. Colin had tried to leave her, and he had died. I would have to be cleverer than Colin, and cleverer than *she*.

I spoke to her, directly.

"Are you there . . . ?" I knew she was. I could sense her, still so close to me, feel her presence, so real.

"Are you there . . . ?"

I waited for her answer. When it came it was a strangely gentle sound; just one little whispered word.

"Always."

Yes, always. True.

"Don't you realise," I said, "I'm *here*. I'm *back*."

"Yes."

Yes. She could hear me all right; she could see me. But she didn't know what was going on in my head. She couldn't read my mind.

"I shall stay here," I said.

Silence.

"Well," I went on, as persuasively as I could sound, "this is my home. It's my *home*."

Then *her* voice. Nearer. "Yes. Yes . . ."

And suddenly her arms encircled me, wrapping me like wings, holding me close, and the fear I felt welled up so that I cried out, "No! Oh, God, No!" and lifted my hands in an attempt to free myself from her embrace. She gave a little cry and her arms fell away from me.

I found I was still holding the sword. Was that what had made her cry out? I was holding the sword by its dull-edged blade, hilt uppermost, so that a cross was formed . . .

I held it higher . . .

"Keep away from me," I said. "Stay away."

I thought of the film I had seen where the man had held aloft a crucifix. Could it be that such a symbol really might combat evil? Had this symbol of the cross I now held had an effect upon *her*? Was she so evil that the goodness it symbolised could cause her fear?—or even pain? I held the cross higher still.

But her fear didn't last. Whatever shock or pain the cross might have given her seemed to be outweighed by her resolve to possess me.

In the next instant I felt a great tug at the hilt of the sword, saw it, felt it move, upwards through my tightly clenching fingers. I gripped tighter, holding on. Still she pulled at it and I felt searing pain in my circled palms as the dull edge of the sword was drawn through them.

I was struggling to hold on, and struggling to ignore the burning in my hands. All I wanted to do was let go, to put an end to the pain, but I mustn't, I couldn't; and all I could do was watch as the sword hilt moved slowly, surely, agonisingly upwards, higher, higher, higher . . .

And then it came back to me, all at once, what Rogers had said: that a ghost, a haunting spirit often lingered in a place because the soul was unaware that the physical body was no longer living. And with the remembrance I yelled out:

"You're *dead. Dead. You're dead!*"

The sword's moving ceased.

I said again, whispering, not relaxing my hold: "You're dead. You must . . . go away from here."

Still no shifting of the sword. I got more courage.

"You must go where you belong. You're dead, Helen—*dead*."

And then the sword moved again. A strong, sudden jerk that took me by surprise and almost pulled me off balance. Still I held on.

It had seemed for a few moments there that she had given in, was retreating. But then, when I had spoken those last words to her she had surged in power again. How . . . ?

And then I realised. *Yes. I had called her Helen.* I had told Rogers, too, that her name was Helen. *Helen*, I had said. *Helen* . . . When all the time I was surrounded by remainders of her *first* name. I said clearly, evenly, my voice low:

"Rose . . ."

There was a moment of absolute stillness. The sword gave one final violent twist, faltered and stopped.

"*Yes!*" I almost shouted it. "It's Rose. It's *Rose!*" I should have told Rogers that—that her first name was Rose. "Rose!" I shouted. I felt suddenly invincible.

"Rose," I whispered from my new-found strength, "you are dead . . . Dead . . . Dead . . . Dead . . ."

"No . . ." It was a whispered, plaintive sound, "No . . ."

"*Yes! dead! You are dead, Rose, Dead . . . Rose . . .*"

I heard birds singing. I followed the line of my aching arms and saw that my hands were held out before me clutching the antique sword. How long I'd been standing there I had no idea. The scent of roses was no longer in the room. She was gone, too.

From behind me I heard a groan. Turning, lowering the sword, I saw Rogers struggling to get up, lifting a hand to his bruised forehead. I knelt beside him.

"Are you all right?"

"I—I think so . . . yes . . ."

"Come on . . ." With my blistered hands I supported him and slowly, painfully he got to his feet. He stood there looking dazed, stunned, and I watched as memory returned, sparking fear into his eyes. He took a step back.

"Oh, God—Oh, God——"

"It's all right . . ." I took his arm. "It's all right. There's nothing more to be afraid of."

He groaned. The fear was still there.

"I didn't have a chance," he said. "She—she came for me almost as soon as I got in the place. I didn't—didn't have a chance . . ."

"It's all right," I soothed him. "She can't hurt us now. She's gone." I added with relief, and a touch of pride: "I did it. I sent her away."

He nodded dully. After a while he asked:

"What will you do now?"

"I'll bring Shelagh back and we'll pack up our things and leave. And after that we'll *never* return."

31

❧ ❧ ❧

No, he said to my suggestion, he didn't need any doctor. I didn't insist. He sat quietly in the car waiting till I'd finished doing what had to be done and then together we set off. I offered to drive, but he said it wasn't necessary; apart from a slight headache, he said, he felt perfectly okay.

He hardly spoke as we headed back to London. He offered no more information about what had happened in the cottage, and I didn't ask. I didn't want to know. It was done with.

Whilst in the cottage I had found, lying on the hall mat, an unstamped envelope. Opening it up I saw that it was a letter from Pitkin. In my rush to get Shelagh away from the danger I had forgotten all about him and the dresser. In the note he asked me to let him know when he could come and collect it; he had tried to phone us, he said, but our telephone was out of order . . . I put the note in my pocket. I'd call him later on . . .

In the city, after our near-silent journey, Rogers headed straight for my hotel. "No, drop me anywhere," I told him, "I'll get a taxi," but he said it was no trouble and I didn't put up any further protests.

Outside the hotel he stopped. No, he wouldn't come in for a drink, he said, thanks all the same. As he reached out to shake my hand he hesitated, seeing the angry scorch marks, the blisters there. Then without comment he gently shook my hand, cupping my palm so as not to hurt.

"I'm sorry I wasn't much help . . ."

I was sorry—for him; his lesson had been a painful one. And frightening. I shrugged, tried a smile. "You did what you could. And I'm grateful. And anyway, the result is the important thing. It's over, that's the thing that matters. You did far more than you think."

When he had gone I went into the quiet of the hotel lounge where Shelagh sat waiting for me. She asked me, a little anxiously, how it had gone. Of course, she meant the meeting with my father.

"Oh, all right. We sorted out what needed to be sorted out."

"And it's finished?"

"Yes . . . finished."

With my words, in a great flood of relief, I put my arms around her, holding her tight to me so that she gave a little cry of surprise. A short grey-haired man sitting in a chair opposite looked at us over his rimless glasses, but I wasn't fazed. I couldn't be, not now. In my mind the words kept repeating over and over: *It's finished, it's finished* . . . There were certainly many whys, hows, whats and whens still to be answered, but even so, they were questions I would learn to live with. The important thing for me, at that moment, was my knowledge that the worst—the threatening horror of it all—was finished. No, the opprobrious glance from the little grey-haired man couldn't touch me at all. How could it? Shelagh was safe from harm, and so was I.

"Come on," I said to her, "let's leave everything here. We'll get a quick snack and get back to the cottage." *The cottage,* I had said—not *home.* I could never call it "home" again; that was something I knew it could never be.

"Are we staying there after all—tonight?"

"No." I knew it would be safe to but I didn't want to. I shook my head, put my hand up to her cheek. "We've got our room here for tonight. We'll just go back and get our things and give Bill Carmichael his car back. Also I have to see Mr. Jennersen at the bank and fix up with Mr. Pitkin about the dresser."

"Okay." She lifted her fingers, pressed my hand. I winced. She asked, looking at my palm: "What have you been doing to yourself?"

I wasn't prepared for her question. " . . . Car trouble," I said.

"Ah . . ." She nodded, looked again at my hand. "Does it hurt?"

"It's all right now." I dismissed it. "It's nothing. It doesn't matter." It didn't.

There had been an accident on the motorway and we got held up for a while. It was getting late and I could see I wasn't going to get back in time to see Jennersen. But we kept going. At the gate of the cottage I dropped Shelagh off so that she could make a start with the packing. "On my way back," I told her, "I'll call in and see if Jean can come up and lend a hand. Anyway, I want to have a last word with her about looking after the place till it's sold."

The bank was closed. Going by my watch it had been closed for ten minutes. I knocked ineffectually on its fortress doors for a few minutes then gave up. Ah, well, I'd have to write to him; it couldn't be helped.

Bill Carmichael was there at the garage, though. Would he still be open in a couple of hours? I asked him; I had a few little trips to run in the car before I could bring it back and settle my bill.

"I'll wait for you, anyway," he said.

"And will there be somebody who can drive us to the station?"

"I'll do it."

On the way back to Gerrard's Hill I stopped off at the Timpsons' little house and asked Jean if she could come up and give us any help we might need with the clearing up. She was happy to, though I found, when we arrived at the cottage, that Shelagh had already made good headway. Her own cases were nearly done, she told me, and soon she'd make a start on mine.

"Let me do it," Jean said, and headed for the cellar to fetch up my empty suitcases. When she was gone Shelagh said, indicating the sword with its broken fastenings, "What happened there?" I'd rehung Sad Margaret's sampler, wiped the smear of Rogers' blood from the wall and cleared up the flowers and broken china; but I hadn't been able to do anything about the sword. I didn't know what to say. As far as Shelagh knew I hadn't been in the cottage since we had left together from London. But she saved me herself from trying to find an answer. She lifted the sword, whistled and put it down again. "My God, the weight of it. I'm surprised it stayed up as long as it did."

Jean Timpson came to the door carrying my cases. "I'll go on upstairs and make a start," she said. "You can get on with whatever else you have to do. I'll manage all right."

"Good," I said. "I want to go down to the cemetery."

She started to turn away, then stopped.

"Oh—Oh, I—I washed your jeans." She avoided my eyes completely. "I'll pack them with the rest of your things . . ." It was the expression on her face that reminded me; she meant the jeans I'd been wearing when I jumped into the pond after her. And with that memory *I* couldn't look at *her*.

"The stuff you had in the pockets—" she nodded towards the mantelpiece, "—I put it all up there."

She went away then and I scooped up the loose change, the dried-out notes and my cheap, throw-away lighter—which surprisingly still worked. Shelagh followed me to the kitchen where I went to get scissors.

"Shall I go with you to the cemetery?" she asked.

"Of course. Why not?"

She picked up her bag while I got together some brown paper. In the garden I cut a large bunch of cornflowers and wrapped them up. Shelagh, taking the scissors from me, cut a perfect white rose—just beginning to open—and pinned it to my lapel. "There . . ." She patted my chest and stood back to admire her handiwork. "Now you look perfect." I didn't want the rose—I didn't like its associations, but I smiled and said nothing.

When we got to the churchyard gates she said, putting a hand on mine:

"You go in on your own."

"Why?"

"You'll want to be alone with him for a while. I'll stay here."

"Okay."

The last time I had been to the cemetery was just the day before, Sunday—when Reese had stopped me from going near the grave, when the place had been swarming with onlookers and officials. I approached the grave now with dread, very much afraid of seeing any signs of the violation that had taken place.

And the signs were there, of course. They were visible in the newly-turned look of the soil, the different positioning of the flower vases—though whoever had cleared up afterwards had tried to make a thorough job of it; even the flowers had been put back, albeit they were wilting.

I threw the dying flowers away and carefully arranged the fresh ones. And then I just stood there, looking down. It was very likely, more than very likely, I thought, that I would never stand there again. Never would I come back to Hillingham.

And that meant that I would probably never find out the truth of what lay behind Helen's death. I would never know, one way or the other, whether or not Colin had been in some way responsible for her violent end. Well, so be it, I said to myself; that was a question I *must* learn to live with. And I would be able to. Somewhere in the more hidden-away recesses of my mind there would be a place for such a question; some place where its nagging would be less noticeable . . .

I looked at my watch. I must go. I would call and see Pitkin, and then Shelagh and I would leave. Goodbye, Hillingham; goodbye, Gerrard's Hill Cottage. Forever.

Stooping, I said a whispered word of goodbye to my brother—for Helen I had no words at all—and then turned away.

As I did so a tall, fair-haired man in blue denims came striding along between the graves. He was holding a small wreath. He walked in my direction, looking straight at me, coming towards me.

He stopped just a few feet away. To my surprise I saw that he was looking at me with disdain. I opened my mouth to speak, but before I could say anything he said:

"Aren't you tired of putting on the act?"

I stared at him in amazement. "What do you mean? Who are you?"

"Oh, my God!" He gave a humourless laugh and put a hand to his forehead in a gesture of hopelessness. "Is that how you manage to keep going—by having this rather convenient amnesia? Or have you flipped out completely?"

His voice—I had heard it before; that same tone, similar words.

"It was you," I said. "It was you who phoned me."

His eyes narrowed. "Are you pretending you didn't know?"

"I didn't know. And I still have no idea who you are. I *can* remember your—slanderous accusations."

"Tough," he said shortly, shrugging it off. "I'm sure you'll learn to live with them. The way you've learned"—here he gestured to the grave—"to live with *that*." He glared at me and I saw hatred in his eyes, and then, with a brief "Excuse me", he brushed past me and crouched over the earth. I watched him as he gently laid the wreath beside the cornflowers. I couldn't see his face but I heard the faint sound of a choked-backed sob and realised that he was fighting tears. Someone else who had loved Helen . . .

Neither of us moved for a while, then I said quietly: "I'm not Colin."

He turned to me and I saw disbelief and puzzlement in his eyes, along with the tears.

"Colin was my twin brother," I said.

He stood up and I took a couple of steps towards him. I saw his eyes flash down to take in my limp, my built-up shoe. Then up to my face again.

"Yes," he said then, "you are different," and continued to study me. He nodded. "Yes, yes, I can see."

A little silence went by. He said, with difficulty:

"I've got nothing against you. It's got nothing to do with you; it only concerns him, your brother." He paused. "Are you staying here with him?"

"I'm staying at the cottage, yes."

"What do you mean? Isn't he there now? Where is he?"

I pointed to the freshly turned earth of the grave. "There."

He didn't know what to say. He looked so completely taken aback, stunned. At last he muttered:

"I had no idea. I'm sorry. I had no idea." He shook his head bewilderedly. "I heard about—about Helen while I was away. I got back to England only a short while back."

"You can't have wasted any time getting on the phone."

"I'm sorry. Really." He raked a hand through his hair. "Since I heard about her I just—just haven't been—thinking straight."

"I have to ask you," I said. "Do you really think—do you really believe that my brother—was responsible . . . ?"

He turned away from me. "What does it matter what I think any more?"

"It matters to me."

"I wish I'd never come here," he said. "But I had

to." He gave a bitter smile. "I'd planned on going up to the cottage afterwards . . ."

"To see my brother."

"Yes."

"What for?"

"It's not important now."

"Isn't it?"

"Please," he said. "To find out I've been hating a dead man, it's . . . I don't know . . ."

"The fact that he's dead doesn't really change anything, does it? It can't alter what he did . . . or what he didn't do."

"No." And then, the words stumbling one upon the other, he said, "I loved her. Then *he* came on the scene. God, I was so jealous. And I didn't trust him. It was all so—so sudden. And in next to no time they're getting married. Not that it would have made any difference to me in the long run. I mean—she'd never loved me."

"Did you know her well?"

"Oh, yes."

"Do you think she—she loved Colin?"

"Yes," reluctantly, and then: "The worse for her . . ."

"You really do believe he killed her."

"I had a letter from her. Not long before she died. I know from that how unhappy she was. But not only that; I know from my own eyes. I'm sure that—from the moment your brother came here she was threatened. I know—I'm certain—that she'd be alive today if they'd never met."

"I don't understand . . ."

"It was just a feeling I had. It's hard to explain, but it was very real, that feeling, that—that sense. It was almost as if he was—trying to drive her out of her mind. Even before I went away from them I saw certain things happen. She kept losing things, mislaying things—and I know it wasn't *her* fault. And then there were all those *other* little things that started to happen to her. The injuries, and so on. And when she wrote to me she——"

I cut in quickly, after his words had registered at last:

"You said, 'Before you went away from them' . . . You stayed here with them?"

"Yes."

I just stared at him, then I said:

"You . . . you're Alan De Freyne . . ."

"Yes . . ."

My mind was whirling like Catherine wheels. I heard myself say stupidly:

"You left your bicycle lamp at the cottage . . ." Inside my brain a voice kept churning out the words. *Alan De Freyne. He's alive . . .*

And if he was alive, then whose body was lying in the thicket grave . . . ?

"I was a fool to come here," he said. "But—well, now there's an end to it all." We looked at each other in silence for a moment. "I'm sorry," he said. "I really am." And then he was turning, and I watched, like someone in a trance, as he left the churchyard, left my sight. Running to the wall I was just in time to see him as, astride his brightly coloured bicycle, he pedalled around the bend in the road. I wanted to shout after him; wanted him to stop, to come back, but I kept silent. After a few moments I walked back to the car.

"Everything okay?" Shelagh asked as I got in beside her. I avoided her gaze.

"Yes, everything's fine." Where was the sense in going after De Freyne? What could it lead to?—only further unanswered questions to add to the tangle of them that already snarled up my mind. And I was through with all that. With all of it. *Through.*

I turned the key in the ignition. "Come on, let's go and see Mr. Pitkin and then get back to the cottage . . ." I put the car into first gear and we drove away.

When I pulled up and switched off outside Pitkin's shop I leaned back, patted my pockets. "I left my cigarettes in the house," I said. "Did you bring any?"

"I smoked the last one while you were there—in the cemetery. Shall I get you some?"

"Thanks." I dug out a handful of loose change and gave some of it to her and she got out of the car and walked away along the street towards the tobacconist's.

I was putting the rest of the coins back into my pocket when I saw that among them was the round piece of metal I had found that day in the garden. There was something familiar about it; I couldn't think what it was.

I still had it in my hand when I went in to see Pitkin. He greeted me warmly as he came towards me. Seeing his limp I reflected briefly on his feelings of guilt he'd been carrying around for most of his life—and said to myself that he, too, in his own way, was another casualty of Gerrard's Hill Cottage.

I apologised for not being there when he'd called; I said we'd had to go out unexpectedly. "Anyway," I said, "if you'd like to fix it up with Jean Timpson she'll let you in. She's got keys to the place. I'll leave word with her that you'll be sending someone to collect the dresser."

"Are you going away so soon?"

"We're leaving Hillingham today."

"And going back to America."

"Yes, tomorrow. We're spending the night in London."

"I'd better write you a cheque now, then," he said. "You tell me how much for . . ."

"No." I shook my head. "You can have the dresser for nothing. You've waited long enough."

His expression of gratitude was almost embarrassing. He kept insisting that I take *something* for the dresser, while I was just as adamant in my refusal. By the time Shelagh came in with my cigarettes though, he'd accepted the gift and was trying to persuade me that we could at least stay and have a cup of tea with him before we dashed off. No, I told him. "Thanks all the same, but we really do have to go . . ." Just to say the words gave me a feeling of relief. In half-an-hour we'd be gone away, forever . . .

In my fingers I had been turning over the piece of metal—and suddenly I realised what it was. I was staring at it when Pitkin's voice came through to me, saying, "You've dropped your buttonhole . . ." and I looked and saw that he was stooping, picking up the white rose that had fallen from my lapel. He stood up straight, put the flower to his nostrils, closing his eyes momentarily as he breathed in the scent. He nodded appreciatively. "A beautiful specimen."

I thanked him and took the flower from his outstretched fingers. He went on speaking but I wasn't really paying attention. I was on the way to the door before I fully realized what he had said, and the significance of it.

I stopped dead in my tracks, slowly turned to face him.

"I'm sorry . . . ? What did you say . . . ?"

And he repeated his words, and he went on talking, and I just stood there, unmoving, letting the words sink in. Then, a moment later I was running outside to the car.

Shelagh had come after me. "No," I said to her, "stay here." I was opening the door, getting in. She looked puzzled into my tight face and began to open the other door. I shouted at her. "No! Shelagh, darling—please! Please stay here!" And I reached across, grabbed the handle and slammed the door shut. I saw her mouth open in bewildered protest, but I couldn't stop to explain. In the mirror, briefly, I had a further glimpse of her as she stood at the kerbside watching while I drove away. I saw how the rising wind flapped her skirt against her legs. In miniature she stood there, a study of amazement, one hand lifted out towards me, fixed, frozen.

32

❧ ❧ ❧

I knew now, at last, the truth.

It had been there before me all the time. All the pieces of the puzzle had been there. I should have realised. I had days ago accepted that fact that the ghost was there, and that, surely, when pitted against our twentieth century demand for scientific logic, had been one of the most difficult factors to come to terms with. Why, then, having negotiated such a major hurdle had I not gone a step further? It would have required only a little more imagination.

But now I had taken that further step. I had been forced to; Pitkin's words came back to me, repeating over and over, and with each echo I was more firmly convinced that now I knew. I knew.

Oh, Colin, how could I have doubted you? How? But no more. And soon I would have proof. Not that I needed that proof. Not to clear Colin's name. *No, Colin, that proof which I shall surely find will put an ending to a story other than your own* . . .

Gravel flew up, spraying, as I turned into the driveway and put on the brakes. I jumped out and went straight to the toolshed. From there I ran to the thicket.

In the clearing I dimly realised that I'd not had a chance to change out of my suit since the trip to London. I was hardly dressed for digging but it couldn't matter less. I threw aside my jacket, rolled up my shirtsleeves, took up the spade and got to work. I worked as if in a fever, sweating like a pig; sweating not only from my exertions, but also from my anticipation and strange, fearful excitement.

I went on digging, methodically throwing up the

earth—far more than I had removed before; that first time I hadn't done enough; maybe if I'd kept on I would have found the answer long before this time.

But I was getting to it now, that answer, and I knelt in the dry, dusty earth, careless of my trousers, and raked and brushed with my hands till I was sure, absolutely sure.

And when I was sure, when I knew there could be no possible mistake, no other possible explanation, I continued to kneel there, while in my mind those twisted tangled threads moved and shifted and became a tapestry, all-telling, so clear, giving me, at last, the whole story . . .

After a while I got to my feet and began to spade the earth back into the hollow. By the time it was done I felt exhausted, though mixed with my fatigue there was elation, great elation; I had the proof I needed.

Yet not *all* my questions were answered. There was still one. How, I asked myself, was it possible for her to have covered up the traces so completely?

I put my jacket on and carried the spade back to the shed. I must get back to Pitkin's shop and collect Shelagh. She would think I was mad, running off like that in that crazy way . . .

At the kitchen sink I washed the soil from my hands. My trousers, I saw, were a job for the cleaners. And still, amongst such mundane preoccupations that same question still kicked. How had she so successfully got rid of the signs that would so easily have proclaimed her guilt? But she *had*—that was a certainty.

I was drying my hands when Jean Timpson came in.

"Oh, I didn't know you were back," she said, and I put on a smile and said, "I'm just going down the road to get Shelagh."

"Your packing's done. Your cases are all ready." She gestured. "They're in the hall."

"Thank you." I nodded vaguely. I was thinking that somehow the answer I sought had something to do with her, Jean Timpson; I saw myself running after her through the orchard, through the gap in the hedge and

down to the water. I remembered how I had plunged in
to bring her up from the bottom of the pond . . .

Yes . . . *Yes* . . .

I hesitated for only moments, then picking up the
towel from where I had dropped it I ran outside again.

Following that same path when I had earlier gone
after her and Reese I hurried across the lawn and
through the orchard gate. I ran past the broken sundial,
through the orchard and then through the gap in the
hedge at the far end. Once, I told myself, the gap would
have been wider, much wider; time had allowed the
brambles to spread, closing the space; but once it would
have been wide enough; it would. Wide enough, too was
the track that led down through the thicket to the edge
of the pond.

When I got to the water I didn't pause at all. I took
off my clothes, everything, and then, quite naked, took
a step down the steep bank and dived in.

This time my view under the water's surface was
clearer; there had been no struggle to stir up the mud. I
knew too what I was looking for and now I headed
straight down, eyes straining to see in the gloomy
depths. Oh, yes, I knew what I was looking for; I had
seen it before, though I hadn't realised what it was . . .

My dive of exploration takes longer to tell of than it
did to do. It took only a few seconds, and in those few
seconds my last question was answered. I found again
the wheel, half-buried in the mud, that had trapped
Jean Timpson in her suicidal jump. And the rest of the
trap was there too, all there. I saw and traced with my
hands the other wheel, the shafts, the main, rotting,
body of the trap, weighted down with the large metal
trunk and the smaller one. There were large stones
wedged in too, ensuring that it could never rise to the
surface. The mud and the thick, grasping weeds had,
over the years, done the rest to keep it hidden.

I'd seen enough. I turned over in the water and
struck out and upwards for the surface.

On the bank I dried myself with the towel, got
dressed and set off back towards the house; not up
through the orchard, though, the way I had come, but

along first by the edge of the pond, then turning so that the orchard was on my left. When I got to the clearing in the thicket I paused for a moment at the spot where Colin had marked out the summer-house, the spot where I'd been so recently digging. I hadn't done too thorough a job of filling it all in again after my work; I could clearly see, beneath a couple of stones, part of the pathetic remnants of Effie's parasol. Her parasol; she'd been so proud of it. Little remained of it now but the ivory handle, a few bits of the ribs and fragments of the discoloured fabric . . . I hooked the stones aside and with the heel of my shoe pressed what was left of the sunshade deeper into the earth . . . next to where Handyman was lying . . .

If I had looked more carefully that first time I would have known. I had been so certain that it was De Freyne's body there; finding his bicycle lamp had convinced me of it. But if I had remembered my lessons in school—and applied a little of that knowledge to what Timpson had told me I wouldn't have been so easily convinced. The roses grew so well, Timpson had said, because of the high acid content of the soil. And that acid in the soil, while it kept at bay the bacteria which would otherwise cause a body to decompose had, at the same time, attacked, by corrosion, the metal of the lamp. The body I had first discovered there had the remains of hair and flesh and clothing, making me assume that it hadn't been there very long, when all the time, over all the years, the acid had been preserving it. That must be it . . . Now, recalling Colin's rambling last letter to me I could see the significance of what *he* had told me. He had written that getting to work on the summer-house had made it all clear to him. It had. He had found the bodies there when he had begun work on the new summer-house for Helen. And obviously, for some reason, he had gone back there at night, using De Freyne's bicycle lamp for light. And he had unintentionally left the lamp there and accidentally covered it up along with the remains . . . But really he had been smarter than I. He had realised at once who lay there. As I had done today so he, earlier, had found the remains of all three bodies there: the animal, the woman and the man. The man with part of his left hand missing . . .

The more I thought about it the more I was aware of all the hints I had had; all the odd bits of knowledge. There had been so many bits of information that didn't gel. Pitkin, for instance, talking to us in the cellar; something he had said then had bothered me. And now it was clear. Bronwen Temple, it was well-known, had been fastidious almost to the point of eccentricity yet when she was found dead—according to Timpson—she had so much dirt and bits of leaves sticking to her clothes, and her clothes themselves were stiff with mud and dried water. And all that was explained now. And I'd even found part of her brooch. Now I really *did* know the whole story . . .

I pictured it all. Like watching a film. I pictured Effie setting out with her parasol and her little tin box, going to the spot, beneath the tree, where she had arranged to meet Handyman. The storm coming on; her growing impatience turning to worry and then, when Handyman still didn't show up, to positive fear.

But in spite of that fear she had been brave enough to go and search for him. She must have done that. And that was when Bronwen had caught her. Had killed her. And by that time, probably, Handyman was already dead. Bronwen had killed her husband rather than let him leave her . . .

Bronwen's task then was to destroy or hide any evidence that would prove that her husband had not left her. And her most difficult job must have been to get rid of the horse and trap in which Handyman and Effie had planned to make their escape. I pictured Bronwen, in the rain, driving the horse and trap through the orchard, through the gap in the hedge and down the wide track to the pond where she unhitched the horse, weighted down the trap and somehow managed to push it down the bank into the deep water. After that she had led the horse up through the thicket to the clearing, and there, during the remaining hours of the morning she had dug the grave next to the summer-house. She must have led the horse into the grave before killing it; that would have been the only way. The bodies of Effie and Handyman would have been manageable.

And how successfully Bronwen had fooled everybody. Her secret had lasted so many years. To this day Pitkin believed that he was responsible for her death. Well, now I could tell him that he was not. Bronwen had not been a murderer's victim. She had been the murderer.

I could see her so clearly in my mind's eye; see her there in the thicket, digging, digging, while the storm raged all around her. I pictured her there when at last her task was done; imagined her standing over the grave, her clothes sodden and mud-spattered, her tired, strained face wearing a look of satisfaction.

But any satisfaction she might have felt hadn't lasted long. The falling tree must have struck her while she was on her way back to the house—perhaps after she had been down to the pond to make a final check. Yes. The tree that had fallen in the storm. It had broken the sundial and it had cracked Bronwen's skull. It was there, where she had been felled by the tree, that she had lost her brooch. Yet even that was not the end of her; she had still managed to crawl back into the house . . .

I took a final look at the area of freshly-turned earth before me, and moved away. As far as I was concerned Handyman and Effie would never be disturbed again.

My main mistake, I said to myself as I walked back towards the house, was in assuming that because Helen's first name was Rose, then she it was who had to be connected with the roses that had appeared on my pillow and in the painting. And of course it was not. It wasn't until Pitkin had handed me the white rose that had fallen from my lapel that I had realised the truth. He had smiled gently at the rose as he placed it in my outstretched hand. "Beautiful . . ." He murmured the word. "Beautiful. Bill Gerrard developed two or three lovely hybrids, but none of them could touch the one he named after his daughter, Bronwen Denise . . ." It was then I knew that it was Bronwen all the time. The white rose was her own, very special emblem. All of it added up with that piece of knowledge—and the remains of her brooch I had found by the broken sundial.

I had blindly attributed everything to Helen; yet there had been indications that it was not she. The alterations to the paintings, for example. That added work was too crude to be *her* work—if I'd realised it at the time.

Poor Helen, I thought. I saw you as the perpetrator of so much evil, when all the time you were just another victim of the spirit of Bronwen; just as Colin was, just as Sad Margaret had been before. I remembered Sad Margaret's sampler with the Keats quotation:

> *And they are gone: ay, ages long ago*
> *These lovers fled away into the storm.*

Margaret Lane had known. Her sampler was stitched in irony—brave irony—before Bronwen had really got to work on her. And when she had, and with a vengeance, poor Margaret hadn't stood a chance. Pitkin had told me that I looked something like John Lane . . . It all added up. Bronwen had wanted *him* and she wouldn't rest until he was hers. Had she actually set fire to the summer-house while Margaret was inside, or had she driven her to do it from madness and despair? It didn't matter how. She had done it, and that was enough. And afterwards John Lane *had* been hers—until smallpox and the lack of any will to live had taken him away.

Then Bronwen had had to wait until Colin came to the cottage. And it was from that time, De Freyne had said, that Helen had been threatened. That's what he had felt. And, I realised now, he had been right. Bronwen had fallen in love with Colin when he came to live with Helen, and from that time Helen's life had been in danger.

I came out under the arch. Hesitating for a moment alongside the sunken garden I looked up at the steep pitch of the roof. Yes, Bronwen had—where Helen was concerned—succeeded in her efforts. Perhaps at the end it hadn't been so difficult. Helen had suffered so much already at Bronwen's hands. I recalled what Reese had said about having to treat Helen for various injuries she had sustained in her work. I couldn't think that Helen was responsible for those injuries; it had to have been Bronwen . . . And then there had been Helen's sleepless nights, her self-portraits mutilated—and her photographs treated in the same way. But she had not seen *them*; Colin had hidden them away. Why? Because he hadn't wanted her to see them? Or perhaps he had thought that Helen herself had done the damage. In which case he must surely have thought she *was* going mad. Yes, Helen had suffered; and in ways I would never know about. How long, I wondered, had he known that Bronwen was responsible? On that last night, though—the last night of Helen's life—he *must* have known about her. And probably poor Helen *was* half-mad by then. Yes. And Colin, beside himself with worry, had asked Elizabeth Barton to come from London. At the last moment he had gone for help. And that was the night it had all ended for Helen. Waiting her chance Bronwen had somehow drawn her out of the house with the belief that the kitten was stuck on the roof. Helen, crazed, had believed it. And climbing up to it she had fallen. Or maybe—*probably*—she'd been pushed. Of course; she'd been pushed just as certainly as Bronwen had driven Colin's car into the beechtree, as certainly as she had torn out his heart. Yes, Bronwen had hurled Helen down to her death on the flower-covered rocks . . .

I turned away, sickened again by the image that sprang into my mind, and moved towards the kitchen door. I must get our luggage and put it into the car. Get away from here. Away from such sad, grotesque images; all those memories of things that showed so clearly the evil purpose that had been in Bronwen's heart. I turned the handle of the door, opened it.

The kitchen was different.

It didn't look any different, but it was. It was the

atmosphere there. It was the welcome that reached out to me; a welcome touched with the scent of roses.

She was still there.

I thought I had banished her. But I hadn't. But there—I had been trying to banish the spirit of *Helen* . . .

Whatever . . . Bronwen was still there. She had not gone. She had never gone. She had merely withdrawn, voluntarily—in order to put me at my ease, *to make me feel safe*. And now she knew that I knew . . . that I knew the truth . . .

The wind had sprung up again and the towel in my hand flapped and billowed out. I stood there with my other hand on the door-handle.

Leave your luggage, a voice in my head was telling me. Leave it. Don't go back inside. Go away from the house *now, forever, but don't let her know that you are going forever* . . .

Yes, yes, I would leave everything there. Don't say a word to anyone. Just leave. Say nothing to Jean Timpson, anyone. Just leave. Bronwen couldn't read my mind. She could hear, she could see, yes, but she couldn't read my mind . . .

I did go inside. I went into the kitchen and hung the towel on the rail. *Move calmly*, I told myself. *No panic* . . .

Jean Timpson came in from the dining-room where I could see she had laid out the things for afternoon tea.

"I made a cake," she said, and I smiled at her and said I could smell it, that it smelled delicious. I couldn't smell any cake; I could only smell the scent of roses. The scent was growing stronger. I said casually:

"I'll just go down and collect Shelagh from the village . . ." *Act naturally. Don't show how afraid you are* . . .Without any show of hurrying I moved back to the door. "See you in a minute," I said as I went outside.

I walked steadily to the car, got in and drove away down the hill. I knew what we had to do. I had to drive with Shelagh straight back to London. We wouldn't stop at the house or anything. Our luggage could stay. Yes.

Our passports were safe at the hotel, as were our tickets and our overnight cases. And I had money. Shelagh might fret that she had lost a few clothes—but she would keep her life and I would keep my freedom, my sanity . . .

I wouldn't even tell her we were going. Not at once. I would lie to her so that she would accept the need for our driving off somewhere else. Only when we were safely out of Bronwen's way would I, *perhaps*, tell her the truth. Anyway, I'd face that problem when it arose.

I pulled up the car outside Pitkin's shop and ran inside. He got up from his old desk and came towards me.

"Where's my wife?" I asked, looking around.

He spread his hands in a gesture of not knowing. "She wouldn't wait any longer. She left."

"Did she walk? She couldn't have done; I didn't pass her on my way here."

"No, Doctor Reese came by. He offered to give her a lift. He said he had to call in at his home first, though." He smiled. "She's only just gone. You'll probably catch her up . . ."

I turned and dashed outside.

33

✧ ✧ ✧

Reese's wife answered the door frowning at my insistent ringing. Her expression cleared when she saw my face, the panic I know I showed there. The doctor had just left, she told me; he'd only stopped to pick up his bag.

"And my wife was with him——?"

"Yes. He was going to drop her off at your house." A piece of newspaper blew against her ankles and she picked it off, raising her voice slightly against the increasing noise of the wind. "Is there anything wrong?"

"No, no, it's all right, thank you."

I left her standing watching me as I ran back to the car.

I drove out of the village with little regard for other motorists or the narrowness of the streets. The wind was really getting up now and the tops of the trees were bending, dipping under the force of the gale. As I turned the car onto Gerrard's Hill the wind buffeted it so that I had to grip hard on the steering wheel.

But I got to the cottage in time. I made it in time. As I rounded the bend I saw Reese's car standing at the cottage gate, and there was Shelagh, next to the car, leaning in through the window. I watched as she straightened up; as Reese's car began to move forward; as Shelagh turned towards the house. I pressed harder on the accelerator and gave a blast on the horn.

With one hand on the gate she looked around. I saw the way the wind whipped up her hair, blowing it across her face. Up ahead Reese's car came to a halt again. I drove on and pulled up just beyond the entrance to the driveway. I wound down the window, put my head out and yelled for Shelagh to come and get in. I had to shout otherwise I wouldn't have been heard over the noise of the wind. She stayed by the gate, waiting for me to get out. I beckoned to her, leaned over and swung open the door on the passenger's side, and the wind promptly took it and slammed it shut again. Leaves and bits of twigs, torn from the surrounding trees and hedges, were hurling past like snowflakes in a snow storm. Shelagh put up a hand, holding the hair out of her eyes and, pressing against the wind, came towards me. She looked puzzled and none too happy. As she came closer I saw her lips moving as she spoke. But I couldn't hear her words.

"What did you say?" I yelled.

She yelled back. "I want to know what's happening. You've got a nerve . . ." The wind was so strong I could barely hear her. I strained my ears to catch her words as she went on: "You left me standing in that shop like a lemon, and now you come blasting your horn at me. What's happening?"

I should have been ready with some story to appease her. *Her and Bronwen.* Bronwen most of all, right now. But I wasn't.

"I've got to go back down to the village," I yelled. It was the best I could think of.

"Well? Have you got to have me with you?" She hadn't got over being left stranded.

" . . . Yes."

"What for?"

" . . . You'll see."

"Oh, come on now." She was in no mood for games.

"Please," I shouted, trying to calm myself inside; the wind wasn't helping, "—please, do as I ask."

"I don't get it . . ." She just stood there next to the car door—which I was fighting to keep from swinging shut. I saw that Reese had got out of his car and was walking towards us. And the last thing I wanted was to get tied up in a conversation with him. I had to get Shelagh into the car and take off. I had to. I forced a smile at her.

"I'm sorry, darling—for leaving you like that." Because of the wind I almost had to deliver each word separately. "Something came up. I'll explain later." I patted the seat beside me. "Come on. Get in, please . . ."

As she still hesitated a shower of broken twigs hurled scattering over the car roof. She moved then, and got in. "Okay," she said, "where are we going? And what's it all about?"

I didn't answer. As she slammed the door Reese came to my window. He was saying something, but I couldn't hear. He tapped on the glass, smiling. I shook my head, turned away from him, released the hand-brake and drove forward a couple of yards. As I glanced into the rear-view mirror I saw the taken aback expression on his face. I didn't dwell on it. I began to reverse into the driveway. Shelagh said, looking at the doctor in surprise and then at me:

"David, what are you thinking of? Are you blind? Couldn't you see Doctor Reese was trying to talk to you?"

I ignored her too. I pulled up sharply, changed to first gear and pressed the accelerator. At that moment I didn't care what Reese thought of my rudeness; I didn't care what Shelagh thought of it either. I just wanted to get us away. I wrenched the wheel round to take the corner back onto Gerrard's Hill . . . and at that moment the cat ran out.

Girlie leapt from among the writhing branches of the hedge right into the path of the car. Shelagh screamed and I jammed on my brakes. The engine stalled. As I struggled, all thumbs, to restart it, she threw open the door and scrambled out. I leaned sideways, reaching to stop her, but my hand clutched only the air. I flung my own door open and leapt out into the wind, which was so strong that I was momentarily knocked off balance and went sprawling across the bonnet.

The cat wasn't dead. As Shelagh moved towards it I saw it get up. Dragging its broken right hind leg, it crawled, mewing piteously, through the fence and into the front garden. Shelagh stopped, standing like a statue, her hands up to her face, staring in shock. Only her hair moved, and her skirt as it flapped against her. Beyond her I saw Jean Timpson appear from the house. She stood on the path, one arm raised, shielding herself from the wind.

Shelagh was crying as her gaze followed the agonising progress of the injured cat. I saw the tears streaming from her eyes, drying on her cheeks. I just caught her words as she cried out hysterically: "Do something! Oh, David, for God's sake, do something!"

I didn't do anything. I just stood there. The little cat appeared in my view again. I saw how her mouth opened and closed with her unheard cries of pain as she slithered through the shrubbery, through the bent and broken poppy stems and onto the pathway. As Shelagh took a sudden step to go after her I reached out and grabbed her arm.

"Stay here! Stay here!"

She tried to shake me off. "David! Let me go!" But I held on tighter and she whirled to face me, her tearful eyes showing horror and disbelief at my callous behaviour. I hardened myself not to give in to her. I held her tighter, leaning to shout into her ear above the howling wind, "Please—get in the car," watching while the kitten crawled by Jean Timpson's feet and into the kitchen. Reese, fighting the gale, came up to us and asked what had happened. "Nothing," I told him, all the time trying to urge Shelagh to get back in the car. Shelagh cried out to him: "It's the kitten. It's hurt." And then to me. "Help it, God damn you. Do something!"

Reese said, "You can't just leave the poor creature if——" and I flung at him, cutting in: "Okay, you're a doctor, *you* do something," and held on to Shelagh while she twisted in my grasp. Raising her fists she beat on my upper arms, my chest, and then with one final, violent movement she was free and running towards the house.

As she got to the door I saw Jean Timpson step into her path, putting up her hands, but Shelagh dodged them, her own arms sweeping, warding off all attempts to hold her. The next instant she had run inside. As I hurried after her Jean Timpson reached out and grabbed my jacket.

"Please—Mr. David . . . don't go in there."

"I *must.*"

"Don't. *She's* in there."

" . . . *She?*"

"The other one."

I stared at her as I shook off her hand.

"You know?"

"For a long time . . ."

"Why didn't you say something?"

"*Who* would have believed *me*? They would have said I—I was mad."

Reese had come up behind us. I heard his voice asking, "What's happening? What the hell's going on?" I didn't answer. Jean Timpson's hand came again to restrain me but I brushed it aside. "Let me get by, Jean . . ."

She shook her head. "Let *me* go in."

"You?"

"Yes. She's got nothing against me. If she'd ever wanted to hurt me she could have done it long before this time."

"You were never a threat to her," I said. "You never got in the way of what she wanted."

At my words she only moved closer into the doorway. "Let me go in," she pleaded. "You mustn't. If you do you—you might never get out again." As close as we stood I had to strain to hear her. The wind just snatched up her words, ripping them away, flinging them into the eye of the gale. Now she turned from me and yelled into the kitchen:

"I'm coming in. I'm coming in to get her. You must—you must let her go."

She turned back to face me, framed in the doorway, her hair flying. Her pink ribbon had come adrift and even as I watched it blew straight out like a streamer and was torn free, to go twisting and turning away with the leaves, grasses and flowers that went whirling by. Against her legs the wind whipped her skirt, showing the shape of them. Over on the edge of the orchard one of the laden apple-trees gave up the struggle and a heavy branch fell, split cleanly from the trunk. On the garage roof one of Timpson's new slates shifted on the pile and crashed down onto the concrete. Others followed it. One of them I saw lifted up as easily as if it were no lighter than a piece of card. In a shower of leaves and spinning gravel it came whirling, whistling by and I watched it rise up, high on the crest of the gale, saw it tossed into the air, higher, higher, then saw it turn, slowly, over and over, and then faster, faster, faster, till its shape was no longer discernible. Up it went, spinning like a disc, skimming over our heads and away, out of sight.

Jean Timpson glanced back into the house, at the same time warding off my hands as I tried to move by her. Then she turned back, one last time, to face me again.

"Please, Mr. David . . . I shall be all right." She gave me a brave little smile, direct into my eyes. "Really I will."

And as she spoke the last word the whirling, spinning blur of grey came screaming, louder than the wind, over the rooftop.

Instinctively I ducked, seeing in the same moment how Jean Timpson raised her hand to protect herself, how she whirled around, turning to face away from the danger. The little cry of fear she gave was cut off as the hard edge of the slate struck the back of her skull, splitting it as a knife will split an apple.

37

❧ ❧ ❧

Blood spurted as she jack-knifed, limbs jerking like a marionette's. Her back arched and her arms flung out sideways, stiff fingers striking the edge of the doorway. Just one more sound she made, short, guttural. For a split second she seemed to hang there, a grotesque, unco-ordinated doll, and then she pitched forward, through the doorway onto the kitchen floor.

The wind had taken the spurt of her blood and sent it in a spray that speckled the wall and drenched Reese's jacket. I could feel it too on my raised hands, taste it on my mouth . . .

I left her in a widening pool of blood while Reese bent over her and tried, hopelessly, to help her. He couldn't help her. No one could do anything for her, that much was clear. She was quite dead. Poor Jean; she had tried so hard to keep me out, but there I was after all, inside the house.

I ran through the dining-room, to the living-room and then back to the hall. Even here, inside, the sound of the wind was deafening. And now there was rain, too, and it dashed itself against the panes so hard that I felt they'd never withstand the onslaught. As I went up the stairs I could sense Bronwen's presence more strongly than ever before. Looking in on Colin and Helen's room I saw white roses on the pillows. Oh, yes, Bronwen was there all right. She had *never* gone. I was a fool to have thought I could banish her so easily; if I *had* banished a ghost then it certainly hadn't been hers. No, she had just used her guile to keep me here. Well, I was here, but she wouldn't keep me. And she wouldn't keep Shelagh, either.

"Shelagh . . . !"

I kept calling her name as I ran from one room to another. No sign of her anywhere, and I turned and hurried downstairs again, all the time breathing in the rose scent and feeling that I might choke on my fear.

As I got to the foot of the stairs Reese came into the hall, a terrible spectacle in his blood-reddened clothes. He looked dazed and totally unaware of what was happening.

"I tried to phone for an ambulance," he said, "but your phone's out of order . . ."

"Help me find Shelagh!" I shouted at him. "Help me!" And then, immediately following my words I heard, faintly in the storm's sudden lull, Shelagh's voice coming from beyond the closed cellar door.

I turned the handle of the door but I couldn't open it. It wasn't locked; it was just stuck. Bronwen again. I called out to Shelagh, "Don't worry, I'll get you out," trying to force calm into my words, then turned and dashed away, out of the house and into the renewed howling power of the driving wind and rain. Although it was still afternoon the sky was dark with heavy clouds that raced by, their shapes twisting, writhing, changing by the moment. I headed for the toolshed, pressing myself against the wind, forcing my way through, while the rain hit my skin like needles. I saw that one of the elms had fallen, crashing through the flimsy orchard fence, and now lay partly across the lawn, partly among the broken fruit-trees. I was reminded again of that other night of storm, when Effie had stood under her parasol, pathetically seeking shelter while she waited for Handyman. But Handyman had never turned up and Effie, going to look for him, had met Bronwen. Bronwen who, hours later, had been struck down by the storm as if by some divine judgement. But by that time it had been too late; Effie and Handyman were beyond saving.

Not so Shelagh. I would save Shelagh. I *would*.

As I ripped open the door of the toolshed the wind tore it from my grasp and flung it back, wrenching it from its upper hinges with a cracking, splitting sound, so that it banged rhythmically, crazily against the side of the shed. I went in, stumbling over the spade, the balls and hoops of the croquet set to the tool rack where I grabbed an axe and a crow-bar.

The wind was behind me as I ran back over the lawn and I was driven before it in a steady pelting shower of driving rain and bits of flying debris. I reached the house and in the kitchen doorway I hesitated, took a deep breath and stepped again over Jean Timpson's body and the pool of blood. Moving to the dresser I ripped open a drawer, grabbed the torch and flicked the switch. Thank God—it worked. In the hall I found Reese rattling and pulling at the cellar door's handle. I pushed him aside, yelled out to Shelagh to stand clear and then let fly with the axe.

It was a stout door, but my fear gave me strength and after a succession of heavy blows I had it open.

The cellar light was *on*—that light that had never worked for me. It was on. Bronwen again? And there in the cold light cast by the single naked bulb I saw Sheagh as she crouched at the foot of the steps, the little injured cat in her arms.

"David . . .!"

She was safe.

Scared and pale-faced she runs up the steps towards me. I see tears in her eyes.

"The door just—just slammed behind me," she cries.

I take a step towards her, holding out my arms. In my head my voice is saying, *You can't do do anything to her now, Bronwen—not as you did to Effie—not as you did to Sad Margaret—not as you did to Helen, and Colin . . .*

"Shelagh . . . Shelagh . . ." I reach out, down, grasping her shoulder, bringing her up to me. To safety.

I've told myself I can't move from this spot until the little spider completes the job he—albeit unwittingly—started. He did the *H*, the *E* and the *L* and then-just went to sleep. That's no good; I have to get home. If I'm not back she'll start to wonder about me. But I can't go yet; not while the spider stays so motionless in the crease of the *L*.

I search around my feet and find a small twig. Gently I prod the spider with it. It moves, a quick darting little run covering about two inches. I guide it—or try to—very carefully. It must touch every letter, only then can I go . . . One more little prod . . . I'm impatient—and too rough and now I've hurt one of its legs. But I keep on and it moves again, although its progress is slow. *Carefully now . . . Careful . . .* It takes great care, an operation like this . . .

As it moves slowly, slowly over the stone its injured leg trails . . .

Looking round I see her there waiting for me on the other side of the wall. I don't know why I was worrying about getting back late to the cottage; she knows I won't be far away.

Her smile, I see, has a touch of sadness, a little disapproval in it; she doesn't like me coming here, I know. But one more minute and I'll be ready. Just let this little spider do his job and then we'll go home together. Home. Together. We'll walk home together through the village. I know what it will be like as we go through the village. There'll be silence. No one will speak to us. They never do. We have no friends here now. No one. Pitkin has never called and Timpson, it seems, never stirs from his house any more. And Reese?—oh, he moved away, quite a while ago.

Perhaps Shelagh's hold on the cat was too tight. Perhaps her sudden movement up the steps jarred its shattered leg. My fingers had just closed around her shoulder when the cat gave a piercing cry of pain and twisted, squirming in her arms. Shelagh faltered in her stride, bending her head to the animal, and I watched as it lashed out, hooked her in the eye and then dragged its razor claws down across her cheek.

With a shriek she let the cat go and clutched at her face. But Girlie didn't fall. She hung on, clinging, claws deep in Shelagh's breast and when Shelagh, screaming, tried to free herself, the cat snarled, spat and clawed her again. Bounding down the two steps that separated us I snatched the cat away. But I was too late. Shelagh, in an effort to escape the pain, stepped sideways, and stepped too far.

Her hand came away from her blood-filled eye socket, reaching out for me. For an instant our hands brushed, and then she had gone over the edge of the staircase.

In the moment it took me to get down the steps I swung the cat—a snarling, spitting, ferocious shape of black fur—back to my arm's length and hurled it with all my force at the far wall. It struck the plaster-covered bricks with a thud and fell onto a pile of old books.

I clambered over a chest, skirted the Welsh dresser and hurried to Shelagh. I found her half-lying, half-kneeling over an old wooden box. But she hadn't fallen very far, only a few feet, and I didn't think she could be seriously hurt.

"Oh, my darling!" I heard myself saying. I saw pain in her face and it brought tears springing to my eyes. Quickly grabbing her by the shoulders I started to lift her up. And as I did so her head snapped back and she let out a scream that made my heart turn over.

"N-o-o-o!" she shrieked. "Oh, God! . . . Don't . . . *Don't! No-o-o-o!"*

There was something digging into her chest. Something that had been left in the box. Some kind of stake . . . And then I recognised the brightly coloured bands of the croquet finishing post. It was upside-down, the sharp end piercing her chest.

I yelled out to Reese as he ran down the steps. *"For Christ's sake, hurry up. Come and help me!"* I couldn't bear to look at the agony in her face, so white, or the blood in her eye or on her cheek where the cat had torn her. Her knuckles were white with the strain of attempting to support herself; she was trying to prevent herself from sinking down and being impaled even deeper. I saw that the colours of the croquet finishing-post were changing; now her blood ran down it, red, red, and her desperate, terrified breathing rasped in my ear; the pain, the fear of death was there in her voice as she cried piteously,

"Oh, David . . . Oh, David . . . please . . . help me . . . Help me . . . David . . . David . . . David . . . David . . ." Her voice went on, speaking my name over and over, and then, her eyes rolling, she said: "*I saw her*. I saw her. She was down here with me, in the cellar. I saw her. Oh, please . . . don't let her kill me . . . please . . . David . . . David . . . David . . . David . . ."

"You'll be all right, darling." What real comfort could I give her. I had no idea what to do. I could hardly speak.

But then Reese was there, bending, kneeling beside us. "Take her weight," he rapped out. "Support her." And he leaned lower, making a swift examination. His head came up and he looked at me over Shelagh's hunched shoulders. The look on his face gave me such a feeling of relief. He said: "I think she's going to be all right. I don't think it's in very deep. Not deep enough to do any real damage, anyway." His hands moved down and groped in the box. "This thing's wedged somehow. We'll have to free it and then ease her up." He spoke then to Shelagh. "We've got to get you free first of all. It'll hurt, but you *will* be all right." He gave her a shaky smile. "Okay?"

She gave the slightest nod. "Yes," she breathed.

And then the light went out.

"Quick!" I said to Reese. "The torch! Get the torch! It's at the top of the stairs. I've got her. *Hurry!*"

It was pitch-dark there now. I heard the sound of his feet as he got up and began to make his way back to the steps. And in the dark, crouching there, I became aware of the perfume. The scent of roses was all around us, stronger than the scent of the musty old books and clothes. Bronwen was close. So close. Watching. Waiting. I shouted to Reese again.

"Hurry! Hurry!"

And all at once I heard a different sound. Beginning faintly, it increased in volume so that I became aware that it had been going on for a few seconds. It became louder than Shelagh's moans, louder than my own breathing, louder than Reese's feet on the stairs. Something nearby was moving, rocking. Something heavy. The sound came from in front of me where the old Welsh dresser stood. It was the dresser that was making the noise. I leaned forward, stretching, reaching out with my left hand. The dresser was moving. It rocked against my fingers. Bronwen's Welsh dresser. Rocking back and forth as if under the power of some unseen hand.

"*Quick! Hurry!*" I screamed the words at Reese. Turning back to Shelagh I said, "Hold on, darling," and took away my right hand with which I'd been helping to support her. As I did so she gave a moan. The sound tore at me but I had to shut my ears to it. I leapt to my feet and in the pitch-darkness put my shoulder against the great piece furniture. As I did so a beam of light struck the wall by the stairs, then circled down, bathing me in it, and the next second Reese was there, holding the torch, dashing down the steps.

"*Help me—!*" The dresser was moving furiously now, rocking, rocking, rocking, gathering momentum, moving faster and further, so that the arc of its swing was getting wider every moment. I couldn't hold it alone; it was far, far too heavy. I yelled again to Reese and he scrambled to the other side of it and threw his own weight against it in an effort to keep it upright. I saw the torch fall from his straining fingers, saw the light go out . . .

Desperately we clung on, pressing with all our might. But there was nothing we could do. The dresser teetered on the edge of balance, gave a final lurch and crashed forward.

The scream Shelagh gave as it hit her made my blood
run cold, ice-cold.

We couldn't lift the dresser. We tried, but we
couldn't.

And then, even as we struggled there in the rose-
scented dark the back of the dresser was struck a heavy
blow that jarred our fingers and rang in our ears. Bang,
bang. The blows went on. Bang, bang, bang, *bang,
bang* . . . making jokes of our strength. Each blow
forcing Shelagh down, hammering her down, impaling
her body more firmly on the pointed stake. Ensuring
that she would never, never get up.

When the light went on again I realised that all the
noise had ceased. In my ears I could still hear the terrible sound of Shelagh's cries; but they were only echoes;
she was quite silent now. Now there was only the sound
of our breathing, Reese's and mine.

Shelagh was completely hidden from our sight. Only
her blood showed as it ran from beneath the dresser and
collected in a widening pool on the cellar floor.

The spider is really moving now. With a little help
from me he practically scuttles back over the letters. I
stop him and he starts again—this time at the *beginning*
of her name. With a little prod from my twig he covers
her name in one fast, simple little run: *S-H-E-L-A-G*
he spells, and finally settles in the cut of the last *H*.

Now I can go. I stand up, brush bits of grass from my
sleeve. I won't bother leaving by the gates; I'll go by
way of the wall. On top of the wall I pause. I sit astride
the old grey stones and look back on the graves. Shelagh, Colin, Helen . . . they're all gone now . . .

But I'm not alone. No. Bronwen comes towards me.
In a minute she will take my arm and we'll go home
together. Home. I'll have a little drink. Try to relax.
We'll be together, undisturbed. *That* we can rely on.

A question nags. I ought to do something—about the
future. But what? I ought to try to find a job of some
kind somewhere. Helen's money won't last forever. But
that's something I can think about. Later on. Give the
matter some real thought. It'll be good to have some-

thing positive to think about. I need something positive otherwise I just get landed with memories all the time.

Oh, Shelagh, Shelagh . . .

I mustn't think of you, Shelagh—not as you were when I last saw you—when Reese and I and the men lifted the dresser. I must think of you as you were at other times. I shall concentrate on other images; I shall see you under the flowered arch in your yellow dress as we set off for our wedding; see you beside the river lifting your beer glass; in the garden with the sun so bright on your hair. In the highlights your hair shone red, did you know that . . . ? Oh, Shelagh, I am not, shall not be, faithless to your memory. I loved only you.

But you are gone. And now there is only Bronwen. She loves me.

Do *I* love?

No. No. But I have no one else.

Though what of my father?

A good question. What, indeed of my father . . . No, I have no one now. Only Bronwen. She offers me love. Of a kind. And it will do—until I grow too tired.

When that will be I have no idea. But until it happens we shall stay together. She won't ever leave, and I have nowhere else to go. And after all, as I said, she loves me. And that's half the battle. It's so important to be loved, to be needed.

But still, you ask, *how could* I stay with her after the horror that has been? It is something I have often asked myself—though much less frequently of late. The horror *does* recede as it becomes more and more a part of the past, believe it; even the most shocking events will cease to shock when seen repeatedly—as they have been in my mind.

And on those occasions when the past does loom up and threaten to swamp me, and I lie in bed while the pictures and the voices churn round in my head, then she, Bronwen, will come to me, and touch me. And I let go then. Completely. I hold back no longer. I can do nothing else when she is with me. And letting go, I let go, too, of the waking nightmares. Soon they dissolve into the past, where they belong.

SPECIAL
SNEAK PREVIEW FOLLOWS!

THE REAPING

BY BERNARD TAYLOR

1

When I found myself staring into the darkness and realized that I'd been dreaming again my sense of relief was indescribable. I lay there in the dark, drenched in sweat and waiting for my heartbeat to slow its pace.

The dream had been much like all the others: the same theme. I had seen so clearly again the faces of the people, the house, the tower, and the familiar grounds. This time, though, I'd been completely hemmed in by the shrubbery and the undergrowth—so thick I could hardly move. And then, quite suddenly, it had all changed and I was running up those steps, round and round and round, seeing no end in sight and feeling as if my legs were churning through treacle.

Some parts, granted, are fantasy. But not all. And anyway the events behind the dreams—the cause of them —are real enough.

Too real for comfort—*still*. But perhaps, I tell myself, the fault lies within *me*, in my refusal to face up to it. Maybe if I faced it all squarely in the day I wouldn't be so plagued during the night—when I'm off my guard. Is that, then, part of the answer?—to talk about it? But where would I start?—it's only in literary, *created* dramas that stories have beginnings. . . .

Though I could use almost anything as a cue. I could, perhaps, begin with one of those times when Ilona was away from London—and choose a particular day of her absence. Yes . . . I'd go back to that day last June—to the day I got her second postcard.

Not that there was anything special about the postcard—there wasn't. It showed a picture of the Arc de Triomphe. The first, a week previously, had shown a view of the Plomb du Cantal in the Auvergne. On the back of both cards Ilona had crammed an enormous number of words into the available space, but for all she'd written very little had been said—and nothing I was really interested in reading. All right, I thought, maybe it *was* hell getting to a phone when she needed one, but at least she might have written a proper letter. But no—just the two postcards. Two in almost three weeks. It hadn't always been like that.

She worked as a make-up artist. Employed on a freelance basis and good at her job she seemed to be forever going off in connection with some film or television production or other. She complained about it often, decrying its disruptive effect on her social life, but nevertheless I was quite sure she derived a great deal of satisfaction from it.

My own feelings about it were unequivocal. Hardly surprising; sometimes many weeks would go by when I'd rarely see her, and of late when she'd been away the contact between us was next to useless. The postcards were an example.

But, I said to myself, I suppose even a postcard was better than nothing at all: at least I could be glad I'd got *that*. It hadn't made me glad, though; it had disappointed me, and my disappointment had hung around. I know it stayed with me for a good part of that Monday.

Disappointment or not, though, I had things to do, and as soon as five-thirty arrived I was at the shop's glass-panelled door and turning the sign so that the *Closed* side looked out onto the pavement. Then I turned and started to give a hand with the last-minute jobs, taking up a duster and wiping it over the counters. Arthur, my senior assistant, was cashing-up at the till while over to one side Alice bent her round body to straighten the stacks of cartridge paper and mounting-card. Brian, looking even more eager than I to escape, hurried into the yard at the back with the accumulated waste paper while Sharon, the youngest, busied herself with the display boxes of paints, brushes and pencils.

The business part of the shop's premises was large, comprising not only the very wide area on the ground floor but also a spacious basement where Enid and Margaret, two other assistants, sold gifts and prints. I employed six people in the shop itself, and one more in the picture-framing workshop half a mile away. I'd worked hard over the years to bring the whole thing to its present state, and as small businesses went it was a successful and profitable one. I didn't, though, regard it with unadulterated pleasure. . . .

Now, all the jobs finished, I unlocked the door and stood aside as everyone trooped out into the sun. I myself left only minutes after them; not to go far, though, but just to let myself through the adjacent door and climb the stairs to the first-floor flat above the shop.

There in my studio I lit a cigarette and surveyed the stacked canvases, and all the paintings, sketches and photographs that hung from the walls. Tomorrow would see the selecting of paintings for the forthcoming exhibition at the newly-built local theatre, and today was the last chance to submit them to the panel. It was at Ilona's suggestion that I'd decided to participate. I realized that I felt an odd little sense of excitement; it had been years since I'd shown anything of my work.

I moved to where four framed canvases stood separately to one side. I turned them around, lined them up against the wall, sat down in the old carver and studied them. There was a landscape, two still-lifes and a self-portrait.

The self-portrait was the most recent of the paintings; I'd only completed it over the weekend. In it I was wearing a favourite old green sweater that had seen better days a long time ago. Its colour made a good contrast with the pale blue-grey of the background. My portrayal of myself was, I thought, a truthful one. There, very accurately, was my thick dark hair—a bit ragged and curling around the ears—and the ears themselves sticking out a bit too much for comfort. There too was the curved, too-large nose and the long, angular jaw. It wasn't, I had to admit, a face I'd have chosen to paint, but it was, nevertheless, one that had the singular advantage of always being available.

I studied the pictures for a long time. There was nothing more I could do to them at this stage, though, I thought—except maybe add a little retouching varnish. . . .

* * *

By six-fifteen I was on my way home, walking briskly the three hundred yards to Lansbury Crescent.

Letting myself in at the front door of the large detached house near the crescent's centre I was greeted by the sound of Em's transistor radio in the kitchen. 'Hello-o-o,' I called out to her and her voice, like an echo over the music, came back to me in reply. I heard, too, movement on the landing above, and as I set down my briefcase Simeon came down the stairs, his shy smile wide and welcoming. When he was close enough I leaned down and placed my hands on his slim shoulders.

'So how have you been doing today?' I asked.

'All right, thanks.'

'Where's your sister? Is she in?'

'No, she's out. Why—were you going to play tennis?'

'Not today. She's supposed to be coming with me to help me with my pictures.'

'Oh . . .' He stepped past me and crossed the hall to the kitchen. 'Aunt Em,' he said, '—where's Julia?'

'Having tea with her friend Joanna.' Following the sound of Em's voice the radio accompaniment of Neil Diamond faded and she appeared in the doorway. 'She won't forget,' she said. 'She'll be here any minute, I'm sure.' Then she added: 'I'm just making some tea. You go and sit down and I'll bring it in.'

As Simeon followed me into the sitting room he said: 'I expect they're discussing their holiday.'

'Yes,' I said, 'I expect so.' I sat down in my armchair, pushed off my shoes and stretched out my legs. Simeon leant against the chair-arm and smiled up into my face. In his blue, blue eyes I could see his mother—so clearly.

'Aunt Em and I have been discussing *our* holiday,' he said.

'Oh, yes?'

'Yes. She says the ponies are wild and that they come into the villages and just wander all round the streets.'

'So I've read.'

His coming holiday in the New Forest with Em and her friend Ivor was very much on his mind. That particular time was in my own thoughts too, for over part of that same period I was going to be in Devon with Ilona.

It had been Ilona's idea. When an invitation had come from the parents of Julia's friend for her to go to Cornwall with them, and at the same time the twins were invited to stay in York with their cousins I'd suddenly found myself presented with two weeks of relative freedom. Ilona, seeing me divested of most of my responsibilities for that time had suggested that maybe she and I could go away together somewhere. I'd jumped at the idea—though we'd have to take Simeon with us, I said. At this point, however, Em had stepped in. Perhaps she and Ivor could take Simeon away with them, she said—which would then allow Ilona and me to be completely on our own for a while. Besides, she'd added, Ivor's son was close in age to Simeon, so they'd be good company for one another. And so it was agreed, and we'd gone ahead and made our various arrangements. Em and Ivor had found a cottage in Brockenhurst for a fortnight and I had booked a week at a hotel in Sidmouth. Ilona's schedule, she had told me, wouldn't allow her to take longer than that—but that didn't matter. We'd have a week of total relaxation; a week of walking, reading, swimming and tennis; a week when we'd be alone together, just the two of us. I blessed Em for her generosity and her understanding. She had known how important it was to me, that Ilona and I get some real opportunity to be by ourselves and sort everything out.

Now Simeon said: 'Aunt Em says the New Forest is a super place. Don't you wish you were coming with us, Dad?'

'There'll be other times,' I said. 'Maybe next year.'

'Next year . . .' he repeated, and then: 'Julia says that next year she might go away to boarding school like Mike and Chris.'

'She's too young,' I said. 'She's not eleven yet.'

'Will I go when I'm older?'

'Do you want to?'

'I don't know. Is it nice?'

The conversation was developing into the familiar question-and-answer pattern which I always felt was his means of keeping a close contact. It ended with Em bringing in the tea.

Over the rim of the cup I looked at my sister as she settled back against the cushions of the sofa. I don't know how I would have managed without Em. Years ago, following her divorce, she had come to work for me in the shop, living in the flat above it. But then, after the death of Elizabeth, my wife, she had moved into the house with me and the children, quietly taking over so many of the responsibilities that had been left unclaimed. Not long afterwards—and so willingly at my suggestion —she had given up the shop altogether.

Now where the children were concerned there was no doubt at all that Em was there to stay; they treated her as much of a fixture as they treated each other and me. We knew, though, Em and I, that the situation could change. It *was* changing. Just before Christmas Em had met Ivor, a gentle, grey-haired assistant bank-manager from Croydon, and their attachment had been steadily growing. And months before that, of course, I had met Ilona. Now both Em and I were having to reconsider the patterns of our existence. Change for both of us could be on the cards. We might remarry. Though I had to admit that of the two relationships Em's was running by far the more smoothly.

She now sat trying to re-attach a loose wheel to a small space-age car of Simeon's while he stood at her elbow intently watching.

She was forty-nine—six years older than I. She didn't look her age, though, I thought. Her body might have thickened somewhat but her hair was still rich and dark, her hazel eyes still youthful and clear. Above all, though, her attractiveness for me came from her warmth; a softness and gentleness that had always been so much a part of her; yet qualities born of strength; she had proved that often enough over the years. I could only applaud the widowed assistant bank-manager's taste.

'There . . .' she handed the repaired car back to Simeon and he knelt and tested it on the carpet. 'And the next time it goes wrong ask your father to fix it,' she added. 'He gets out of too much by insisting that he's useless at anything mechanical.'

As Simeon wandered away out of the room Em asked me whether my pictures were ready to be taken to the theatre. I told her they were. Then she asked whether I knew yet when Ilona was returning from France.

'I should think it would be another week yet,' I said. 'I just wish she'd give the bloody job up. It's such a fly-by-night kind of existence, isn't it? Here today and gone tomorrow. I can't even *begin* to understand its attractions. Or even that whole scene—everything connected with the film and television industry. It all seems just too far removed from—reality.'

'Only to you,' Em said, '—but that's just *because* you're not interested.'

I shook my head. 'I never have been. That's why we hardly ever talk about it. I just can't—relate to it.'

'So what would you like her to do instead?'

'Who knows . . . I suppose it makes as much sense as anything else—in the long run. I suppose I get mad because of what it does—keeping her moving around all the time.'

There was a little silence then Em said:

'How do you feel about things?—are they going any better?'

I thought about it for a moment. 'I can't really tell,' I said. I told her about the picture-postcard I'd received that morning, my disappointment. 'Perhaps I'm expecting too much. . . .'

'I'm sure it'll work out all right,' she said.

'I hope so. Things certainly can't stay as they are.'

My relationship with Ilona seemed to have no *stillness* about it. It seemed to be moving all the time—and I didn't like to think about the direction it might be taking. Our coming holiday together, I felt sure, would be the turning point; everything would be made clear then. . . .

Em, as if reading my thoughts, said: 'You wait until the two of you get away together on your own. You'll get things sorted out then.'

Yes. It would be a make-or-break time, I was certain.

But even so, there were two months to go before then; anything could happen in that time.

2

Soon after Julia arrived home we had dinner and afterwards I got the Citroën out of the garage. With Julia sitting beside me I drove up to the High Road and parked around the corner, not far from the shop. Up in the studio I briefly surveyed the pictures once more and then picked up the two smaller ones, the still-lifes. I'd pack them together, I decided.

Julia, having spoken a little of her forthcoming holiday with her friend, went on to give me a run-down on her friend's record collection; it seemed to be made up of stuff by groups with strange-sounding names I'd never even heard of. I realized just how quickly now she was growing up.

A tall girl for her age, her hair was as fair as Simeon's and fell down loose and flowing past her shoulders. The effect was not as neat as with the plaits she'd worn till lately, but in her own eyes it was a vast improvement on such a style. She had the same blue eyes as her mother, but her bone structure owed much to the Rigby side of the family. On her, though, I was glad to see, it emerged—as with Simeon—with a promise of refinement.

Now as I wrapped the paintings she wandered around the studio (it had once been Em's sitting room) peering into the various jars and tins, and studying the pictures that crowded the space. Practically the only other times she had been there were on those occasions when she'd sat for me. She'd proved to be one of the most restless of models, though, so those occasions had been few.

'Mummy. . . .'

I heard her say the word in a small, surprised little voice. Looking around I saw her crouching, a couple of canvases leaning against her knee. Her eyes were fixed on one that leant against the wall in front of her. It was one that had come from several batches of old works that I'd kept tied in bundles and shelved, unlooked-at, for several years. It was only recently that, out of curiosity, I had taken two or three of the bundles down, dusted them off and glanced through them.

I watched now as Julia leaned forward, her blonde hair hanging down like a curtain, hiding her face. She was the one of all my children who constantly filled me with surprise—because she was female, I supposed. Who would have thought that I should have had only one daughter among so many sons? But there, we Rigbys had always sired more male children.

Putting the picture-wrapping aside I went over to her and looked down past her head at the portrait of Elizabeth. It was not by any means a good painting, but nevertheless there she was. There was the smooth cheek and the blue eyes, their expression hinting at the warmth and humour that had always marked them in life; there too was the thick fair hair, so like that of her daughter who now gazed at her image.

My glance went back to Julia. I could see her face now, but I detected no sign of distress. She was quiet, subdued, yes, but she didn't seem inordinately moved. A sign, I thought, that she was over the tragedy. And it had been that. I could remember only too clearly the effect it had had upon myself; how it had affected my children I could only guess at. . . .

'She looks so . . . young,' Julia said, and then: 'Daddy, I've never seen this picture of her before.'

'No. She was *very* young then. It's an old painting. Done before you were born. I only recently came across it. All those there—' I indicated the many other pictures stacked in groups, 'are old ones. From my student days. They've been packed away for ages.' I hovered above her for a while longer and then moved back to get on with my work. A few seconds later her voice came again.

'Who's this?'

This was a picture I had forgotten had even existed. Recognizing it I moved closer. It was of a slightly younger woman, no more than in her early twenties. She wore a white blouse and blue jeans and had long red hair and green eyes. I found myself gazing at the portrait in a kind of awe.

'Where did you find it?' I asked.

'It was here—in another bundle at the back. Who is she?'

'Just a girl I used to know. A long time ago.'

'Where?'

'Where? In Brighton as I recall. Yes—Brighton.'

'We've been there—Brighton. What's her name?'

'. . . Rosalind.'

'That's a nice name. Rosalind what?'

After a moment's thought I had to admit that I couldn't remember. Julia then said:

'Did you know her before you knew Mummy?'

'Yes, some time before.'

'And wouldn't she marry you—Rosalind?'

'Marry me?' I grinned. 'The question never came up.'

'Didn't you want to marry *her*?'

All the questions. 'It never occurred to me. We didn't know each other for very long.'

'Where is she now?'

'I have no idea.' I glanced at my watch. 'Hey, we'd better get a move on or we'll never get to the theatre in time.'

As I started to turn away she asked:

'Are you going to marry Ilona?'

So was that what all the questions about marriage had been leading up to? She'd had no real interest at all in the long-departed Rosalind; the focus all along had been on Ilona. I realized I wasn't prepared for the question. Instead of answering, I said:

'Do you like Ilona?'

'Oh, yes, she's a lot of fun.' She paused for a moment then asked again: 'Do you think you'll marry her?'

I supposed that a preoccupation with marriage and love could be a part of her growing up, of her increasing awareness. The question now, though, was too close.

'I'll have to give it some thought,' I said and turned back to the task of packing the pictures.

When I'd secured the last knot I handed her the smallest of the three packages, flicked off the lights and followed her down the stairs and out into the street.

* * *

On Thursday morning I received a card from the chairman of the exhibition committee telling me that all four of my paintings had been accepted and would form part of the exhibition that was to open on the following Saturday. When Saturday came I left the shop in the afternoon and went along to see what the show—and my paintings—looked like. There, surrounded by the other viewers I stood in the foyer of the new theatre and looked around me.

The pictures had been hung on the walls and on screens, and whoever had done the hanging hadn't had much idea or experience. Far too many pictures had been displayed and they'd been packed into the available space with too little room between them and too little thought as to the general appearance.

Looking at my own pictures my spirits were not lifted in any way either. Apart from being as hemmed in as were the rest of the works there my paintings appeared to have been given the worst possible place in the whole show. There was so much light reflecting from the canvases that it was necessary to stand to one side and look at them from an oblique angle to get even a half-reasonable idea of what they were like.

My greatest disappointment, though, came from the company in which my pictures were hung.

The space on the right of the area allotted to mine boasted a still-life of a misshapen jug and two bilious-looking apples with white, glistening highlights. Below that was a badly composed landscape replete with purple shadows and trees that defied specification. Over on the left were two truly horrendous portraits. The rest of the stuff on display was, on the whole, no better.

I left and went back to the shop.

Later, when I'd closed up and the others had all gone I sat on a stool at one of the counters and looked around me.

Was this, here, I asked myself, what I had studied for? Was this what my parents had worked and saved for?—to send me, their youngest son, to art school so that I could end up serving in a shop? All that promise I'd shown, leading to my years at the Slade; what did it count for now?

When I'd married Elizabeth I'd been so full of plans

as to how I'd provide a good life through my work as a painter. But it hadn't happened. Almost at once she had become pregnant and the time for risks was over. So, scraping together what capital we could, we had bought the shop. It was meant to be only a temporary measure; after a time, I was determined, I'd get back to my *real* work. But that hadn't happened either. The other children had come along while at the same time the shop went from strength to strength, developing into the very profitable concern it now was and bringing in an income that allowed me to run a large, comfortable home and send my children to decent schools. While that had happened the artistic ambitions I'd nursed were relegated to the sidelines. I'd still kept the dream, though. *Someday*, I would tell myself . . . *someday.* . . .

But now, I realized, it was too late. That someday had come and gone. My visit to the art exhibition had made me aware of that. I'd missed out and now it was too late to do anything about it.

I mentally shook myself. I had too many responsibilities for the luxury of self-pity, and besides, it had all come down to a matter of *my choice*—and I'd long since opted to keep to the *safe* way. I had some nerve, I thought, questioning Ilona's choice of career.

*   *   *

Ilona telephoned me that evening.

Beyond the sound of her low, clear voice I could hear music and the clamour of laughter and talking. She was calling, she said, from a small café just outside of Boulogne.

'How did it go?' she asked.

'How did what go?'

'You'll have to speak up,' she said, '—there's such a noise in here.'

I said: How did *what* go?'

'The *exhibition*. It opened today, didn't it? They did show some of your paintings, didn't they?'

'Yes, they showed them.'

'—You don't sound too happy about it.'

'It was a complete waste of time.'

'Oh, don't say that. —What was the rest of the stuff like?'

'It was rubbish. Ah, but what does it matter?'

'It *does* matter,' she said earnestly. 'You're a very talented painter; of course it matters.'

'Maybe.'

I asked her then when she was coming back. She replied that a few more days should see the whole thing finished.

'Look,' I said, '—give me a number where I can reach you in the meantime. . . .'

She gave a hopeless-sounding sigh and said, 'Oh, God, I wish I *could*. But this itinerary is all up the creek, and I can't seem to get a straight answer on it from any-body.' She paused and then added warmly: 'Be patient, Tom, just a while longer. I'll see you very soon.'

And I had to be content with that.

*   *   *